Shadows
OF DOUBT

Shadows OF DOUBT

MELL CORCORAN

Copyright © 2013 by Mell Corcoran.
www.mellcorcoran.com

Mill City Press, Inc.
212 3rd Avenue North, Suite 290
Minneapolis, MN 55401
612.455.2294
www.millcitypublishing.com

All rights reserved. No part of this publication may be reproduced, stored in a retrieval system, or transmitted, in any form or by any means, electronic, mechanical, photocopying, recording, or otherwise, without the prior written permission of the author.

ISBN-13: 978-1-935204-78-7
LCCN: 2013900764

Cover Design by Alan Pranke
Typeset by James Arneson

Printed in the United States of America

For my Mom. My biggest fan, my toughest critic, my best friend.

Acknowledgments

A very special thanks to the Los Angeles County Sheriff's Department for all your hard work, inspiration and for putting it all on the line every day.

I would like to thank my uncles and aunts for all their support during this journey. If I were to thank each of you for every little thing you did for me, that would be a novel unto itself. I am so blessed to have a family such as mine.

Thank you to my best-pal, Shelley, for putting up with me through all of this. Your patience and humor kept me sane and I adore you.

To my cousins, especially Sara, for supporting me and putting up with all my Facebook stuff. I love you guys tons!

To the rest of my family, there is far too much to say to fit on one page.

Finally, to MK, thank you for your unwavering belief in me and absolute support. This simply would not have been possible without you.

Mom, my partner in crime, you are my strength and my laughter in all things. No one in the world is as lucky as I am to have such a phenomenal mother. Thank you.

Prologue

It is a simple thing to know one's place in this world, provided you have a pulse and your gray-matter is intact. Whether your name is on the V.I.P. list or you are required to wait in line behind the velvet rope with everyone else depends entirely on your place in the social food chain. This pecking order is entirely different from the true ecological food chain. The natural order of things such as spider to fly, cat to mouse, cheetah to gazelle. Survival of the fittest has given way over time from the physical to the fiscal and become the driving force behind modern civilized society.

Let us be completely honest here, it is only opposable thumbs and the invention of gunpowder that has given humankind the illusion they are king of the evolutionary mountain. Little worry of being ambushed and devoured by a pride of lions on one's way to a mani-pedi or power lunch as far as the natural selection aspect is concerned. So completely taken for granted by modern culture, the social food chain is rarely, if ever, given actual thought. Who is at the top of the chain rules all and those at the bottom have little choice but to either accept their fate, scraping the boots of those on high, or bite and claw their way up the rungs by whatever means possible. An individual's moral compass is all that dictates whether the biting and clawing is metaphorical or literal. It is in that simple distinction that we have the modern struggle of right versus wrong, good versus evil. This entire concept is just a given course of tides in our society, rarely thought of, questioned or challenged. It simply "is" and has been for thousands of years. Until it isn't.

For a select few, whom we shall not necessarily call a "lucky" few, all illusions are shattered and the social food chain is properly pushed to the back of the line behind the natural order. By a simple twist of Fate in the guise of bad timing, a lapse in judgment, a wrong turn, or a simple mistake, the comfy cozy illusion of life as one knows it can be forever altered and replaced by a reality that only some know to be the truth. In that split second of wrong place at the wrong time, the fragile human psyche can fracture irreparably, leaving the ill-fated individual facing a rapid end to their life. Or, in the alternative, a permanent state of drooling and a long, fruitless existence filled with pudding cups and anti-psychotics administered at regular intervals. Once in a while, however, the unfortunate soul holds, absorbs, processes and actually survives not only the physical assault, but the psychological cataclysm of this encounter. Either way, life is never the same. Every rule, social norm and expectation is warped, flipped and contorted beyond comprehension. Here it is back to the natural order with a variable never before known in the average every day in a life. In a nutshell, adapt and fight or die.

On this particular day, this particular instance, it would most certainly be die. After all, this was not an encounter created by the Fates, twisted though it may be, it was careful design. He pondered that a moment with a twinkle in his eye as he looked at his fly writhing and wriggling in his meticulously woven web. Even from a distance he could feel the terror radiating from the young, petite blond that was brutally bound to the wooden chair in the middle of the room. A shiver

Shadows of Doubt

of excitement slid up his spine as he leaned against the doorjamb staring at her, savoring the moment. Even obscured by her bonds she was lovely. Pale blond curls, only slightly matted, tousled about her heart shaped face, spilling down over her bare, bronzed shoulders. Delicate shoulders, he noted, though probably formed more from malnutrition and copious amounts of crack than her having a naturally slight frame. Such a romantic, he thought to himself. He would rather look upon her as a delicate fragile beauty than the abject hollow crack whore that she was. Worn and overused at such a tender young age. Had she said she was twenty when he asked? Or was it twenty-one? It mattered little. He was sure she was lying for his benefit as would any semi-experienced underage harlot to a nervous John. How thoughtful that was, he mused with a smirk. Her selfless attempt at making him feel comfortable with the transaction. He would have to remember to thank her for that at some point between the bouts of unconsciousness that were about to befall her and surely before he finally ended her pathetic and useless life.

He moved toward her slowly, taking delight in the desperate flare of her nostrils as she struggled for air. Smiling softly, he stood over her and continued to observe the panic washing over his little fly caught in his web. With a tug of his sash and a roll of his shoulders, the rich brown silk robe he wore slid to the floor like a puddle of melted chocolate. He stood bare before his prey breathing in deep the scent of her fear. Almost tenderly, he reached out to stroke a stray curl covering her face. "I wish I could say that I am sorry this is going to hurt you, my dear." His voice was soft, low and musical with an accent she had never heard before. "But I must admit to you now, before we get started, that it truly brings me joy. So please, don't hold back on my account..." He reached around her head and unfastened the buckle of the thick leather strap that mercilessly dug into her flesh. The strap was tethered to the ball-gag that was brutally shoved in her mouth. Once undone, he tossed it aside then sighed almost wistfully before he continued. "Scream my dear, scream all you like."

She felt the air shift and something quickly brush against her chest, a surge of heat, something warm and wet. A coppery smell filled her nostrils as a searing pain snaked its way up her neck and wrapped itself around her skull with an agony she could scarcely believe possible. To his delight, the screams began.

Chapter One

January in Southern California was nothing short of meteorological schizophrenia. Thursday the snow levels had dropped to twenty-five hundred feet with temperatures topping out at a whopping forty-three degrees through the weekend. Now, the amazonian lap dancer passing as a weather anchor buoyantly reported the forecast for Monday as above average highs in the low eighties. Detective Lou Donovan stood four feet from the flat screen television staring, highly annoyed. She looked down at herself, growled, then violently yanked the heavy wool turtleneck from her body.

Born Tallulah Louella Donovan, the petite homicide detective went strictly by "Lou" to anyone other than her mother or uncle. Those others who preferred keeping all their teeth securely in their mouths called her "Lou". Haphazardly pulling sweatshirt over t-shirt, she caught the disapproving gaze of her cat out of the corner of her eye. "What?" she demanded from the glossy black puff of fur sitting in the middle of the doorway. The feline simply tossed his nose up at her then sauntered off to find a patch of sun to lounge in. "Everyone's a fashion critic." she muttered and proceeded to pull on her boots. Though Lou would never be mistaken for a fashion model, she was a far cry from plain. Rich auburn hair, cut in a severe a-line bob, framed delicate almost elfish features. Sharp green eyes, the color of good imperial jade, could spot a mouse hiccuping fifty yards away in the dark. At a mere five feet, four inches tall, she could take down and hog tie a two-hundred and fifty pound tweaker in under a minute. It was well known among the ranks that this fifth generation cop was all business and not someone to be taken at face value. Despite her uncle being a highly decorated, now retired, detective with the Los Angeles County Sheriff's Department, and her father having been gunned down in the line of duty when she was only two years old, Lou earned her own way, on her own merits, and everyone in the department knew it.

"Good morning sunshine!" Lou exited the closet with one pant leg inadvertently tucked in her boot to meet the sound of her mother's voice. "I heard you come in around four this morning so I figured the sooner you got this in you, the better for the planet." The cheerful woman handed her one of the two mugs of coffee she was holding and leaned in to kiss her daughter good morning.

"Have I told you today how much I love you?" Lou took the offering with both hands as if it were the most fragile thing in the universe then returned the ritual morning kiss before bringing the mug to her lips. She nearly inhaled half the steaming contents in one gulp. "Ahhh... thank you, thank you, thank you." She followed her mother to the sitting area of her room and plopped down in one of the overstuffed chairs. "Sorry for waking you. I was helping out one of the guys from narcotics who was sitting on a house waiting for some jackass he's been trying to pin down for almost a month." She drank deeply from her mug and flashed her mother a weary smile. "The moron finally came out around three, stark naked, to get a pack of smokes out of his car and we scooped him up." Lou snorted a laugh recalling the events. "Rico had me rolling, yanking the guy's chain telling him he was going in naked as a jaybird. The twit was seriously freaking out over that more than the fact that he was facing fifteen to life."

"Morons have their priorities too, dear." Her mother noted as she grinned and leaned over to pull Lou's pant leg from her boot. "You didn't wake me though. Joe had to catch a red-eye flight at two this morning. I couldn't fall asleep after he left." Her mother was referring to her husband, Lou's step-father, Joe McAllister, who despite being rich enough to hire Donald Trump to do his laundry for him, still worked harder than any man she had ever known. "He'll be in Bangladesh or Bangalore or wherever the hell it is until Thursday."

Shevaun McAllister was more then Lou's mother, she was her best friend and biggest fan. With a short fringe of strawberry blond hair, her face always reminded Lou of a fairy queen. Regal petite features, with gently sculpted cheekbones, a slight upturn to her nose and a smile that never failed to make Lou feel like everything in the world would always be fine so long as her mother kept smiling. Her slight, athletic frame was wrapped in her favorite fluffy purple robe as she curled up in the chair opposite Lou. "So anything juicy on calendar for today?" Her sapphire blue eyes twinkled with curiosity.

"Nothing exciting on tap so far. I'm gonna take the train in, get some paperwork done and see what Vinny has cooking." No sooner than she spoke his name, Lou's cell phone began to play the theme to the movie "Godfather", which she had set as her partner's specific ring-tone. Her own little personal joke. "Speaking of angels." She popped up from her chair and retrieved the phone from the bedside table and snapped it open. "Yo! Vinny!" She answered his call as she often did, imitating a thick Brooklyn accent. On the other end should could almost hear him roll his eyes.

"Yo yourself, Kiddo. I can tell you're coffee has started kicking in." Sergeant Vincenzo DeLuca had been a part of Lou's life for longer then she could remember. He had come up through the academy with her uncle and had been his partner in Narcotics Division for several years during which time a friendship of enviable proportions had been forged. When her uncle retired early, after nearly being blown to pieces during a raid on a major methamphetamine lab, Vinny transferred to homicide. Almost losing his best friend shook him more than he would ever admit, so he opted for the slower pace of the dead squad. Once Lou had put her time in at Narco, she transferred over to Homicide herself and Vinny had made it his personal mission to keep as close an eye on Lou as humanly possible. "We got a messy one. I'll text you the address but you want me to swing up and grab you? You really awake?"

"I'm awake, I'll meet you there." It was Lou that rolled her eyes now. "Whereabouts am I headed?" She looked at her watch to calculate her arrival time.

"Sherman Way and Jordan, the alley behind a little bookstore. Uniform has the street blocked waiting for us so you'll spot 'em."

She furrowed a brow and sighed. "I love that bookstore, damn. Isn't that LAPD's turf?"

"I'll explain when you get here." He grumbled.

"Okay, I should be there in ten." She snapped the phone shut and started to gather up her things. "Looks like we got a juicy one after all, Momma." She pulled her holster over her shoulders and adjusted herself before tossing on her jacket. "Although juicy as in messy, or so Vinny says."

Her mother scrunched her nose at the visual that popped into her mind. "That's not the kind of juicy I was looking for but, oh well." She hopped up and kissed her daughter's cheek, then headed down the hall. "Be safe and check in with me later if you get the time. Love you!"

"Love you too!" Shevaun was already gone from the room by the time Lou snatched up her bag and headed out.

About nine minutes later Lou was walking up the back alley of the funky bookstore she frequented every now and then. It was an older section of town that the city had tried to revitalize by emulating the Melrose Avenue boutique feel. Unfortunately, the city kept the rehab to face value and the backsides of the shops were in worse than sad shape. Jury-rigged power lines buzzed audibly as they twisted from one main pole that towered at the far side of the alley. The cables looked like dirty clotheslines slung almost low enough to touch as they splayed out to the back of each shop. Crates, boxes, rubble and waste were piled everywhere due in some part to the fact that the graffiti riddled dumpsters overflowed with all manner of refuse. The stench of rotting produce and spoiled fish from the Asian market's repository wafted through the air along with undertones of urine and wet asphalt from the previous night's rain. Lou knew the area well. Just two blocks north was a notorious drug area with its low income housing and heavy gang presence. During her time in narcotics, she and her former partner had spent many a day scooping up junkies and tweakers that had violated their probation or parole by inevitably crawling out of their holes to score from the drive-up dealers that hung out on every other street corner. Finding a dead body from an overdose was not uncommon in this area so, naturally, that is what Lou expected to find. When she rounded a rusted out dumpster behind the bookstore and looked at the scene, it was clear this wasn't that simple.

"Yeah, that's what I said." Her partner grumbled, having apparently read Lou's mind.

"Well this is different." Lou looked down at the body of what had once been a rather young blond female. At first blush Lou surmised that if this were a cartoon, the voluminous injuries inflicted upon the victim were the result of being repeatedly dragged over a giant cheese grater. But this was no cartoon and there was nothing even remotely humorous about what had happened to this girl. The naked form had more slashes and slices from head to toe than could be counted without a great deal of time and effort. It was apparent that the body hadn't been dumped willy-nilly in this location but had been carefully placed there. Behind a dumpster, the girl lay face-up on the asphalt with her arms arranged deliberately so they crossed over her pubic area in an odd show of almost modesty. The dead eyes were open and already clouded over which told Lou right off that time of death was more than three hours prior to their arrival. Pulling a pair of gloves from her pocket she glanced up to notice the baby-faced Deputy that stood off to the side of the scene and was a curious shade of greenish gray.

"So why is this ours and not LAPD?" She asked her partner.

DeLuca simply looked at her with mild annoyance then to the bright and shiny rookie. "Ask him."

Making note of the name on his tag she snapped the gloves on. "Brooks, what's the deal?"

Deputy Brooks averted his eyes from the victim and turned sheepishly to face Lou. "Ma'am, my partner and I were on our way to serve subpoenas just up the street when the owner of the bookshop, a Miss Sue Shuster, came bolting out of the alley, into the street right in front of our cruiser. It was approximately 6:13 a.m. at that time. When we got out of the car to investigate, she informed us of the body which she discovered just moments prior. Ms. Shuster stated she arrived early to do inventory and when she approached the back door of her shop, well, there it was." He gestured with his thumb to the corpse.

"She said she immediately started yelling for help and ran out into the street to try and flag someone down and we happened to be right there. When we confirmed there was in fact a body, we called in to dispatch at approximately 6:20 a.m. for Homicide detectives and backup to assist with securing the alley. Rather than have the witness sit out here, my partner escorted her to the front entrance and is presently waiting with her inside." He looked now at the body and swallowed hard.

"You are aware that this should have been called in to LAPD since this is on their side of the line?" She asked.

The Deputy blew out a breath and looked at her partner. "I am painfully aware of that now, ma'am."

"I checked with the brass. Captain said we deal with it for now, contact LAPD later and pass it off if they want." Vinny's tone of voice matched the annoyed expression he wore.

"Alright, fine. Anything else Brooks?" She asked, trying to mimic her partner's tone.

"Ma'am, Shuster did indicate to me the owners of the Asian market were here before her. She says they get here at dawn and are always here before her. However, Ma'am, the dumpster appears to block the view from their side, they probably never saw the body when they got here."

"Probably, but we'll need to confirm one way or the other." She squatted down closer to the corpse. "Alright then, lets get this party started, shall we? ETA on the crew?" She glanced at her watch and noted the time being 6:48 a.m.

"Should be here in a few." Vinny replied as he donned his own gloves. "They got the buzz when I did. This girlie got one serious working over, and it wasn't done here, that's for sure. I'm not seeing one speck of blood anywhere besides whats on her and even that ain't much." As two more deputies arrived on scene Vinny immediately proceeded to bark various orders at them and then instructed Deputy Brooks to get statements from the Asian market proprietors. It was highly unlikely the market people saw or noticed anything. No one had even bothered to peek out their back door to notice it was a crime scene. Lou had learned very early on as a rookie that there were two kinds of people in this world, those who would go out of their way to do anything they could to help, and those that couldn't be bothered to pee on you if you were on fire, dancing a jig smack in front of them. In this neighborhood she expected you were going to find more of the latter then the former.

While her partner walked methodically over the area, Lou leaned over the body and looked closely. Head to toe the girl was covered with dozens upon dozens of lacerations ranging from less than one to ten inches long. Some of the slices were clean, almost surgical while others were jagged and rough. The wound that stood out the most, however, was the gouge across the throat. It appeared as though someone had literally tried to rip her throat out. While scanning the injuries to the arms she could clearly make out track marks between and beneath the slices. "She's a junkie." Lou noted aloud so her partner was apprised. "Long time user by the tracks."

"I got a bag over here." He announced and she looked over her shoulder to see her partner's find. The bag was between the size of a duffel and a purse, large and well used. What little of it that wasn't filthy showed a faded floral print that Lou thought at one time might have been considered festive and cheery. Vinny carefully shuffled through the bag and recited the contents. "We got a pair of heels, a shirt... No, wait... it's one of those spandex dress thingies, I think. Got antibacterial wipes, a wide variety of condoms, some deodorant, mints..."

"Sounds like a working girl's bag to me." She stood up and walked toward him as he continued.

"Yeah, would be my take too. Okay, here we go, we got a wallet. Last year school ID, Santa Monica High, says she's Angela Talbott... ahh hell..." He paused to take a breath. "Kid's sixteen years old for Christ's sake! Still in high school!"

"Obviously not or she wouldn't be here." Lou turned back to the body.

Vinny looked at the dead girl and shook his head in disgust. "Where the hell are these kids' parents." It was a statement, not a question. One Lou had heard him make on an almost daily basis. "I know I've said it before but it bears repeating, you need a license to drive a car, but any mental defect can pop out a kid."

"Yeah, ain't that the truth." As her partner bagged and tagged the contents of the purse as evidence, Lou looked the victim over again while she waited for the Coroner and Forensics team to arrive. Even under all the wounds it was hard to believe the girl that laid in front of her was sixteen years old. She was young, Lou agreed with that, but this girl was worn, haggard and used. At best, for a junkie prostitute, Lou would have put her at a rough twenty-five, if she had to guess. To know that in a perfect world this girl should have been getting ready for school at this hour, with her worst worry being who was going to ask her to the winter formal, that just sucked.

Deputy Brooks returned from questioning the proprietors at the Asian market faster then they expected. Still trying to avoid staring at the corpse, he glanced at his notes and began to relay his findings. "Owner of the market is John Xian. He arrived with his son, John Jr. at approximately 4:25 a.m. The father stated that it was no later or earlier than that because they barely made it into the store and got the lights on before the delivery guy started banging on the front door."

"The front door?" Lou wondered why a delivery would be coming in the front.

"Yeah." He continued, understanding her question. "Seems the alley back here is too narrow for most delivery trucks to fit so they come through the front. Mr. Xian said it was pitch black when they parked their Prius over there. The only light was from the streetlamp out over on the side street. They were in a rush because his kid overslept so he didn't see anything out of the ordinary." He paused a moment to notice the gray SUV pulling up within the perimeter.

"Here comes the Coroner and Forensics crew." Vinny announced. "Is that it, Brooks?"

"Well, sir…" Clearing his throat he continued. "… as far as any of the other shops or possible witnesses, it appears none of the other shops on these two blocks open before 10 a.m. Between the fencing and tree line, no one in those apartments would have a line of sight to see anything down here. Not much left to canvass…"

Lou stood up abruptly from the body and looked hard at the deputy. "I know that doing a boring canvass on a homicide pales in comparison to the exciting work of serving subpoenas, Deputy. However, there is the annoying little matter of procedure!" Lou was up on her toes, in his face now and the baby-faced deputy didn't dare make eye contact with her. "I shall not even get into the fact that you saw fit to skirt protocol and failed to notify LAPD since this is their jurisdiction! So, since we are now all bright eyed and bushy tailed here, lets do the damn job and do it correctly!" She noted the light bulb, however dim, go off over his head. Deciding her point was made she took a step back. "Local bums hit the dumpsters regularly in this area. Its also not entirely out of the realm of possibilities that someone's pitbull or chihuahua needed to take a leak during the night so I want you to grab a study-buddy and canvass the buildings within a three block radius." She caught the stifled grin on her partner's face out of the corner of her eye. "If you see anyone dirty pushing a shopping cart filled with everything but groceries, talk to them! If we have to pass this to LAPD we are sure as hell not passing them a half-assed investigation." She turned her back on the deputy and for some inexplicable reason he saluted her then scurried off.

"What?" She feigned a scowl at her partner as he looked at her with a smirk.

"Study-buddy? That's priceless. Where the hell did that come from?" Vinny was clearly amused.

"I don't know, maybe because he looks like he's twelve years old." Her scowl gave way to a grin as she looked up at the new arrivals. "And the cavalry has arrived. Good morning kiddies!" Following with the grade school theme she greeted the Coroner and Forensic teams that miraculously arrived at the same time. Various grunts and nods were tossed back at her as they all got right down to business.

Deputy Coroner Caroline Devereux sauntered up next to Lou and draped an arm over her shoulder while looking down at her latest charge. "Well, someone is not having a good morning." Caroline had been with the Los Angeles County Department of Coroner as long as Lou had been with Homicide. The two had shared their first crime scene together and been fast friends ever since. Caroline's parents, particularly her mother, had far different plans for their only child than her communing with the dead for a living. Hailing from Savannah, Georgia, and looking every bit the part of the Southern belle, Caroline had been born and bred from the elite of blue-blood stock and very very old money. Much to her parent's chagrin, the five-foot, ten-inch, platinum blond, violet eyed beauty seriously upset family tradition by becoming a doctor, rather than marrying one. To escape the constant disapproval of her mother, she left Georgia for Los Angeles and tried very hard to not look back. Now, sighing, she started to glove up in preparation for her duties. "And someone clearly was unhappy with services rendered." She knelt, opened up her case and began.

"Who'd you piss off to get sent out here?" Vinny asked as he jotted notes in his little black book. "Thought we would get that new guy, whats his name? Crap-ass?"

Caroline snorted. "His name is Carpesh, geez Vinny!" She tried to stifle her laughter, knowing it was utterly inappropriate. "He seems like a good sort so be nice! Anyway, I didn't piss anyone off. I was free when the call came in, so thought I would get some fresh air and slum it with you guys for a bit."

"What's a kid from Santa Monica doing around here?" Lou considered as she backed up to give Caroline room to deal with the victim.

"Some low-life John brings her out to party; halfway through she becomes the party favor." Her partner tossed out a theory. "Things get out of hand, tweakers go too far with one cut too many and she bleeds out, whoops. Its not like she's gonna be pissed about not getting a ride home. Speaking of rides, since you have you're own, I'll head over to the local and see what I can pull up on her. See you when ya get there. Take care Doc, nice seein' ya."

"Nice to see you too Vinny." She tossed him one of her sunny, Georgia peach smiles. "Give my love to Vera."

"I'll bring coffee on my way in." Lou nodded to her partner as he took off. She knew there was little they were going to get from the body until Caroline had processed it fully. Lack of blood evidence, no video surveillance, no cursory signs of anything other then the bag that was tossed in the dumpster. Little was going to get put together sitting in the alley all morning. Lou would wait for a preliminary time of death then meet up with her partner.

Unfortunately the mutilation and death of a teenage junkie/prostitute in Los Angeles was not an unfamiliar sight. The length and breadth of the depravity in this city knew no bounds. Wanna-be stars, runaways, the used, abused and neglected child all too often wound up on a slab in the City of Angels. It had been the children that made Lou decide to leave narcotics nearly five years ago. Babies crawling around on filthy floors in diapers that hadn't been changed in days, while the parents cooked up batches of meth in the kitchen. The screams of a child as his or her parents were hauled off to jail and they themselves were hauled off by Social Services. The last straw was when a mother offered Lou her two year old baby boy if she would just let her get high one more time before they took her in for her third strike. Lou could handle the grown ups, it was the innocent kids that got under her skin. As she stood now, looking over Caroline's shoulder while the body temperature was taken to calculate time of death, Lou knew that this victim hadn't been dead or innocent for a long time.

"I can give you a preliminary T.O.D. of between twelve and two this morning." Caroline snapped off her gloves. "She's too much of a mess for me to give you anything more than that here. I'll need to do my business back at the shop before I can give you anything definitive."

"I figured as much." Lou removed her own gloves then stuffed her hands in her jacket pockets and let out a sigh. "We'll do the run through on her but I am not expecting a whole hell of a lot to pop. She's close enough to crackville that it could have been a dump from there but her I.D. puts her out of Santa Monica. I'm gonna head over to Lost Hills and see what Vinny has on her. Let me know when you get something will you?"

"Don't I always?" Caroline gave her that signature smile then turned back to resume her business of the dead as Lou headed out to deal with her own.

Los Angeles County Sheriff's Homicide Bureau Detectives were a bit like temps. Though the bureau itself was based out of Commerce, the detectives went where the work was, or rather, where the bodies were. In this case the crime scene was closest to the Malibu/Lost Hills station. Lou liked working out of Lost Hills because it was close to home and she knew just about everyone. It was also a big bonus that getting to and from Lost Hills was almost always opposite the throng of traffic. When she arrived, her partner was on the phone so she set his coffee in front of him, made a call to check in with her Captain and set up her laptop on the communal desk opposite Vinny. She was just settling in when he finally clicked off the phone, removed the lid from the paper mug she had brought him and drank deeply.

"Ahh, nothing like a caramel macchiato to smooth out the edges." He smiled with satisfaction. "Thanks, kiddo."

Logging into her computer, she glanced up and grinned at the whipped cream mustache on Vinny's lip that he was completely oblivious to. "My pleasure." She grinned and resisted the urge to hand him a napkin. "Got anything on our victim?"

"We gotta confirm with Caroline since her face was pretty much ground beef, but with the ID from the bag, I'm pretty sure I got our victim here." Leaning back in his chair and after one more long draw from the paper mug, he began. "One Angela Talbott born May 3, 1993, aka Amethyst Sky. Lists a Francine Lobler, aka "ChiChi", as mother and nada as father. Over a dozen juvenile offenses involving drugs and alcohol by the time she was fifteen. Her mother is doing twenty to life up north in Central. The name sounded familiar so I looked it up and remembered it was a big meth lab bust up in Palmdale that got ugly about seven years ago. Lobler was the old lady of the main ass-hat running the production. She decided to stand by her man, literally, and the tweaking sons of a bitches unloaded their MP5's at our boys and girls rather than come along quietly." He blew out a breath in disgust and ran his fingers through his hair.

"So..." She chimed in to give him a moment. "Angela got kicked into the system at ten. You pull anything up on that yet?" She asked, looking up from her own findings on her laptop, and noticed he looked tired. Even with the whipped cream mustache he was a formidable looking man. His thick, shoe-black hair was mercilessly slicked back as usual, but the silver at his temples seemed more prominent today. His aquiline features screamed of his Roman heritage. In fact, Lou had once asked her step-father why he had a marble bust of Vinny in his study, only to be told it was a bust of Augustus Caesar. Today, however, he looked like a tired Caesar.

"No, was just about to." He scrubbed a hand over his face then looked at the whipped cream in his palm and scowled.

"I got it up already." Trying to hide her amusement, Lou began to give him the rundown. Angela Talbott had been removed from her mother's custody by Social Services at age ten and put into foster care where she had been bounced around like a pinball ever since. She had thirteen months to go before she was legally on her own and no longer the State's problem, as if the State was doing a bang up job taking care of her. Social Services had noted numerous complaints from the fosters about drugs and suspected prostitution but Angela would run away before anything could be followed up on. Inevitably she would wind up in juvenile detention, then placed with a different foster family before any sort of intervention could be done. It was an all too familiar story with a new face.

"Looks like her last two arrests were by the same uniform out of the Venice sub-station. Maybe they have a story on our girl that we don't already know." He picked up the phone and started dialing.

"Her file lists her current foster on Pearl in Santa Monica. No missing persons report on file. I'll give a call while you check with LAPD." Lou pulled out a fresh notepad and hunkered down to make the call.

By 2 p.m. they had logged over a dozen calls apiece and knew two things for certain. Angela Talbott at the tender age of sweet sixteen was a hardcore junkie that would do anything for a fix and no one, but no one was even remotely surprised she was dead. Not a soul was sad or sorry or even had the decency to fake one or the other. Not one person, not even her social worker could give a known associate or a place she frequented other then the general vicinity of Santa Monica Beach or Venice. Like that narrowed it down or something. Apparently, it wasn't unusual for Angela to drop off the grid for a couple weeks at a time. So far, everyone they spoke to hadn't seen her in over a week, some said it had been over two. Vinny had gotten the blessing from LAPD to have a go at the case but they didn't relinquish jurisdiction. Not like that was a big surprise. They did say they would do what they could on their end and get back if anything popped but for us not to hold our breath. Right. Intra-agency cooperation was just grand. So basically Lou and Vinny had zero. They decided they were going to have to head down to the Venice Boardwalk and see if anyone at all had seen their victim or could give them any solid lead to follow. On the bright side, it was a beautiful day to head to the beach.

Halfway down PCH Lou's cell rang. It was Caroline. "Give me some good news, girlie." she answered hopefully.

"Well, I wish I could." The southern drawl on the other end sounded less then enthusiastic. "I can confirm cause of death as exsanguination and though I've documented over three-hundred and forty-seven cuts, slashes and slices, the laceration to the neck was the coup de gras. It was a painful, long drawn out process. You might be interested to know that for a junkie her preliminary tox-screen is oddly clean. By all indication she hadn't used in anywhere from seven to ten days."

Lou pondered the implications of that for a minute. "No traces of methadone or LAAM?"

"Honey, she wasn't in rehab if that's what you're thinking." Caroline was quick to answer. "Aside from the multitude of lacerations, she's got severe ligature marks on top of severe ligature marks at the wrists, ankles and across the forehead. Based on the discoloration, I would put the oldest injuries at about five to seven days and the most recent within the past twenty-four to thirty-six hours."

"So she was restrained for a week?" Lou grimaced, waiting for Caroline's confirmation.

"By all indications, yes. And whoever did this to her wanted her sober so she could feel the pain." Caroline sucked in a long breath before continuing. "Also, there was bruising around the mouth and horizontally thereabouts, I'd say classic ball-gag on a strap based on the buckle impression on the back of her skull. The one front tooth she had left had traces of urethane rubber that's used in just about every ball-gag manufactured in the country. Other than that her body is oddly immaculate. We've swabbed every inch of her and come up clean save for the tooth with the urethane and one other wound and that is both weird and a dead end. But we are quadruple checking that now."

"Wait, are you serious? There is nothing else?" The frustration in Lou's voice was more than apparent. "What's the other piece? And why is it a dead end?"

"Amylase was found in the neck wound. Specifically at the area around the severed carotid and no where else. The sample is clearly saliva but its too degraded to even tell whether its human or animal. It's bugging me because the wound was inflicted less then twenty-four hours ago. If it was some critter like a rat that wandered by for a nibble after she was dumped, how could it be so damn degraded? Why is there no evidence of animal activity on the body? I am going to go over her again to see if I missed any gnaw marks from even a gnat, but so far there is nothing to support that and it's really odd. We've been able to take three separate samples so far with the same results and the new guy, Carpesh, is running the fourth himself. I'm sorry, Lou, but we've got nothing for you on this so far."

Lou blinked a lot, as if that would help make sense of anything. "Well, hell. What's you're bottom line here?"

"You're the detective but it looks to me like some neat-freak sadist went to town on her. Maybe a dealer she ripped off or some sick twisted John, but what do I know?" Caroline seemed to be at a loss. "I've e-mailed you my findings but I knew you wanted to know what I had so far right away. If Carpesh's run comes up with anything new, I'll call ya."

"Thanks Caroline, I appreciate you pushing this through and getting back to me. I'll check in with you later." Lou snapped the phone shut and looked at her partner who had just scored a prime parking space at the end of the boardwalk. Once the engine was off he turned in his seat and stared at her.

"So you're gonna tell me we got bupkiss?" Vinny could read the expression on her face clearly.

She stuffed her cell into her pocket and relayed Caroline's report nearly verbatim, with a few colorful expletives tossed in. "Well isn't that just dandy. I'm tellin ya Lou, if we don't get something solid on this within the next twenty-four hours, psycho-sadist or not, the captain is gonna have us box it."

"Yeah, I know." She agreed as she peeled off her sweatshirt and put her jacket back on, grateful she pitched the wool sweater that morning.

"No next of kin other than her mother, who forgot she even had a kid. So far not a single soul has batted an eyelash that she's dead." Locking up the car they headed toward the boardwalk. "Hell, the social worker couldn't hide her relief that she didn't have to deal with her anymore."

Vinny shook his head as they walked. "Nice legacy to leave. Maybe we'll find a fan or two around here that can give us something to go on."

They started at one end and worked their way through to the other, stopping only briefly to grab a hotdog. The Venice boardwalk was a colorful and always bustling stretch that ran parallel to the Pacific Ocean. A wide expanse of walkway and bike path separated sand and sundries. Vendors and street-hawkers sold everything from crappy hand made jewelry, incense, second hand Jimmy Hendrix t-shirts and shoes made of hemp to high-end Italian leather goods and Murano glass sculptures. They talked to every last vendor and the best they got from any of them was that they may have seen her around, but that was it. Lou and Vinny were able to squeeze a little more information out of a few beach rats and skels that habitually loitered on the boardwalk. Those that recognized her, knew her or would actually admit to knowing her, confirmed she would do anything to get high. The limited info on her suppliers was that those she scored off were far too brain damaged to be violent towards anyone.

Lou and Vinny came upon one young girl who sat on a colorful woven mat along the sidewalk making her living by braiding customers hair with pretty thread and beads for five bucks a braid. The hemp-clad urchin informed them that Angela would come around every few weeks or so to get some "sparklies" woven into her curls. The girl said Angela had told her once or twice that the freaky tricks paid more, so she could spring for the braids. Kink tipped big it seemed. Aside from the hippie-chick, no one knew anything more. No one even knew of anyone that might know more. Angela had no friends and no regular hangouts. She was a face some people recognized but not enough to give a when or where. Even the two guys that Lou and Vinny suspected of supplying Angela's habit were oblivious and both claimed nearly identical stories. She would turn up once in a while but never long enough for them to even learn her name.

It was well after dark by the time Lou and Vinny got back to the car and most of the shops had long since closed. They had been at it for nearly seventeen hours straight and were both cranky, frustrated and tired. They headed up the coast, then through Malibu Canyon Road talking it out, trying to find something to grab on to. By the time Vinny pulled up behind Lou's car in the station parking lot, they had worked it every which way they could think of. No matter how you sliced it, what it came down to is they had spit. Literally. Useless, degraded spit.

Peter Carpesh was what many would consider a slight man of five-feet, seven inches in height. His rounded face with its apple cheeks gave him a jovial look, even at his most serious, like now. He leaned his face closer into his laptop and spoke urgently to the five men on his screen. "I took a sample and tested it myself! There is no doubt that it is one of ours, but more than that, I am certain it is him."

Chapter Two

Los Angeles was roughly twenty-seven hundred miles from Washington D.C. but through the wonders of technology, Peter Carpesh frantically relayed his report to his superiors via live video stream. Five imposing men sat silently at a long mahogany conference table and watched the oversized face of the Ukrainian born medical examiner as he detailed recent events. It was clear to them all that Carpesh was a bit panicked at the situation given the way his spittle was hitting the screen and he was all but shouting at them.

"I was not on duty when the case came in. However, I reviewed the initial findings and then I was able to play the helpful colleague and offered to assist so I could take a sample to test myself!" It was amazing how Carpesh's accent had grown thicker and thicker in just the past five minutes. "I have no doubts whatsoever on this!"

"Peter..." The man seated at the head of the conference table leaned forward, interrupting Carpesh. "You need to take a breath and calm down. And you need to sit back and stop shoving your face in the web cam. For Christ's sake I can see your nose-hair."

Snickers and chuckles stirred from the other four men but Carpesh finally leaned back and took that deep breath, raked his fingers through his hair and gathered his composure.

"My apologies, Dominor. I simply had not expected to encounter this and am not certain how you wish me to proceed."

"We need to discuss that. Someone will get back to you shortly. Now calm down and get back to your normal routine until we contact you."

"As you will, Dominor." Carpesh bowed his head respectfully before the transmission was cut off and quiet contemplation blanketed the room.

The conference room was a classic, old world law office with several high-tech touches. The long mahogany table monopolized the center of the room and was encircled by sixteen high-backed oxblood leather chairs on swivels. The eastern wall was a long expanse of glass that looked out over the snowy landscape of Georgetown. At one end of the room the sixty-five inch video screen, where Peter Carpesh's face had been moments ago, was flanked by floor to ceiling bookshelves stuffed with various legal publications. The opposite wall was fixed with an ornate mahogany bar that housed a huge, gleaming gold dome espresso machine and baskets that overflowed with fresh fruit and pastries. The wall that separated the conference room from the rest of the floor was also glass, but was set to privacy. With the touch of a button the usually clear glass instantly turned opaque, making it appear frosted, providing privacy from curious onlookers. It also helped that the room was soundproofed for complete confidentiality and discretion for the firm's clientele.

Maximilian Augustus Julian, the commander-in-chief of the law firm of Julian and Associates, among other things, sat at the head of the conference table with his hands folded pensively under his chin. He was an imposing man of nearly six-feet, five inches with a shoulder span that would make any NFL linebacker feel a bit puny. The bespoke three-piece cashmere suit of dark umber complemented his rich olive complexion and golden-amber eyes with an understated sort of poshness. His dark sable hair had been slicked back making it look a glossy black. This only added a regal polish that softened the dangerous fierceness that was unmistakable in the man. Flanked on both sides by his equally fierce and imposing lieutenants, Yuri Markovic and Finn Erikson seated to his left, Niko Gattilusio and Connor McManus to his right. They all sat quietly for several minutes before anyone spoke.

Finn was the first to break the pensive silence. "Okay, I'm on it."

"No, I'll go." Connor chimed in next.

"No. No, I'll do it." Yuri followed suit.

The four lieutenants began to argue about who was going and why it should be one or the other until Max raised his hand in a halting gesture and silence filled the room once more. All eyes rested on him as he pulled his cell phone from his pocket, pressed a button, then spoke to whoever had answered the other end.

"We're going to Los Angeles. Make the arrangements. I want to leave in the morning." He listened briefly. "However long it takes." He ended the call and placed the phone back into his suit pocket.

"With great respect, Dom..." Yuri looked at his associates, then back to Max. "I hardly see why it is necessary for you to make the trip. Any one of us can handle this."

"Things are out of hand out west as it is. We all know it." Max pushed himself away from the table and started to rise before he continued. "It's long overdue that a formal assessment is made. This isn't simply about verification of Carpesh's findings. I don't want to discuss this any further up here, we'll take it below and get things sorted." Turning for the door, he paused to press an inconspicuous button underneath the edge of the conference table that set the glass wall back to clear. As he exited the conference room with his lieutenants in tow, Max was met by an efficient looking woman who was dressed more like a Victorian era librarian than a top-of-her-class Harvard Law graduate. Her mass of brown hair was pulled into such an impossibly tight bun, it literally made Max's head hurt to look at. It simply had to be painful. The clippity-clap of her sensible shoes rang out as she tried to keep up with Max's stride.

"Mr. Julian..." It was a question, not a statement, that the woman often greeted him with rather than a hello. Max found her at-the-ready personality both comforting and annoying at the same time.

"Hanna, the boys and I will be out for a while. Please make sure things are handled while we are gone would you?"

The young office manager nodded enthusiastically, forcing her to push the thick horn-rimmed glasses back up onto her face. "Absolutely sir. Is there anything you need me to take care of while you are out?"

"Actually..." He broke stride and paused to face her eager, yet utterly professional face. "A matter has come up that requires my presence in Los Angeles, immediately." He tried not to grin when panic washed over her face.

"Los Angeles? Sir did I miss something? I wasn't aware of any pending matters in Los Angeles! If I mishandled something..." The poor woman began to stutter. Hanna Brown made it her life's work to know every speck of firm business so that it was handled quickly and efficiently. A point of pride with her was that she would already be on top of something before Max ever asked about it. However, she had no clue about any business pertaining to Los Angeles on any docket and she felt herself start to freak out.

"No! Hanna its nothing you missed, I assure you. Now, I'll need you to handle things for me in my absence. If you don't feel comfortable dealing with something yourself, pass it off to one of the boys here or one of the senior associates. I am not sure how long I will be gone so if you feel you need assistance, hire someone."

"Sir?!" The woman nearly fell over at that suggestion. Did he think she was incapable of handling matters on her own?

"Hanna!" He placed a gentle hand on her shoulder before she jumped out of her own skin. "I am well aware you work your ass off for me and this firm nearly twenty four hours a day, seven days a week. While I am gone you will need to handle everything in my absence. This does not mean overload, it means delegate." Max could see her starting to calm down at his reassuring words. "If you need an assistant to take the menial work off of your hands, you have my blessing to hire someone. Make sure they are properly vetted. Mr. McManus can handle that for you." After giving her a light pat on the shoulder, Max turned crisply and the five men continued down the hall leaving the young woman standing with her mouth agape.

The law firm of Julian and Associates was the oldest in the state, the most respected, and had owned the building where it was housed for as long as the Capitol itself stood. Granted it had been modernized along the way, but it held that enduring aura of rich, judicial tradition with its well worn hardwood floors, mahogany walls and oxblood leather accents. With a staff of over one-hundred-fifty that included the best and brightest legal minds in the country. One would expect to see a gray-haired old codger at the helm of the firm rather than the elegantly dangerous man who now strode through the hall toward the elevator. The gleaming brass doors to the lift opened as soon as they reached it and the five men stepped inside. Once the doors closed, Max placed his hand on the mirrored wall to the right of the doors and a faint glow emanated from beneath his palm as it read his hand print. He then leaned in and a tiny, nearly invisible hole in the mirror gave off a blue beam of light as it proceeded to scan his eye. The cleverly camouflaged security devices verified Max's identification and the elevator car began its descent. Though the digits above the doors listed nothing lower then the basement level, the elevator kept going down. In fact, the lift was sinking to a depth nearly ten floors below basement level. When the car finally came to rest, the doors opened up to a large corridor leading to a giant steel door flanked by two very large, very heavily armed men. The men were dressed in immaculate black combat uniforms, complete with tactical combat vests and stood vigilantly in port arms stance. As soon as Max and his lieutenants came into view the two guards snapped to attention. They instantly lowered their weapons, placed their left fists over their chests and bowed their heads in perfect synchronicity and salute. Once the five men exited the car, blue beams of light emanated from the ceiling and proceeded to move down horizontally along the walls, finally disappearing into the floor. With the scan of the men completed, the heavy door opened for them and they proceeded forward, past the guards and into a buzz of activity. The heavy door opened to reveal an expansive room about the length and width of a tennis court. Computers hummed, phones rang and a melody of half a dozen different languages could be heard amidst the organized chaos. On each side of the room were two doorways spaced evenly apart and flanked by two workstations, each diligently manned. Only a single set of double doors stood at the far end of the room but they too were flanked by desks on either side. A man speaking Russian into his headset sat on the left, and a woman who appeared to be mumbling various obscenities at her computer screen sat on the right. A few paces from the entrance to the room was an impressive circular desk where a petite woman sat twirling around in her chair. Her flame red hair was expertly pulled back into a high ponytail and whipped around as she spun faster and faster. She was screaming to someone named Karl about the significant differences between the color pink and the color fuchsia and why he had better learn said differences if he wanted to continue being a fully functional male. Upon spotting the men entering the room, the woman's face lit up with an enormous grin. She began clapping her hands merrily as her chair came to an abrupt halt.

"Well hello boys! I didn't think you were going to grace us with your presence today!" She clutched at the edge of the desk for a moment to regain her balance, then gleefully popped up and out of her chair. After grabbing a clipboard from a drawer and what appeared to be a stack of sticky-notes at least an inch thick, she pulled a pencil from behind her ear and skipped over to the men that hulked over her by well more than a foot. "Well?" She tapped the eraser of the pencil to her cheek and offered it to them. One by one, starting with Max, each of the men bent down low, kissed her cheek and grinned.

"Abby, these public displays of affection are highly damaging to our bad-ass image." Finn said as he leaned down to give her his kiss.

"Not to mention undermine our authority." Max added with amusement.

The pixie of a woman snorted and swatted at Max's shoulder. "Oh silly boys! You're bad-assness and authority will be undermined the day I hit five feet tall, without heels. Besides, if anything, it reminds people you are not complete ogres." She smiled up at Max sweetly. He couldn't help but laugh at the statement while the other men attempted to restrain their own chuckles and snorts.

The large circular desk where Abigail LaRue sat at the helm was known simply as "Admin". The central hub of the hive. All of the desks in the room were high-tech, high-gloss black and sat atop plush black wall-to-wall carpeting. Soft, soothing indirect lighting bathed down along the brushed silver walls and a long silver backless s-shaped couch sat in the middle of the room for the rare visitor to wait comfortably.

Abby was the Executive Administrator of all things. She was the Gatekeeper who would either handle a matter herself or filter things as needed to a specific department of which each lieutenant was in charge. Each lieutenant had two administrative assistants, or "ad-asses" as Abby liked to call them. These were the ones who were seated at the desks flanking each of the five doorways. Much like sentries at the gate. The doorways off to either side led to each department's command center then further on to each lieutenant's private office. The double doors at the far end of the hive, however, were where the buck ultimately stopped. As Dominor of the U.S., and the whole of North America for that matter, everything lived or died by Max's word, or fist. Whichever the case might require.

Max headed toward his doors with Abby at his side and his lieutenants close behind him. Abby pointed to the "ad-ass" known as the apparently colorblind Karl. He nodded, knowing that this meant he was to watch the gate while Abby was with the Dom. As they walked, Abby slapped sticky-notes, one after the other, to Max's chest while rattling off the current state of affairs, bringing him up to speed. She was the only person in the universe who could get away with such shenanigans with Max. Though he grimaced with each slap, he endured the torture, peeling off each note as they came, giving it a cursory glance. Max truly adored Abby's sense of humor and looked forward to seeing her every day. He often felt she was the daughter he wished he could have had.

"Abby..." He tried to interrupt her rant. "... Abby..." The double doors to his office opened before they could break stride and Abby continued her dissertation and sticky-note dispensation, unaffected.

"... then your video conference in an hour with London and I am fully aware you are leaving for L.A. tomorrow for an undetermined amount of time." She ended her rant with the knowledge of events that had only minutes ago been decided.

"Oh?" He stopped and stared down at her with raised brow.

"I know. Frankie notified me immediately so that I could assist with logistics and supplies. "Her sweet smile was forced this time and he knew it. She hated it when he was gone.

"It shouldn't take long. "He offered the small consolation. "I will conference with you every morning, I promise."

"Oh I know. That doesn't mean I have to like it." She turned her cheek to him and he smiled softly as he bent down to give her another kiss. "If you were the all supreme genius Dom that I know you to be, you would take me with you."

"Abby, how could I feel comfortable, ever, leaving all this without you here to oversee things?"

"That's a load of crap, with all due respect, my Dom. You know perfectly well that I can do what I do here while doing what I need to do for you, with you." The batting of eyelashes was added to the sweet smile for dramatic effect.

Niko plopped down into one of the overstuffed sofas and grunted. "What are we? Chopped liver? Last time I checked the four of us were the Aegis Council, no?"

Abby walked over and patted Niko softly on the shoulder. "Of course you are, Niko, of course you are." She spoke in a deliberately soothing, tone as one would to a small child.

Finn plopped down next to Niko and slung an arm around his comrade's shoulder. "Bro, you and I both know damn well that half the time we can't find our own asses without calling Abby for directions."

Niko smiled wide and looked up at Abby, echoing her words to Max only moments ago, imitating her voice uncannily. "Oh I know. That doesn't mean I have to like it."

Laughter erupted around the room and Max shook his head and grinned as he moved around to his desk, slapping the pile of sticky-note down on his blotter. "Abby, my sweet, would you please get Frank? I need both of you to come take a seat with us. We have business to discuss. Also, have Drew hold everything but the London call, have him buzz when that comes in."

"You betchya my Domaliscious." She twirled around and skipped out the door as only Abby could.

"Domaliscious?" Max looked at his lieutenants. "I know I should be offended by these pet names…"

"Its Abby, she can tell us to go screw ourselves and we think its cute." Niko smirked. "And I say that from personal experience."

Yuri snickered and nodded in agreement. "She is a treasure. I would rather lose my foot than her."

"Which brings me to an issue we are going to have to face, gentlemen." Max took his seat in the large glossy black leather chair that sat behind his enormous ebony wood desk. "If my suspicions about the West Coast are confirmed, the time may have come to erect a formal operations base out there." He could see the disgruntled looks pass between the men and was not surprised in the least. The process of establishing a formal base out west meant massive logistics and massive manpower. "This isn't a new issue." He continued. "We've been mulling things over for well over a decade now. I need you all to be thinking and preparing for that time. Whether or not it is now, it is coming."

"We know that Max, but its not something we really are looking forward to." Niko shifted in his seat uncomfortable with the topic.

"We have a tight ship here." It was stating the obvious but Max felt it bore acknowledging. "Abby has this administration running like a dream, as she continually reminds us. If we find that Los Angeles is necessary, seating a new council could play in perfectly with the longevity issues."

The implication of Max's words had them sitting up in their seats, muttering and looking at each other in shock. The normal course of seating a new council meant splitting them all up, the two senior lieutenants being assigned to the new council and a new Dominor, which meant someone that was not Max.

"Splitting us up? But we are the Aegis! No, we are family!" Connor looked sad as he admitted the weakness they all shared. There was more then camaraderie, there was true family and admiration among them and that was a precious thing in their world.

"Dominor! A new council?!" Niko struggled to find the appropriate words. "Max, I pledged my fealty to you! You cannot expect me.... us..."

"Wait, wait!" Max interrupted him even though it did his heart good to see the loyalty and care in his First Lieutenant's face. "It may not be necessary to split the council." The four men looked at him curiously. "At least not permanently. There are a few provisions in the Law that actually work in our favor here. I won't bore you with specifics right now but the bottom line is I will petition the Senatus to allow me to preside over both councils. In similar fashion to what was done with Canada. If that is acceptable to you all. It must be unanimously agreed by each of you, of course."

"Holy crap don't do that to me bro! Of course we agree!" Finn stood up and went straight to the bar across the room, pulled a large decanter from the fridge and poured himself a drink.

"No shit man!" Connor rose from the couch and followed Finn to the bar. "Pour me one of those, would ya?"

Finn grabbed four more glasses as he saw his comrades approach. "I think we all could use a drink after that little hiccup." He pointed a finger at Max and motioned for him to join them.

"You all realize it will be more work for all of us, not just me. I also need you all to keep a lid on this until the time comes. Abby will freak out a thousand times worse than any of you just did and she won't calm down unless my petition is granted." All four of his lieutenants nodded in understanding and with that Max rose from his chair and strode to the bar. "And I am sorry. I obviously didn't articulate my thoughts very well. I should have opened with the provisions rather than the way I did." Although he was their leader, they were very much his brothers after all these years and all they had been through. It couldn't have been any other way. He raised his glass to them. "Brothers, aeternitas!"

"Aeternitas" The men echoed his words, clanked their glasses together then drained them dry. They all slammed their glasses down just as Abby and Frank entered the office, securing the doors behind them. Abby skipped up to the bar and looked at the empty glasses with a pout.

"Aww, I missed a toast!" Looking at Finn behind the bar with puppy dog eyes, he grabbed a pair of fresh glasses and poured her and Frank a drink.

"My Dom, my Lords." Frank greeted the men with the formal fist-over-heart salute and bowed his head respectfully before stepping up to the bar stoically. He was a well built man of six feet, two inches and looked every bit the Irish boxer he once was. Waves of chestnut hair fell in choppy layers to frame the strong angular face and wily hazel eyes.

"All the arrangements have been taken care of, my Dom." There was the faint lilt of Ireland in his voice. "All your usual personal effects are packed and ready to go. All the gear you may or may not require is packed and ready to go as well. The jet leaves Dulles at 12:00 p.m. Eastern time and arrives in Burbank rather than LAX at 2:43 p.m.

Pacific. Your preferred suite at the Chateau is being prepared according to usual specification as we speak and I've arranged for a separate car to take your things to the hotel since I was certain you would want to deal with business immediately."

Max nodded in approval. "And the meetings?"

"My Dominor, ass kissing shall commence in you're suite at precisely 7 p.m.." Frank's face remained formal and all business as he continued his sardonic recital despite the muffled snickers and snorts within the room. "With an estimate of one hour for each report and ritual brown nosing, I anticipate that you're ass should be thoroughly kissed and tuckered out by 1 a.m.."

"Excellent." Max had long grown accustomed to Frank's colorful embellishments and only cracked a slight grin. "Grab your drinks and let's get down to business. We have much to discuss and sort out before I leave."

Weather conditions in Washington had been close to blizzard-like and delayed their departure by several hours. With that and the infamous Los Angeles rush hour traffic, they were seriously behind schedule when they finally arrived at the Department of Coroner well after dark. Peter Carpesh ushered Max and Frank nervously through the corridor and back into a large storage area that was icy, smelled of antiseptic, formaldehyde and death. The walls were lined with cantilevered shelving, stacked with dozens of bodies stuffed in bags either waiting to be claimed or otherwise disposed of. They approached the stainless steal rolling cart that the body-bag in question was placed on and Carpesh unzipped it to reveal the body of one Angela Talbott. Max's body began to vibrate with rage as he took in the level of brutality inflicted upon the girl. Though there was no signature left by the killer, Max knew instantly from the very depths of his core that this was his guy.

"And what of the previous victim?" Max growled.

"Mm.. my Dominor..." Carpesh stuttered nervously and shrank at the anger in Max's voice. "...that was over two months ago. No next of kin was located, no one claimed her. There was little I could do to stall so she was cremated a few weeks ago." The Ukrainian's eyes darted about as he tried to think of something that would appease his Dominor. "But! Detailed photos are in the file I sent, along with copies of all reports, as well as my notes." He looked at Frank apprehensively.

"The report is at the suite along with copies of the data on this one here." Frank interjected on Carpesh's behalf, which was clearly appreciated.

"I contacted the local agents, three times before the body was disposed of." Carpesh's accent was growing thicker by the minute once again. "No one came or followed up with me. So when this girl came in, I contacted the Council directly. Miss LaRue requested everything I had and then, well, you know the rest since you are now here." Stuffing his hands into the pockets of his crisply ironed lab coat, Carpesh waited for Max to begin reprimanding him.

"Frank, bring the car up and make sure our guests for this evening are on time." Max's eyes never left the body of the brutalized girl as Frank nodded, then hurried out of the room to comply. "Mr. Carpesh, I am deeply disturbed that you were not properly addressed by our agents here." The small man winced at first, then looked up at Max with puzzlement. "I want a detailed report by the end of the week of any and all other instances when local agents neglected to respond to reports out of this facility."

"Ye.. yes... Of course my Dom." Carpesh stammered. "You will have it without delay."

Max turned and met Peter Carpesh's wide eyed gaze. "I promise you there will be no further dereliction, ever. You have done well here and I am pleased with entrusting you with this station."

"My Dominor." The little man seemed to grow in stature before Max's eyes as he gave him the fist-over-heart salute and bowed his head. "You honor me with your words."

"You honor yourself by your diligence." Max spoke sincerely then turned toward the exit pausing once more to look at the body of Angela Talbott. "Keep me apprised of anything further. You know how to reach me." Without waiting for a reply, Max made his way out.

Though time held little meaning for the dead, it had been an important factor in planning Max's visit to the morgue. Fewer employees roaming about meant fewer chances for someone to question who he was and why he was there. Fortunately, a lone man in coveralls diligently mopping the main corridor and Peter Carpesh had been the only two people Max had encountered on his way in. Unfortunately, on his way out, Max stepped through the double doors into the main corridor just as a woman was entering. Noting the worn jeans and clunky boots she was wearing, he deduced she was not an employee who would question his presence in a restricted area and was therefore of little concern. But as they came closer to one another he couldn't help but take notice of her. She was a petite young woman, perhaps thirty years or so if he had to make a guess. She strode through the hall with a strong and confident gait, shoulders back and head held high. Her hair was cropped in sharp angles, a style reminiscent of one many women had worn in the 1920's and 30's. The glossy color was that of rare, well aged cognac and contrasted nicely with her lightly bronzed skin. Though her clothing was grubby (the jacket she wore looked to be a man's second-hand blazer that was at least two sizes too big for her) there was something elegant and regal about her. Her nose was delicately carved and balanced nicely with her fine cheekbones. The line of her jaw was strong yet graceful and her lips were full and lush with the perfect hint of cupid's bow. Just before they passed each other he caught her eyes looking back at him. The piercing green caught him and for one instant he felt his heart skip a beat. The shock of it made him look forward immediately and he picked up his pace as he headed down the hall, resisting the urge to look back. What on earth was he doing? A woman making his heart skip, an average stranger; it was nonsense. Pushing the door to the parking lot open with conviction, he scolded himself for his momentary lapse into the ridiculous. Frank stood at the car with the door open, waiting for him.

"Let's get out of here." Max ordered with a grumble as he lowered himself into the back seat of the town car.

"With pleasure." Frank slammed the door and walked around to the other side, slapping his hand on the roof of the car before he slid in, indicating to the driver they were ready to go.

Lou walked into the morgue more than a little off her stride and it annoyed her to say the least. It was just a guy. An extraordinarily well dressed Greek god sort of guy, but still just a guy. He had been coming down the hall when she was coming in and normally she would never have even glanced his way had it not been for how tall he was. He had to have been six and a half feet and built to accommodate every inch. He wasn't one of those vein-popping, muscle bulging types that absolutely turned her off, definitely not. Instead, he was statuesque with perfect posture, seriously broad shoulders and long legs all wrapped in one hell of a wrapper. The man wore an impeccably tailored three-piece suit, the color of burnt sable, topped off with a dark caramel three-quarter length overcoat that could only have been the finest cashmere. His hair was almost the same color as his suit, intensely dark chocolate with a few strands of gold here and there for good measure. It was just short enough not be trendy but long enough to make you want to yank it while you planted a wet one on those perfectly strong and purposeful lips. Oh and that face, pure chiseled marble that even Adonis would envy. His strong angular jaw and carved cheekbones along with that aquiline nose created a perfect balance between beauty and strength. He was definitely a pretty-bad-boy who never had to work a day in his life to be pretty. But it was the eyes that had gotten her. A fringe of impossibly thick black lashes framed those heart stopping golden eyes, the color of warm honey. They only flashed at her for a split second, but when they did, her heart nearly stopped dead in her chest. It took everything she had not to look back once he had passed her. "What the hell!" She scolded herself out loud as she walked into the morgue offices and the doors were safely closed behind her.

"What?! I … err.. I..." Peter Carpesh spun around, more than startled when Lou walked in, nearly shouting. "Uh.. I..."

"Oh, crap..." Her partner's nickname for the new Deputy Coroner flashed in her head immediately. "I mean... shit! Uh, I was yelling at myself." Lou tucked her hair behind her ears and forced herself to get a grip and focus on why she was there. "I was just coming to get a file that Caroline left for me. Sorry for scaring you Carpesh, I didn't see you there."

"Oh!" Relief washed over him instantly. "Yes, you did startle me Detective." Chuckling, he walked over to Caroline's desk to look for the file.

Before she could even think about what she was doing, it slipped from her mouth. "Hey, who was that guy that just walked outta here?" Wincing, there was no taking the question back.

Carpesh froze. He had been caught? "Err...uh... Which guy?" He needed a moment to think of something.

Since she was stupid enough to let her hormones take control of her mouth, she may as well see it through. "The well dressed man, blackish hair, tall, early forties?"

"Uh... Hmm..." Think, think, think! He demanded himself. Suddenly the lie formed crystal clear in his head. "Oh, that man. He was just dropping off the necessary papers so his grandfather can be flown home for burial." Brilliant, he thought to himself, that will work.

"Ah. Flown back?" Dear God she had lost her mind. Carpesh was going to put the screws to her inappropriate questions and she would never be able to walk into this office again.

"Er... Uh... Back east, Washington I believe." His Dominor would surely have his head for spouting out a piece of truth.

"Oh. That's a bummer." What was she saying? "I mean that his grandfather died." Good God she needed to shut up. "Let me help you look."

"No!" He shuffled papers around on Caroline's desk desperately looking for the file so he could get the detective the hell out of there before he signed his own death warrant with his own tongue. Audibly sucking air in when he found it, Carpesh spun around and launched himself at Lou. "I got it!" He shoved a manila envelope at her, physically moving her backwards.

"Oh great! Thanks. See ya." Lou was too mortified by her own school-girl stupidity to notice Carpesh's agitated state. She hauled out of the office as fast as she could and didn't stop until she was safely behind the wheel of her car, at which time she proceeded to berate herself out loud. When Lou realized she must have look like a schizophrenic off her medication to anyone walking by, she promptly decided it was better to yell at herself while driving home.

The minute Lou had left the morgue office Peter Carpesh began pacing and biting his nails. After several moments of wearing a path in the tile floor, he pulled his cellphone from his pocket and dialed frantically.

Max looked at the ID on his phone when it rang, grumbling as he answered. "Carpesh?"

Shadows of Doubt

"My Dominor, please forgive this intrusion so soon but..." Carpesh had forgotten to breathe since he took his cell phone from his pocket and was nearly gasping for air between words. "... you said that I was to contact you if anything came up and..."

"Carpesh, breathe. Take a moment to breathe, nice and slow, that's it." Max glanced over to Frank just in time to see him rolling his eyes. He couldn't blame him, Carpesh was extremely excitable over just about anything, it seemed. "Now, tell me what came up."

"A detective came in shortly after you left inquiring as to who you were."

Max stiffened a bit in his seat. "And what did you say?"

"My Dom, I had little time to think and was ill prepared but I said that you were just a family member of a recently deceased, dropping off papers for their transport home for burial." With a gulp of air, Carpesh continued. "The detective asked where the transport was to and I wasn't thinking, I said back east, perhaps Washington. Please forgi..."

"Carpesh, stop. Just tell me what was said."

"Well nothing really, my Dom. The detective expressed some pity at the loss of the loved one but that was all, really."

It was Max who rolled his eyes now. "Did they ask my name or any specifics?"

"Oh, no my Dom. The detective was here to pick up a file, but I..."

"This detective was there for something other then to inquire about me?" Max was patient with the man, barely.

Carpesh blinked several times as things sunk in. "Yes, precisely. But.."

"I was a civilian, unescorted after proper business hours in a restricted area, correct?"

Carpesh suddenly realized how ridiculous he was being. "Yes my Dom, this is true."

"So, naturally someone might be curious, correct?" Max's tone was becoming increasingly patronizing.

"Well, that would be logical, yes my Dominor. I was just..."

"Carpesh, please do not make me regret giving you my private number. I need you to think before you panic from now on. Alright?"

"No! I mean yes!" Carpesh sighed heavily as he slumped into a chair. "I am so embarrassed. Please accept my apologies, its just when I blurted out Washington, I did indeed panic."

"Do you know this detective?"

"Yes! Detective Lou Donovan of Homicide..."

"Alright..." Max cut Carpesh off. "... if this Donovan comes back asking specifics about me or any of our people, then you contact me. Is that clear?"

"Crystal clear, my Dominor. Again may I say how sorr..." Carpesh heard the line go dead before he could finish apologizing, again.

Max stuffed his phone back into his pocket while he listened to Frank chuckle. He would look into this detective Donovan just to be cautious but from what he had come to know of Peter Carpesh, he was as high strung as he was meticulous with his work.

"Call Abby and have her get some sort of drugs sent to that man to settle him down. We can't have our primary in there flying off the handle every time he's asked a question." Max sighed and tried to relax for the duration of their drive to the hotel.

"Right away, Domaliscious." Frank grinned as he started to dial Abby.

Max turned his head and stared at Frank. "She can get away with it. You, I will hit."

Frank laughed aloud knowing full well that despite the fact that Max could take him out by batting an eyelash, he hadn't thus far.

Shadows of Doubt

Stuck behind a sea of cars on the 118 freeway, Lou continued to berate herself for her foolish behavior. Perhaps it was due to the fact that she was really tired and had a crappy day that she had fallen to such juvenile depths over a perfect stranger she passed in a hall. Her day up to that point had been as futile as banging her head against a wall. She had started at dawn trying to find anything or anyone that would give a clue as to how Angela Talbott ended up in that alley. Lou had dug for one single scrap of something that would tell her where she was that led to the girl finding herself strapped down and being tortured. At this point Lou couldn't even be sure the girl knew she was being tortured. For all she knew she had been hired for some freaky S & M party and had expected to get paid big bucks for letting whack-jobs cut her up some. It could have been exactly like Vinnie had theorized when they were at the scene. Some clean cut, well-to-do sickos pick up a nobody hooker outta nowhere to get their rocks off and it goes way too far. Or it was one sicko with a lot of energy and a lot more knives playing Benihana on her. Regardless of what it was, the powers that be had given Lou and her partner until the end of the day to come up with something to justify their taking jurisdiction of the case. Since they had come up with zero, the case went back to LAPD first thing in the morning, where it had belonged in the first place. The same LAPD who had done such a bang up job on the last case Vinny and Lou had to pass over. She had followed up on that one and found that it had been only four days before those detectives slapped a cold case sticker on it and sent it to archives.

As she started up the drive to her parents' sprawling estate which she called home, Lou was damn good and cranky.

Casa de McAllister was a sprawling Spanish-Mediterranean labor of love that Joe McAllister had built for Lou's mother for their twenty-fifth anniversary. Set on several acres of land nestled up against the northwest hills that separated Los Angeles and Ventura counties, the nearest neighbor was currently a quarter of a mile away.

Joe McAllister had made his original fortune the good old Texan way, in oil. Then, like any shrewd businessman worth his salt, he went global. Branching his empire out into real-estate and shipping on what seemed to Lou a galactic scale. He was currently worth about a billion and change, liquid. Lou's mother had commuted back and fourth from Galveston for twenty-five years to be with her husband when he wasn't traveling for business. When he was away she would come back to be near her family who all resided in Southern California. Lou had moved back to Los Angeles after high school to go to college then enter the Sheriff's Academy immediately after graduation. It had been very hard on both Lou and Shevaun to be separated from one another. When Lou's uncle Seamus was nearly killed in the line of duty several years ago, Joe decided being close to family was the most important thing and set out to finding the perfect place where he and his wife could live, love and laugh surrounded by everyone they held dear. Three years later, and after more than plenty of sneaking and plotting on the part of Joe, Lou and her uncle, the twelve-thousand square foot compound was planned, built and ready for move-in on Shevaun and Joe's twenty-fifth anniversary. One of the things Joe had insisted on was that Lou move in with them. He had even specifically had a second master suite built on the opposite side of the house to afford Lou privacy, but keep her close to her mother which was one of the most important things to Shevaun, and also to Joe.

Lou barely remembered her birth father since she was only two when he was killed in the line of duty. Joe McAllister had been her father ever since she could remember. He had fallen madly in love with Lou's mother the minute he laid eyes on her and subsequently with Lou, as if she was his own daughter. Lou's mother, however, was not so easily swayed. She had resigned herself to being a widow and it had taken Joe nearly three years to win her over. But the second he did, they were as tight as any family could possibly get and perhaps even more so. To Lou, Joe and her mother were her best friends and the most important people in the world. As she rounded the drive and headed for the garages in back, she saw the soft glow of lights from the magnificent house that was filled with so much love. Her crankiness seemed to melt away in remembering how truly lucky she was and how much Angela Talbott was not.

Lou's mother was cozied up with a book in the sitting area of Lou's room when she finally made it inside. As she often did, Shevaun had a steamy cup of tea waiting for Lou along with that brilliant reassuring smile.

"Hey Momma." Lou kissed her mother hello before anything else. "How are you?"

"I am terrific! Thanks for asking." Shevaun watched her daughter sigh as she tossed a large envelope on the coffee table then disappear into the walk-in closet. "But the more important question is, how are you? Any break in your case yet?" By Lou's lack of immediate response, she knew that her daughter was not a happy camper. She closed her book and set it down on the table then retrieved her cup of tea, sipped slowly and waited until her daughter was good and ready to vent about her day. It was a ritual they shared regularly.

Lou emerged from the closet a few moments later wearing gray sweatpants, a ratty old Los Angeles Kings hockey jersey that was about four sizes too big for her and fuzzy black and white convict style striped socks.

"Uh oh." Her mother groaned.

"What?" Lou asked while she placed her holstered gun in the drawer of her bedside table.

"It was a bad day. You're wearing the socks." Her mother eyeballed her over the rim of her cup and sipped slowly.

"It wasn't that bad. Ok, it was bad enough." Lou plopped into the chair across from her mother and picked up the cup of tea that was waiting for her. "I got nothing. We got nothing." She paused to take a sip and savored the warm comfort as it flowed over her tongue. "The captain gave us today only to find a legitimate reason to keep her, which we didn't. So now we have to pass it back to LAPD since she was their jurisdiction to begin with."

"You know my feelings about the LAPD. No offense to the officers, but the bureaucrats there, well never mind." Shevaun was clearly disgruntled. "I understand the socks now."

Lou chuckled and looked at the manila envelope that she had put on the coffee table. The message she had gotten from Caroline that evening had been a little vague. Caroline had said that the degraded saliva on Angela Talbott had been annoying her so she ran some searches to see if she could find anything to help explain things. Caroline had indicated that she found something odd and would leave a copy of her findings for Lou on her desk since she herself was leaving early because she had an engagement that evening.

"Caroline called me while I was in with the captain. Left a message saying she might have something but it was already too late. I picked this up from her office on my way home." Lou set her cup down, grabbed the manila folder and pulled out the file.

"Oh coroner stuff! You know how much I love those things." Her mother grinned and nestled down into the chair with a cheery grin.

Lou went through the file with her mother snuggled into the seat across from her with wide eyes as though she were a small child being read a bedtime story. The victim was a Marjorie Scott and had been found on October twenty-seventh, just after dawn in

Lake Balboa Park. The crime photos showed the woman laying face up, naked with limbs carefully arranged. Her legs and ankles were set tightly together and her arms were resting snugly at her sides. The palms of her hands were upturned so that you could clearly see the gashes in each wrist. What you couldn't see was any blood, at all. Though the death had been ruled as a suicide, there were obvious holes that didn't seem to matter to the investigating officers. No clothing found at the scene, no tool or weapon used to make the wounds, no evidence as to how the woman got to the location, nothing. A lot of obvious, gaping holes. The coroner assigned to the case had ruled it a suicide with exsanguination from self-inflicted wounds to the wrists. There was evidence of scarring to the wrists from a from a previous suicide attempt which was in the woman's record from when she was seventeen. The LAPD detectives had put in their report that the lack of clothing or ID was likely the result of theft given the numerous vagrants that were known to roam the park regularly at night. They also explained away the body being staged under the tree next to the lake as being another random vagrant's disturbing the scene of the suicide. It was so bloody thin that it made both Lou and her mother grunt and groan at the report.

Marjorie Scott had been a recent transplant from Chicago with no family or ties to speak of. She had been working as a massage therapist for a less than reputable massage parlor in Studio City for only a few months. Her presence in the universe seemed to be so insignificant that neither her employer, landlord, nor any one of her acquaintances had ever bothered to report the woman missing. Given all of that and the statements gathered, it actually was understandable how the investigators let things go as suicide along with the coroner's findings. It was all plausible when stacked up, which is why it stuck and ultimately got the case closed. Aside from the lack of blood at the scene, the body being face up when it was placed and the fact that no one gave a shit about the woman, there was nothing to tie Marjorie Scott and Angela Talbott together. But it was one single line in the the coroner's report that made Lou understand why Caroline pulled the case file and passed it to Lou. Traces of amylase were found at the wound on the left wrist. Said trace was too degraded to extract any DNA or even determine whether it was human or animal.

"Now that is a coincidence isn't it?" Lou's mother said, even more wide eyed than she had been before.

"Don't start doing the conspiracy theory thing on me yet, Momma. There are a thousand reasons why the saliva could have been degraded."

"Well Caroline obviously thought it probative enough to pull the case for you." Shevaun was clearly thinking on the same lines as Caroline Devereux had been. "Why don't we call her and ask her? It's not that late, she'll still be awake."

"Mom, she's at some charity thingy. I am not going to call her tonight on this." Lou considered the situation. "I'll call her in the morning to get her take, then if she's planning on backing me, I'll take it to the captain."

"You could go down there and bring her those croissants she loves and schmooze her into backing you up." Lou's mother was a brilliant extortionist when it came to knowing people's culinary weaknesses. She had the best bakeries and restaurants on speed-dial for just that reason. It worked like a charm when she was hitting up deep pockets, fund raising for her church.

"Okay, now that you've made me hungry, lets put this away for the night and go raid the fridge." Lou pulled the file together and stuffed it back in the envelope.

"Oh goodie!" Her mother clapped her hands happily as she sprang up from her chair. "I brought one of those chocolate cakes home from Romano's!"

"Did you eat anything with nutritive value today?" Lou sometimes wondered who was the parent and who was the child.

"Of course I did!" Shevaun perched her hands on her hips and gave Lou a scolding look. "I had an apple martini and fried mozzarella sticks for lunch. That's fruit, grain and dairy!" She spun around with conviction and bolted out the door, yelling as she ran down the hall. "Last one to the kitchen does the dishes!"

Lou rolled her eyes and grinned but didn't bother to race to the kitchen. Her mother always cheated when they raced and Lou was always last and always got stuck with the dishes.

Max sat comfortably on the pewter couch sipping from his glass as he listened to Agent Martin Gilroy ramble his report. The man stood in front of Max looking every bit the wanna-be Hollywood playboy complete with horribly over-done highlights, a fresh coat of spray tan and clearly over-priced, over-grunged clothes. To make matters worse, Gilroy had brought his assistant Vito with him. The greasy looking man stood near the entry door with his arms crossed over his chest and a look on his face that made him appear like he had eaten bad clams for lunch. Max supposed the man was trying to look imposing but he simply came off looking like an extra from a Sorano's episode that spent more time at craft services than at the gym. Max barely glanced at Gilroy as the agent continued to pontificate about how tight he had the west side running and how everything was smooth as silk, blah blah blah. Max glanced at his watch then to Frank who stood in the back corner of the living room, stoic and brooding. With the slightest lift of Max's index finger, Frank nodded and pulled the phone from his pocket and proceeded to type on its miniature keyboard. To his credit, Max noted that Vito had picked up on the signal and shifted his stance. When the knock on the door came several minutes later, Vito looked to Max with eyebrows raised and Max nodded to him to open the door. Gilroy never broke from his dissertation as four very large men in impeccable black suits entered the suite, saluting Max without a word. The four men stood shoulder to shoulder a few paces behind Gilroy. Vito tried to move to the side, clearly out of his element.

"What of Carpesh's inquiry? Max interrupted Gilroy finally as he set his glass on the coffee table.

"Who?" Was all Gilroy said.

"Peter Carpesh. Our man at the Coroner's office." It was only then that Max bothered to make eye contact with the man.

Gilroy strained a moment. "I don't know that I received an inquiry from any Carpesh."

"You did. Three actually." Before Gilroy could speak, Max cut him off again. "You are being relocated, effective immediately."

"What?! But... You... Now wait a minute Julian..."

Before he could blink, let alone utter another syllable, Max was off the couch, in Gilroy's face and had him dangling with one hand by the throat. "That would be Dominor Julian, you incompetent, self-important toad."

Vito jerked but stood where he was as he visibly began to shake. The man could only watch as his charge was being manhandled.

"Now I could very easily, and with great pleasure I might add, pop your head off like a soda cap right this instant. But since I am very fond of the décor in this suite, these men will escort you, and your unfortunate troll here, out. A jet is waiting to take you immediately to your new station where you will be assisting the agent in charge." He let go of Gilroy and turned before the idiot hit to the floor with a solid thud. "If I so much as hear you blinked in the wrong direction, you're next assignment will be to fish your head out of your own ass." Max turned his attention to Vito this time. "As for you, I strongly recommend you pick your employers more carefully in the future. Frank will see you out."

Frank appeared out of nowhere behind Vito and firmly took the man by the arm. The four well-suited men yanked Gilroy to his feet and dragged him out the door while Frank followed with the unlucky Vito. Martin Gilroy was a moron on so many levels that it upset Max deeply that such a twit had ever been given a position as an agent. Correcting his error, Max had arranged for Gilroy to be shipped directly to Alaska and the agent stationed there had assured Max that Gilroy's existence would be made a living hell, albeit a very frozen one.

As for Vito, it had been another brilliant display of bad judgment for Gilroy to hire an outsider without Council vetting. After some checking, they had learned that Vito had come into Gilroy's employ several months ago, was new to the area from Brooklyn with no family on record. Max could trust that Frank would give Vito a good enough crack to the back of the head that it would give medical feasibility to the amnesia Vito was about to suffer. It was messy, it was so unnecessary, and it would sure as hell never happen again.

Glancing at his watch Max noted that he had approximately twenty minutes before an instant-replay of recent events would take place, only with a few different cast members. There were several more agents on schedule this evening. Max was looking forward to it. He was seriously pissed now.

Chapter Three

Caroline took another bite of the fresh baked croissant and considered the situation carefully while she chewed slowly, savoring the flaky goodness. It was an excellent bribe, but really unnecessary.

"I don't know what I can tell you here Lou." She took a sip of coffee to wash down the rest of the croissant. "I'll put whatever I can in the report to help but the bottom line is it's weak as hell. Degraded saliva on two bodies found three months apart does not a serial killer make."

"I know! I know!" Lou was exasperated and she was running out of time. "I know it's weak but it might give me just enough to convince the Captain to let me follow up on this and not have to hand it over to LAPD."

"Lou, you also have to consider that the other case belongs to LAPD. To them its closed and long put to bed." Caroline eyed the pink box where the other half-dozen croissants waited, quietly whispering her name. Instead of giving in to their call, she shoved the box to the other side of her desk and focused on Lou. "Fat chance in hell they are going to let you keep a case that should have been theirs in the first place, then hand over a closed case based on some suspicious drool. It would be different if I could come up with something to explain why the saliva was degraded and the explanation was consistent for both of the bodies. You get what I mean?"

Even though she hated what she was hearing, Lou nodded in understanding. "This is almost as weak as LAPD's theory on how Marjorie Scott wound up near the lake with zero blood anywhere. I know they are going to pull the same crap with Angela Talbott and just write her off too." She sighed with resignation. "Well, thanks for trying. I better get this over with."

Muttering some choice expletives under her breath, Lou stood up and opened the pink box she had brought for her friend. She quickly snatched one of the baked goods and stuffed half of it in her mouth as if to mask the bitter pill she was having to swallow.

"Hey!" Caroline protested. "Indian giver!"

Lou grinned as she chomped on the croissant, waving to her friend and headed out the door.

Captain Sam Davidson was a no-nonsense man who walked the line between cop and bureaucrat with precision and grace. He knew when to go to bat for his deputies but also knew how to reign them in to keep things neat and tidy for the bean counters. Lou had managed to talk her way into seeing him before he left for a meeting at City Hall, which explained his being dressed in full uniform. The military-sharp man sat behind his desk and listened to her intently as his keen blue eyes carefully scanned through the files she had handed him before she began her report. His weather beaten face was expressionless as he listened. When she finished laying out her case, she could read nothing from him. She simply stood silently for several long moments and watched her silver haired superior mull over the data.

"Sir, if I could just get the okay to requisition the full file from LAPD rather than hand over this case." The silence was too much; she started on him again. "If I could get a closer look at this, I'm sure I can find a solid link between the Scott and Talbott women." Lou tried to not sound desperate.

"What does your partner think about this?" Davidson never looked up from Caroline's report as he asked.

"Sir, your orders yesterday were for us to wrap it up for LAPD so we could hand it over first thing this morning. I didn't bother DeLuca with the information the coroner gave me because I wanted to make sure it was staying in house before bringing him in."

Davidson's sapient blue eyes peered up at her from beneath his bushy pewter eyebrows. "So, if I am reading this correctly, the only thing you have with these cases is unidentifiable amylase? Degraded saliva?"

She shifted slightly but stood her ground. "It's the fact that the saliva on both victims is exactly the same in its unidentifiability, Sir." Okay, so now she was making up words. This had gone so much smoother in her head.

"Detective Donovan, I can see where you are going with this but I have to say, this is quite a stretch here." He began to put all the documents together neatly then placed them back into the folder. "The first victim could have been munched on by a rabid squirrel for all we know. Or those ducks!" He slammed his fist on his desk with a heavy thud, startling her. He was patronizing her now and she knew it. "Those ducks are mean over there! One attacked my grand-kid last summer!"

"Sir..." Lou gritted her teeth at his poking fun.

"As for our victim from the alley..." He cut her off cold. "Detective, you and I both know that was more than likely a rat. We just do not have any justification to withhold the Talbott case from LAPD; it's their jurisdiction. Then to hit them up for records on a closed case because of spit? Spit that the coroner states definitively that she cannot narrow down a species for. Without even that much you are completely screwed in finding a source for it. Christ, they could turn around and blame us with mishandling evidence as far as Talbott goes."

"Yeah but if I had more time I could..." She was definitely sounding desperate now.

"Its making a case out of spit and chewing gum, almost literally! The District Attorney would laugh you out of his office!" He leaned back in his chair and looked at her flatly. "Lou, you're a good detective, a smart one. I know you think you are seeing something here but you're not. Even if there is something here, it's for LAPD to handle. Pack it up and hand it over." He glanced down at his watch and cursed under his breath. "Now that I am ten minutes late for my lunch meeting, dismissed Detective."

"Sir. Yes Sir. Thank you for you're time Sir."

Deflated, discouraged, and angry, Lou left her captain's office and headed back to Homicide. He was probably right but she didn't have to like it. Then there was the fact that she just had a gut feeling and couldn't shake it. By the time she got to her desk and sat down, she was flat out sulking. It was several moments before she noticed her partner was making a painful attempt at sitting Indian-style in his chair. His eyes were closed and he was rolling what looked like two silver golf balls around in his left hand. The balls even appeared to be making some sort of chiming noise.

"What the hell are you doing?" She asked him.

Vinny didn't flinch at her question. He continued without pausing but peered at her through one eye before closing it again. "I am meditating."

Lou blinked rapidly several times. "You are what?"

"I am meditating!" He took a deep breath and kept rolling the humming balls in his hand.

"Vinny, what the hell are you doing?" She was seriously trying not to laugh at this point.

He stopped, unfolded his legs, pausing briefly to work out a cramp in his hip, then planted his feet firmly on the ground. With a huff, he rolled his chair up to the desk and slammed the silver balls down on the blotter. After looking around to see who was within earshot, he leaned in and looked her square in the eye.

"Vera's pregnant." No beating around the bush on this one. He picked up the silver balls and carefully placed them into a satin lined box then put the box into his desk drawer. When he looked back at Lou he noticed she had turned a few shades of pale and hadn't yet blinked. "Yeah, no shit!"

"Holy crap, Vinny!" Was all Lou could come up with.

"My sentiments exactly kiddo! You know she's twenty years younger than me so now she's on this kick to get my stress levels down and get me all healthy and shit for when the bambino arrives." Vinny scrubbed his hands over his face. "She also wants me to take the exam."

"When? How? I mean…" Lou flopped back in her chair completely dumbfounded by her partner's news. "You mean the Lieutenant's exam?" She was still stuck at the part about the baby.

"Yeah. I didn't know how to tell you. Any of it. Christ I'm 50 for crap's sake! Do you realize I'll be 78 by the time the kid gets outta high school? This is nuts, Lou!" He blew out a long breath. "Top that off with you goin' off doing something with Caroline and not telling me. Everything is just screwy, and weird. I'm freakin' out over here!"

"Oh crap, Vinny! I wasn't doing anything behind you're back! I just didn't want to drag you into something until I had something to drag you into!" Lou gave him an apologetic look and was really glad she had decided to keep him out of her fishing expedition. He didn't need any sideways glances in his direction if he was going for a promotion. "Now when is Vera due? And shit, are you happy? Is she happy?"

"Yeah, yeah! She's over the moon about it. But its a major rethink I gotta be doing on my end. I mean you're my partner, my friend, my best friend's niece! I got a responsibility here too. And riding a desk permanently... Shit, Lou."

Lou smiled at her partner. Boy, had he worked himself into a tizzy over all this. It was so like Vinny to put his own forthcoming baby after his sense of duty to Lou and her uncle. That would certainly change once the little rugrat arrived, though. She would miss having him as a partner but he bossed her around so much anyway that having him as her lieutenant wouldn't change things much. It suddenly occurred to her that the poor guy must have passed up the exam a few times so he could stay with her on the streets. It was time for some changes and she was going to shove his chicken-shit, petrified ass in the right direction, starting now.

"Okay, I took the train in so you gotta drive me home." She got up and started gathering her things. "We can cut out early and miss the rain. Besides, Mom's got Romano's chocolate cake at home." She grinned as his eyes lit up at the mention of chocolate cake.

As he hurried to gather his things he looked up at her suspiciously. "You gonna tell me what you were doing in the captain's office?"

She tossed the manila folder at him that contained Caroline's data. "You read while I drive. We can talk about that and the rest of it over cake and coffee."

"That sounds like the best offer I've had all day. Is this something that Shevaun would call "juicy"?" He tossed her the car keys.

"I thought it might be, but its looking pretty damn dry." Lou paused a moment and took a deep breath. She had to force that feeling in her gut to let go so she could move forward. "Okay, let's go, partner."

The coffee table in the middle of the suite had been turned into a mini-command center with Max at the helm sitting in the white leather armchair. A dual-screened communications hub sat back at the far end of the table so that he could talk to more then one person at a time while having complete access to the touchscreen system in front of him. On either side of the touchscreen were mini-systems that were both controlled by the single wireless keyboard Max was currently abusing. With the thump of a key he switched from one system to the other and processed the data that flashed across both screens with lightning speed.

"Dominator..." Abby's face pouted on one of the communication screens while his Aegis Council sat around the conference table staring at him from the other. "I don't understand."

Max felt the vein on the side of his head twitch ever so slightly and set the keyboard down on the table next to him. It had been an infuriating twenty-four hours but he had made up his mind on how he was going to rectify the situation and make some drastic changes. Now it was a matter of figuring out how to get it done, and fast.

"Abigail." His tone was nearly a growl. "Disconnect this transmission, go into my office, secure the room and then establish a new connection from my desk. How difficult is that to process?" He wasn't being intentionally curt with her, he just didn't want, nor did he have the time, to go through her usual 'not comfortable fiddling with your stuff' crap again. He needed her to step up, and step up right now.

Clearly wounded, she bowed her head before cutting the transmission without a word. Once that line was officially dead, he turned to the other screen and looked at the men.

"So it's seriously that fucked up?" Finn asked again.

"Lets put it this way..." Just as Max started to elaborate, Frank walked into the room with a silent nod. "I had an emergency video conference with the Senatus Imperium at four this morning to get official sanction for five terminations. I obtained all five but with the clear understanding that they must be carried out by the letter of The Law. You all are well aware that means they must be carried out by the Aegis Council."

Things got very quiet in the conference room. When a soft knock broke the silence, Frank opened the door to the suite to find a crisply dressed bellman waiting with a service cart. Frank stopped him short and handed him a large tip before ushering him back the way he came. He rolled the cart in and up next to the coffee table himself.

Max's expression brightened instantly at the sight of the absinthe service, complete with fountain. "Frankie, sometimes you are just my hero."

Frank only smirked, then began to prepare the ritual for the two of them. It was going to be a long night for everyone, so he felt a little decadence would do very nicely in smoothing out the rough edges.

"So..." Max resumed his attentions to his lieutenants who sat quietly on the monitor. "There was no hesitation by the Senatus once I detailed the offenses. They were mollified with being formally included and the whole thing is on record. However, given they were agents, the Senatus wants this handled with honor despite the offenses. The Piaculum Sanguineus must be made. As you all are aware, pursuant to The Law it can only be offered by the Aegis." Immediately various groans and grunts of objection erupted from the lieutenants.

"I have no problem with knocking some ass-hat's block off Max, not in the least." Finn's voice rang out over the discord. "What I don't understand is why they get any comfort after they fucked themselves into this corner and never even thought about how that would jeopardize the entire Sanguinostri." He leaned heavily forward on the table. "They pissed on our legs and kept walking! I say we stuff their heads up their own asses and let them rot."

"I agree bro." Connor shifted in his seat uncomfortably. "My Dom, these are people that took the oath. They were given everything. They swore on their blood and the blood of our elders to protect the Sanguinostri and instead they used it, spat on it! From what you've told us, they were not only shocked but indignant about getting their wings clipped. How is it acceptable that on top of all that, they are to be afforded eternal honor?"

The room erupted in a chaotic chatter of concurrence. Max watched the screen as the men argued and postured, understanding their feelings more then they knew. But they were all bound by The Law. Before Max could speak up, it was Niko that silenced them when he stood up and slammed both fists on the table.

"Enough!" This was the reason Nikandros Georgaes was Max's first lieutenant. "You all know why! Because that is The Law! And it has been Law since the day our Elders suffered through their first Lunation!"

"Niko speaks wisely." Max interjected. "The Laws are eternal. We do not have the luxury of re-writing or interpreting them in a way that lends itself to loopholes or to suit our whims. Protect, Provide, Prosper. Anyone who betrays or threatens our way of existence is a traitor! And in our world, traitors cannot be allowed to betray a second time because it could mean our demise. But these men were not common and we must abide the honor that comes with that fact." They all listened to him intently, absorbing every word. "We... I chose these people to ascend to the station of Agent." The lot of them tried to interrupt him immediately but he halted them with a raise of his hand. "There was something noble and good in them at one time which brought them to us, and the Senatus wants that remembered. I, as always, am ultimately responsible for their station and their failure at it. This is on my hands and that will clearly be remembered as well."

"My Dominor..." Niko wouldn't stand for that. "I was the one who vetted Gilroy. I was the one who brought him to the table for ascension. I am to blame for him, not you."

"I let him and the others have all the rope in the world and never tugged it back." Yuri added, given he was in charge of domestic operations. "If anyone is to wear disgrace, I am the one."

"Okay!" Max shouted before they could get started again. "Before we all get into a rousing game of who screwed up worse than whom, I need to remind you all that I am responsible for each of you as well! So shut it! Now lets get back to handling business."

At that moment, the other communications screen beeped, indicating Abby's incoming transmission.

"Now watch yourselves, Abby is linking up again and I don't want to freak her out. Is that clear?"

"Yes, my Dom." The men answered in unison.

Max hit a button and Abby's face came into view again. She seemed impossibly small sitting in his chair, behind his desk in his office as he requested. She clearly did not look comfortable in her compliance.

"Alright Max, now just what the hell is going on that I need to go all Cone of Silence?"

"A lot Abby, and I am going to need you here in Los Angeles." He sighed and sat back in the chair trying to think of how he was going to pull this one off.

"I told you to take me in the first place!"

"Abigail..." He only called her that when he was either dead serious or angry with her. "I am going to need the boys too, which means I need you to pick someone who can sit in your stead and for you to assist them in doing the same."

"For how long?"

"That's uncertain, which is why you need to approach this as though it were permanent. Be certain. Be absolutely certain whomever you pick can be trusted and is competent enough to handle the pressure. Let me explain what we are looking at here and why we have no time to waste."

Max spent the next hour relaying the extent of incompetence, corruption and deception he had uncovered since he arrived in Los Angeles. Martin Gilroy, the agent entrusted with handling most of Los Angeles County, had basically neglected any and all enforcer and administrative duties. Instead, he utilized Sanguinostri resources to play the high-rolling Hollywood playboy. In his utter neglect and dereliction of duty, underlings were left to their own projects which consisted of drug dealing, prostitution rings, and all manner of illegal activity that put the Sanguinostri at risk. Unfortunately, Gilroy was not the only one. From San Diego to San Francisco, California was a mess and all of its agents had been lying, falsifying documents, records, reports and paying administrators off to keep the Council from finding out. It was little wonder their rogue had decided to set up shop here. That was the whole reason Max had come to L.A. in the first place, to deal with the damn rogue. Now he was stalled on that by having to clean house first.

"We'll need to work concurrently and fast." Yuri told them. He knew precisely how to handle a sweep of this magnitude. "Once the head is cut off the word will spread like wildfire and rats will scatter. We will have to take the high-profiled agents' zones first. Go in with sweepers and enforcers who can shore things up concurrent to the agents' termination."

"Agreed." Max referred to a jurisdictional map he had up on screen. "San Francisco, Sacramento and here, in Los Angeles, are our main messes. Sacramento is critical given it bleeds into governmental branches. I will entrust that to you Connor. Get a team together fast."

"As you will, my Dominor." Connor nodded and began fiddling with his Blackberry, presumably getting contacts for his team ready.

"Yuri, you and your team will deal with San Francisco, which may take a while, but I know you have the patience for it. Finn, you can take care of San Diego." Max looked at Niko, then Abby. "We have more than just bullshit here in Los Angeles and the outlying areas. I have confirmed that our rogue is working out of here." He turned his attention back to Connor, Yuri and Finn. "I will need the three of you here as soon as you are done with restructuring your assigned regions. Get things on auto-pilot then get here as fast as you can."

Max felt better once things had been laid out. He leaned in and softened his posture a bit as he addressed Abby once more. "You are from Los Angeles. so I am going to need your insight as well as your administrative genius to get things secure here before we go after the rogue."

Abby chewed on her lip a moment before answering him. "Its been a long time since I left L.A., Max. Based on how the tabloids and magazines read, it is a totally different place from when I was there. But I will do my best."

"You always do." He gave her a quick wink and her face lit up with a huge smile. He knew he was forgiven. Turning once again to the men, he was all business. "Frank has assembled a solid bunch of guys that are dealing with the wet work. However, Niko, I need you here to help me get things cleaned up and get new agents in place. There are no two ways around it, we are going to have to spend some quality time to avoid this happening again. Frank is going to get me some possibles on property so we will have a permanent residence rather than over-using the Chateau's generous hospitality."

"Oh oh! I get to decorate it!" Abby bounced happily.

"Abby, get the stand-in's up and running, then we will discuss it." Max rolled his eyes at her immediate pout.

"I actually have several good places for you to look at when you are free." Frank set a folder on the table next to Max.

"Good. Alright, we know what needs to be done immediately so lets get to it. I'll need daily reports to keep me apprised every step of the way. I also want e.t.a.'s on each of you by the morning."

After they had set everything in motion and the video conferences were done, Max and Frank sat quietly for a while, sipping absinthe by the fire. Frank hesitated a bit longer but knew if he didn't get the lastest developments out, it would only further sour Max's mood.

"So, we might have a problem."

Max snorted. "A problem? Singular? Did you not arrive on the same flight I was on?"

Frank grinned. "Yeah, well... it may just be a case of Carpesh being wound too tight per usual, but erring on the side of caution might be wise right now."

"What's the problem?" Max sipped the last of the opalescent liquid.

"The deputy coroner, Caroline Devereux, pulled the file on our rogue's first victim. Carpesh thinks that was what the detective picked up yesterday, the one who was asking about you."

"That Lou Donovan guy?"

"That's the one. Carpesh can't be sure so he's going to try the helpful, friendly co-worker approach to see if he can get something out of Devereux to confirm things. We have a bit of good fortune here with her though."

Max raised an eyebrow. "How so?"

"She's originally from Savannah." Frank could see Max was not seeing the significance so he continued explaining, but in a mock female southern drawl. "...of the Savannah Devereuxs..." He waved his napkin like a kerchief for added dramatic effect. "... as in the niece of Richelieu Devereux." Frank grinned when he saw Max's eyes go wide.

"Our Richelieu?" Frank nodded and sipped his drink. "How did that slip by us? How long has she been in Los Angeles?"

"Actually, Rich himself informed us about six years ago. She bolted from Georgia after she did her internship and came out here. Her parents had planned to initiate her but she took off before they had the chance. Apparently, the old pomp and circumstance of the southerners didn't appeal to little Caroline. Which is understandable since she hasn't a clue about us." Frank got up from his chair and retrieved Max's empty glass, then headed for the serving cart.

"I don't know if that's lucky or if it complicates things." Max pondered the development.

"Well, considering Carpesh's temperament, and the volume that department handles, she could be a huge asset to us. As it stands now, she is just a nose snooping around where she doesn't belong." Frank came back to the table handing Max his refilled glass and the folder with the property research he had requested earlier. "I have Richelieu and the parents on standby, ready to come out at you're order."

"Lets get things cleaned up and Abby out here before we go there." Max began to look through the folder.

"I don't see how we are going to get around setting up shop here permanently one way or another. Circuit management has been solid up until now. Our Canadian divisions, the Midwest and East Coast all are reliable. Even the Pacific Northwest is solid as a rock, but here?" Frank stretched out on the sofa and took a long sip from his glass. "It's just too much to leave in the hands of others when temptation is like a marketing strategy out here."

"Don't make me repeat myself. One thing at a time." Max knew Frank was right but couldn't think about it now. Getting a handle on things and getting his hands on the rogue were the priorities at the moment. The rest he would deal with once his people were by his side.

"Oh hey, before I forget, remember a guy named von Massenbach?"

Max turned to Frank with a look of surprise. "Of course. We served together on the London Aegis Council. What about him?"

"Apparently word of you're arrival on the West Coast has spread. A messenger delivered an invitation this morning to some gala at the Museum of Art next week. He's the host. I put it on your dressing table but he had a hand written note in it. He looks forward to you attending."

"Send word that I'll be in attendance. It will be nice to see him again and it will be smart for me to be seen after the sweep, as a bit of an exclamation point to things." Max was actually looking forward to it. "What about this detective?"

"Donovan is Los Angeles County Sheriff, not LAPD, I know that much." Frank answered while fiddling with his Blackberry. "I checked with our boys at LAPD and they assured me that the Scott case is now buried, so it will stay off the radar. They don't know why this Donovan guy still has Talbott though. The body was found in the Valley, on LAPD turf, so it should have been turned over to them. I'll check in with whoever we have at command in the Sheriff's Department and get it out of his hands. Our guys in LAPD will take care of it quickly once they get it."

As Max continued looking at the property information, he thought a drive to the Valley might be called for. The south side of things had gotten a little crowded for his liking since the last time he had been in Los Angeles. A large enough estate in this area was going to be in paparazzi riddled territory which was entirely counterproductive to covert operations. Something on the outskirts. Privacy. Land. Yes, land. "Find me lots, parcels of land, so we can build to suit. Then tonight we'll go take a drive and see what our choices look like."

Frank started typing madly on the tiny keyboard of his Blackberry. "On it, my Dominator."

Max grunted.

"Okay, so it is what it is." Lou shoveled another piece of chocolate cake in her mouth as they considered the situation.

Washing down far too big a bite, Vinny looked at her with a grin in his eyes. "It's scary as shit, is what it is!"

"Well ya, but it's also fantastic! You're going to be a dad! You know you'll make an awesome dad, Vinny. You have to know that."

"Ah, hell I don't know that! Who can know that?" Huffing with uncertainty, he forked another too big a bite into his mouth.

"I know that!" Stabbing her fork at the air as if to accentuate her point. "Geez, Vinny! Look at how you take care of me! We both know you do, so don't even try to deny it."

The two of them sat together at the island situated in the center of the kitchen that was nearly as big as Vinny's house. Though it was a massive expanse of space, the soothing honey-colored wood and chocolate granite counters, accented by hand-forged wrought iron touches, made it warm and inviting. Lou and Vinny had spent many a night solving the problems of the world sitting at that island devouring baked goods. It was one of the rituals they had, similar to those Lou had with her mother. When Shevaun walked in to see the two huddled over plates in deep discussion, it was a familiar sight that she secretly enjoyed very much.

"Uh oh, whats going on?" She teased as she dropped her bag on the island, then proceeded to kiss each of them on the cheek. "Glad to see that cake wasn't wasted. Now spill it." She stole a curl of chocolate off her daughter's plate.

Lou looked at Vinny as if telepathically trying to get permission to tell her mother the news of his pending fatherhood.

"Vera's pregnant." He blurted it out before Lou could.

"Holy shit!" Shevaun nearly fell over.

"That's exactly what I said." Lou laughed.

"Well, it's a freaking miracle!" Without any further hesitation, Shevaun tossed her arms around Vinny and hugged him tight. "It's about damn time you got your own kid!" She let go, then swatted him playfully on the shoulder. "How is Vera doing? I should call her... Oh she's probably sleeping... We need to shop!... Is it a girl or a boy?"

Lou gave Vinny an 'I told you so' look and quietly chuckled at her mother as the woman rattled off questions.

"Shevaun, Shevaun!" He grabbed the over-excited woman by the hand. "You have plenty of time to have your fun. Relax. We won't know if it's a boy or a girl for a couple months, I guess."

Lou's mother stopped dead in her tracks and glared at Vinny. "Why the hell didn't Seamus tell us? When did this happen?"

It was a well known, yet unspoken law among Shevaun's family that you never kept secrets, especially juicy ones such as this.

"I haven't told him yet." He gave her a sheepish look. "You and Lou are the first to know outside of Vera, me and her doctor. Well, and her sister. We wanted to wait until... well until it stuck I guess."

"Well, he'll be right pissed when he finds out we knew before him." Grabbing the cordless phone out of its cradle, Shevaun started dialing then hit the speaker button and set it on the counter as it rang.

"Ah Jesus, Mary and Joseph." he blew out a breath. "I'm gonna need more cake."

Lou laughed out loud and went to fetch Vinny another piece of cake as she heard her uncle's voice on the line. It was very clear that any discussion about Caroline's findings or Lou's meeting with the captain was never going to make it to the table tonight. It was actually better that way, Lou thought as she sliced her mother a piece of cake and slid the last hunk onto Vinny's plate. His becoming a dad was far more important than her spit hunch. There was nothing she could do about it anyway now that it was going to LAPD. When she heard her uncle's thunderous belly-roll of laughter fill the kitchen from the tiny speaker in the phone, she smiled to herself. Yes, this was far more important. Family always was.

He circled her slowly, enjoying the cool feel of plastic as it crinkled under his bare feet. The poor girl was exhausted, he could tell by her soft low whimpers that came fewer and further between now. She had struggled so hard the first several hours after her arrival, it was a wonder she was awake at all. As if by some subconscious need to comfort her, he reached down and twirled one of her long, glossy ginger curls around his finger. She stiffened instantly at his touch and tried to hold her breath, the panic and fear ushering in a second wind. A smile spread wide across his tight, thin lips. Who was he kidding, he didn't have a comforting bone in his body. He existed solely for moments such as these, where the foreplay of pain was danced out like a carefully choreographed tango. Ah, how he loved to tango. He stopped in front of her and closed his eyes, swaying his hips to the music that began to play in his head, lost for a moment. The silk robe danced across his skin like a soft caress as he moved, prompting him to hum his tune aloud. The robe he donned this time was a deep jade color, in honor of his guest's stage name. He wore it open and loose, unabashedly. Despite a few minor inconveniences, it had all worked out rather delightfully, after all.

He opened his eyes and looked at the girl who was naked and bound in the chair before him. Her body strapped in to conform to each spindle of the wood. Leg to leg. Arm to arm. Her head strapped snugly to the high straight back. Restricting movement was a critical component of the experience, after all. It added such a wonderful undertone to the panic, much like cherries did to a good cabernet. She was far more intoxicating to look at than drinking any amount of wine could ever be for him. Such pale skin for a Southern California girl. Those long curls spilling wildly about like the petals of a giant sunflower. Her blindfold was still secured, as was the ball-gag, which only heightened her feeling of vulnerability. What a rare vintage this one was. Studious urchin by day and lap-dancing harlot by night. It was just too delicious. His mouth literally began to water. When he pulled the blindfold off of her, it took a few moments for her eyes to adjust to the light. When she finally saw him, taking him all in, her eyes went wide with horrifying realization. God he loved that look. If he hadn't been impotent, he imagined it would have made him rock hard on the spot. Despite that minor hiccup, he knew she could see his excitement. It made her breath accelerate and she fought fitfully to draw air through the ball-gag. This was why he particularly enjoyed the ball-gags. Another oppressing factor for her to struggle against. It was all about layers of suffering, and he enjoyed them all deeply. Unfortunately, as much as he liked playing with his food, she was not a dish best served cold. It was time to dig in.

He took a step back from her and watched those cute little nostrils flare then pinch as she struggled to take in as much air as possible. He rolled his shoulders and the robe slipped off of his body, puddling at his feet like a pond of tropical water. Stepping forward, he leaned down and took her by the chin then caressed her cheek gently, almost lovingly.

"My rare, beautiful Jade. I have so enjoyed the intimacy of our courting these many hours. However, I think it's time we take our relationship to the next level." He pressed his thumbnail to her cheekbone and began to carve a slice very slowly across its curve. "Don't you?"

As the blood began to drip down her cheek, he reached behind her head and unfastened the ball-gag so that he could hear her answer. She sucked in as much air as she possibly could with a fitful gasp, then released what would be the first of many, many screams.

Chapter Four

The blaring melody of the Godfather theme scared Lou out of a dead sound sleep. She couldn't remember what day of the week it was, let alone focus enough to see the time displayed by the clock on her nightstand. She finally found her cell and managed to hit the right button to answer, but she forgot she was supposed to actually speak.

"Lou? Wake up, Lou!" Vinny's voice shouted at her.

Wincing, she sat up and tried to get her bearings. "Wha... what time is it?" She finally croaked out.

"It's almost 5:30."

"Shit! You let me sleep all day?" Leaping out of bed, almost dropping the phone, she wondered why it was still so dark. "5:30?"

"In the morning kiddo! Its barely dawn. We got a call from Metro deputies, they got a body. The tunnel down the hill from your place, Old Santa Susanna." Vinny laid on his horn as someone cut him off. "I'm en route. Get dressed and I'll pick you up in 10."

Vaguely aware of what was going on now, she scrubbed a hand over her face. "Oh shit, thank God. I mean, not the body, the time!" She grumbled and looked for a light switch. "Whatever... okay, yeah, sounds good. Drive slow and there's coffee in it for you."

"Not like I can go any faster than slow. Freaking traffic is killin' me.

Splenda, no sugar. Am cutting back." He clicked off before she could think of anything witty to say.

She was grateful she had taken a shower before she went to bed as she stuffed herself into a semi-respectable pair of jeans.

"Its going to rain today, and be cold all day." Her mother startled her as she came into the walk-in closet holding out a mug of coffee.

God she loved her mother. "Thanks Momma." She took the mug and guzzled half of it down, nearly scalding her throat in the process. "You got enough for a couple travel mugs?"

Shevaun smiled brightly. "Two waiting for you on the table in the foyer. If you're racing this fast, no way Vinny would let you drive so I assumed he would be picking you up."

"Huh, with a brilliant mom like you, it's no wonder I'm so good." Lou grinned as she juggled the mug to pull on a black turtleneck then a quick balancing act to pull on her boots. "How bad is the hair?" She dragged her fingers through her hair and did a little twirl so her mother could inspect her.

"Bed-head suits you. No one will make fun of you, I promise." Her mother took the now empty mug from Lou and handed her a coat. "I'm talking 40's cold today. It may even snow here tonight."

"Oh for pity's sake, would the weather please make up its mind!" Lou hauled out of the closet and gathered her things as she stuffed one arm into the coat. "Okay, gotta go." She gave her mother a quick kiss on the cheek then hustled to get out front before Vinny had to hit the horn.

Lou stood in the early light of dawn shivering. It was so cold that she'd been staring at the huge fountain in the middle of the circular drive, certain the water was going to freeze any second. When her partner finally drove up, she got in the car and handed him the travel mug while he laughed at the chatter of her teeth.

"You wouldn't last a second back east, you know that?" He shook his head and put the mug in the cup holder before heading out.

She reached over and turned the heater to full blast. "For Christ's sake its gotta be two degrees!"

Rolling his eyes he decided to endure the blasting heat for the short drive to the crime scene. They drove down the road and out the massive gates that guarded the hidden niche of sprawling estates and grand mansions from the rest of the universe. Close enough to still be considered Los Angeles County, but far enough removed that it seemed like a country all its own. Vinny really loved the drive and the scenery up in Lou's neighborhood which is why he always volunteered to drive. It was an easy excuse to steal a few moments to enjoy the peace, quiet and the view.

Just under ten miles later they approached the Topanga/Santa Susanna intersection but rather than turn right, Vinny kept going straight.

Still rubbing her hands together in front of the vent, she shouted at him. "You passed it!"

"No I didn't! Jack gave me a heads up that they have it jammed. As you can see, he was right and it's basically a parking lot! So we use the old road entrance."

"Oh." Was all she said but slumped down in her seat, slightly embarrassed.

At the bottom of the hill he made the right onto the old road and when they rounded a curve they saw what seemed to be a small army of law enforcement, Metropolitan Transportation Authority and Amtrak officials.

"They must have car pooled." Lou snickered.

They pulled off to the side and just watched for a moment.

"Well crap!" Vinny pulled the keys from the ignition. "Since the train crash a few years ago, anyone sneezes near the tracks and these guys start swarming."

"Yeah. You got any gloves?" She looked at him pathetically.

"Its called a 'glove box' for a reason kiddo." Reaching across her lap he opened the glove box to reveal that it was stuffed with several pairs of gloves, all identical in color. He noted her expression had gone from pathetic to puzzled as she stared. "Its a Vera thing. She worries I'll catch cold. I got three jackets, two sets of sweats and a survival kit in the trunk too."

"Seriously?"

"Seriously. And a 6-pack of socks." Not giving her the opportunity to make a wisecrack, he hopped out of the car and headed toward the scene. She caught up to him quickly but didn't utter a word. "You're not gonna make a crack?"

Buttoning her coat as high as it would go, she glanced at him. "Why the hell would I?" *I could friggin kiss Vera right now.*

The section of tracks that had become a crime scene ran parallel to the old road on one side and the new road on the other. The old road inclined and wrapped around on a hairpin curve over the train tunnel to the east, and ultimately merged into to the new road further to the south. From Lou's vantage point it looked a lot like terraced steps. Old road, tracks, old road, new road. Though, with all the people looking down from each level, it kind of reminded her of an amphitheater. Whatever. She knew she was grateful to be at the bottom because they had a chunk of old road taped off, which meant those people would have had to hike down the hillsides to get to the tracks. Clopping through the gravel in the dim light of dawn, Lou noted something else, and it was odd.

"Where's the train?" She whispered quietly but got only a shrug in response.

They came upon the throng of officials and observed that the crime scene tape had been anchored to folding plastic barricades that blocked off both road and tracks to the hillside then down to the tunnel itself. There were at least fifty people there, but only coroner jackets were behind the tape. Lou caught raised voices from some suits talking to the men with Amtrak logos on their jackets and more raised voices from the suits talking to men with MTA logos on theirs. It was a zoo. Through the crowd they spotted the Metrolink deputies heading their way and offered hands when they stepped in front of them. Lou recognized one Deputy as the ever-helpful Jack, Vinny's buddy that had tipped him to the parking lot situation. Once the pleasantries were out of the way, Vinny asked them what the story was.

"The suits demanded no one touch anything until the coroner determines whether or not it's homicide by train. So far, all we've got is the guy that lives in a house down there was heading to work about 4 a.m.. He comes around the bend here and spots something in the road..." Jack gestured in the direction of the tarp spread out. "... so he puts it in park, gets out to see what it is and he nearly shits himself when he sees it's a human leg."

"Just a leg?" Vinny asked.

"There, yeah. This guy though, he's part of the Community Watch over here and has us on speed-dial because of the kids that screw around in the train tunnel. So he instantly thought some kids had been partying in the tunnel and one got crunched, so he called us."

"Okay, that makes sense." Lou said as she stuffed her hands deeper into her coat pockets. "So you two were first on scene?"

"Affirmative. The second we saw the leg we called in to get a road block topside but we put cones and flares right away since it was black as pitch down here. My partner and I started a cursory grid search and that's when we found the rest of her. Main chunk is between the tracks. I'm no forensics guy but I knew right off, she wasn't killed by the train and she sure as hell wasn't killed around here. That's why I called you."

Vinny raised a brow. "What makes you so sure?"

The Deputy looked around to see if anyone was listening then leaned in closer to Lou and Vinny. "Zero blood on scene."

"What?" She hadn't meant to blurt it out. "You said it was black as pitch, how can you be sure?"

"Look, you'll see. I am telling you that either train may have pinched that girl's legs off but she was there, dead as a doornail, without a drop of blood in her before those trains left whatever station they were coming from."

"Those trains?" Vinny and Lou asked at the same time.

Jack nodded and jerked his head toward the mob and lowered his voice a bit more. "Only two trains have been through here in the last six hours and they both went through within an hour of the call in. One Amtrak and one Metrolink. These yahoo's have both trains stopped at stations. The Metro is at the Chatsworth station and the other at Union. They sent forensic teams to both to determine which clipped her." As if it were possible, he lowered his voice even more before he spoke again. "I got a buddy over at Chatsworth and he just texted me like five minutes ago that the Metro has tissue, but preliminary tests show impact was postmortem."

Lou looked at Vinny then back to Jack "Which means it's like you said, she was already dead."

Vinny peered over Jack's shoulder to look at the coroner team working. "Isn't that Caroline and Crapass in there?"

Both Deputies erupted into laughter, drawing disapproving looks from the hoard that loomed about. They tried to stifle their laughter but were failing miserably. Lou backhanded her partner across the chest.

"Its freaking Carpesh, not Crapass." She scowled at him. "You are going to slip one of these days and call him that to his face!"

Vinny looked at her, unaffected. "And your point being?"

Jack snorted then looked at his cell phone. "Hey, one of the guys is making a coffee run. You two want in?"

"Tell him to bring a tanker-truck. Vinny, pay the man." She smiled, winked at him, then scooted up to see if she could get Caroline's attention. Lou didn't expect Caroline to respond, knowing full well with all these eyes on her, no way Caroline would let anything distract her from the job. It was a classic case of hurry up and wait.

Lou shuffled her feet and loitered at the edge of the crime tape waiting for any sign of where this case was going to land. Dawn had broken but it was dim and grim under thick cloud cover that really looked quite threatening. How bad would it suck if the skies opened up on the scene right now as Caroline and her team combed over everything? Lou wouldn't have minded watching the bureaucrats get soaked, but that would mean she would be too, so she skipped that thought. All she knew about the scene for sure was it was a female and it was probably a dump job if no blood turned up. Lou started to ponder the possibilities then talked herself out of them since that would only make her more antsy waiting. So in a juvenile attempt to keep her mind off the crime that they may or may not be handling, and while she waited for her tanker-truck of coffee, Lou decided to do a head count. She started with the closest people to her first, then worked her way up the amphitheater steps. LAPD, Sheriff, Metrolink, suits, Amtrak, more suits. But on the upper step she noticed one of those suits in a really nice three-quarter length overcoat and thought of how you never see men dress nice like that in L.A. She looked harder and froze. Holy shit, it was him! Yummy morgue guy! Her breath caught and she looked up at him and squinted like an idiot to try and be sure.

It was still so dark and the glare from the portable lights shining down to her right onto the crime scene had her moving forward to get a better look.

"Hey!" Vinny caught her by the shoulder before she breached the tape and wandered into secured area. "What gives, kiddo?"

She glanced at Vinny then noticed what she was doing and stopped but that had only exacerbated her fluster. "Its gotta be him!" She barked as she quickly looked back up only to find whoever had been there was now gone. "Shit!"

Vinny followed Lou's gaze to see where she was looking and only saw Amtrak suits gawking from up on the road. "Who? Shit, what?"

"Yummy morgue guy!" It left her mouth before she could stop herself.

"Uh..." Vinny grabbed Lou by the arm and led her away from earshot of the several men who were currently staring at her. "Kiddo, you wanna qualify that statement? And maybe quietly?"

She suddenly realized that once again this perfect stranger, if it had been him at all, had reduced her to behaving like a moon-eyed teenager. She roughly stuffed her hair behind her ears and tried to regain her composure as she yanked her partner by the arm to an oak tree across the path.

"Okay..." She wagged her index finger under his nose as if it were the barrel of a gun. "... but I am telling you right now if you mock me or breathe one word of this I will never, and I emphasize the word 'never', babysit for you. You understand?"

"Yeah, okay."

Her partner leaned against the tree trunk and listened to her recount, in full-blown babbling idiot detail, her complete forty-seven second path-crossing with the well dressed, yummy smelling, perfect man in the corridor down at the morgue. The several minutes of continued babbling idiocy with Carpesh and her schizophrenic self-berating drive home. She clammed up the instant Jack started walking up to bring them their coffee and noticed her partner was grinning at her like the fool she felt like.

"Thanks Jack." Taking the coffee and drinking deeply she glared at Vinny over the plastic lid.

Never bothering to wipe the grin off his face, he took his cup when Jack passed it and thanked him as well.

"Hey Jack, you mind giving Lou and me a few minutes? I'll catch up to you when we are done." There was a decidedly jovial ring to Vinny's voice.

Jack flushed a little, realizing he had again interrupted them. "Oh! Sure, sure! I'll check in and see if there's anything new." He hurried away and met his partner up the path by the corner of the crime tape.

"Thanks buddy!" Vinny shouted after him then turned his wicked grin back to Lou. "Go on. And don't even dare try to blow it off and change the subject."

Lou rolled her eyes and slumped her shoulders. "Geez Vinny! Don't make me feel like more of an ass than I already do!"

"Keep dreaming kiddo. I'm gonna milk this one for all its worth. Now you shouted 'It's him!' when I came up, what did that mean?"

"Some freakin' detective you are! I meant it was him! Up there!" She pointed to the upper portion of the old road where Vinny had caught her staring. "At least I thought it was him. I am pretty damn sure."

"Watch it wise-ass. Now either it was him or it wasn't, which is it?"

"It was him... I think." She stomped her feet like a petulant child. "I don't know!"

"Well now who's the brilliant detective? Come on, what made you think it was him to begin with?" He sipped his coffee while he waited for her to think.

"The coat. Yeah, I noticed the coat."

"What about the coat? The color? Some logo on it?"

She blew out a breath and hesitated to answer. "It was really nice. One that no one in L.A. wears and it dawned on me, so I looked at the face."

He cocked his head sideways at her. "What the hell dawned on you exactly?" He watched her stuff her gloved hands into her pockets and shuffle her feet. "Hello? Spit it out Lou!"

"Okay! Okay!" God, this was embarrassing. "In the hall at the morgue, the first thing I remember catching my eye were the shoes. Then as my eyes worked their way up, the man was dressed so perfectly."

"You realize in the past twenty minutes you have used one form or another of the word 'perfect' about a gazillion times in reference to this mystery man?" He was so milking this for life.

"I know!" She blew out a breath. "Okay so he was dressed exactly how I would love a man to dress but they simply don't! So it made me look up and then he hit me square in the gut."

"He hit you?!" Vinny nearly dropped his cup of coffee.

"Not literally! Oh come on Vinny! I don't know how to explain it! You know me, I don't go all gooey-eyed over men, its not my style. Hell, I haven't been on a date in what, eight years? And we remember how that turned out don't we?"

Vinny remembered exactly how it turned out. The date that turned nightmare, quite literally. When Lou turned down a second date, the guy had gone psycho-stalker on her and nearly killed her twice before they finally caught him. It wrenched his gut just remembering it. "Yeah, I remember."

"Christ, I've been trying to forget this stupid... juvenile... whatever it was the other day! Then whammo! Either my subconscious is

Shadows of Doubt

playing one hell of a game or he was up there. I don't know what the hell I am doing."

"Christ is right Lou. Cut yourself some slack! So your hormones got a little shock treatment. Its about time!" He ruffled her hair as if she was a child. "I am pretty hurt though."

"What the hell for?"

"The whole nice dressed bit. I ain't no slouch ya know, my suits are Italian!"

Now it was Lou that cocked her head at him. "Vinny, just because the label has an Italian sounding name on it doesn't make it an Italian suit, and you know it."

Vinny huffed, slightly insulted. "We've strayed off topic here. So if this guy was making arrangements like Crapass said, why would he be here?"

"I have no idea! Which makes me second guess myself as to whether I really saw him." She didn't even bother scolding him about his slander of Carpesh's name.

"Lets say for argument's sake that it was him. Maybe Crapass mixed up the guys. Maybe he's some new admin down at the morgue and he came up here to bean count!" Vinny was proud he had a plausible theory for her.

"Maybe..." That would be easy enough for her to pin down and find out. "Caroline would know for sure!"

"Absolutely. If he's as yummy as you think he is, she would have sniffed him out the second he landed." He noted as Lou instantly frowned. "What? Whats wrong?"

"You're right is what's wrong. She would have sniffed him out by now and I would have heard about him, so that can't be it."

Neither of them noticed when Jack walked up. "Hey guys..."

"What?" Both Vinny and Lou said in unison, and both with an abrasive edge to their voice.

"Uh, sorry to interrupt but I thought you would want to know..." He pointed to the hoard. "We got a ruling as you probably can tell."

Lou and Vinny looked toward the crime scene and saw that a dozen or so suits were hiking up the hill along with all the marked Metrolink and Amtrak personnel. Caroline was waving at them from behind the tape with her Georgia peach smile, the brightest thing in Lou's day so far.

"I was right, neither of the trains were cause of death so the scene is all ours. Our forensics should be here soon."

Vinny gave Jack a pat on the shoulder. "I think the day is lookin' up my boy!" Grinning at Lou, they all headed towards Caroline and their crime scene, finally.

Max stormed into the suite and began pacing like a caged tiger. What the hell was wrong with him? How the hell could he lose control of himself like that? He went to the bar and poured himself a stiff drink. Who the hell cared what time it was, he needed to calm down and get things under control. Collapsing into the chair, he took a deep swallow of the 30-year old whiskey and cringed as he reviewed the morning's events in his head.

Things had started out promising enough. Well, not for the dead woman but nothing could be done about that. Carpesh had called shortly after four that morning from a homicide scene where the high-strung coroner had known immediately that the body was the work of their rogue. Frank had driven at break-neck speed to get them there and even with that, the scene had been swarming with transportation officials and law enforcement by the time they got there. It worked out in their favor though, allowing them to blend in since many of the officials were wearing suits. Frank had driven them in from the upper road which had given them a bird's eye view of the scene. The red-headed woman, or what was left of her, had been laying in the middle of the tracks, her legs sheared off just above the knees. He assumed the two pieces of tarp were spread out, one to the east and another to the south, to cover the severed legs. The sight of it had made his body tense with rage. He wanted information from Carpesh. Wanted something to get him on the path of their rogue, but Max had no choice but to hang back. Observe and wait. So that is exactly what he did, he waited. While waiting, he watched the officials and officers, transit authority etc., meander about while they waited for bureaucracy to dictate protocol. Max could have left, they didn't have to stay. Carpesh could have called them with any information later but at the time Max felt he needed to be there. Dammit, he should have left then and there! Even now, sitting in the hotel suite alone, he could scarcely believe how foolish he had behaved. Like some switch had gone off inside him the second he had seen her. All reason flew out the window.

The small figure had only been vaguely visible through the trees when they approached the scene. He had recognized her gait immediately. That strong stride, even next to the man that towered over her, she was unmistakable. Max's rage had all but vanished as he had watched the pixie of a woman and the man talk to uniformed deputies. It was then Max realized he had classified the man as her partner so they must have been cops. He truly hadn't been thinking clearly when he had ordered Frank to find out who they were. Frank hadn't questioned him, he simply took off to comply immediately.

Thinking about it all now seemed somehow worse. Not even the bite of the whiskey could take the edge off of Max's embarrassment. He could have lived with it had things stopped there, but no, he went on, continued to an even lower depth of... What the hell was it anyway? Hormones? He wasn't a teenager by a long, long, long shot but that is exactly how he had been behaving. He pictured himself standing up on that ridge, staring down at her like some dumbstruck juvenile. He had noted her hair was a bit of a mess compared to the other day, but that had only made her look more charming. What the hell had he been thinking? He was a Dominor. He had a job to do, not fawn over some strange woman. He remembered thinking that at the time but then he had been distracted, noticed she was wearing gloves that were far too big for her. It made her look impossibly fragile and vulnerable. She must have been cold and borrowed the man's gloves. Max remembered that he felt the instant need to give her his coat, to warm her, wrap his arms around her. He had even started to take a step forward before he caught himself. Or rather she had caught him.

That had been when he started his nosedive into the ridiculous, as if it hadn't been bad enough. She had looked straight at him. While that should have mortified him sufficiently to snap him back to his senses, he ducked and ran instead. The Dominor for the whole of North America, and formerly Britain, ducked and ran for cover! For the love of all things sacred, what in the hell had he been thinking? But he hadn't been thinking, had he? If he had been, he wouldn't have needed, yes needed, to know what she and her partner scurried off to talk about, would he? He wouldn't have run down the road like a buffoon, slid down the hillside unnoticed so that he could skulk around oak trees in the gloom of dawn like a common thief. All to eavesdrop on a total stranger! It made him cringe to think about it. But that hadn't been the end of his folly, oh no. He recalled slinking through some oaks to get close enough to listen to their conversation. His cell phone had begun to vibrate and scared the crap out of him. Replaying it in his head, he may as well have screamed like a little girl, it would have been par for the course! But the shock had come when he finally answered. Frank hadn't even waited for Max to say 'hello' before he started yelling in his ear.

"That's Donovan and her partner!" Frank had told him, managing to shout and whisper all at once. Max thought at the time he had heard wrong but Frank repeated it with emphasis as though reading Max's mind. "You heard me! Carpesh's 'Detective Lou', as in Detective Tallulah, Donovan and her partner, Sergeant Vincenzo, aka Vinny DeLuca." Frank had then muttered something about meeting at the car and abruptly clicked off.

Max should have left immediately. He knew it then. He knew it now, but he hadn't. Instead he plastered himself to a tree and listened to the woman recount their chance path-crossing the at the morgue to her partner. He listened carefully, to his shameless delight at her fluster and bewilderment that mimicked his own. He listened to her exasperation at her lack of rationality. He listened with more than a little amusement as her partner ribbed her. What the hell had he been doing allowing himself to muse that way! It was absurd at best. If not for the other cop interrupting Lou and her partner, Max probably would still be there. But somehow he still had enough sense to seize the opportunity to get the hell out of there and make a beeline for the car.

Frank never asked him a thing the whole way to the hotel. They had ridden back in silence. And now, an hour later, here Max was, staring into an empty glass and feeling like a complete fool. He couldn't help it. She was all he could think about.

The smack of the file landing on the coffee table startled Max out of his pity party. It hadn't even registered with him that Frank had entered the suite. Boy, was he off his game.

"Okay so here are the specifics on our Tallulah Donovan." Frank plopped down on the sofa and kicked his feet up. "Sure didn't see that coming. I expected a fat old rumpled dude, not a girl!"

Max didn't mean to laugh, but he did so with a snort even. Christ he had to get himself focused. "I was expecting the same thing so don't worry about it. Now what the hell are we going to do to get this case out of her hands before she and Devereux add that to their little mystery?" This was good, talking things out was getting him back on track.

"I wouldn't worry too much about that." Frank grinned like the Cheshire Cat.

Max quirked a brow. "Care to enlighten me, oh faithful sidekick?"

Now it was Frank that snorted. "I have my scanners set up in my room. While I was pulling up Donovan's data, an LAPD car called in on an abandoned vehicle in a grocery store parking lot. A couple bags of rotting groceries and a purse were on the front seat. So, I called one of my guys to trot down there and check it out. Turns out one of the cashiers knows the owner of the vehicle and its been there for three days."

Max furrowed his brow. "And this helps us how?"

Frank resumed grinning. "Well, while you were in here doing whatever it is you've been doing, Carpesh called with an ID on train-wreck-girl. Seems train-wreck-girl and the owner of the abandoned car are one and the same. And..." he continued before Max could cut him off. "...that makes the primary crime scene the parking lot which is LAPD's turf which means it's an LAPD case. Voila! I give it a few hours before they put it together. I'm a bit brighter than most."

Max placed his empty glass on the coffee table then sat back in the chair. "She is not going to like that one bit." He smirked ever so slightly..

Frank caught it then but played dumb. "Who?"

"Lou... er... Donovan" Oh to be a fly on that wall when she threw her fit. He bet she was adorable when she was pissed off. "Why does she go by, Lou?" He hadn't meant to say that out loud.

Bells were definitely starting to go off in Frank's head but he simply shrugged. "Dunno. But I will in a couple hours. By then I'll know what brand of cat food she feeds her cat."

"She has a cat?" Again, he needed to control the mouth and not just blurt things out.

Oh yeah, this was going to get good, Frank thought to himself. "I dunno. Don't all single women over 27 have cats?"

"Don't be an ass, Frankie."

Frank shrugged and bounced up" from the sofa and headed to his room. "What can I say, I'm a stereotypical pig about women." He chuckled as he disappeared through the doorway; he had some serious plotting, planning and flat out work to do now. He laughed some more.

For another hour, Max sat in that chair. This time however, instead of brooding over his idiocy, he went through the preliminary file Frank had pulled together on one Tallulah Luelle Donovan, also known as Detective Lou Donovan, Homicide. Such a frilly name and such a petite frame for such a tough cut of woman. By the time he had committed the contents of the file to memory, he was absolutely certain he needed to know more. It was time to take a little drive, by himself. But given recently gleaned information, he needed to make certain he was invisible. He pondered for a moment then headed into Frank's room with a knock that was more for show than courtesy.

"I'm borrowing some clothes." Was all he said as he started to rifle through Frank's closet.

Frank was so startled when Max entered the room that he nearly fumbled swapping screens on the computer so Max couldn't see what he was really doing. "What? My clothes? You hate my clothes. And my pants are way too short for you, nothing is gonna fit right."

"I need to do some recon. Need street clothes." Max pulled an olive drab commando sweater, a desert combat uniform jacket and tan tactical cargo pants from Frank's things.

Frank watched as Max made his careful selections. "Street clothes, huh?"

"What size boot do you wear?"

"Same as you." Frank tried so hard not to grin while Max grabbed his tan tactical boots. Street clothes, his ass.

"I'll have these cleaned and back in you're closet in a few days."

Getting up from the workspace, Frank fished a pair of thick tan socks and a tan watch cap from his drawer, then tossed them to Max before he left the room. "Gotta color coordinate, ya know."

Max only nodded as he left the room and headed to his own to change.

Frank knew something was going on for sure but needed to be patient and diligent to figure out what it was. He knew it had something to do with that detective, so that was the place to start. Frank had called a couple of his contacts to get data on her and had been running searches when Max had come in to raid his closet. All of that was going to take some time and again, patience. While looking over the educational data that scrolled across the screen, Frank heard the door to the suite slam. When he got up to see who was there, he discovered no one was, not even Max. Now that was something, wasn't it? Max rarely, if ever, took off on his own or without a word to Frank on where he was going. A man of Max's position was a target. It was Frank's job to have his back and to not know where he was going, or with whom, made it very difficult for him to do his job. This was not good.

A quick call down to the concierge to find out what vehicle Max had taken only made the plot thicken. Frank was informed that a motorcycle had been delivered a short time ago and Max had just left on it. It took a few minutes, but after some phone calls and some ingenuity, Frank was on the phone with the very helpful gentleman that brokered the sale and was obtaining the GPS data on the MV-Augusta F4CC. So, a guy screaming through L.A. in desert camouflage on a $120k motorcycle was apparently considered covert recon. Max was off his game and that bothered Frank a lot. Max was never off his game, that's why he was who he was. Max was the master of details, rational planning and patient execution. For him to take off and not follow normal protocol confirmed any suspicion Frank had that something was definitely up.

After a few minutes more, Frank had the map up on his cellphone showing the blip that was Max heading northbound on Laurel Canyon. At least he was taking back streets. It took another six minutes but Frank had called down for his SUV to be brought around. He grabbed some gear and was on the road and hot on Max's trail. Well, not too hot. If Max caught wind of Frank following him there would be hell to pay. As Frank finally exited the highway, turned and headed north up Topanga Canyon he found himself whistling the theme to Mission Impossible. He had a gut feeling he knew where Max was headed now and things were going to get tricky.

Caroline and Carpesh had taken what was left of one Janine Winslow, stage name 'Jade', back to Mission Road nearly an hour ago. Her prints had been in the system for a DUI she got popped for a while back which made the identification relatively quick. The young woman hadn't been a prostitute or a junkie. She had been an art history student at California State University Northridge and was taking a full load of classes during the day. At night, she danced at a fairly decent strip club in West Hollywood that had been made trendy a few years back when it was featured in some movie. There was nothing trendy about where Janine was going now.

Despite having been run over by a train and having her legs chopped off, Winslow's wounds were superficial and minimal, save for a gouge in her upper right thigh that had clearly severed the femoral artery. Several slices on each side of her face were arranged methodically and asymmetrically. They looked to Lou much like Native American Indians would wear war paint, only sliced into the woman's face with some kind of straight edge. The cuts were made with care, patience and no hesitation. Other then the wounds to the face, there were no other marked injuries. Only mild abrasions from being dragged. Across gravel most likely.

Lou had stopped being able to feel her toes about an hour ago. They were waiting for the deputies that they sent out to call in with the measurements from two trains. Determining which one sheared off the girl's legs was key for their time-line.

"Hey do you know if coyotes will eat something that's been dead a while?" Jack asked them while he walked the perimeter, double checking for evidence.

"How the hell would I know? Google it!" Vinny grunted and continued writing in his notepad.

"That would be carrion, and yes they do." Lou chimed in. "And they are prolific in this area so if Caroline doesn't find any evidence of wildlife feeding on our victim, our dump window just got a lot smaller."

"Clever girl." Max whispered to himself regarding Lou's remarks. He had hidden the motorcycle in a dilapidated barn about about 300 yards to the west and traversed the hillside to get close to the scene with relative ease. Perched between two boulders, he managed to disappear into the landscape because of what he was wearing. Even his Leupold tactical binoculars faded into the stone. He was close enough that he could hear them clearly so if he restricted his movements, he

Shadows of Doubt

should be perfectly safe from detection. Max took note of any data he gained from the conversations, perhaps to justify his being there as a covert op. He tried not to think about it too much because the truth of it was far less noble and more to the asinine. He wanted to see her. He wanted to observe her movements, how she worked, who she was. This was a start.

"So we are going with the theory that she was laid very carefully like this…" Lou laid down crosswise on the tracks with her legs slung over the east rail about mid-thigh. "… Metro trains do an average speed of fifty-five miles per hour so let's say thirty five to forty since it was approaching the tunnel and that evil curve is on the other side."

Vinny walked over and looked down at her positioning. "That seems about right. I can check with the conductor and get the logged speed for the train once we know which is our clipper."

"Yeah, okay. So she had debris pushed up against the right side of her torso, which is consistent with the directionality of the train."

Vinny's face looked pained. "I am sensing a 'but' here."

Lou hopped up off the ground. "The femoral wound." She said while dusting herself off. "Not even touching the fact that there is zero spray or spatter, directionality of that slice is inconsistent with the path of the train. If something from the undercarriage of the train snagged her, it would have been from her right to left. The actual wound shows a left to right rippage."

"That is not a word." Vinny scoffed.

"It is now!" She stuck her tongue out at him then maneuvered around to the location where the first leg was found. "I'll bet you one of Wicked Jack's chocolate rum cakes that the femoral wound was sustained before she hit the tracks and a pot of Kopi Luwak that cause of death is a bleed out from the same."

Vinny snickered. "You're on, Sherlock."

The deputy hurried up to them with a look of panic on his face. "What the hell! Rum cake? I don't bake!"

Both Lou and Vinny burst into laughter which only made him blanch more.

"Wicked Jack's rum cake ya dork! Its a brand name, we didn't mean you, Jack!" Vinny shook his head and resumed laughing.

"Oh." The color returned to Jack's cheeks. "Is it good?"

"As the name would imply, it's wicked good. The original is a must but the chocolate is to die for." Lou thoughtfully explained as her partner merely moaned.

Jack nearly moaned himself. "Man that sounds good. So whats that poopieloo-whatever?"

The two laughed again as Lou's cell started to ring. "It's Caroline."

Vinny took the opportunity to explain the pricey coffee and its origins to Jack while Lou took the call, pacing while her friend relayed the preliminary findings. Lou mostly listened until Caroline got to the part where she said she thought they had their mystery saliva again. That's when Lou yelled, very loud.

"Are you shitting me?!" Vinny and Jack turned to look at Lou when they heard her shout but quickly turned their attention to the four arriving vehicles, two of which were LAPD cruisers.

Max wondered who it was Lou was talking to on the phone and what it was that would make her shout. He thought perhaps she was being notified about the jurisdiction issue that Frank had the inside scoop on, but the cars that had pulled up after her exclamation made him think again. "Well, let's see how well you do under pressure my dear." He whispered to himself and settled in to watch the show.

Lou clicked off her call, stuffed her phone back in her pocket and watched as the four uniformed LAPD officers exited their respective cruisers. Behind them came two men who looked like department brass to Lou, exiting a cliché blue Crown Victoria. Then to her surprise came her captain, who got out of his departmental issue brown Accord looking less than pleased. This could not be good, she thought to herself. As if in a gesture of solidarity, Vinny and Jack flanked Lou's sides and waited for the posse to land.

It was their captain that walked up to them first. He had apparently asked the others to hang back so he could speak with his team privately.

"Alright, we have a development with this case." He ushered them off to the side and instinctively they all huddled together.

"Whats going on, Captain?" Vinny was the one who asked, but they all wanted to know.

"Lou, since you're tight with Devereux, I'm sure she has notified you by now that the victim was not killed here. Preliminary findings state she bled out through the severed femoral artery, the wound to the thigh.

Lou smiled wide at her partner. "Coffee and cake at my house tonight!"

The Captain rolled his eyes and continued. "Time of death is placed between 8:00 p.m. and 11:00 p.m. last night. She was only dumped here. And here's where it sucks hard..." he blew out a breath and scrubbed his face with his hands. "victim's car was found at a market not too far from here. Purse and groceries purchased three days ago were on the front passenger seat."

"Do not even tell me we are tossing this to LAPD." Lou's back was up instantly. She knew where this was going and she was pissed.

"I know this bites harder because of the Talbott case, Lou. But it is what it is and it's LAPD's case. So wrap it up, give them what you've got and go home, get some rest."

"Are you fucking kidding me?" Vinny got a pointed glare from the Captain but did not back down. "Listen Cap, we have spent all day, freezing our asses off, the first half waiting for a ruling that hit to us and now because the side of the parking lot she was snatched from is LAPD's half?"

"That's the way it is, Sergeant. Now I won't say it again. You're hereby ordered to wrap it up, pass what you have to those detectives, then I am giving you the rest of the day to be pissed wherever you wanna be pissed. But not here." He turned and walked to the LAPD detectives and spoke with them a moment while Lou, Vinny and Jack just stared the death stare in their general direction. Lou turned her head so none of them could see her lips when she spoke.

"We have all our crime scene photos packed up already, yeah?" She took the grunts as a yes. "All our sketches and everything are in your car, Jack, we put them there when it started to rain earlier. Forget they are there."

Jack turned his head to look at her with wide eyes.

"I'll get them from you later and turn 'em over like the captain ordered, but I want to look into a couple things first."

It was Vinny that looked at her now. "What you got going on in that messy head of yours?"

She gave him a solid stare before she spoke. "Follow my lead on this will you?"

"Sure but..."

"There are things I didn't fill you in on last night that will make all this clear. Just take off. Get my coffee and cake and meet up at my place in an hour."

The LAPD detectives approached them and civilized introductions were made. They made halfhearted apologies but got to the meat and potatoes real fast and demanded all data handed over. Max knew this was where Lou would show her true character. How she reacted to being booted out of her own case. He looked through the binoculars so as not to miss every expression that would pass over her face if she did what he was hoping she would.

"Hate to take all your grunt work and run, but, protocol dictates." The one named Pearson said in a not so subtly smug tone.

"How many times you think he practiced that on the ride over, Lou?" Vinny's smug tone wasn't meant to be subtle.

"Four, maybe five? What do you think Jack?"

Jack yawned and shrugged. "Don't really give a shit."

Lou snorted, then, with a good bit of dramatic flourish, fell into a professional persona. "Well, would love to help you boys out but we basically haven't done shit. We don't get to work until after the donuts arrive and…" She looked at the watch she wasn't wearing. "Deputy Fife hasn't come back with them yet."

"Oh! He called!" It was hard for Vinny to keep a straight face.

"He did?!" Lou went overboard with the look of surprise.

"Yeah, he called and said Aunt Bee burned the first batch so it was gonna be a while longer." Vinny spit to his left, then walked straight through the men, patting one on the back as he slipped through. "Good luck y'all!"

Both Lou and Jack followed Vinny to Jack's cruiser and ignored the shouts and threats that the LAPD boys were tossing at them.

"Jack, get directions from Vinny and get up to my place as soon as you're officially off duty. Bring everything. Don't say a word to anyone. Got me?" Lou looked at him sternly, waiting for his response.

"Roger that! This is the most fun I have had in a long time. See ya!" Jack grinned from ear to ear as he got in his cruiser and took off.

As Lou and Vinny walked to his car, she started to consider everything that Caroline had told her. "Vinny, you go get my cake and coffee and then get back to my place."

"I got it! Cake and coffee! I don't welch on a bet and you know it, But…You gots some splaining to do Louseeeee." He loved using his

Ricky Ricardo imitation on her whenever he got the chance. "Lets get you home and warm."

"Nah, I'm gonna walk."

"Walk? Its like ten miles! Nobody walks in L.A.!" Vinny's face was aghast.

"There's a trail back up through Santa Susanna. Its not that bad. Besides, I have to think some things through first."

He blew out a breath and ran his fingers through his hair. "I don't like it. What if you get eaten by a mountain lion? You know I can't bring rum cake home. Vera will kill me."

She rolled her eyes at him and started walking up the embankment. "GPS on my cell is active. If I'm not home by the time you get there, track me."

Max watched his spitfire detective disappear into a gap in the hillside with a grin plastered on his face. The Mayberry references almost made him laugh out loud. She was quick, and smart, and she sure as hell was not going to let this case go. It was going to be a major fly in the ointment dodging this woman while trying to put an end to his rogue. But he had a very strong feeling he was going to get a kick out of it.

Frank had tracked the motorcycle to an abandoned barn but there was no Max in sight. He knew he was close, though. The crime scene was about 400 yards to the east so doubling back was the best course of action. Frank parked the SUV down the canyon then hiked up to the peak where he could get a decent vantage point. He had brought his Steiner binoculars and his Phantom IR Thermal Binocular, so if Max was in there, he would find him. Frank started to hum the Mission Impossible theme again and had to admit he was having fun.

He watched the detectives and the uniform do their thing but he couldn't see any sign of Max at first glance. He slowly and methodically scanned the landscape with the binoculars to try and spot his man. The clothes Max had worn were made for this terrain. He would be blending in perfectly. Tricky bastard. But then Frank saw it. A faint flicker in a boulder formation on the hillside above the scene. Confirming with the thermal, it was Max. He was so perfectly wedged between the rocks that Frank could have walked right by him and never seen him. The watch cap Frank had tossed him was a brilliant touch, he had to admit. So what the hell was Max doing? This was seriously covert for just surveillance on a couple cops. What was the big deal? Frank watched Max carefully through the binoculars, zooming in as close as possible to try and read his expression. Was Max grinning? Frank scanned over to try and figure out what could possibly make Max grin. It took only a second for the scene to come into focus. Frank zeroed in on the woman. Donovan was laying across the railroad tracks as her partner walked up to her, then the uniformed deputy. They appeared to talk a bit but there was nothing overtly amusing. It was then that it hit him. It wasn't what they were doing, it wasn't even them, it was her! Max was grinning at her! It all made so much sense now, even the odd concern over her name and the cat thing. Max was sparked! Devout to being the lone wolf tough guy. Refusing any semblance of an advance for what everyone thought was the sake of his position. Max had the great wall of no-romance-whatsoever built so thick and high around him for as long as Frank could remember. There was absolutely no way in hell he was letting this opportunity slip by.

Frank scrambled from his perch and reached for his cell phone while he sprinted back to the SUV. He hit speed dial, tossed his gear into the back of the truck then hopped into the driver's seat. Someone finally answered on the other end.

"Invoke a Cone of Silence and call me back immediately! This is a code pink!" He clicked off and burned rubber hanging a U-turn to head back to the hotel. This was going to take a lot of finesse but he wasn't going to get another chance like this again so he had best make it good.

While he drove he propped open his laptop in the passenger seat and started issuing it verbal commands. Naming files, transfer locations, then his cell phone rang and he hit speaker.

"You clear?" Was how he answered.

"What the hell? Code Pink?"

Frank was nearly humming with excitement. "You heard me right, girlie!"

"That's our secret joke, not a real code Frankie."

"Abby, its a real code now! You will not believe what I just saw! But you need to make sure this is all secure. Plausible deniability if it goes south."

"Again I say, what the hell?" Abby was more confused then ever with Frank's cryptic ramblings.

"Listen to me!" He shouted at her. "We have very little time to pull this off so I need your genius, like now. Get a pen and take notes on what I am about to tell you and make sure no one can hear you! Use your secret encrypted shorthand or whatever it is."

Abby was really curious now, and a little excited, she had to admit. Code Pink was a joke she and Frank had come up with ages ago when they were trying to play matchmaker for Max. Max refused even the slightest attempt at any matter of the heart after his betrothed had died eons ago. But it had been way too long and Frank and Abby were worried for him. Max deserved love and happiness more than any of them. At least that's how Abby and Frank felt. So Abby and Frank made a pact that if ever there was a glimmer of hope to get Max hooked up, it was a Code Pink and took priority over everything.

By the time Frank was pulling up to the hotel valet, he could hear Abby literally bouncing up and down with excitement. "Focus and get it done Abby. I gotta go and get my end set. Keep your fingers crossed and your mouth shut, you hear me?!"

"You have so got it, Boy Wonder! This is gonna be awesome!" Abby clicked off before Frank could so he knew she was going to go mach five to get her end set up. He handed the keys to the valet and noted it was only half past one in the afternoon so getting what he wanted set up was entirely doable. He just had to do it before Max got back. With that thought, Frank literally ran for the elevator.

Chapter Five

The drive from the crime scene was roughly ten miles to the McAllister compound whereas the hike through the hills and into the hidden valley of estates was about half that. By the time Lou made the descent into the backside of their property, she was less livid over having the case yanked away than she had been. It was still freezing but the hike had done her good, warming her up and bringing her focus back. Had it not been for the feeling that she was being followed by a hungry mountain lion or something, it would have been a perfect hike home.

When she hopped off the last boulder, it wasn't the all-terrain golf cart that startled her her so much as the two uniformed men who stood crouched with their weapons trained at her head. It took her a second but she soon recognized them to be the roaming security detail for the estates.

"Hey Lou! We thought you were some creeper sneaking around." The security officer she knew as Bob, holstered his weapon and smiled pleasantly. "What the heck are you doing coming in this way?"

"Sorry guys, I had a crime scene local so I decided to hike home, since it's such a lovely day." Lou smirked and the two men laughed. "Have you guys spotted a mountain lion around recently?"

"Not in a couple months." The other officer Lou knew to be Jose answered. "It probably headed to Florida for the winter! Hop on and we'll give you a ride the rest of the way before it starts to rain, or snow, or whatever the hell it's planning to do."

"Thanks! This weather is starting to get to me." Lou noticed she still had Vinny's gloves on and was grateful for it.

"It'll be spring before you know it. Hang on tight, ride is a little rough heading back to the road." Bob strapped himself in then started the engine of the stout little vehicle.

Lou grabbed on to to the crossbar and gave it a good hug as the man put it in gear and they started the haul through the dirt. When her cell rang she was surprised to hear Caroline on the other end.

"What the hell Lou?!" the southern drawl on the other end exclaimed.

Lou rolled her eyes. "So you heard?"

"I heard! LAPD took over our case! I don't want to deal with them on this! This was our thing! Why did you let them take it?"

"Like I had a choice! The captain came to the scene himself to drop the bomb." Lou's voice shuddered a bit because of the bouncy ride.

"Where are you?" Caroline could hear the engine in the background.

"Security is giving me a ride home. As soon as you can get out of there, head up to my place. Oh, and if copies of all your stuff on Winslow could manage to find its way up here too..."

"Already in the works." Caroline cut her off because she had been planning the same thing Lou seemed to be. "They've bumped me for Carpesh on this but easy-peasy to snag duplicates. I am just waiting for the tox report, then I can be outta here."

"See ya when I see ya then" Lou stuffed the phone back in her pocket and got a better grip on the monster truck of a golf cart. It really was very clever for security to have the sturdy vehicles, given so much of the area was still undeveloped and would hopefully stay that way.

The rain had just started to come down when they pulled up to the McAllister steps. Lou thanked the guards then headed inside. She noted it was almost three in the afternoon and heard her mother's voice coming from her office. Before heading upstairs she popped her head in to see Shevaun on the phone scribbling furiously in a notebook. Her mother looked up briefly and waved at Lou but was obviously on an important call given she waved her daughter off. Lou would find out what was up soon enough, so she decided a long hot shower was in order before her co-conspirators arrived. One of them with rum cake and coffee.

It was half past three when Max walked into the suite. Abby and Frank had spent the last hour and a half working magic and it was all lining up brilliantly. All Frank had to do was keep his composure until the mouse went for the cheese. The mouse being Max of course. Abby spent the last twenty minutes lecturing Frank about remaining calm and not giving anything away or blowing it. That was easier said than done. But when Max walked in, Frank was cool as a cucumber and had everything in play. All he had to do is get Max to take the bait.

"Hey. How'd it go?" Frank looked up casually from his papers to greet Max.

"Hey. Ah, was a dead end. Whats going on around here? Anyone check in?" Max removed the watch cap and jacket, then plopped down on the couch.

Dead end my ass, Frank thought to himself and tried with all his might not to grin. "Yeah everyone did. Abby expects to be here by tomorrow afternoon. Niko may be here in the morning."

"Good. What about Finn and Yuri?"

"Finn just secured the last Piaculum Sanguineus and is preparing the transport. Once he's made sure they've been received by the

Registrar, he'll be on his way." Frank double checked the file to make sure it was all in order before he got the show on the road. "Yuri is having some minor issues with one of our Congressman so he's going to get that cleaned up and should be here by Monday."

"Good. Things are coming along then." Max felt a slight twinge of guilt that he had allowed himself to become distracted while everyone else had been following through on orders so diligently.

"Actually..." This was it. Frank got up and set the file in front of Max. "They are coming along a little faster and smoother then I expected. You're going to need to change, we have a meeting."

"A meeting?" Max reached for the file. "About?"

"Well, after you took off and during my research, I came across the perfect location for a permanent residency here. The problem is that in order to meet our specs, we need to merge four separate lots, which normally wouldn't be a problem..."

"But?" Max really could have cared less about all this.

"But it's in a very exclusive and guarded area and the Association has to sign off on the reassignment of the lots."

Max set the folder back down without looking at it. "You handle it, I trust you."

"Well that's real sweet and all but you are the principal and they need to meet with you, personally. I think they want to be assured you're not going to build a pig farm or a porno amusement park or something.

"Christ Frank, I can't be bothered with this trivial bullshit."

Frank tucked his hands in his pockets and crossed his fingers. "It won't take long. Its a perfect set up, you just need to schmooze for an hour, then we can come back. Its only about 10 miles north-ish from that crime scene we were at today. There is another industrial zoned area within your preferred range for a build to suit tech-ops. Really a perfect situation if we can get it."

Max quirked his brow, grabbed the folder and started flipping through pages. When Frank saw Max close his eyes as if recalling something, he knew he had him. "What time is the meeting?"

It took everything Frank had not to grin. "Seven. So put on a spiffy suit and polish those pearly whites so we can get this deal done and get on with things."

"Alright. I'm going to check my messages, then take a shower. I'll be ready in time."

"Sounds good." Frank grinned from ear to ear the second Max was safely out of the room.

By the time Vinny got there, Lou had showered, dressed and gotten plates and mugs set up for her guests in the family room. The room was cavernous but cozy in its tones and décor. It made you feel as if you were in some grand Tuscan estate with its cathedral ceilings, old stone, distressed hardwood floors and massive iron candeliers. Two giant chocolate chenille couches, heavily laden with overstuffed pillows, flanked each side of the majestic fireplace that was currently ablaze. The coffee table between the couches was equally massive and was constructed of a similar cocoa colored wood as the beams in the ceiling and iron as the chandeliers. It was a soothing ensemble of earthy taupes, rich browns, creamy ivory and dashes of burnt umber for good measure. It was one of Lou's favorite rooms in the whole house.

Not only had Vinny come through with the coffee and cake, but he had brought two pizzas loaded with nearly everything as well. Lou set up both work and food stations on the coffee table while Vinny took off his coat and got comfy.

"Okay Lou, so what the hell have you not been telling me here?" Vinny eased himself down on the couch opposite Lou and waited for her to spill the beans.

"Caroline is on her way over. I would kind of like to wait until she gets here so that we are all on the same page."

"Same page?" Vinny proceeded to remove his shoes and wiggle his toes. "I ain't even in the same bookstore as you! Ya gotta give me a clue here kiddo."

"Alright, well you remember the saliva that was found on Angela Talbott?"

"Yeah, the stuff was too degraded to even get an animal, vegetable or mineral type off it."

"Right. Well..." The sound of the doorbell cut Lou off. "That's gotta be Caroline. Here, take a look at this while I get the door." She handed Vinny the file on Marjorie Scott, then headed for the door.

By the time Lou got there her mother was opening the front door to reveal a completely sopping Caroline Devereux.

"Its raining, in case you were wondering." The sarcasm dripped off Caroline almost as much as the rain.

"Good lord Caroline! You are soaked to the bone!" Lou's mother ushered her into the house and shut the door behind her.

"Yeah well I ran out of gas three blocks from the damn gas station just as the skies decided to pee all over me!"

Lou snorted. "Its been one of those days all around I guess."

"Come with me dear..." Shevaun took Caroline's hand. "We'll get you some dry clothes and dry that hair, then you can be comfortable while you kids take over the planet."

"Thanks Momma. We're in the family room when you're cleaned up. Vinny brought pizza, too."

"Oh cool! I'll be down lickity split. Thanks Mrs. McAllister."

Lou listened to her mother scold Caroline for not calling her Shevaun all the way up the stairs. Looking out the window Lou thought about what her mother had told her about the possibility of snow tonight. The way it was looking, she may very well turn out to be right. She gave a little shiver then headed back into the family room to see Vinny scratching his head.

"You seeing it?" She asked him.

"Well, I think I see what you think you're seeing. If that makes any sense."

"Yeah it does." She copped a squat on the floor and flipped open one of the pizza boxes, inhaling the delicious aroma deeply. "Man you get the best pizza."

"I'm Italian, what do you expect? Pass me a slice while you're in there." He continued looking at the Scott file while she put a massive slice of the pizza on a plate for him.

"Caroline spotted the same anomaly on Scott as she had with Talbott." Lou handed him his plate and a napkin.

"Yeah but with Scott it could have been duck spit. You ever have a run in with those ducks? Those guys are mean suckers!"

Lou rolled her eyes. "You sound like the captain. He said the same thing about the ducks."

"See! I'm not the only one who knows how vicious those buggers can be!"

"Oh Vinny..." Lou's mother came into the room, pulling on her coat. "... babies are only vicious until they are done teething." She grinned and leaned down to kiss Lou on the top of her head.

"Oh great, I was talking about ducks and now you toss that at me!" Vinny paled a little as he considered Shevaun's words.

"I was kidding you." She grinned and winked at Lou. "Okay I will be back in about an hour or so."

"Where the heck are you going in this weather?" Lou was obviously not pleased. "I thought Joe had a car bringing him from the airport?"

"Its an emergency Association meeting at the Gould's." Shevaun sighed. "Some God knows who wants to buy the five lots adjacent to the west of us, consolidate them into one lot, then build God knows what."

It was Lou's face that paled now. "Are you serious? I thought Joe was going to buy those and keep them natural? For the animals?!"

Shevaun patted her daughter on the head. "I know baby but Joe isn't here is he? So Momma's gotta go and scare the mean man away." She smiled sweetly, then turned to leave. "Don't worry, it should only take an hour. Save me some cake!"

Caroline came into the room as Lou's mother was going out. She looked like she was ten years old wearing a pair of Lou's pink sweats and oversized fuzzy bunny slippers.

"I'm staying the night. And maybe forever." She declared as she plopped down on the couch behind Lou.

"Fine with me. But you take a guest room, ya ain't sleeping in my bed. Angus barely lets me sleep in it." Lou was referring to her highly territorial cat.

"Yeah I could see how that would be a problem. He was sprawled out on the comforter when I went in there. How the hell does he stretch out so long? He didn't even bother to look up when I said hello."

"Okay ladies, can we get back to business here before my wife calls and smells the pizza and cake through the phone and I get royally busted?"

The two women snorted and chuckled at the grown man's blatant fear of his wife. Then Lou shoveled a piece of pizza out for Caroline and they all snarfed the pie down in record time. Between bites, Lou filled Vinny in on how Caroline made the connection between the Scott and Talbott women and when he was finally up to speed, including her conversation with their captain, Lou turned to Caroline.

Shadows of Doubt

"Okay so you found something on this one too, right?"

Vinny held a hand up. "Wait, I think I'm going to need coffee for this. Go over the salients on today's victim while I play barista." He got up and headed to the bar where he had put the bag of exorbitantly expensive coffee. Joe McAllister had spared no expense on appliances for the house and had over a dozen coffee makers, espresso machines and other caffeine producing equipment installed throughout the house. Behind the bar was one of Joe's prize acquisitions, a beautiful Belle Époque espresso machine that gleamed of copper and brass. Vinny absolutely coveted the thing and knew how to operate it like a master. Lou had to admit, Vinny and Joe did make the best damn coffee in the known universe.

Caroline pulled out a file and notepad from her bag while trying not to over-salivate at the smell of the luscious coffee. She proceeded to read them the data she was able to snake from Carpesh and then started in on information she had gleaned from eavesdropping on the LAPD detectives that had been in the morgue before she left.

"Okay so Janine 'Jade' Winslow was a student and stripper. You both knew that though. Resided at the Chatsworth Glenn Apartments on Canoga, Apparently she left her place of employ, the Body Shop in West L.A. just before midnight on Monday. Manager stated she had a test the next morning so she cut out early. From there she went to the twenty-four hour Grocery Mart just up the block from her apartment. Apparently this was a common practice for her, according to the checker on graveyard shift who knew her as a regular. She would go in on Mondays and sometimes Fridays. Checker said she went through her line at 1:23 a.m. according to the register log which technically made it Tuesday. She paid with a Visa so it was easy to pull up." Caroline paused to take the cup of coffee Vinny passed her. "God bless you sir."

Vinny chuckled. "You're welcome" He passed Lou her cup and Lou smiled brightly but looked at Caroline with a suspicious eye.

"How the hell did you get all this from eavesdropping? Its a full freaking investigation report." Lou was rather impressed.

"I have big ears. And they sat at Carpesh's desk while they waited and went over everything with one another. I just happened to be within earshot, in the storage closet." Caroline beamed proudly at herself. "Anyway, the checker usually parks in back so it wasn't until today that she noticed Jade's car in the parking lot and saw the stuff on the front seat. Purse, the two bags of groceries she left the store with Tuesday morning. She calls it in, LAPD rolls up, gets the ID on the car and makes it for the point of origin for the crime. Thus, you guys getting snaked, again." Caroline sipped her coffee and moaned almost obscenely. "Mother Mary this can't be legal coffee."

"Kopi Luwak" Vinny said proudly.

Caroline looked at her cup then back at Vinny. "Seriously? That stuff from the Bucket List? The beans the cats crap out?"

Lou sipped from her cup and smiled. "One and the same."

Caroline looked back at her cup. "Ya know, when I heard that I thought there was no freaking way anyone would get me to drink it. Now that I have, get that cat some laxative and keep it coming!"

Both Vinny and Lou laughed, Lou nearly spilling her cup and its precious contents.

"Come on, lets get serious. So we know how we got snaked so lets skip that part. What did you find from the body?" Vinny demanded as he sat back in the couch and enjoyed his own coffee.

"Well, time of death was between 9:00 p.m. and 11:00 p.m. Wednesday night. That's as accurate as I could get given the weather and before they yanked me off the case. Amputation of the legs was certainly from the train, the Metrolink one by the way. Cause of death was definitely exsanguination from the femoral artery. Now, here is where it gets odd and where I get pissed because I can't do the tests myself, and I don't know what the hell Carpesh is going to do on it. First, we have the same degraded saliva on the femoral wound. That wound was made by God knows what. There are no discernible kerf marks or anything identifiable that I could get to before I got yanked. The wounds on her face, those were made by some sort of dull slicing implement but no tool marks there either. But!" She paused to take another sip of coffee. "This is what's going to fry your asses. There were traces of keratin in both the femoral wound and in all of the facial lacerations."

"Keratin?" Lou and Vinny both asked in unison.

"Yeah, keratin. But that's not all of it, the keratin has the same degraded bullshit situation as the spit! I can't tell you if it was a horse hoof, a fingernail or some weirdo knife made out of horn."

Vinny huffed. "So what are we looking for? A freaking serial killer reindeer with a drooling disorder?"

There was silence for a moment, then all three of them burst out laughing. It was a long belly rolling hysterical laugh fit that they all desperately needed.

"Okay..." Lou spoke up when she finally caught her breath. "I think it's that time in the program where we take a break, let things sink in, gel a bit while we get drunk on rum cake. What do you two think?"

It was unanimously agreed.

The house was tastefully done in French colonial architecture with impeccably manicured grounds, much like its owners. Phoebe and Carl Gould were a cheerful couple of a certain age that refused to appear as such. It was nice that the two were going through their mid-life crises together. Carl was dressed in a modern cut navy blue suit that Max felt was far too narrow for his frame. The Louis

Vuitton loafers were from the Summer 2006 line and bore the enormous "LV" buckle that you couldn't avoid seeing even if you were blind. Phoebe was not quite as subtle, donning a brown and pink Juicy Couture jogging suit with its gold foiled branding strategically placed on her backside. She wore enormous hoop earrings encrusted with stones in the same pink as the trim in her jog suit and the pink theme was carried out with the over-glossed, over-injected lips. They had greeted Frank and Max warmly and welcomed them graciously into their home. Once inside, the couple took them around and introduced them to the other Board members that had arrived. The weather appeared to be delaying two or three residents so Mr. & Mrs. Gould played the proper host and hostess with a small offering of canapes, an assortment of cheeses, wine and a lovely little coffee bar set up.

Max took the opportunity to, as Frank so eloquently put it, schmooze and put the Association members on his side of the voting column while they waited for the latecomers. The usual questions were asked, as they always were, and Max let his cover story flow with little effort. Over the years it was only little touches that had changed but the basic story was always the same and iron clad if anyone, including MI5, the CIA or any other top level security agency felt the need to check. A great majority of the story was true at this stage in the game. He was the senior partner of the oldest law firm in Washington D.C. and was planning on opening up a small annex of said firm here in Los Angeles. True too was that he was from very old money and station. As often happened, and to Max's mild amusement, when old money was alluded to, people became much more friendly. It was transparent, but it was the nature of the human beast, it seemed.

When the last of the members arrived, they were all urged to have a seat so that the meeting could commence. Max had noticed that one of the late arrivals was a very elegant looking woman who reminded him of the gilded fairy queen from a Shakespearean tale. There hadn't been time for formal introductions before the meeting was convened but he felt an odd familiarity to the woman that he couldn't place. Brushing the thought aside, Max directed his attention to the all-important matter at hand. As was another usual routine, Frank took the lead on technical specifics and explained to the assembly that the lots were to be merged simply to provide for a larger landscape for a private residence. When the direct questions and answers were posed, it was Max who answered and much to his amusement, the feisty fairy queen who asked them. It was clear that he had a bit of schmoozing to do with this woman as she was very unsettled with his proposal. Every time Max thought they had the sign off sewn up, the woman would toss out very articulate and possibly deal breaking questions. She clearly did not want him procuring the land. When the frustration of the assembly had reached a certain level, the glossy Mrs. Gould suggested a break be taken so that everyone could stretch their legs. Max decided it was an excellent opportunity to get to know his adversary and win her over.

Approaching her cautiously, Max knew now that this woman was not of the type to be taken in by his charm or his pleasant looks. It was time to take a cerebral tactic and appeal to her intelligence.

"Mrs. McAllister, we didn't have the opportunity to be formally introduced so please allow me do so now. I am Max Julian. It's a true pleasure." He extended his hand as he would have to a gentleman adversary and she quirked her brow as she accepted, apparently appreciating the gesture. "This is my aide, Francis Sullivan."

Frank followed Max's lead and offered the same handshake as he had done. "Call me Frank, please."

"Gentlemen." She spoke with the slightest hint of Texas in her voice and there was a familiarity to her that Max still could not place.

"I had expected to see you're husband tonight. Might I ask where he might be?" Frank asked.

Both Max and Shevaun looked at Frank with a bit of puzzlement.

"My husband? You know my husband?" She queried.

"We know her husband?" Max queried as well.

"Of course! This is Shevaun McAllister, Joe's wife." Max couldn't be sure but he could almost swear he saw a twinkle in Frank's eye.

"You're Shevaun McAllister?" Max was obviously taken aback by the sudden smallness of the world.

"Why yes, but how do you know my Joe?" Her brows knit, she was seriously suspicious now and Max was certain that was not a good thing.

"Why you're husband and I have been business associates for ages. My family has done work with the McAllister clan for as long as this great nation has been alive." Max gave her an easy smile. "Perhaps the name of my family's law firm is more familiar, Julian and Associates, in Georgetown?"

The connection was made and flashed across Shevaun's face instantly. "Oh my! You're Max!"

"Well I think I did mention that was my name, yes." He grinned and winked, perhaps a little of his charm might be useful at this point after all.

"I don't know why I didn't put that together earlier!" She seemed a bit embarrassed now. "Joe speaks of you endlessly and is so very fond of you and all your people. He actually is annoyed with me that I've never made the trip with him to Georgetown to meet you myself."

"Well I hope he'll be pleased we have rectified that situation. Where might the fine gentleman be tonight? I would love to see him." Max knew that dealing with Joe McAllister on the property would be a cake-walk compared to his wife.

"He has been in Bangladesh for the past few days." Her sigh gave away that she clearly missed him. "He is due back on the red-eye."

Max nodded. "Must be the Patel-Sanger merger. He contacted me a few months ago on some international legalities regarding the company."

Shevaun was beaming now. "Why yes! That is exactly what he's been there for."

"Well..." Max saw an opportunity for a lethal strike. "It would have been lovely to have been neighbors but I can see you are passionate about the properties. So out of respect for you and your husband I will withdraw my bid."

Shevaun's expression blanched. "Oh. But... well let's just see a moment, shall we? Let me just get perfectly clear on what you plan to do..."

In that instant Max knew he had her.

For the first time all night, Frank breathed easy. He had started to panic just before the break that his plan was not going to go off the way he had hoped. Shevaun showing up to the meeting in Joe's place had been something he hadn't expected. Frank had known Joe would have vouched for Max but Shevaun had been highly opposed before she had ever walked in the door. Now that the connection between Max and Joe had been uncovered, it was smooth sailing all the way. They detailed to her that the majority of the property would be landscaped and assured her that it would be fluid to the natural environment. Once it was explained that the necessity of such a large amount of property was to allow for the home itself to be set back as far as possible into the landscape, leaving the feel that there was no other structure around for miles, the woman was clearly pleased. Shevaun was enthralled and very happy with the idea now that she had actually been listening, as opposed to readying for battle.

"Oh that sounds perfect, and my daughter will be so pleased. She and I both love the land up here so much that we hate the idea of it being overrun by houses, and the animals getting landlocked." She was a totally different person than she had been several minutes ago.

"Your daughter?" Frank asked, already knowing what the answer was going to be. It was all part of his evil genius plan.

The pride for her daughter radiated out of Shevaun's pores when she spoke. "Yes! My daughter lives with us at the house. She's a detective with the Sheriff's Department. Though I am sure Joe has mentioned her hundreds of times. He's more proud of her then I am."

A vague bell started to go off in Max's head. "I am sure he must have but I simply don't recall the tales of a Detective McAllister from our Joe."

Shevaun continued to smile brightly although a faint flash of sorrow seemed to wash over her briefly. "Oh no, Tallulah kept her birth father's last name, Donovan. Though he passed away, God rest his soul, when she was only two. Joe has been her father ever since."

Frank imagined it took ever fiber of Max's being to keep his face impassive. He knew because it was taking every fiber of his own not to bounce up and down like Abby would have if she were there, watching their brilliant plan unfold so perfectly.

Despite being dumbstruck, Max was able to keep his composure. "Detective Tallulah Donovan. Now that has a ring to it doesn't it?"

With a melodious trill, Shevaun laughed at Max. "Do not ever let her hear you call her that. Only her uncle and I are allowed to call her by her given name. She goes strictly by 'Lou' anymore. A shortened version of her middle name, Louelle."

These were the little things that Max had so wanted to learn about his detective. This was a most auspicious evening after all. Meeting her mother who was all too willing to brag and impart little personal tidbits about the woman who had slammed him like an eighteen-wheeler.

By the end of the meeting, Frank had all the necessary paperwork signed and thanks to the use of the Gould's fax machine, was able to get copies off to all relevant parties in order to have the property secured by no later than noon the next day. Max and Frank were the new darlings of the community and Shevaun had insisted that Max join Joe and her for dinner at their country club the following evening. Max had desperately wanted to ask if her daughter would be joining them, but he managed to show a modicum of restraint and didn't. Once a toast had been made to the new neighbors, and all proper farewells had concluded, Frank and Max were able to head back to the hotel.

"How did we miss that Donovan was Joe McAllister's daughter?" Max demanded of Frank.

Frank bit his lip and continued to drive and only once his cool had returned did he respond. "It had to be the fact that she has a different last name. I didn't look at her residential information yet. That's all in the details file I was compiling before we had to leave for this meeting. I know we knew, it's on record somewhere. We have details on everyone but there are volumes so it's hard to remember them all. I thought securing properties for residence and the business front took priority over the cop?" Frank couldn't resist touching that nerve.

If Max squirmed, he did it on the inside. "Absolutely, but I expect you to be mindful of all operations at all times."

Frank took his lump, knowing damn well Max gave it only to cover his own guilty conscience.

"Do we have a front property for the firm's annex yet?" Max skillfully shifted the focus now.

"Abby has that in the bag. Got a historic old bookstore near the design center in West Hollywood. Its going to take some retrofitting and such but once we offered them the ground floor at a peanut lease, they jumped on it. Oh, and we had to stipulate to keeping the garden and some ficus tree."

Max gave Frank an odd look. "A ficus tree?"

"Yeah, its a new-agey place that's been there since the 1970's. Has a huge following. One of our local trainers has strong ties there so it really works as a great front diversion." Frank was so proud of how well things were coming together on the West Coast. Once the dust had settled and Frank was able to hammer him over everything, he knew Max was going to be proud too.

"Hanna stays in D.C." Max was finally focusing on matters that were seriously in need of resolving. "She runs that office far too well and I can trust her to be even more ruthless with it in my absence."

"So you're planning on making this coast your primary?" Frank feigned surprise.

"Its far more volatile out here. I should have discussed this with you, I know you have a life back there." It occurred to Max that he hadn't considered anyone else but himself since he became obsessed with Lou Donovan.

"Yeah, I do." Admittedly, Frank was milking it a little. "However my life is yours, my Dom. I am where you are always, you know that."

Max looked at Frank thoughtfully. "I do know that."

"I am sick to death of the snow anyway, so this works out just fine with me." Frank turned to smile at Max briefly then turned his attention back to the road.

"Do you think the others will be as amenable? Picking up and taking off just like that?" Even though it was the wisest thing to do, it still was not lost on Max that it was a substantial uprooting.

"My Dom, it's what is right and best for the Sanguinostri. That makes it a no-brainer." On so many levels Frank was absolutely right.

They looked like those sea lions that hauled themselves up on the rocks at the beach. Lou knew she felt like one and really wished she hadn't had that second piece of cake. Maybe she should have just chewed it then spit it out and she wouldn't feel like she was going to burst at the seams.

"Dear God in heaven, the pain." Caroline gurgled.

"I think my stomach is so full that it's shoved my liver into my sinuses." Vinny informed them. "I smell the glass of wine I had last night."

"That is so lovely, Vinny." They all turned their heads to the sound of Shevaun's voice. "I think all our days are a little brighter having been given that information."

Caroline snorted but winced immediately after. "Ow!" It hurts to laugh."

"It hurts to breathe." Lou said while trying to sit up so she could shove the last piece of cake over towards her mother. "So how did it go? Did you scare the mean old developer away?"

Shevaun smiled at her daughter as she picked up the plate, then sat down next to Vinny, being sure to give the cushion a little extra bounce so that he grumbled in pain. "Well it would appear that I panicked without good reason."

"So he's not buying?" Lou allowed herself to fall over on her side making no effort to straighten up.

Her mother carefully selected which side of the cake to start from. "Oh no, he's buying. Probably bought by now."

Lou shot straight up, despite the pain it caused. "What?!"

Shevaun refused to answer with her mouth full and smiled gently as she continued to chew.

"Mother! Hurry up and swallow and tell me what the hell happened!"

"Hey!" Vinny tried to sit up, he really did, but his belly was in the way. "Don't shout at your mother like that!"

Lou scowled at him. "She's dragging it out on purpose to get me all riled. You know how I hate it when she does that."

Vinny and Caroline both nodded and muttered. They knew Lou's mother made a hobby of getting Lou riled just for fun.

Shevaun finally swallowed and grinned. "Okay! Well, it seems the man is a long time associate of Joe's! He is only planning on building on one of the lots, the rest will be landscaped in keeping with the natural surroundings. Its really going to be very lovely. I'm excited about it now."

Lou grumbled. "How do we know he's not going to build some monstrosity or a log cabin?"

Her mother laughed out loud as she forked another bite of cake. "Oh he is so definitely not a log cabin man."

"Oh?" The tone of Shevaun's voice definitely got Caroline's attention. "What kind of man is he then? Hmm?"

Lou's mother laughed, then took one last bite of her cake before she started gathering all the dishes. "He's not enough of a bad boy for you, Caroline. I think his aide would be more your type though."

"His aide? What's that, like a secretary?" Caroline got up to help Shevaun with the dishes and get more of a scoop on the new men in the neighborhood.

"Oh sweetheart, I double dog dare you to call him a secretary to his face!" Shevaun laughed at herself. "They both are lovely, very refined men but the aide definitely has a mischievous side to him. I got the distinct impression that he is a bit of a bad boy, though well mannered. Impeccable manners now that I think of it."

"Well that's a rarity in L.A." Caroline scoffed. "That's one thing I do miss about Savannah, Suth'n gentlemen." She exaggerated her drawl.

"Well I am going to take these to the kitchen and catch a catnap before Joe gets home. Sweet dreams everyone. Give Vera a kiss for me, Vinny." Shevaun blew a kiss to everyone, then took her leave.

"Night Momma." Lou shouted after her. "Okay, kiddies. What are we going to do about these cases?"

Vinny blew out a breath and struggled to put on his shoes. "Not sure there is much we can do. None of them are ours so we can try and work them under the radar until we come up with something solid."

"That's three bodies in four months." Lou pointed out. "Two of which were killed within a week of each other. This guy is escalating and no one is cluing in to this except us."

"They may catch on." Vinny shrugged.

"Well you guys are officially screwed with these going to LAPD. Not like you can go plop down at their desks and peruse their files. Me, on the other hand..." Caroline flashed a cheesy smile. "Its perfectly normal for me to be roaming around. Plus Carpesh and I get along pretty well so I can snoop, bat my eyelashes and see what I can get."

Lou looked at her slyly. "You think you can get something more off that keratin thing?"

"You bet you're ass I'm going to try!" Caroline looked over at the grandfather clock. "I should probably hit the hay so I can get in before Carpesh and dig."

"Oh geez!" Vinny looked at the time and sprang up so fast it scared Lou. "I am so late, Vera is gonna beat me senseless."

Lou rolled her eyes and relaxed. "If she was pissed she would have called here fifty times by now. You're cell hasn't even rung once."

He ignored her and raced to grab his coat. "You don't understand, she will guilt me over this for a week, at least. Don't get up! I know the way out! Night, girls. I'll pick ya up around eight, Lou."

"Okay, drive carefully." Lou waved lazily.

"Night Vinny!" Caroline shouted as he flew out the door. "Okay so now that he's gone, whats the deal with some guy you saw when you were getting the file I left you?"

"Oh geez!" Lou folded her arms over her face.

"Don't be like that! Vinny seemed concerned. He asked if there was some new fancy dressing admin then told me the story, sorta. So whats the deal?"

Lou sighed and then proceeded to recount every embarrassing detail, as she had with Vinny. Including the seeing or not seeing him at the crime scene earlier that morning.

"Well, shit..." Caroline began after Lou had finished. "We need to find out who the hell this guy is!"

Lou sat up and looked at her friend like she had two heads. "What the hell for?"

"What do you mean, what the hell for?" Now it appeared to be Lou who had two heads.

"Why would I want to know who this guy is?"

Caroline threw one of the pillows at Lou's face. "Because he makes you a blathering idiot! That's why!"

Lou threw the pillow back at her. "That is precisely why I do not want to find out who he is and forget it ever happened."

"Lou..." Caroline scooted right up next to her friend and slung her arm over her shoulders. "I know you had that scarey crap happen what, eight years ago? Don't answer that. I know that in all the time I have known you I have never seen you even bat an eyelash at a guy. Hell for a while there I thought you were gay and couldn't come out!"

"What?!" Lou shoved Caroline's arm off her shoulder.

"Oh come on! The point is, this guy made you're toes curl, and not in a Gerard Butler sorta obvious way. You noticed the shoes first and everything else stacked up. I am a firm believer in Fate. If you saw this guy today, there is a reason your paths are crossing and we need to find out who he is."

"Crap, I hate it when you do that." Lou sulked and laid her head on Caroline's shoulder. "But how the hell am I going to find out anything?"

"Shit, are you not a detective?" Caroline swatted at Lou and made her grin. "We just do it. Hey! I'll tell security someone hit my car the day and time he was there and see if there is any security footage of him!"

Lou looked Caroline in the eye. "Damn, you should be the detective."

The two women laughed then decided it was time to get to bed. Once they cleaned up the place and were heading upstairs, Lou stopped and turned to her friend.

"What happens if we find him?"

"Who? Yummy Morgue Guy or the rabid reindeer serial killer?"

Lou rolled her eyes and laughed. "Yummy Morgue Guy."

"Well ya get married and live happily ever after, or so the books say." Caroline scrunched her nose, pondering a moment. "How about we just find him first. From there, we do a full background check. Then you can ask me that question when it comes back spotless. Sound like a plan?"

Lou grinned. "Sounds like a damn solid plan." She turned and resumed heading up the stairs, lucky to have such a good friend.

Chapter Six

The first glimmer of dawn began to silhouette the mountains in the east. Fading just the edges of the blackened night. Max had been sitting on the terrace in the icy darkness for hours trying to get his head on straight. It was better, but by no means perfect. He couldn't wrap his head around why this woman had gotten under his skin. Things like this simply did not happen to him, affect him, faze him in the least. Yet here he was trying to put an absolute stranger of a woman out of his head so he could focus on the voluminous matters at hand. It was a bit easier to control now that he at least knew where she was, or at least where he could find her. Not that he intended to, that would be absurd. It was just having the option left open that made him feel more at ease. The real kicker, the one that had him unable to sleep, was how this woman kept flying in his path, literally from the moment he arrived in Los Angeles. First it was at the morgue, then at the latest crime scene. Now with Frank finding the perfect piece of property and it's smack at this woman's back door. The cherry of all cherries on top was that her stepfather was a long trusted ally of the Sanguinostri which meant she had been right under Max's nose for all this time. If there was one thing Max had learned so very very long ago, it was that there was no such thing as coincidence. For whatever reason the Fates were weaving this woman into the fabric of his world and he would know why soon enough.

Now as the cloud-wrapped glow of dawn crept out, turning the black of night into the gray gloom of day, there was much work to be done and one serious pain in his ass to be rid of. This damned rogue had been plaguing their world for far too long now and it was time to get a fix on him and remove him from the face of the planet once and for all. His latest victim needed to be looked at carefully. Aside from the degree of torture being minimal compared to all his past victims, there was something different with this one, but Max couldn't put his finger on it yet.

"You know what I love the most about L.A.?" Niko appeared out of the shadows and laid down in the chaise next to Max.

"No, what do you love the most?" Max smiled, glad his friend was finally there with him.

"I can pack my surfboard and my skis, hit the beach for some waves at dawn, then head up and watch the sun set from the slopes. That's just sweet, bro."

"Niko, you can pack your skis and your board on the jet and do the same thing anywhere in the world you like, right now."

He gave Max a disapproving look. "Its not the same and you know it. Packing up the Jeep, heading out, disconnecting from everything for a solid day and hitting surf and snow in that same day. Loading up on crap coffee and snacks at the mini-mart. Its a real grounding thing. You gotta do it with me one day before the snow melts."

"So does that mean you wouldn't hate hanging here for a while?" Max knew Niko was making this easy for him. He appreciated it, but he needed to ask just the same.

"Hell no!" Niko chortled, snuggled into the chaise and closed his eyes. "Its dead of winter and here we are hanging outside. I mean it's

Shadows of Doubt

crisp and all, don't get me wrong, but this is as bad as it gets for L.A. It sure as hell beats shoveling snow. Not that I've shoveled snow myself in ages, but you know what I mean. Besides, this is the only place in the world where it's cool to be a freak." They both chuckled, then were quiet a while, just taking in the calm before the storm.

Niko finally broke the silence. "So you think he's escalating because he knows you're here?"

"I'm thinking he escalated to get me here. He's been under a long time. He has patience and he's smart. He'll let me know one way or the other and it will be soon. I have a feeling there will be something with this last woman. Something that I better damn well not miss this time." Max reached for the phone and dialed room service. "You want coffee?"

Niko pulled out a small antique silver case from his coat pocket and retrieved a slender black and gold cigarette from within. "Coffee wouldn't suck." He lit the cigarette and inhaled deeply while Max finished ordering, then hung up the phone. "Abby has everything in order back east. She's like a bloody machine with her efficiency. You going to want to bring bodies over for the annex here or hire fresh?"

Max had managed to consider that over the past several hours. "Given this is an entertainment town rather than political, I'm going to have Hanna research some top talent for that genre. Then we'll need to see who's recruitable. I think Frank's renting some office space in Century City until the new building is finished."

"How are we going to handle putting a new Council together for D.C.?" Niko took another long draw from the cigarette.

"I want each of you to pick two possible choices. Either from your own team or from one of the subs. Ultimately it will be up to me to pick, but we'll work them out together here while we are reorganizing. See how the dynamic goes. We'll use the alternates here for local enforcement. This place is a fucking mess and it's my fault for not doing this a long time ago." Max accepted he had failed. All fifty states were his responsibility but he had gotten lax over the years with California. He had faith that his local agents were doing what he had entrusted them to do, accepting reports at face value. He knew better now. Max was going to have to spend some serious live and in person time making sure people were doing exactly what they were being paid very well to do.

"You want me to hang back in D.C. and make sure things get settled the way you want them to?"

That was something else Max had considered carefully. "I think I need you here Niko. Finn likes the crap on the hill so I think I'll have him hang there and supervise the transitions."

"You know this is gonna scare the crap out of the Canadian offices. They are going to tighten thing up so hard on their own so that not a hair is out of place. Those guys would spontaneously combust if they thought even one pencil was out of place for you." The two men chuckled at the thought.

"Yeah, well we have good people up there. Plus each of us making rounds up there regularly makes them keep things tight. Its a point of pride with them that things are run like clockwork." Max appreciated the Canadian Provinces being straight laced and old world minded. Most of the agents up north came from first generation stock and had been raised to the highest standards of the Sanguinostri. He wished he could poach a few of them to fill spots back in D.C.

"So you ever going to fill me in on what's going on with you? I know its more than this rogue business and the free-for-all out here." Niko looked at Max and studied him carefully. They had known each other for far too long and Niko could see what no others could in his eyes.

"How about I get back to you on that when I figure it out?" Max didn't even attempt to lie.

Niko crushed his cigarette out in the large stone ashtray that sat on the table between them. "Fair enough, but I know something is weighing on your gut, so don't take too long to figure it out. Bad for business." He hauled himself up off the chaise and stretched out a bit. "Mind if I grab a shower in your room before coffee gets here? I took the red-eye coach so Abby could come in on the jet this morning. The guy next to me fell asleep and used my shoulder as a pillow. I think he drooled on me."

Max laughed out loud at the image of his hulk of a friend wedged into a coach seat with some strange man dribbling on his shoulder. "Of course! That's classic though. Why didn't you thump the guy and move his head off?"

Niko shrugged. "He was flying in because his wife went into labor early. Figured it would be the last sleep the guy got for about eighteen years so what the hell. I'm getting soft in my old age I guess. I'll be back in a few." Niko disappeared into the suite to get cleaned up, leaving Max to ponder what the hell he would say to him about the detective if he had to say anything at all. There really was nothing to say other than perhaps he was behaving a tad like an adolescent psycho stalker.

Max had a grip on himself now, or at least he would keep telling himself that. Things would take on a new dimension now because of his relationship with Joe McAllister, and now the one he was establishing with the detective's mother. It was easy to see the resemblance between Shevaun and his detective once he discovered the kinship. Shevaun had that same fiery tenacity that he had observed in her daughter. Both carried petite frames, although neither of the women were waifish or frail. They were strong, fierce and undeniably female in their small packages. Shevaun was nobody's fool, that was clear from the start and it was only the miraculous stroke of luck that she was the wife of Joe McAllister that had given Max half a shot at getting in the door with her. Fortunately he had seen that opening and it had actually worked.

He had known Joe McAllister for ages and liked the man very much. The McAllister family had been extremely valuable, loyal and diligent stewards of the Sanguinostri for generations. Max needed to make sure they had been properly rewarded for that through the years and if not, it would be an excellent opportunity for him to start taking care of that at dinner later that evening.

"If you want your coffee, you come and get it. It's too bloody cold out there. It'll freeze, or I'll freeze before I make it to the table." Frank yelled at Max from inside the suite, the door opened only enough for his mouth to fit.

Max rolled his eyes and checked his watch as he got up. It would be another half hour before the sun was actually up so he had a bit more time to relax and enjoy his coffee before the day got rolling.

When he stepped inside he was taken aback by all the bags piled at the entrance to the suite. Frank emerged from his room carrying more bags and sat them on the existing pile with a huff.

"What the hell?" Max looked at Frank as though he were insane. "What's all this?"

Frank plopped in a chair and retrieved his coffee from the tray on the table. "I'm moving across the hall with Abigail and Niko is parking it in here."

"Why? Why doesn't Niko bunk with Abby and you stay put where you are?" Max was clearly puzzled.

"Yeah man, that doesn't make any sense." Niko emerged from Max's room toweling his hair dry and wearing nothing but a pair of well-worn jeans that he hadn't managed to button up all the way. "I can bunk with Abby."

Frank snickered. "Well thanks for adding the protection of your virtue to the list, Mr. Modest. Abby considers me her little brother so there's no worry of her attacking me like she would you. Especially if she got a load of you like that." Max looked just as Niko looked down at himself.

"Okay, point taken." Niko said as he finished buttoning up his jeans.

"Then there is the practicality of it" Frank added. "You two can talk war all night like you usually do while Abby and I can deal with the administrative minutia that has to get handled, and fast." He sipped from his cup and looked at the two men, hoping they were buying his story. "Maid is coming in any second to clean up the room so you'll be good to go within the hour.

Max wasn't entirely sure this was the best set up. "What if I need to toss things at you on a moment's notice like I have been?"

"I am just across the hall and that's primarily for sleeping purposes. I'll be hanging in here most of the time and we'll probably just prop the doors open since we have the whole floor to ourselves anyway. The other two suites are already blocked for us for when Connor, Finn and Yuri arrive."

"Alright. Actually that is a good thing. We can put guards at the elevator to secure the whole level and just prop our doors open." Niko felt better about the arrangement now.

"It's only a temporary set up" Abby said as she stormed through the door with two bellmen at her heels and another dragging a fully loaded luggage cart behind them. She pointed to the door across the hall. "Over there, and haul all this crap in there too, please." Peeling her gloves off she walked to each of the three men and offered each a cheek. They each gave the customary kiss without hesitation, then she went straight for the coffee tray where Frank had already started to pour her a cup. "Good morning boys. Glad to see you are all up and at it since it's nine in the morning to me with that stupid time zone crap." She took the cup that Frank had prepared for her and drank deeply as she scanned her surroundings. She walked across the hall to the now open suite and barked a few orders to the bellmen then returned to Max's suite. "Okay, so what do I need to know that I don't already?" She asked while she sat down in the soft pewter couch and studied the three men. Her gaze paused to look at the shirtless Niko and give him a once over with her salacious gaze.

"See!" Frank snorted.

Niko immediately went and dug a t-shirt out of his duffel bag and pulled it on. Max only chuckled.

"Oh get over it! Abby swatted a hand through the air. "You all know I am what I am, so get over it already. Besides, its too early and I need way more coffee than this to actually be a threat to any male species. Now answer my question."

"You probably know everything already except that Max has a dinner engagement this evening. We need to get all the paperwork pushed through on the estate property today, so that's our main focus besides getting the building plans done and approved." Frank paused to take another gulp of coffee and Abby continued where he left off.

"My guys are already handling the lot line adjustments. Those should be recorded before the offices officially open, and ownership is already done. I got that taken care of once you faxed me copies last night. You own it all, lock, stock and smoking barrel and have since 11:14 P.M. last night." She smiled sweetly then sipped from her cup.

"That was excellent work, Abby. I have no idea how you managed that in under twelve hours." Max never ceased to be amazed at how

Abby could get things done in the blink of an eye. Especially when the normal course of something would usually take weeks or months to get through. It was good to have power, connections and unlimited resources. The Dominor and his Aegis Council irrefutably had all of the above.

"I have had a team of architects working around the clock for the past three days and should have four sets of plans delivered here by eight for your approval." She got up and retrieved her laptop from one of her bags, flipped it open and booted it up. "I have virtual renderings of all the proposed plans here so you can take a look now and perhaps even have a choice made before the architects get here. That way we can spend an hour going over any changes you want so I can make my meeting with the architectural committee, get them to sign off and get the plans through with regional planning by no later than noon. But I don't think you'll make any changes since I have had my hands on them already." She smiled sweetly again then turned the screen so Max could see.

With the magic of technology and Abby's laptop, Max was being taken on a virtual tour of an old world Mediterranean style structure that reminded him of a place he often loved to visit in Sardinia. It was perfect aesthetically for the area and had just enough opulence without being tacky or overdone. Stone and stucco exterior with cobblestone drive and walkways, tiled roof, iron gates and storm shutters. There were plenty of bedrooms, a guest house, massive arches and vaulted ceilings with exposed dark-wood beams. It all spoke to him of his old country and he fell in love with it immediately, just as Abby knew he would. But it was the things you didn't see on the surface that were the true beauty of the plan. Abby had worked her genius within the architecture to make the estate more secure then Fort Knox. The walls were reinforced with steel, windows were bullet proofed and everything that needed to be and even those that didn't were blast proof. The technical aspect of it all had the entire estate capable of total lock-down at the touch of a button. Two massive generators, very cleverly hidden, would provide full power to the residence for over a month. A fully appointed wine cellar was simply a false front for the basement command center that would be decked out with more high-tech equipment than he expected the Pentagon had. It was all brilliant. One thing he noted as the tour brought him to his master suite, which was a masterpiece in itself and exactly his taste. But it was its placement and positioning in relation to the land that made him pause. He studied it carefully and two of the four walls were made up of folding glass so that when open, the suite simply flowed out onto the pergola covered terrace that wrapped around the southeast corner of the house. The southeast which was the exact view to his detective's balcony.

"I don't need to see the others. When can we get this started?" He turned and looked at Abby who was smiling wide. Obviously very pleased with herself.

"I'll see if I can get my meeting with the architectural committee moved up, get this signed off then then get it sent to regional. Our people are standing by with the stamps and permits ready. With approval from the architectural committee we can start soil samples and surveying so grading etc. can start Monday."

"How long will it take to get finished?" Max wanted to be in the house by the time the weather turned.

"Do I have carte blanche for palm greasing? Twenty-four hour crews, gift baskets to all residents impacted by said twenty-four hour crews and then I am thinking we should purchase the parcels up next to the road and make it a park with a pond or little lake, and even a little pergola. Dedicate it to the community, then all the residents will be so grateful to you that no one will bitch. So you giving me a green light on the green or what?" Abby batted her eyelashes.

Max considered for maybe half a second. "Make sure the maintenance of the lake and park are handled by me indefinitely. And get one of those bronze plaques set in stone like we did at that memorial park in Virginia. Make it something poetic without being cheesy. We'll have a little gathering for all the residents for the dedication, those tents and twinkly lights, a string quartet, champagne, yada yada, you know what I mean."

She smiled at him brightly. "I know exactly what you mean. We should have a bridge go over the lake or pond or whatever. Hmm... maybe we need more land."

"Abby, how long for the house to be habitable?" He brought her back to the original question.

She scrunched her nose at him. "Do you want it done fast or do you want it done perfect?"

"I want it both and you know better than to ask that question." His tone was a little sharp with her so she reigned in the sassy factor and gave it to him straight.

"I'll be conservative and say four months. But I am sure I can bribe the association to allow restricted construction on a twenty-four-seven basis."

"I had an idea for CCV feeds that cover the entire area." Frank interjected. "We could donate some fabulous hand-made old style gas streetlamps to the community that just so happen to have hidden cameras in them for our perimeter feed. But we tell them its for the community's security & just tap into it."

Max nodded. "I like it. Do it. Do it all. Do whatever it takes to get this done perfectly and fast. You have carte blanche."

Frank and Abby gave each other a high-five and gathered their things to get started.

"Abby, Frank..." Max had them stopping in their tracks. "I need a list of all our people in the region. I want dates of when they landed here as well. Addresses, aliases, full detail on everyone and I need it this afternoon."

"You'll have it. I need to get set up and cracking. You all know where to find me." Abby headed across the hall, snatching up her laptop and coffee as she went with Frank following right behind her.

Niko sat in the chair across from Max and refilled his cup of coffee, one eye on the cup, the other on Max. "So what's on the agenda for today?" He asked.

"I need you're gut instincts on this changing of the guard, so to speak." Max leaned back in the chair and ran his hands through his hair. He was really trying to get a grip on things but he wanted to delegate so he could focus on the rogue. "You good with how we've left D.C. for the moment?"

"Abby is as shrewd and ruthless as she is freaking adorable. She has exactly who should be in place and I agreed with all her choices from the get go. As for a new Council, I think we need to call in a couple of old schools. You're going to have to take that up with the Senatus, though." Niko got up to get his cigarette case from his coat. "They may not dig on us fishing outta their pond but I personally think it's long overdue that things got mixed up a bit."

Max held out a hand towards Niko. "Give me one of those would you?"

Niko quirked his brow. "You know they say these things will kill you?" They both chuckled as Niko passed his friend one of the fancy cigarettes and lit it for him, then sat back down in the chair before lighting his own.

"What do you mean by mixed up?" Max asked, then drew deeply of the smoke.

"You know I'm pretty tight with guys in other Councils, yeah?"

Max nodded, it was one of his ways of knowing what was going on within the other circles, the gossip that Niko would feed him. "You have unique insights there."

"Well I have a few buddies that would jump at the chance to get out of their stations to relocate to D.C., but you will want to meet with them first and get a feel. See if they fit with your style." Niko watched the smoke drift through the air as he pondered. "They each have great admiration for you. One still wishes you had chosen him to make the crossing originally. It's kind of a constant joke he pulls on me that I beat him out of his spot."

"You think he could make a trip out here or should I go there?"

"Given you're poaching, I think you should set up the meetings there. Then you can address the Senatus in person once you're certain you want to poach them."

"Talk to your guys. See if its worth me making the trip or if they are just blowing smoke." Max crushed out his cigarette. "I want you to come with me to make some rounds today. People know I am here. I want to get in some faces, especially local distributors and havens. I want to find out why no one felt any need to inform us this place was becoming a shit hole and all our laws were deemed optional."

Max reached for a folder that was sitting on the coffee table and perused its contents for the fifteenth time since the night before.

Niko glanced over to see the crime scene photos. "That his latest victim?"

"Janine Winslow, went by the name of Jade. She was twenty-seven and lived in the Valley." Max got up, walked over to the window and looked down across the boulevard. "She worked right over there as a dancer most nights. I may have very well been standing right here when she walked to her car for the last time." Max shoved his hands into the pockets of his robe and sighed with disgust.

"No way you could have prevented this, Max." Niko got up and stood next to his friend. "You think he knew you were here and pulled her because she was in the line of sight? Just to piss you off?"

"Yes and no. He didn't snatch her from here, he waited and made sure she was a safe distance away. But he knew I would eventually be sitting here doing exactly this. Staring out the window to where she worked. He likes rubbing my nose in it."

"Yeah, but this one wasn't an urchin. She was bettering herself, that's off pattern. Even the London victims were unfortunates but this one was a student who was just working in a trash-pit to make ends meet." Niko had a point, and a point that Max was well aware of, which is why he was all the more bothered.

"That is precisely why I know he's escalating. He waited a long long time to pick up where he left off." Max turned back to the coffee table and picked up his cup. "The timing is key. He started in London right after I was tapped as Dominor. That went on for, I don't want to think about how long that went on. But once I clued in and we started hunting him, he made it more of a game. He got more careful. Then when I got reassigned to the U.S., he stopped cold. Nothing, or so we thought."

Niko sat on the arm of the chair and skimmed over the open file on the table. "Those scattered single kills all over the planet. You've always felt those were him. Taunts."

"Exactly, just to remind us he's still out there and there's nothing we can do about it. But now, he's in my face again. I'm not letting him float away this time, Niko. I can't. If he does, I will step down as Dominor."

Niko grumbled. "That's crap Max. You can't let this ass-hat undo all the good you have done all these years. Just because the West Coast got a little out of hand. He's taking advantage of that and pushing your buttons, but you can't let that work."

Max stood up and stretched while he considered Niko's words. "I want to shake some trees and see what falls out on this bastard. Someone has to have noticed someone acting a little too innocent or a little too guilty, not putting in for deliveries on a regular basis or something else out of the norm. There has to be something." Max looked at the clock and was glad that it was later than he expected. People would be waking up and available. "I'm going to shower and get changed, then you and I are hitting the streets."

Lou came out of the bathroom squeaky clean, warm and cozy, wrapped head to toe in fluffy white terrycloth. She could hear Caroline rummaging and cursing in her closet and for some reason that made Lou smile. It served Caroline right for being so damned tall.

"What are you grinning at?" Lou's mother walked into the room carrying a lovely tray filled with a coffee service and scones.

Lou jerked her head in the direction of the closet. "Caroline is raiding my closet. By the sound of the expletives coming out of there, not having much success."

"Ah, I see." Shevaun nodded as she arranged the tray on the coffee table. "It's her own fault for having those damn long legs of hers."

Lou snorted and bounced to her mother, kissing her on the cheek. "That is exactly what I was saying to myself just before you walked in. Thanks for this, Momma. I was just gonna hit the Keurig for a couple cups before we headed out."

"Joe did it, I just carried it in here. He's all excited for dinner tonight so he was looking for ways to burn time before he could head to the office. He sends you kisses and was sorry he couldn't wait until you were out of the shower to say hi and bye."

"Dinner tonight?" Lou asked as she poured herself some of Joe's amazing brew. She so missed his coffee while he was gone. "You didn't mention you were going out tonight."

"Didn't I?" Shevaun fixed herself a cup then sat on the edge of the ottoman. "Oh, well, we are taking our soon-to-be neighbor to dinner at the club. Joe was so thrilled when I told him about the meeting last night. He is so happy I finally met his business buddy and that we hit it off so well. You want to go with us? He's a lovely man."

"I really can't, Momma." Lou unfurled the towel from her head and combed through the damp mop with her fingers. "I have a bunch of stuff I need to do after I'm off the clock on this Winslow woman since it's no longer our case."

Caroline stepped out of the closet wearing a triumphant look on her face. "Tada!" She said as she did a little twirl. "How's this look?" She had finally settled on distressed black jeans tucked into tall black leather boots that reached just below her knee, and a gray chenille tunic.

"Well that looks adorable! Perfect for casual Friday on a rainy day." Shevaun complimented Caroline's ensemble. "Are those Lou's jeans? I can't believe they're not too short on you, and that top too."

Lou scowled at her mother. "That top is a sweater-dress on me. I usually wear it with tights and those boots, which go over my knees!"

Caroline snickered. "Yeah and these jeans are like pedal pushers on me. Without the boots you'd see they only hit me mid calf. But it works!"

Shevaun laughed but tried not to. "Oh honey, she's more than six inches taller than you and I so don't feel bad. At least we can call her a bitch to her face!"

They all laughed as Lou took her turn in the closet. She tossed on some boots, jeans and a sweater herself, then the three women sat and enjoyed their morning coffee together. One would think three women would be talking about the latest fashion or gossiping about someone or another, but not these three. Janine Winslow and how she came to be bloodless and legless on those railroad tracks was the topic of their conversation.

The three agreed that it had been premeditated, not a spur of the moment snatch and grab. No robbery since her purse was found in the abandoned car untouched. All three of them felt that the killer knew her or at least enough of her routine. Grabbing her when she came out of the market was the perfect window of opportunity. It was what they didn't know that was the big issue. Her body hadn't been on those tracks for very long, which meant that she had been dumped there three days after her abduction.

"You know what this means then, right?" Caroline's eyes were as big as saucers.

Lou nodded, knowing exactly what she was thinking. "It means if this is one guy, he took Winslow within twenty-four hours of dumping Talbott."

"Holy marigolds, and you don't think LAPD has a clue the two are connected?" Lou's mother broke off another piece of scone.

"Not as of the time I left Mission last night." Caroline stated as she tied her platinum mane in a tight knot at the nape of her neck. "When the Chief came in and had me pass off Winslow to Carpesh, I told him about the anomalies and the keratin and he said he would follow up on them, but I could tell he was basically slotting it the same way your captain did." Caroline got up from her chair and began to gather her things.

"Damn, I wish there were a way to get those samples re-tested." Lou looked at the time to gauge if she had enough of it to indulge in one more scone.

"Oh darlin'!" Caroline spun around and looked at Lou with that beaming Georgia Peach smile. "I plan on just that! I stuffed my own samples in a drawer and am having them sent to a buddy of mine over at Quantico."

Lou nearly choked on the bite of scone she had just taken. "Why didn't you tell me that last night when we were plotting with Vinny?" She said through coughs.

"I didn't? Well I was focusing on the fact that we have no hand in any official part of the investigations anymore. If my friend gets anything off my samples, I have no idea how I'm going to inject myself officially without getting my ass handed to me for going off the reservation. Its a sticky situation we're in here." Caroline leaned over and kissed Lou's mother on the cheek. "Thank you so much for everything. Those scones were dreamy."

"You know its always a pleasure to have you here, Caroline." Shevaun's cell phone beeped with an incoming message. "Oh dear, I need to get over to the Goulds. Joe needs me to sign some papers on the new neighbors and they can't wait until he gets back up the hill. I'll walk out with you, Caroline."

"Give me a kiss goodbye now, Momma. I'll be gone by the time you get back. Hey tall bitch, you coming back here after work?" Lou got up and kissed her mother before she could bolt out the door.

Caroline laughed at Lou. "Yeah I'll bring Chinese from that great place we love. Make sure there's cake." She waved as she and Lou's mother headed out the door.

It seemed that for the first time since Lou woke up it was quiet. As she walked over to her balcony doors, she wasn't sure if she liked it better this way or not. There was something very comforting in the hustle and bustle of a busy morning that seemed to take the edge off knowing the coming workday was going to suck. She stared out into the gloomy morning and was surprised the skies hadn't started dumping more rain already. The one consolation with so much rain was that the meadow would be blooming crazy with flowers come spring. Lou had a spectacular view of the meadow that spread wide and deep all

Shadows of Doubt

the way to the hillside. A pang of sadness hit her as she realized the new neighbor would be trashing her meadow. Soon she would be looking at some hideous house in the distance. He would probably even tear out her giant oaks that she loved. Damn, she was thoroughly depressed now.

The sound of clanking cups startled Lou from her brooding and she spun around to see Marta, their housekeeper, collecting the tray that Lou's mother had brought in.

"Oh!" Marta shouted, obviously as startled by Lou as Lou was of her. "I am so sorry, Miss Lou, I didn't see you in here! Please forgive me!"

"Don't be silly Marta, I'm sorry for scaring you. I can bring that down." Lou started to help the woman stack the cups and plates onto the tray.

"No no, I have this, but thank you very much." The plump and cheery Portuguese woman smiled brightly at Lou. Her hair was pulled back into a pompom of a ponytail and she was dressed in her usual white smock over black pants and impossibly white tennis shoes. While the McAllisters had no requirement that Marta wear any sort of uniform, the woman had said that it made her feel more official to wear something appropriately professional. She was a darling woman that had been working for Joe since before Lou and her mother had come along. She was family and Lou cared for her very much. "You need to go and catch bad guys and leave these things to me." Marta gave her a wink, then hoisted the tray up and headed out of the room.

Noticing the time, Lou decided she had better get downstairs and wait for Vinny there. She grabbed her gun, badge, cell phone and other essentials and tossed a coat over her shoulder, then headed down. When she hit the foyer the doorbell rang and Lou was certain Vinny was going to bitch that he had to get out of the car to ring the bell. She yelled to Marta that she had the door and ran before he could ring again. To Lou's surprise, the person standing on the step was not Vinny at all but some woman who amazingly enough she stood eye to eye with. Lou noted right off that she was lovely and impeccably dressed with a decidedly sassy style. Lou would have liked to steal the woman's flame red coat but it would be a shame since it matched the woman's hair so perfectly.

"Can I help you?" Lou asked the woman.

"Hello! I am looking for Shevaun McAllister. Would that be you?" She beamed at Lou.

"No, I'm her daughter. She's not here at the moment. Can I help you with something? Miss...?" It was definitely a questioning tone that begged for an answer.

The woman shuffled some cardboard tubes under her arm then quickly peeled off a glove which was the same flame color as the coat and her hair. "Where are my manners? I'm Abigail La Rue." She offered her hand to Lou and Lou accepted it with a certain hesitation. "I was sent to have the architectural committee sign off on these plans. For your new neighbor?"

"Oh, well, crap..." realization dawned on Lou. "You know what, come on in. I think there was some mix-up because she just left for the Goulds apparently to meet you. Let me call over there and get her back. Please, come in!" Lou waved the woman inside, then bolted for the phone. "Make yourself comfortable, can I offer you some coffee or tea?"

Abigail smiled brightly. "Oh no, thank you, I'm great. I am so sorry for the mix-up."

"No worries, give me just a sec to call her." Lou began dialing as the red-head took a seat.

Abby knew Max would be livid when everything came out but

Shadows of Doubt

she couldn't resist getting her eyes on the woman who had sent her and Frank into an actual, real Code Pink. She wasn't sure what she had expected, and she would never admit out loud to anyone that she was hoping not to like her. But there was something about this Lou person that Abby instantly liked, and it made her very happy. She sat quietly and folded her gloves while she listened to Lou tell her mother that she had someone waiting for her. Glancing around the McAllister foyer, she could see that tastes ran similar between them and Max. That was going to be convenient. When Lou came back into the room, Abby stood up and resumed smiling.

"Apparently you just missed each other. She's heading back now so it should only be a few minutes." Lou gestured towards the sitting room off to the left of the Foyer. "Why don't we wait over here. Any chance I could get a peek at those plans? Since I'm going to be staring at it every day, it only seems fair." She grinned.

Abby grinned back. "I don't see what the harm would be. Are you excited for new neighbors?" She decided to do a little fishing while she had the chance.

Lou sighed. "I probably will get in trouble for saying this but I was just thinking about it while I was upstairs staring out my windows. It's actually rather depressing!"

Abby blinked. That was not what she had been expecting to hear. "Why is it depressing? I won't let on you told me, I promise." She lied. If it served Abby's purposes she would tell anyone she needed.

"Well..." Lou hesitated for a moment but felt compelled to tell this woman the truth. "I love the natural state of things up here. That meadow in the spring is just amazing with wildflowers. Once someone builds there, they are going to grade it and landscape the crap out of it and it's no longer nature, it's just someone's yard." She shrugged and waited for the woman to laugh at her.

"Can I let you in on a little secret?" Abby leaned toward Lou with a glimmer in her eye and passed her business card to her. "I'm responsible for the landscaping plans so you tell me what you want to see and I'll make sure it makes the plan."

Lou looked at this Abigail LaRue and couldn't help but smile. "How the hell are you going to talk this guy into just accepting what you put in the plan? He has to have ideas for his own yard."

Abby just kept smiling as she unrolled the structural plans. "Lets just say I have significant pull in the aesthetics. Right now his plate is very full, so he is trusting me with a good chunk of the project."

Lou looked at the plans and really wanted to hate everything about them, but she just couldn't. It was just like her mother had said. The actual structures were going off and to the back with the majority of the land left undeveloped. In fact, when she looked at the orientation of the main house, Lou would only be able to see a third of the actual house at most.

"Are you leaving the oaks alone?" Lou looked at Abby pleadingly.

"You want him to? What about a good trim now and then, that okay?" Abby was moved by the depth of Lou's appreciation for the trees and land in their natural state. She was not what Abby had expected for an L.A. girl, or a detective.

"Oh, that would be so awesome! I know it sounds strange but I am pretty possessive of the area up here, including the animals. I grew up in Galveston and got a healthy respect for Mother Nature and her creatures at a young age. I was a self proclaimed 'warrior protector of the sea turtles' when I was eight years old." Lou laughed at herself, not even remotely sure why she was spilling her guts to this stranger. "Here it's the ground squirrels, bunnies, frogs, bobcats, skunks, basically any four legged or feathered creature."

Just at that moment Lou's cat decided it was the perfect time to introduce himself by jumping up on Abby's lap.

Shadows of Doubt

"Well hello there!" Abby greeted the friendly feline.

"Angus! That is so rude!" Lou reached for the cat but Abby instantly wrapped her arms around the black ball of fur and snuggled him.

"No! I love him!" She cooed and the cat started to purr in kind. "Oh isn't he just the sweetest baby!"

Lou had never met anyone who showed no shame in their love of an animal the same way her mother and she did. Seeing this woman adore her cat as if it were her own struck such a hard chord inside of Lou that it was all she could do not to hug them both and cry. Lou was a hard-ass without question the majority of the time, but when it came to her cat or any of her adopted animals, she was as mushy as mush got. "Wow, he loves you. Now you're screwed."

Abby looked at Lou suspiciously. "Why am I screwed?"

"Because you're going to have to come back and visit him or he's going to drive me crazy with his whining." Lou gave Abby a sincerely warm smile and she knew at once they were going to be friends for a very long, long time. Max was definitely keeping her whether he knew it yet or not.

Shevaun came into the room and stopped dead in her tracks to see Angus being groped and snuggled by some strange woman and her daughter not ripping the woman's head off for it. Whoever this woman was, Shevaun liked her already.

"Well isn't this cozy." Lou's mother spoke with laughter in her words. "You must be Abigail. I am so sorry for the mix-up. I would offer my hand but I think Angus might bite me if I make you stop snuggling him."

Abby laughed and gave the cat one more smooch then shifted him to Lou's lap despite the protests. "Its a pleasure to meet you Mrs. McAllister." Abby offered her now free hand to Shevaun. "Please, it's me who should apologize. I must have misunderstood the instructions.

But I have to admit I am glad. It gave me the opportunity to meet your lovely daughter and her precious cat."

Shevaun beamed proudly. "Yeah, I am pretty fond of 'em. Well the cat anyway." She winked at Abby.

"Oh nice! Thanks, Momma." Lou sat Angus on the floor and got up from her seat, glancing down again at the plans one more time. "You really think you can save the oaks and stuff?" She asked again.

Abby's smile for Lou was as bright as the sun as she nodded in the affirmative. "I can pretty much guarantee it. You call me if you think of anything else. If your mother signs off on these, we hope to get started right away, so don't be shy and hesitate!" Without really thinking, Abby stepped in and gave Lou a warm hug then stepped back, still smiling. "It was really wonderful to meet you."

Perhaps Lou should have felt odd with a total stranger hugging her out of the blue, but she didn't. Instead she felt really happy, at least for the moment, before she heard the shrill of her partner's horn blasting at her from the driveway.

"Oh shit... err... excuse my language." Lou blew out a breath. "It was wonderful meeting you too. I'm sure I'll see you again soon. I gotta go before my partner shatters the glass with his horn." Lou leaned over and gave her mother a quick kiss then raced for the door with a wave. "See ya! Oh Momma, the plans are awesome so just sign them." Lou winked at Abby before she closed the door behind her.

Shevaun stared at the front door for a moment in shock at her daughter's complete turn around on the new neighbor. "Well, those must be quite some plans for her to say that."

Abby turned her full attention to Lou's mother now. "Well, as I told your daughter, I have significant pull in the design and planning so you two just tell me if there is anything I can do to make things more agreeable. I have a very strong feeling we are all going to be very good friends because of this little venture."

"Well that sounds lovely. Lets get a good look at these plans and see if we can start your prediction off on the right foot, shall we?" Shevaun sat down and picked up where her daughter had apparently left off.

Abby was confident that Lou's mother would approve of the plans just as Lou had, so she settled herself and waited to field any questions Shevaun might have. In the meantime she was bubbling inside over having met the object of her Dominor's distraction and the fact that she liked her. She couldn't wait to call Frankie and tell him about her not so accidental mix-up and meeting Lou face to face. Frankie would probably have a fit over Abby taking such a risk but he would get over it. She needed to know if this mystery detective was worthy of her Dom and if she warranted all of Abby's considerable skills to make the stars align properly for this match to be made. As she listened and answered all of Shevaun's very articulate and intelligent questions, Abby was certain this was a worthy cause.

Chapter Seven

Lou had prepared herself for a perfectly dreary Friday morning stuck in traffic with her partner complaining as usual, but Vinny had decided they were taking the scenic route to the station. By scenic route, he had meant by way of the Chatsworth Glenn apartments to talk to Janine Winslow's roommate. Carla Schwartz had not reported Winslow missing because she herself had been out of town at a training seminar for her vocation which was as an instructor at the local beauty college. Ms. Schwartz, despite her gleaming plum hair, was what Lou considered a chihuahua of a person. She was shaky, bug-eyed and would not shut up. Fortunately, her continuous chatter yielded them some crumbs of information that gave them a clearer picture of who their victim was.

Janine Winslow was a decent young woman who had moved to California when grandmother, her only living relative, passed away after a long battle with lung cancer. Janine had dreamed of being a dancer since she was a little girl and had taken classes up until her grandmother took ill. After playing nursemaid for several years, Janine took what little inheritance was left to her and came to California to finish her education so that one day she could fulfill her second place dream of working in a museum or art gallery. She had answered Schwartz's ad in the paper for a roommate nearly three years ago and they had been residing at Chatsworth Glenn ever since. Winslow had started dancing at the strip joint because the price of her education was far more than she had expected, along with the cost of living in Los Angeles. Schwartz stated Janine was emphatic about keeping 'Jade', her dancing persona, entirely separate from the rest of her life. What little time Winslow had between classes and work she spent volunteering for her professors on various projects. According to the roommate, Janine had been helping one of her professors with some sort of big event that was taking place at some museum in the next week or so. Although that was vague, it would be easy enough for them to track down which museum was holding an event that qualified as big.

Once Lou and Vinny left the roommate, they were able to track down the professor and sketch a decent time line of Winslow's movements for the week prior to her abduction. They just needed to confirm her comings and goings from work to fill in the gaps. Unfortunately, that was going to have to wait since they had put off checking in at the station as long as they could. Fortunately, the club was in Sheriff's jurisdiction and being acquainted with the establishment from their days in narcotics, they knew they had a few hours before anyone would be there to answer any questions. So the two of them headed to Homicide to finish up their official paperwork on Janine Winslow and ship off copies to the investigating officers at LAPD. Before they had the chance to stew about how much they hated shipping those reports off, they got a call to a neat and tidy little crime scene that provided a perfect time filler.

They arrived at the one bedroom apartment to find a frail and weathered fifty-something woman who looked like she had been repeatedly dropped face first off the balcony, then kicked down the

Shadows of Doubt

stairs several times for good measure. The woman sat silently with a detached expression. Staring off into the long distant nothing while a uniformed deputy stood over her. Lou and Vinny walked past her for the time being to get a look at the scene. The apartment looked like it had been picked up and shaken like a snow globe. Furniture flung, fragments of some sort of crockery everywhere, even a piece lodged in the wall. The sofa was on its side and askew by the door to the apartment which made it appear as though it had been used to barricade the door from the inside, unsuccessfully. The door itself had been hacked nearly to splinters with a gaping hole where the doorknob had once been. Later, Lou and Vinny were informed that the victim had indeed hacked his way through the door with an ax when the suspect had barred his entry by whatever means she could. When they finally saw the victim among the rubble, it appeared as though he had been both stabbed in the chest with a bread knife then smashed in the head with a cast iron skillet. Lou couldn't help but think of the old adage, if first you don't succeed, try, try again. The victim was an enormous man, who amazingly enough, beyond the smell of blood and brain matter, reeked of tequila. He easily outweighed the suspect by one-hundred pounds and was still clutching the ax in his right hand and a tattered copy of a Restraining Order in his left.

It had taken them about two hours to make sure everything was done by the book but once all was said and done, it was a clean case of self defense. The real victim, Lupe Gonzales, had been a repeated victim of abuse at the hand of the now deceased George Perez, her former boyfriend. The apartment had been the location of over a dozen domestic violence calls over the past two months and the officers on scene knew that if George didn't drink himself to death first, either he or Lupe was going to wind up dead by the other's hand. The sad part was that Lupe had been really trying to do the right things since her last release from the hospital two days prior. She had gotten counseling. Found someone at Legal Aide that helped her with the paperwork and finally gotten a restraining order against George. He had been served that morning and that had set off the latest and fatal attack. Lupe had called 9-1-1 when George started hacking at her door. The operator could hear him screaming that he was going to kill Lupe through the phone even over Lupe's own cries for help. It was all on the 9-1-1 recording. Clear as day for everyone to hear. Even the part where George had broken through the door, told Lupe she was going to die and even still when he yelled at her for stabbing him and told her he was going to rape her dead corpse. It was neat and tidy from a legal standpoint but it was a safe bet that Lupe Gonzales would be a mess forever.

"God, I really want to go home and kiss my wife." Vinny finally spoke once they left Homicide after filing their reports and talking to the powers that be to make sure Lupe Gonzales wouldn't have to spend the night in lock-up. Lou didn't say anything. She simply stared out the side window. "Ah shit, you okay kiddo?" Realization struck Vinny that this sort of case was way too close to home for Lou.

She looked at him and smiled solemnly. "I'm good." She turned back to stare out the window.

Lou hadn't dated when she moved back to California until eight years ago when she unwittingly agreed to go out to dinner with a ticking bomb. The guy had seemed nice enough. A new clerk at the downtown courthouse. But Lou had known after dinner that he wasn't her type and that he was a little too clingy out of the gate. She had thought they parted ways that evening well enough and when he had called to ask her out again she simply told him she was really busy with her career and it wasn't a good time in her life for any sort of dating. The man apparently had other plans for her. He had hacked her email, broken into her apartment, even tried to storm the station she was working out of at the time. She got a restraining order and he broke it the same day he was served, very much like George Perez had done to Lupe.

It had been on a Wednesday night when Lou had been wearing her headphones and had her back to the door of her apartment when he picked the lock, snuck up behind her, then proceeded to beat her to a pulp. Her uncle had scared him off when he came by unexpectedly to check on her, finding the door open and Lou unconscious on the kitchen floor. That was when Lou's uncle made her move in with him and her aunt. They picked the psycho up the next morning but a handy and hefty trust fund had the bastard out on bail before the weekend.

His second attempt on Lou's life was when she was driving home from the station the Saturday night after he made bail. It was simple and efficient planning on his part. He waited until she pulled up to the stop sign less than a block away from her uncle's house and when she started to go through, he and his rented Hummer were careening into her car at over sixty miles per hour. The impact was so violent that it shot Lou out the passenger side of the car, along with the door that had blown right off it's hinge. The moron hadn't counted on his own airbag knocking him out so he was still at the scene when Lou's uncle Seamus and Vinny ran up on him after hearing the crash. No one ever questioned how the son of a bitch was so banged up and bloody even though there was no evidence of blood inside his car. It was obvious, or so the District Attorney had argued at the trial. He had sustained his injuries when he attempted to flee the scene and fell, several times.

Vinny didn't press Lou to talk about it now. He remembered that the bastard was going to be eligible for parole at the end of the year and that was probably why Lou wasn't shaking it off like she normally would. Instead, Vinny thought it best to shut up and get her home, safe and sound.

"Hey!" She shouted at him. "You missed the turnoff!"

Vinny nearly sideswiped the car next to them when she shouted at him. "What the hell, Lou?!"

"We're going to the strip joint, remember?"

"Seriously? You still wanna do that tonight?" He glanced at her quickly, not wanting to take his eyes from the road for too long.

"Seriously! What are you thinking? We can't wait on that! LAPD will be all over the place. We can't afford to wait until after they're done. We'll draw too much attention if we wait."

So maybe getting her head into Winslow was a better idea then her stewing at home. Grinning at his tough as nails partner, he got off at the next turnoff and headed to the strip club.

Max stood watching the city go by from his terrace already polished, pressed and nervous as hell. He had well over an hour before they had to leave to make his dinner engagement. It irked him beyond belief that he was nervous over something as simple as having dinner with the McAllisters. Especially since he had spent the better part of the day scouring the underbelly of the city in search of a ruthless sadistic killer without batting an eyelash. The foolishness of it was that Max had known Joe for all of Joe's life and was his superior after all. But now things were decidedly different. Now Max knew that they were Lou's parents. Granted, Joe was technically her step-father but he had raised her for the majority of her life and from all of Frank's research, Lou regarded Joe as her father. So it was indeed very different, if only to Max. These were the parents of the woman that had knocked the wind out of him. Without warning, without want. He had resigned himself that it was pure stupidity and nothing would ever come of it,

Shadows of Doubt

but deep down in his core he was powerless to it. He mulled it all over in his head when all of a sudden, as if the Fates needed to highlight the point, there she was. He thought it was his own head playing tricks. Forcing him to see her in random people but when he saw her brawny partner join her on the street corner a block or so over

"Un-bloody-believable!" Max hissed through his teeth.

"What's up Boss?" Frank asked as he handed him a snifter of cognac of which Max drained in one gulp. As Frank followed Max's gaze he had to restrain himself from flat-out giggling when he saw Lou Donovan and her partner standing on the corner near a strip club. He checked himself quickly and put on his best grimace. "What the hell are they doing there?" It was a rhetorical question. "You don't think its over the Winslow woman do you? I mean this is Sheriff's turf so maybe it's something else."

Max turned to Frank and scowled at him. "Isn't it your job to find out? And get me Carpesh on the line right away. I want to know if Caroline has been snooping." He stormed off the terrace and disappeared into the suite with his empty snifter. Frank just looked back at the two detectives on the corner and did in fact giggle, quietly. After a few seconds, he ran to Abby and his suite to fill her in on the latest development.

Six minutes later, Abby walked out onto Max's terrace to find him staring across the block at the strip club with a half empty snifter of cognac. She quickly staunched her grin and cleared her throat.

"I have Carpesh on the line for you, my Dom." She handed him the cell phone and played it formal because she knew he was having an internal struggle at the moment and was seriously grumpy about it.

He snatched the phone from her with barely a glance. "Peter, what's the status on Devereux? Is she minding her own or what?"

Abby took three steps back and tried to decipher the content of the conversation based upon Max's facial expressions. From what she could see, it wasn't good. Max even dropped the phone to his side for a moment and made a sound that Abby often described as a growl. She could hear what sounded like Carpesh's faint stutter coming from the phone before Max put it back to his ear.

"Carpesh... Carpesh..." Max rolled his eyes. "Peter! Stop! Breathe!"

It would appear that Peter Carpesh was panicking again and Abby literally had to bite her lip so that she wouldn't laugh.

"I will handle it. You do your job and do it meticulously, that is all. Do you understand?" Max was straining to not bite the man's head off. "No, you leave that to us. You simply contact me, Frank or Abby immediately if anything else pops up like this. But Peter, think before you dial that phone, make certain it's a legitimate call and not paranoia, do you understand me?" Max listened for about three more seconds then actually attempted to strangle the phone before he resumed speaking to Carpesh. "This was not paranoia. This should have been relayed to us immediately. Do you see the difference? Good. We'll be in touch." Max calmly pressed the disconnect button then turned and pitched the phone somewhere in the direction of Roxbury Road. It appeared as though he contemplated tossing his snifter as well but he thought better of it then turned back to Abby. "Sorry about your phone."

"Oh don't even worry about it! That wasn't my phone." She gave an impish grin. "That was Frankie's second line. He's in our room talking to a stripper named Jiggles, if you can believe that." She made a shimmy attempt that had Max grinning despite himself. "He said he'll be in to update you as soon as he gets the four-one-one. You look very handsome, by the way." It nearly brought tears to her eyes when she watched Max fluster and blush then try to hide it by looking down to straighten his jacket. In all the years she had known him, and they were many, she had never seen him fluster or blush. Max could be gruff or intense, but always in complete command of any situation.

Shadows of Doubt

"Uh... Thanks I guess." He paused a split-second as though something occurred to him. "Do I normally not look handsome?" He looked up at her with an expression that made her think she could almost imagine what he looked like as a little boy.

"No no! You do always look handsome. You just look extra handsome tonight!" She was so moved by the man she could barely stand it. "I'll go see what's keeping Frankie." She hurried off the terrace and out of the suite before he could notice her emotions spilling over. She waved Frank off as she passed him in the doorway and went straight to her room.

"Everything alright Boss?" Frank approached warily, not noticing that Niko had come in and was following behind him.

"Carpesh says that Devereux took her own samples of the saliva and the fingernails. He cannot find where she stashed them." Max turned back to look over at the strip club but he couldn't see his detective or her partner any longer. They must have gone inside or left. "Which means Donovan and her partner are over there asking about Winslow, not another case."

"Well I happen to know where she stashed them." Frank held a hand up when Max tossed him a death look. "Hey I just got the call! She sent them to a friend of hers at Quantico. Fortunately he passed them to one of our people for analysis so we have it covered."

Niko sat on the edge of a chaise and proceeded to light one of his fancy cigarettes. "I can handle the detectives." He said coolly.

"No!" Both Frank and Max said at the same time. Frank's face flushed and he took a step back, deferring to Max's orders. "Forgive me, my Dom."

"No, its alright. It's Devereux that's the key on this. Those two are thick as thieves so if we can pull Devereux back I think she can get Donovan to back off as well." Max considered for a long time while the two men watched him pace back and forth. It was a huge decision to be made but it was a little easier in knowing that Caroline Devereux's lineage was Sanguinostri and her family had intended on initiating her before she came to Los Angeles. Better late then never, Max supposed. "Call Richlieu and her parents. Get them out here immediately. Get two bungalows next to each other here at the Chateau." He wasn't going to let his plans for the evening get disrupted over this. "Frank, you stay here tonight and make sure all of this is handled. Niko, can you make yourself available to Richlieu and the Devereuxs while they deal with their daughter?"

Frank interrupted immediately. "I can handle that!" He caught himself after it left his mouth and realized he had spoken out of turn, but he may as well run with it. "I have dealt with these types of things countless times and am familiar with the whole Devereux Donovan deal so it only makes sense not to bother Niko with this when he's got the whole replacement counsel to deal with, among other things."

"It's not a biggie to handle but Frank has a point." Niko laid back in the chaise. "I really wouldn't give this the delicacy that it deserves."

Max nodded, agreeing with all points presented. "Right, good call Frank. Make it happen." He looked at his watch and had a few more minutes before the car would be waiting to take him to dinner. "Follow up with our people at Quantico and make sure those samples are dealt with properly. If Devereux is initiated this weekend, then we don't really have to worry all too much. Find out who her 'person' is over at Quantico so that doesn't backfire."

"Right away." Frank bolted to his own suite to make the calls and get Abby up to speed.

"I hate to throw another wrench into the works but there's this whole matter of protocol that we need to address." Niko pulled out a cigarette for Max and held it out to him, then offered a light once he accepted.

"You're a bad influence." Max said while blowing out a thick stream of smoke. "Alright, elaborate with the protocol. Given what we are into here that could mean at least a thousand things."

"Protocol dictates certain things when you, being the Dominor, arrive on scene. A sort of 'I have arrived' dinner, banquet, ball, whatever. Remember when we came to the U.S. back in the day? Although I am sure everyone and their dog knows you're here by now. It's still proper form for you to make a formal appearance as the head honcho of all things cool and fruity." He crushed out his cigarette and continued. "The word around the water cooler is that the blue-bloods are already scoffing at the fact that you haven't sent a formal invitation yet. Given the fact that you're planning on asking the Senatus to install a West Coast counsel, it would be wise to follow protocol to the letter so they have no excuse to deny you."

"I had thought about that but was hoping we could get construction done so we could hold a formal banquet at the new house, but you're right. That would be serious bad form to wait that long. The sneers and snickers are already starting. We can't delay on that. There is some sort of gala that Albert von Massenbach is throwing next weekend. We'll need to have invitations sent before then if we're to follow proper form."

"It will be tight but if anyone can make it happen..."

"Its Abby." Max finished Niko's sentence for him and grinned. "You want to ask her or shall I?"

A wide smile spread across Niko's rakishly handsome face. "Please allow me the pleasure of seeing Abby's face light up when I tell her she has to plan a party."

Max snorted and passed his barely smoked cigarette to Niko. "Have at it. Tell her to make sure she does it up so that all the snobs won't have any critiques to pass abroad in their gossip sessions. Make sure she invites our Canadian delegation too." He checked his pockets to make sure he had everything, then started to head for the door. "I'll be back in a few hours, you have the comm Number One."

Niko chuckled at the Star Trek reference. It was a little known fact that Max and Niko would on occasion spend hours watching marathons of the old sci-fi series, reciting the dialogue as it went. Niko finished the cigarette then headed in to give Abby the good news.

As decided, the doors to the suites were propped open and two large men stood to either side of the elevator, securing the entire floor of the Chateau for the counsel's private use. The problem was that Niko was the stealthiest damn person next to Max and walked into Abby and Frank's suite without detection. He arrived just in time to hear Abby asking Frank how they were going to get "her in his face again" and that had Niko wondering. When the two conspirators turned to see him standing there, he quirked his brow and watched both of their faces turn an ashy white.

"Oh this is going to be good." He snickered and plopped himself on the couch. "Spill it. All of it. Now." He ordered.

"Shit!" Was all Abby could say while Frank stammered, uttering nothing intelligible.

"If you don't tell me and get me in the loop now, I am going to ruin whatever it is you are up to by cluing Max in and you know it. So spill it all. Bring me in and we go from there."

Frank and Abby looked at each other with desperate expressions. They knew they were caught, but for the life of them neither could come up with anything to bullshit Niko and cover themselves.

"Ah, hell, just tell him Abby." Resigned, Frank sank down into one of the arm chairs.

"Me?! You're the one that called the Code Pink! You do it!" Her face rose in color, making Niko grin.

Shadows of Doubt

"Code Pink?" Niko sat up as the words registered in his brain. "Who?!"

Frank and Abby looked at each other with more desperation and a wash of shock. "How do you know Code Pink?" Abby demanded.

"Abigail, it's my job to know everything. Especially when it comes to anything that directly involves the fate of my Dominor. Besides, you two need to turn lights on and clear rooms to effectively invoke any cone of silence. I was sitting in the library when you two came in like little girls to make your pact on the Code Pink like a hundred years ago."

"Ah, hell." Frank repeated himself and looked back at Abby for guidance.

"You didn't tell anyone did you?" She gave Niko a threatening look.

"Who are you talking to?" Niko tilted his head sideways at Abby's ridiculous question. He was the soul of discretion and more secretive than the entire counsel and the Senatus combined. "Now tell me who and every last detail before I shut you two down without any consideration."

Pondering briefly, Abby knew it would only be to their advantage to have Niko on their side and working with them on their little conspiracy. Now it was just a matter of telling him everything in the proper way so that he would be sold. "Frankie, lock the door and get us all a real drink. Has Max left for dinner?"

Niko nodded to her. "He left before I came in."

"Alright then, but you have to swear by blood that either way you go with this that you will never reveal it to Max." She walked over to a silver tray on the coffee table and picked up a small knife and held it out to him. He rolled his eyes but took the knife and slashed his palm without blinking an eye. Abby took the knife from him once he was finished and slashed her own palm and then the two locked hands.

"I swear by the Blood of the Ancients I will not reveal what you tell me about this Code Pink to Max under any circumstances..." He smirked at her. "Until you tell me I can."

"Fair enough." Abby smirked back at him. "Alright then..."

Frank returned to the table, carefully balancing three crystal wine glasses and their crimson contents, offering one to Abby, then one to Niko. He sank back down into the arm chair and drank deeply as Abby began telling Niko the sequence of events that led them to this point in time. She recounted everything down to Max's facial expressions that had Abby welling up with tears again as she had earlier in the evening. Emphasis was put on the ironic connections to the Sanguinostri, Joe's family connections, the Devereuxs, right down to Lou standing on the corner a little more then an hour ago. Frank watched Niko's face for any telltale expression but his face was stone as he listened intently to it all. When finally Abby was done, Niko sat forward, resting his elbows on his knees, apparently digesting everything he had just heard.

"Hmm." He grunted and sat for a good while longer until he finally scrubbed a hand over his face. "How are we going to get her in his face again? It has to be soon."

The strip club where Janine Winslow was previously employed had recently undergone a makeover after a rather convenient fire toasted the place. Unfortunately the decorator must have been blind. The place was an assault on the eyes even with the lights down, and the overall vibe was pretty damn sleazy even as strip joints go. It always struck Lou funny that given the law of no alcohol in an all-nude establishment, management would instead serve energy drinks to the customers. The whole visual of wired perverts flicking out dollar bills in rapid succession like a speed-freak just cracked Lou up. Even while they waited to talk to the manager, Lou noted at least seven guys tapping their feet like hummingbird wings, completely out of time with whatever it was that was being pumped out of the sound system.

The manager was the final person they needed to speak to about the last night Janine worked. None of the other dancers had seen anything out of the ordinary or anyone unusually creepy. Given the nature of the beast, it was hard to expect anyone to actually identify anyone as being creepy, unusually so or otherwise. The bartenders that were on duty hadn't seen anything out of the ordinary, either. The only thing they remembered was a large group of college guys that the bouncers had to deal with several times before they finally asked them nicely to leave. Lou figured it would have been easy to go unseen with a bunch of frat boys drawing all the attention. Very convenient to say the least. When the manager finally arrived he had little more to add to the consensus that Janine was a nice girl who worked hard and kept it clean and professional. He gave her plenty of leeway with her schedule to accommodate her schooling because she was a big draw and brought in a lot of faithful customers. It seemed that Janine was rather popular because she actually danced, rather than just jiggle, fondle herself and do the splits over and over again. The one thing that the manager did add that was of interest was that security usually walked Janine out to her car but that night, because of the unruly frat mob, they had their hands full and Janine opted not to wait, leaving alone. Janine also parked her car regularly in the parking lot across the street rather than in the back alley which was reserved for staff. She took a chance of being towed but she preferred blending back into the Hollywood shuffle, or so the man recalled.

Lou and Vinny left the club and walked to the corner to trace Janine's last exodus from the club. They stood a while watching the continuous throng of traffic pass by.

"No way in hell he could have nabbed her here. Way too many people and it only gets worse at that hour." Lou turned and looked from all angles but paused after a moment. She knew it was ridiculous but she couldn't help but feel she was being watched, which was entirely likely because there were a bazillion people driving by.

"That's a well lit lot over there." Vinny had to shout over the din or cars. "Manager said she parked smack under the light too, every night. All those businesses in there are closed when she's on so easy peasy to get that spot regularly." He walked to the curb and surveyed the area with her. "Pretty smart if ya ask me."

"If he followed her from work, he probably parked down there." She pointed down the side street which was canopied with giant magnolia trees. "Crappy lighting. If he got the spot up front there, on the street, he could easily see her crossing here and get his engine running, waiting for her to pull out of the driveway."

Her partner nodded as he came back to the corner. "That's what I would do if I was a creepy scumbag stalking serial killer." He glanced at his watch. "Hey isn't Devereux meeting you at your place tonight?"

"Crap! She'll be there by seven, what time is it?"

"Let's go, we should make it in plenty of time. It's only quarter to six." He fished his keys out of his coat pocket as they headed to the car.

They talked it out as they drove and both of them were pretty damn certain their guy followed Winslow from the strip joint to the market. It was an easy drive to keep a tail on someone, mostly freeway with just a couple of surface streets to and from. He knew her routine and could have waited in the parking lot of the market. Half the fun was the build up, the control of following without being noticed. He may have even waited until she parked so he could park next to her. Snag her as soon as she loaded the bags and her purse onto the seat. Easy to scoop her up and into his own car that way. It was late, no one around in the lot or even in the market at that hour. Both Vinny and she thought it may have been likely that he went into the store and bought something just because he could. They had gotten their hands on copies of the security footage from the market and it was simply crap. You couldn't make out a fly if it landed on the lens. All they could say was that fifteen people had come and gone, including Janine Winslow. Not even the finest tech equipment in the world would make it possible to identify one of them. All they had was a theory of the 'how' and were just as clueless as to the 'why' as they had been before they ever set foot on the crime scene.

By the time they pulled up in front of Lou's house, Caroline was sitting on the stoop eating out of a Chinese food container with chopsticks.

Vinny snickered. "Oh geez, you're gonna catch serious grief for this one kiddo."

"Well crap. I wonder how long she's been here." Lou had called the guards ahead to let them know she was expecting Caroline and that it was okay to let her in if she got there ahead of Lou.

"You'll be able to tell by how far down the carton of chow mein she is." Both of them chuckled. "See ya kiddo. Call me if ya get anything new. I'll be hauling all my crap out of my hobby room for storage. We're gonna turn that into the nursery."

"Don't pop your back. Get my uncle and nephews to help. Give Vera a kiss for me." Lou hopped out of the car and ran up the steps to one very annoyed Caroline Devereux. "I am so sorry but traffic was a bitch." Lou peeked into the carton to see how much chow mein had been consumed and saw it was nearly full and steam was still rising off the noodles.

"I know about the traffic, I drove in it too remember?" Caroline stabbed the contents of the carton with her chopsticks then handed it to Lou. "Now hurry up and get me inside so we can eat while we watch the security discs to find Yummy Morgue Guy!" Jumping up and down, Caroline could barely contain her excitement.

"So you're not pissed?" Lou pulled her keys out and unlocked the door then dashed for the security panel.

Caroline hurried inside right behind Lou, closing the door after them. "Not at all! But I had you fooled, huh?" She didn't bother containing her giggle.

Lou punched in her security code then stuck her thumb on the little blue circle next to the keys. After a second, the panel beeped three times and the previously red LED light turned green.

"Even Vinny thought you were pissed. You got security to give you the discs from the other day? How'd you manage that? You wanna watch them in my room or the media room?"

"Your room, I'm spending the night again and I want to change before we snarf so we can expand cozily as we eat." Caroline dangled the bag stuffed with more Chinese cartons and what appeared to be a pink bakery box.

Lou smiled wide and ran for the stairs. "Last one up forfeits the extra egg roll!"

"Cheater!" Caroline yelled as she scrambled for the stairs, nearly falling on her face at the second step.

Twenty minutes later, both women were sitting indian-style in the chairs of Lou's sitting area wearing nearly identical sweatpants and oversized t-shirts shoveling noodles into their mouths.

"There!" Lou shouted with her mouth full. "That's him!"

Caroline nearly dropped her carton of noodles trying to grab the remote. She finally found the pause button. "Holy crap!" Caroline managed to mumble without food falling out of her mouth. She swallowed hard and looked at the image on the screen, rewinding a bit so they could see from the moment he exited the building.

It was a night and day difference between the resolution of security footage from the market Winslow had been in to the footage from the morgue. Lou had told Caroline exactly which door she had come in and he had gone out so that she could get the precise camera feed. Despite it being night time, there on the screen, crystal clear, living color they saw a black town car pull up and a tall, well built man with reddish-brown hair dressed in all black get out from the rear driver's side of the car. He wore wrap-around sunglasses so his face was relatively obscured, but by movements it appeared to Lou that he was scanning the area as he walked around the car and waited. The camera angle was elevated from the second floor of the adjacent building so it caught the rear view of the car clear enough that Lou scrambled for a pen to jot down the plate number.

"Geez, that guy is pretty damn hot." Caroline sat on the edge of the chair, leaning towards the screen and squinting as if she would see more if she did.

As the time display on the feed ticked off the seconds, Lou found herself holding her breath as she waited for her mystery man to appear. When the man waiting at the car moved and opened the rear passenger door, the glass door of the building swung open and out came Lou's Yummy Morgue Guy.

He was everything that Lou remembered and more. Now that she had the luxury of taking her time to ogle him, she got up from her chair and moved to stand near the flat-screen so she could examine him closely. As he stepped out of the building, his overcoat swooshed in the breeze and his hair tousled around his perfectly chiseled face. It was a distant angle so it was hard for Lou to make out the finer details, but she could tell his expression was intense with those perfectly arched eyebrows knit, giving his eyes a fierce look. He scanned the area in a similar fashion as the other man had done. Lou noticed his rich olive complexion was clean shaven so that his chiseled features were a play of light and shadow. He was tall as Lou had remembered and had a build underneath that immaculately tailored suit that made her mouth water. His stride was dangerous. Feline graceful as he moved toward the car with purpose. He reached up and raked his fingers through his hair which made Lou noticed his elegant, strong hands. His mouth moved so she knew he was saying something to the man who stood waiting, She couldn't help but wonder what his voice sounded like. It was probably deep and rich, she thought, and would more than likely make her toes curl when he whispered. She lost herself for a second in the thought of what whisper would sound like but was jarred back to the moment when he slid into the car. The other man shut the door and walked around to get in himself.

"Christ." Was all Lou could say.

"Holy shit, Lou..." Caroline stammered as she rewound the tape to replay the scene again. "... no freaking wonder you went all pudding cup over this guy!"

As they watched again from the moment the car pulled up, Lou tried to remember the smell of him as they passed each other. Her body started to hum as the memory of him so close saturated her senses. Never, ever, had a man affected Lou like this. It was disconcerting at best and horrifyingly frightening to her. She didn't want it, or need it despite what anyone said. Lou was perfectly content with her life alone and had no desire to disrupt her routine with a man in her world. But the thud of her heart as she watched this person exit the morgue for the twelfth time was telling her something entirely different.

"Run it!" Caroline's voice snapped Lou back to the present.

Lou turned to see her friend licking the filling from a cream puff. "What?"

"Run the damn plate to the car, Lou!"

Lou had forgotten all about jotting down the license plate. "Oh shit, yeah!" She whirled around to grab the piece of paper she had written it on, then dashed for her laptop.

It took a few minutes to boot up, get the program loaded and log in to the system. She input the plate number and waited, hovering as if staring at the monitor would make the data appear faster. Finally there was an audible beep as the information came up on screen. The car was registered to a rental company, as both women had expected. There were half a dozen branches in the metropolitan area. Caroline ran for the phone, peered over Lou's shoulder to read off the contact numbers then started dialing madly.

"What the hell are you doing?" Lou demanded as Caroline stuffed the phone into her hand.

"I am calling the company so you can find out who the car was rented to!"

"They aren't just going to tell me that over the phone!" She pressed the off button on the hand-held and got up from the desk to pace.

Caroline studied her friend a moment. "Lou, you're a cop, of course they are going to give you that information."

"No, genius, they won't." Lou walked back over to her chair and plunked down. "Think for a second. Anyone can call up and say they are a cop. Besides it's after ten, no one of authority who can give me that info will be there. I'll have to go down there and bully it out of them."

Caroline skipped over and plopped down into her chair next to Lou with a devilish grin on her face. "Can I play bad cop?"

"What are you talking about?" She stared at Caroline, trying hard not to be caught up in her infectious enthusiasm.

"Well I am going with you, as soon as they open tomorrow. Don't even think about arguing with me on this, we are going." Caroline tucked her legs up back into an indian-style sitting position and wiggled to get comfy. "Oh, I forgot to tell you, I am going to be incommunicado tomorrow night."

Lou looked at her suspiciously. "Why for?"

"While I was waiting for you to get home I got a call from my parents." She paused and sighed with annoyance. "They are coming in with my uncle tomorrow morning and want me to have dinner with them. I'm pretty sure they are going to try to con me into moving back to Savannah or something stupid like that. No biggie though. Just call me when you get back from your Sunday golf thingy with your parents and I'll fill you in."

"Well that's kind of out of the blue isn't it? Isn't this the first time they've come out since you moved here?"

"Exactly, which is why I know they are plotting something. But I can handle that. We have far more important things to focus on like your Yummy Morgue Guy." After rewinding the security footage so she could remind Lou of the more important matters, she picked up another cream puff out of the pink box, carefully peeled the pastry top off, of then proceeded to lick the filling out.

Lou looked down at the open box and noted that out of the ten cream puffs that filled the box, two were hollow pastry shells. She couldn't help but laugh out loud.

The Indian Falls Country Club was everything you would expect from an exclusive five-star club. The facade was immaculately groomed with abundant trees and shrubs, carefully obscuring any view from outsiders who might want a glimpse of the recreational habits of the elite. Max was impressed to see a club in Los Angeles that held to the old traditional country club vibe. When he stepped into the main entry hall of the facility he noted the butter toned marble floors were polished to a mirror finish and swathed in elegant hand loomed rugs. Rich dark wood wainscoting wrapped the walls with the remainder awash in a soft glowing butter that blended perfectly with the marble. Elegantly carved sideboards were strewn with massive fresh floral arrangements while gleaming brass and crystal chandeliers illuminated everything in a flattering warm incandescence. As he continued to take in the décor, a pleasant looking woman dressed in proper dinner attire approached him carrying a leather bound folio.

"Mr. Julian?" When Max made eye contact with her she immediately snapped her fingers and a young man of perhaps seventeen years, at most five and a half feet tall and eagerly polished in his formal waitstaff uniform appeared out of nowhere. "We are so pleased to have you with us this evening. Allow Daniel to take your coat for you." The young man bent slightly at the waist and then assisted Max with removing his coat.

"Thank you, Daniel." Max smiled genuinely at the boy. He had a soft spot for youth that held to manners and tradition. It was a rare thing to come by these days.

"My pleasure Mr. Julian. I'll have it for you when you're ready to leave. Enjoy your time with us, sir." The boy smiled earnestly then scooted down a hall and out of sight as quick as a wink.

"My name is Elaine Price, I am the Club Director..." The woman handed him her business card which she had at the ready. "... Mr. and Mrs. McAllister requested that I see you to their table."

Max walked with the woman as she led him up a sweep of steps and down a hall that was lined with portraits of what he assumed to be a long line of former and current members. "Thank you, Ms. Price. This is a lovely facility you have here."

The woman blushed as if Max had complimented her personally. "Please, call me Elaine. Mr. McAllister didn't mention how long you would be in Los Angeles but we would be honored to have you as our guest during your stay. We have fourteen tennis courts, all lit and available to you at any time. Complete and comprehensive spa and gym facilities as well as indoor and outdoor pools and whirlpools. We also have our famed east and west golf courses at your disposal. Both are championship courses that I am certain you will enjoy very much." It was clear to Max this woman had done her homework on him and knew he was a sucker for golf.

"That's very kind of you, I may take you up on that. As it so happens, I may be making my stay more permanent and would need to make arrangements for membership for myself and my staff."

"Oh! How delightful! Might I ask how many of your staff you would be considering?" To the woman's credit, she restrained her excitement very well.

"At the moment there would be six but we are expanding the firm to include Los Angeles so there may be a dozen or so more within the next few months. I would also need an inclusive allowance for bringing clients and guests without restriction so you may want to revise your figures taking all of that into account." Max tapped a finger lightly on the leather folio the woman was clutching and gave her a warm smile. He had negotiated thousands of membership deals over the years and was well accustomed with the discreet sell they always tried to give him. He found it so much simpler and amusing to cut them off at the pass.

"Uh... I... of course! I would be happy to prepare a proposal for you. Tailored to your specifications, of course! Is there anything you would need from us that I should handle for you?" The woman gracefully recovered from stumbling on the step as they entered the formal dinning room.

"I think that about covers everything. Just make sure that usage of all facilities is included, without restriction. The total fee as well

Shadows of Doubt

as a direct telephone number for you so that I can have my assistant handle all of the details and finances, please." He smiled once again as they approached the McAllisters who were seated at a table next to the rear wall of windows. The table provided for a stunning view that looked out over the immaculately groomed 18th hole of the east course.

"I'll revise this and have it ready for you by the time you are ready to leave us this evening." She all but sang with excitement. "Here we are. Mr. and Mrs. McAllister, Mr. Julian..." The exuberant Ms. Price nodded to her left and a waiter whooshed in to pull out Max's seat and stood by at the ready to place his napkin. "Please enjoy your evening and let me know if there is anything you need." She backed out and nearly sprinted from the dining room.

Max approached Joe McAllister who had stood and come around the table to greet him. He took the hand Joe offered and embraced the man warmly as a dear old friend, rather than an operative.

"Max it is so damn good to have you here. I was completely thrilled when Shevaun told me you were not only here but were going to be our neighbor!" Joe patted Max on the back enthusiastically.

"Well I am sure she told you I was equally thrilled when I discovered she was your Shevaun at the meeting last night. You kept this brilliant jewel a well guarded secret all these years." Max was oozing charm as he approached Shevaun and leaned down to greet her with a kiss on her cheek and a squeeze of her delicate hand. "It is lovely to see you again. You look simply gorgeous this evening."

Shevaun's smile was sincere and stunning, sending a pang in Max's gut since it reminded him so much of her daughter. He could only imagine what Lou would look like dressed in finery as her mother was now. Elegant and understated, putting the other women in the dinning room to shame.

"You are too kind and very full of it, but thank you Max." She waved her hands in a gesture for both of the men to sit. "We're so glad you could join us tonight. The food here is truly excellent."

Max took his seat and observed the couple together for the first time. He had known Joe forever but had never envisioned what his mate might be like. After meeting Shevaun the night before, seeing how beautiful she was and that she was also a truly lovely person, it made Max look at Joe with entirely different eyes.

Joe McAllister was a handsome man in his mid sixties who may have looked younger than his years if not for his time under the Texas sun. He had crisp blue eyes that twinkled with pride when he looked at his wife, and strong angular features that softened profoundly when he smiled. His choppy dark blond hair was silvering at the temples and suited him nicely. His hands were well manicured but had clearly seen their fair share of hard work and he wore a single Irish knot-work wedding band on his left ring finger. The bespoke charcoal gray suit complemented his wife's pewter satin dress perfectly. Joe and Shevaun were an unassuming couple with impeccable taste and Max already enjoyed their company immensely.

They chatted and laughed over bad business trips while sipping martinis when Shevaun excused herself to visit the power room before their first course arrived.

Max leaned in towards Joe and lowered his voice "I really would have liked to discussed things with you prior to this dinner, Joe. I realize that your wife knows nothing of the true nature of our relationship let alone anything about the Sanguinostri so I am at a bit of a disadvantage here."

"I know my Dom..." Joe dragged his fingers through his hair, clearly frustrated. "I apologize profusely for the inconvenience of it all. I truly hate keeping my two worlds separate from my wife. It's agonizing on a daily basis dancing around the truth with her. I feel like such a shit."

Shadows of Doubt

"Its a long time to keep such a big secret from someone you obviously adore. She's quite exceptional Joe." Max stabbed the olive in his barely touched martini and swirled it in his glass.

"I know she is, which makes it all the worse! But first it was about our daughter. I couldn't expect Shevaun to deal with my world with a baby girl that's the center of her universe, could I? That was simply asking too much. I know damn well I will always be second in Shevaun's life and I am totally okay with that." Max continued to fidget with his skewered olive while Joe vented his predicament. "Then Lou grows up and follows with her family tradition of being a cop. How the hell was I going to explain all this to the two of them and it not totally blow up in my face?" Joe's expression was one of pure exasperation. "I would give anything to be able to come clean with them, but how the hell do I do that at this stage in the game?"

Max looked to make sure Shevaun wasn't returning, then responded. "We may not have a choice Joe. Lou is poking around in Sanguinostri issues without knowing it. You and I are going to have to have a discussion about this in private. The sooner the better." Knowing he was going to need it, Max shoved his martini in front of Joe then signaled to the waiter for another round. "Don't stress over it now, this could actually be a very good thing for you, so don't panic just yet. Lets just enjoy the evening, then we can discuss everything in the morning at my place, alright?"

Joe drained the martini glass Max had passed him and pulled the clean toothpick from his mouth while he nodded. He nearly choked on the olive when Shevaun suddenly returned to her seat and eyed him suspiciously.

"Did I miss something good?" She asked the two men.

"Not at all..." Max took the lead on the cover-up as their first course was served. "...we were just discussing boring business matters which

I apologize for bringing up. Lets get back to more enjoyable dinner conversation, shall we?" It was clear to see that Joe was having a difficult time shifting gears as he aimlessly stabbed at his field greens. "So I hear the courses here are quite spectacular?"

"Oh that's right!" She bounced in her chair. "Joe tells me you are a huge golf buff, is that true? I bet you're an outstanding player."

"Well I wouldn't go that far but yes, I am quite fond of the sport." In fact, Max was a golf nut and had been for eons. He had a private golf memorabilia collection that rivaled anyone in the known universe. "Your Ms. Price is actually preparing a package for me to consider. I'll have to find some time to actually play the courses here so I can make an informed decision."

"The weather is supposed to be lovely this weekend, you should come out and play! Joe and I usually make it a family Sunday with our daughter. We have brunch, then play at least 9 holes, depending on how stuffed we are or what the weather is like. You should join us! Tell him Joe!" Shevaun poked her husband in the arm repeatedly. It was seriously difficult for Max not to panic at the thought of coming face to face with their daughter and actually having to converse with her.

"Darling..." Joe patted his wife's hand to get her to stop poking. "I am certain Max will join us if he is able but you must remember he has a good deal on his schedule." Joe had apparently recovered his composure given his handling of his wife's demand. "As a matter of fact he and I have a rather serious matter we have to deal with first thing in the morning. So let's wait and see how he feels, alright?"

Shevaun was suddenly embarrassed by her over-exuberance and became notably quiet. Max realized the situation was delicate in more ways than he had ever imagined, but gaining Lou's mother's trust and acceptance was critical to him.

"I truly would love to, but I cannot make any guarantees. Is it just the three of you that play?" He specifically looked to Shevaun to answer and he could tell it made her feel more at ease.

"Yes, just the three of us. The weather has been so dreadful that I am so looking forward to a decent day out. Even if it's gloomy I won't mind, so long as it's not freezing or raining."

"You need to remember I come from D.C. and will admit I've even attempted to play in the snow. Weather wouldn't prevent me from joining you, I can assure you." Max's smile was kind and sincere. He truly would happily play in a blizzard with them but he just was unsure of how he was going to handle himself in front of Lou. "Would it be alright if we played it by ear? You tell me when you plan to tee off and I will be here if I can break free?"

Shevaun was clearly pleased. "That would be perfect. I do hope you can make it though."

The salad plates were cleared. The next course was served and the remainder of the evening's conversation was, much to both Joe and Max's relief, monopolized by golf tales and debate over various players. Who would win the Masters and other benign chatter. The food had been excellent, the service impeccable and the company more than pleasant.

Max found himself musing the entire ride back to the hotel over how much he looked forward to his next dinner with the McAllisters. He tried very hard not to think about how that may never come to pass if things did not go well with him and Joe in the morning. It was going to be tricky as hell. Especially since Max had not a clue what he wanted to do about his infatuation with the detective. He truly couldn't understand how he had come to this point. He should not have cared one iota about this total stranger let alone be tap dancing and weaving his plans for Los Angeles around the possibility of her.

But she wasn't really a total stranger was she? Tallulah Donovan had been on the fringes of his world for so long without him ever knowing it. When Joe had confided to Max about the situation at dinner, Max had vaguely recalled it had been something they discussed before but for the life of him Max could not recall Joe mentioning a daughter or any details or specifics. Joe had made mention of his predicament in the past but it was cursory and Max had always made light of things, telling Joe things would work themselves out. He had really paid little to no attention to Joe's personal dilemma and for that he was now facing it head-on. There was a vested interest in how things played out but he was thoroughly irritated with himself for it. If anyone ever knew Max Julian, Dominor of North America, was a complete blithering idiot over a woman he did not even know, he would be a laughing stock.

Chapter Eight

The woman behind the counter at the rental agency was less enthusiastic about Lou's request than she was about being at work on a Saturday morning. The lack of any make-up, the haphazard way her ponytail had been fastened and the rumpled, misbuttoned blouse were dead giveaways that she had overslept for work.

"I know there is some sort of procedure I need to follow for stuff like this. Don't you have to have a warrant or something?" The bleary eyed woman asked Lou.

"That would be if your vehicle was involved in the accident or directly involved in a crime, which I'm sure you can see if you look, it wasn't. The person who rented the car from you may have been a witness to an accident and we just want to get in touch with them and find out." Lou tap danced and continued to sell her story that she and Caroline had come up with on the ride over. "All we need is the contact information, that's all."

"Well, I guess since it really doesn't involve the company." The woman finally caved and pulled up the information and printed it out for them.

"Thank you very much for your cooperation." Lou smiled thoughtfully as she took the printout from the woman.

"No problem. I hope you nail the bastard that hit that old lady."

Lou looked up at the woman, wondering what she was talking about until she remembered Caroline's fabricated sob-story. "Oh yes, we will. Thanks again."

With the information in hand, Lou and Caroline walked out of the rental agency at a fast clip and headed for the car.

"Holy cow, you were right. That wasn't as easy as I thought it would be." Caroline hopped into the passenger seat and flipped open her laptop.

Lou rolled her eyes. "I told you. Its not like what you see on television. I thought for a minute there we were screwed and she was going to demand a warrant, or call her manager who would." She got in the driver's side and handed Caroline the paper. "It says the car was rented to an Augustus Industries with a contact name of Frank Sullivan. There are two phone numbers. One local and one with a 202 area code. Where is that for?"

"Hang on, I was looking up the company info first but let me do the area code." Caroline typed away then waited a few seconds. "That area code is for Washington, D.C." She looked at Lou with a puzzled expression. "What the hell?"

"Look up the company, Augustus Industries." Lou tapped her fingers nervously on the steering wheel. "Frank Sullivan, you think that's his name? Kind of anticlimactic don't you think?"

Caroline laughed at her friend as she continued her search for data. "What did you want? Some fancy name like the male version of Tallulah?"

"Har har, very funny." Lou tweaked Caroline's ear.

"Ow! Don't do that! Anyway, I think it's a nice strong Irish name." Rubbing her earlobe, Caroline pondered a moment. "Can't be his name."

"Why not?"

"Precisely because it is an Irish name. Yummy Morgue Guy is no way Irish with that hair and skin."

That was a good observation on her friend's part, Lou thought. "Maybe his mom was Mediterranean or something and his dad was Irish."

The sunny blond shook her head then cursed under her breath at the laptop. "Nuh uh, I know my men. He's Spanish or Italian or something like that. The other guy looked Irish, but not your guy." Cursing once again she resumed typing and clicking away.

"What's wrong?" Lou asked, noticing her friend was getting annoyed.

"I get tons of crap on Augustus but its like everything on their branches and divisions. Shipping, finance, global this and global that but I cannot find names. No board of directors info. There isn't even a personal name on the different contact pages for the various divisions that do happen to have a web-site. I'll say one thing though, its a freaking massive company." She sighed and slammed the laptop closed. "Lets call the local number."

Lou's eyes nearly popped out of her head. "Are you out of your freaking mind?"

"Of course, but what does that have to do with anything?" Caroline fished out her cell phone.

Lou yanked the phone out of her friend's hand and looked at her with a death stare. "Hello? Caller ID? And what in the hell do you plan on saying? 'Hi, are you Yummy Morgue Guy?' I don't think so!"

Caroline hated that Lou had two very valid points but smiled as an idea hit her when she looked toward the gas station next to them. "Give me a quarter."

"What for?"

"Just give me a quarter."

"No, not until you tell me what for."

Caroline blew out a breath and shoved the laptop back in its case and started fishing in her purse. "Never mind. I'll find one." She got out of the car with the contact information tucked under her arm and walked to the pay phone at the gas station, fishing out a handful of change from her purse as she went.

"Wait!" Lou yelled after her then jumped out of the car to follow. "What the hell are you doing?"

"You'll see." She dumped coins in the slot, then dialed.

"Holy crap, you are nuts!" Lou scrubbed her face with her hands and began to pace.

The phone rang three times before a deep voice answered on the other end. "Yeah?"

At first Caroline said nothing, then it just came out. "Mr. Sullivan?"

"Yeah?" The baritone voice answering and asking with one word.

Lou bolted next to Caroline so she could hear. "Frank Sullivan?" Caroline asked.

"Yeah? Who is this?" The man at the other end demanded.

"Uh..." Was all Caroline could say before Lou slammed her hand down on the hook. "What the hell, Lou?"

"What the hell is right! What the hell were you going to say?! Never mind! Get in the car and let's get out of here before he..."

"He what? Traces the call in a nanosecond and teleports over here to see it's us calling him?" Caroline slammed the receiver onto the hook.

"Exactly!" Not waiting another second, Lou yanked Caroline and high-tailed it to the car. "Lets go."

"Fine, but you're buying me breakfast for that."

Lou looked at her friend incredulously as she pulled out of the parking lot. "How can you be hungry? You ate like eight of those cream puffs last night!"

"I did not! I only ate seven." She pouted. "Besides I only ate the filling and that's mostly air!"

Lou tried to remain serious but couldn't. Thinking about what her friend had just said, and truly meant. All Lou could do was burst out laughing.

It had taken about an hour and a half to bring Joe McAllister up to speed on the reorganization of the West Coast and then the whole matter of their rogue. Max had recounted all the other murders around the globe in graphic detail, to stress the gravity of the situation. He went step-by-step on how Lou and Caroline Devereux were involved and how despite the fact that all three cases were LAPD's now, they were still investigating. Joe was floored to find out that Caroline was of the Richlieu Devereux line and that the parents and Richlieu himself were arriving at any moment. They would be dealing with Caroline's indoctrination into the Sanguinostri that evening. It was a lot to take in, Max admitted, but here they were and things had to be dealt with before their rogue struck again. Of course Max omitted any hint of his infatuation with Lou and that he had a secret personal stake in the dilemma.

"This is really bloody complicated!" Joe got up and began pacing. "Caroline and Lou are very close, almost sisters. Hell, Caroline has spent the last two nights at our house and I think she's with Lou right now!"

Frank walked back into the room, stuffing his cell phone into his pocket. "Yes, she is. They are eating pancakes at a cafe in Tarzana at the moment."

Joe looked at Frank, stunned. "You're having them followed?!"

Max got up from the chair and put a hand on Joe's shoulder. "If we know they are poking around at the rogue, its not impossible that he knows that as well. Its for their own protection, I assure you."

Joe looked Max in the eye and thought for a moment. "Yes, of course. Thank you for that, my Dom."

"Now come back and sit so we can continue." Max steered Joe back to the couch. "The matters at hand are all intertwined and require careful consideration. Whichever first step we take will be critical for all other outcomes."

Joe nodded in understanding. "Caroline will never lie to Lou. That will be a sticking point with her. That much I do know."

"Which is why what I am about to propose may be difficult for you." Max had thought about it over and over and knew that he had to just get it out. "With my Council and I shifting bases to California, and our need for solid people in key positions, it has occurred to me that your daughter may have been put in our path for a reason." Max waited for the underlying meaning to hit Joe. When Joe's head whipped around to stare at Max, he knew that it was understood.

"You mean indoctrinate Lou?!" Joe got back up to pace again.

"I realize you have kept the Sanguinostri a secret from your wife and daughter all these years for a reason, and I am sorry for putting you in this position, but..."

"But it was because of Lou that I never put Shevaun in that position when we first met!" Joe cut Max off before he could complete his sentence. "Lou was far too young to understand and Shevaun was... hell she is devoted to her. There was no way I could be so selfish tas o tell her. To ask her to join us with a baby girl that was her life. But now Lou is grown. Strong. Smart! She is dedicated to the pursuit of justice and the protection of the public. If you were to explain that is exactly our role, our code but on a grander scale, she would understand and couldn't help but want to be a part of it!" Joe's eyes were wide and sparkling now as he talked it out and paced back and fourth. "But her indoctrination would be contingent upon her mother knowing! Of course she'll be pissed as hell that I've kept this from her and I've been a part of it all my life, but she'll understand once she thinks." He moved to sit next to Max and nearly grabbed him by the collar. "Don't you see? All this time I have hated having to keep two lives. Lying to Shevaun. I've wanted nothing more than to tell her, to explain. Yes, yes and there was the hope that perhaps she would turn with me but even without that! If Lou joins, then there is no way Shevaun would not!" He nearly started to laugh as he looked around the room, to Frank, then back to Max. "And then Caroline wouldn't have to lie and …." Joe stopped himself, then smirked. "…and you already deduced all of this yourself, haven't you?"

Max smiled at Joe brightly, then couldn't help himself. He pulled him into a hug. "I needed you to pull it together yourself Joe. I needed to see your reaction as you came out with it. To know you were alright with it. I consider you family, Joe. I will protect yours as though you are my own."

Joe was so moved by Max's words that his eyes welled with tears. "My Dominor, I am so honored by you. Thank you."

Max patted Joe on the shoulder again and grinned. "Don't thank me yet! We need to make this work the way we think it will. It's going to be tricky and timing is everything.

"Speaking of timing…" Frank interrupted. "The Devereuxs have arrived at the Chateau. They are being shown to their bungalows and should be settled shortly."

"Right then." Max clasped his hands together. "Joe, would you mind assisting me with this? I'll need to explain everything to them and given you probably know their daughter better then they do at this point in time, you could really help me here."

"It would be my pleasure to assist with anything, you know that."

Max did know that, which made his stomach flip-flop a little at the thought that Joe would lose all respect for him if he found out how he felt about Lou. He swallowed hard and let that thought pass. "Frank, have a nice coffee service sent to Richlieu's bungalow and then inform the Devereuxs that Joe and I will be down soon." Frank nodded to Max, then left the room. Max had thought long and hard about the entire situation. He knew that there was a very small window of opportunity here and regardless of his personal feelings, and fears, he needed to meet Lou face to face and be sure that his gut instinct that she was fit to be brought into the Sanguinostri was correct. "Well then, it looks like we are on for golf tomorrow, after all."

Joe had to laugh. "Christ, I forgot all about that."

"Its a good opportunity for me to meet Lou. Be certain we are doing the right thing. That I am doing the right thing. Ultimately, you all, every last one of you are my responsibility. That is why we have our laws about indoctrination."

"Oh I completely understand that. But I know in my gut that Lou would be one of the greatest assets we could ever have." It was the father speaking now and it warmed Max's heart to hear.

He turned again to Joe and looked at him thoughtfully. "Joe, you need to be prepared if this doesn't fall our way. If Lou wants no part of it, we will need to wipe her memory of the discussion and things will go back to as they are now. Do you understand that?"

"I know, I understand." Joe's shoulders slouched just a bit. "But the Fates can be kind sometimes, can't they?"

"Yes." Max smiled softly. "Yes, they can sometimes. Let's hope that this is one of those times."

Shadows of Doubt

Lou had been grateful for Vinny's call that afternoon. While Caroline had managed to pack away a not-so-short stack of pancakes at breakfast, Lou's mind had been racing and she had more or less just shoved her food from one side of the plate to the other rather than eat it. When Vinny called stating he needed an escape from nursery prep and suggested they go out for some beer and barbeque, Lou immediately began over-salivating. As far as she was concerned Vinny couldn't get her there fast enough.

The restaurant was a definite dive but it was also a coveted local institution that had been family owned and operated for nearly a hundred years. Tucked back on a side road nestled between the foothills and a reservoir, it was probably the only joint in the universe where bikers and cops hung out under the same roof in relative harmony. Whether perched at the bar or parked at one of the family-style tables made from old railroad ties, rookies, seasoned detectives and hard-core leather clad dudes alike kicked back to have a few beers and partake in some of the heavenly concoctions the old man cooked up at the ten foot barbecue outside. The building itself had once been an old barn that had been converted by Jeremiah Jackson Sr. about a hundred years ago to accommodate his entire church congregation for regular Sunday barbeques. His wife, Sarah Ann, had become legendary for her sauce and cornbread, so Sundays expanded to include Wednesdays with a donation jar to help recoup the cost for the meals. From there it snowballed into a full time pit-stop for the entire town. Since then a full kitchen was installed and revamped several times over the decades. The barn had been retrofitted to accommodate the forty foot bar and a small stage where local musicians cranked out everything from blue-grass to speed metal depending on the day of the week. Jeremiah Sr. and Sarah Ann were long gone now but his son Jeremiah, Jr., at the spry young age of eighty-two, his wife Maggie and their four kids, Jeremiah the 3rd., David, Johnny and Annie all ran the local treasure together like a well oiled machine. Cooking up the same amazing food every day of the week.

    Watching Vinny slather yet more sauce on his sandwich, Lou smiled to herself, knowing Vinny's wife would have a fit to see the mess he was ingesting. This was definitely not something in the healthy eating category. After double-dipping one of her huge steak fries in ranch dressing in almost an act of solidarity, Lou looked around the expanse of the barn and marveled at the variety of people gathered. Rumpled business suits, uniformed deputies and LAPD blues. Leather motorcycle pants as well as some jeans that looked like they were so old and filthy they would stand up on their own. One table near the barbeque patio was filled with a group of women who appeared to be nurses, given their green scrub pants and trademark floral and cartoon scrubshirts. They were laughing uproariously at something one of them had said and were ogling the Hulk Hogan look-alike that had just strutted back from the bar in his well-worn jeans, shit-kicker boots and nothing else but an open leather vest. He had foregone the draft mug and was drinking straight from the pitcher as his bronzed abs twitched with each gulp. It was easy to deduce that whatever the women were going on about, it was definitely not PG-13.

    Lou munched another french fry while Vinny ranted about his impending fatherhood and the implications of green versus yellow paint for a nursery while her eyes continued to peruse the packed house around them. At the far end of the bar, obscured by a group of most-likely investment bankers, she thought she caught a pair of men staring at her. When she eyeballed them directly they appeared to be talking amongst themselves but Lou felt the hairs on the back of her neck stand up for no apparent reason. Casually she tried to get a good look at the two but neither of the men looked even remotely familiar to her, aside from the standard visage of blue-collar grease monkey.

"Can I get you two another beer?" The lanky bartender's squeaky voice jerked Lou's attention away from the dubious pair.

"Not me, thanks though." Lou smiled politely at Jeremiah number three who in turn gave her a nod.

Vinny picked up his mug and drained the last gulp before sliding it to the man. "One more, then the bill if ya don't mind, JJ. Thanks." He mopped his face with his napkin and eyed Lou wearily. "Any idea who they are?" Lou looked at him with a crooked glance, only semi-surprised he had caught the two grease monkeys looking their way.

"No bells going off." She picked at another fry as she glanced back to the end of the bar just in time to see the two leaving. "Guess it was nothing."

"Maybe, but they seemed fishy." Vinny watched the pair head for the door as Jeremiah the younger plopped down his foamy draft and the bill. "Thanks JJ. Tell your mom and pop it was delicious as ever. Hey, you happen to know who those two guys that just left were? That were at the end of the bar?"

JJ looked in time to catch the backsides of the men in question stepping out the saloon style doors. "Nah. They're not locals for sure though. Been hanging around just about a week, I guess and not exactly the friendly type if ya get my drift." The sound of breaking glass drew JJ's attention and a scowl to the opposite end of the barn. "Hey! You break it you bought it!" He shouted over their heads. "Duty calls. Take care you two." The man rushed off to handle the scuffle leaving Lou and Vinny with their suspicions of the noobie grease monkeys and the unpaid bill. They each fished out a twenty and stacked it over the check, leaving well more then the standard fifteen-percent gratuity as was well deserved.

"Probably just that parolee-vibe, ya know what I mean?" Vinny speculated as he took a sip from his mug.

"Maybe." Lou conceded, not wholly convinced. "So, Vera won with the yellow despite your bitching?" She brought the topic back to a more pleasant one. Dismissing the strangers that were now gone.

"Yeah but I still think it's a girlie color. Too damned perky!" Vinny grumbled.

Lou chuckled at him. "If you two are set on not finding out if it's a boy or a girl, then you gotta go neutral. It's not banana yellow or anything, right?"

"Nah, Vera says it's buttery. Whatever the hell that means. The name of the paint she picked is called spring serenity or some shit like that. Here! Look!" He shoved up the sleeve of his shirt to show her the yellow paint splatters on his skin. "See? That's it here."

Lou looked at the soothing pale yellow and nodded her approval. "That's a nice color."

"Yeah I guess." He rolled his sleeve back down, took another slug from his mug then plunked it down on the bar with a thud. "She says she wants me involved in all this but you know as well as I do she's gonna pick everything the way she wants it no matter what I say. I don't know why the hell she even asks me!"

"Because she wants you to feel included but knows you're crap at things like that." Lou gave him a gentle nudge. "It's a girl thing, Vinny. She's nesting or whatever it's called. Find your patience and avoid the stress."

Vinny shoved his half-empty mug away and mopped his face once more with his napkin as he rolled his eyes at her. "Words of wisdom, grasshopper. Easier said than done! I better get you home and get myself back to the nest before momma-bird decides to clip my wings once and for all."

Lou snorted at his all-too-accurate bird analogy as she got up from the bar and made her way for the door. For some odd reason the image of Vinny in a Woody-Woodpecker costume popped into her head. By the time they got to the car she was chuckling out loud at the visual.

"What's so funny?" Vinny asked as he fished his car keys from his pocket.

"Nothin', Woody." She chortled.

"Huh?' He stared at her with confusion for a moment. Lou heard a pop then suddenly Vinny dropped to the ground with a thud.

"Vinny?!" Lou shouted as she rounded the back of the car towards him but was slammed to the ground by some unseen force just as she reached the driver's side. As Lou tried to get up and get her bearings she heard an unknown voice from behind her shout to someone to get the car. Glancing up she saw Vinny pushing up off the ground and getting to his feet. "Vinny?" She croaked this time, only semi catching her breath from whatever blow she had taken to the gut. Since there was no blood and she was already able to move to get back on her feet, she deduced it had to have been a bean bag or a low-dose stun gun that nailed them.

"Behind you, kid!" Vinny shouted as he came to attention and reached for his gun.

"Don't even think about it!" The male voice from behind Lou was gruff and gravelly, sounding like a two-pack a day smoker's voice. "Hands up, both of you!"

Lou turned slowly to face one of the grease monkeys who was now standing in front of them with his Glock pointed at them. Still no bells ringing as to who the man was, Lou figured grease monkey number two was the one getting the car and she had precious little time to waste getting this guy out of their faces.

"Hey Einstein, you got about thirty seconds before the three dozen or so cops that are inside there come out and turn you into swiss cheese." Vinny's colorful yet accurate observation bought Lou the second she needed when the man turned his head to look at the restaurant.

"Duck!" She shouted at her partner as she pivoted on the ball of her left foot, swinging her body around and nailing the asshole hard with a solid roundhouse kick. The blow knocked the gun from his grip and sent it and him skittering across the dirt. Lou did an almost perfect pirouette, righting herself above their would-be attacker who was now face down on the ground, choking for breath. She straddled him, yanked his arm up behind his back almost popping it out of it's socket while placing her boot firmly into the small of his back.

"I got him." Vinny assured her as he planted himself on top of the man's back and reached for his handcuffs. Lou glanced over her shoulder to see the herd of charging cops approaching as promised. She quickly turned to catch sight of the dust cloud approaching from what could only be the second grease monkey in the requested vehicle. As the beat-up sedan closed in, Lou reached for her gun and relinquished her hold on the first asshole to one of the uniforms that was now assisting Vinny. In what could only be described as a twisted game of chicken, Lou took several strides head-on towards the sedan, aiming her gun dead at the driver. With a jerk of the wheel, the sedan skidded sideways and the driver pointed his own gun likewise at Lou through the open window and popped off two shots in her direction before he hit the gas and sent yet more dirt billowing into the air, obscuring Lou's sight. She ducked instinctively and fired her own two rounds before the sedan's wheels caught hold of the loose dirt and started making it's getaway.

"Go! We got this one!" A uniformed deputy shouted, sending Vinny in a sprint for their car.

"Let's go!" He demanded of Lou as he cranked the engine and flung the passenger door open for her. Before her butt was even in the seat, Vinny floored it and they were in hot pursuit of grease monkey number two.

Although he had a mild lead on them, it wasn't difficult to deduce the direction their man had gone. The trail of dust had them heading southwest along the old road then hanging a prompt left onto Box Canyon.

"Ah crap. I got a bad feeling about this, Lou." Vinny grumbled as they headed into the pitch black of the windy canyon road while Lou called in to dispatch and relayed recent events.

"Not allowed to have a bad feeling Vinny. Vera will kick my ass if you aren't safe and sound to finish that nursery tonight." Lou tried to make light of the situation with her joke but she too had a bad feeling as they headed further into sketchy territory through the canyon. "Fifty bucks says we hit the pass."

Vinny snorted at her comment. "That's a sucker bet."

Sure enough, the faint red glow of tail-lights ahead of them pulled right onto the Santa Susana Pass which as both Vinny and Lou expected would inevitably lead them into the infamous territory of the former Spahn Ranch. Once a location notorious for filming such classics as the Lone Ranger and Bonanza, the deeds of Charlie Manson and his "family" had forever scarred the location and made it a well known campground for crooks and kooks alike. Despite it falling victim to Manson and numerous wild fires, the ranch that was now part of the Santa Susanna Pass State Historic Park still held dilapidated outbuildings, makeshift shanties and enough hollowed out car carcasses to make it a tricky place to chase down a suspect at night. Lou knew once they turned off onto the old dirt road that was exactly what they were going to be doing and relayed such to dispatch right before Vinny slammed on the brakes to avoid rear ending the ratty sedan that was now at a standstill, driver door agape and still running.

"Dammit!" Vinny grumbled as he unhooked his seat-belt and bolted from the car.

"He's not heading into the hills, you know that, right?" Lou followed her partner to the back of their vehicle where Vinny was already pulling a shotgun from the trunk.

"No shit, Sherlock!" He gave her a wry smirk as he clipped his flashlight to the barrel of the shotgun. "I'll go left and come up the rear. You good?"

"I'm good. Heading up the middle. Watch your ass." She retorted as she stuffed an extra magazine in her pocket and flipped on her flashlight.

With that, Vinny nodded and headed to the left side of what appeared to be an old double-wide with various plywood modifications. The kicked up dust from the vehicles tasted salty on Lou's tongue and among the smell of dirt, old wood and sagebrush was the stench of piss and stale beer. The faint note of a chemical smell pulled memories of meth-lab busts from Lou's mind and she wondered if there might be enough crap left to cause an explosion if a bullet caught the wrong target. Just another fun and exciting fly in the ointment of what had been a perfectly lovely evening up until a little bit ago. She proceeded cautiously through the burned out hull of some sort of outbuilding, possibly an old barn or corral once upon a time. Any trace of daylight was long gone, making anything five feet in front of her lost in the pitch black of the moonless night. Not a sound stirring, not even a shuffle from Vinny in the distance as she carefully climbed over a pile of wood that appeared to have once been a barn door. She could smell stale hay and kerosene as she ducked under a collapsed rafter, proceeding deeper into the ruins and trash. He was in here. She could feel it and she shut off her flashlight so as not to give him a spotlight on his target. Slower and more cautiously she hugged the right of the structure as best she could. Ducking and weaving silently through the wreckage of the corrals that perhaps once housed the horses for Little Joe or Hoss from Bonanza. Man she really loved that show when she was a kid and what a crush she had had on Pernell Roberts. She tried not to snort as she realized where her mind had wandered while skulking through the dark in pursuit of an armed twit that had only just minutes ago taken a couple shots at her. Surely Ben Cartwright would be impressed with her nonchalant attitude in the situation.

Hunkered down in the darkness, positioned behind an old rusty oil drum, grease monkey number two stood silently with his gun aimed at the only way in to his location. He had worked it out in his mind that once he capped the chick-cop he would squeeze through the hole in what was left of the wall and haul ass for the car. He didn't move as he let his eyes adjust to the darkness. He had seen the glow from a flashlight a few moments ago but now it was black again and all he could see was the narrow walkway that funneled towards him. As soon as he caught sight of her he would blow her away. He just needed to be still, silent and keep the gun steady and trained on that spot until she made her way towards him. He could hear his own heart pounding in his ears as he watched his hands tremble lightly with anticipation. Before his brain had even a second to acknowledge what was happening, a pair of hands came from behind him, wrapping around his own and the grip of the gun. He saw the gun tilting upward, towards him. Closer until he sensed the barrel pressing underneath his chin. So fast. Bang.

Niko carefully slipped back through the hole from whence he came and let the body of the would-be assassin slump into a heap. He swiped a gloved hand over his face in a futile attempt to remove the blood and brain matter that covered him. Without a sound, he hit full stride in less than a second and made his way through the brush, thicket, pitch black night. Back to the motorcycle that waited, hidden, off the side of the road. He had calculated carefully that he had parked far enough away that the sound of the motorcycle would be drowned out by approaching sirens and that he was off the main road enough that his exit would be undetected. He was really glad he had indulged his curiosity about this woman after learning of the Code Pink from Abby and Frank. She was lovely. Quick witted and shrewd from everything he had observed since he spotted her at the restaurant with her partner. Now, she was very much in danger and that simply would not do for the object of his Dominor's affection. Niko needed to find out who these assholes that had targeted her were, and make sure they were shut down permanently. One down, one to go.

Lou had seen the muzzle flash before she heard the shot and had made a bee-line for the source. Her heart was in her throat but she knew better than to yell out for her partner and give away her position. When she felt close enough, she flipped on her flashlight and caught sight of grease monkey number two splayed out on the ground, gun still in his hand. The top half of his skull was blown clean off.

Clearly no longer a threat, Lou shouted out for her partner. "Vinny?!"

"I'm here! You okay?" Vinny climbed through a hole on the other side of the structure and trained his flashlight on the corpse. "Freakin' cheeseball! Guess it was gonna be his third strike then, huh?"

Lou snickered and turned her head towards the sound of approaching sirens. "Crap, this is gonna suck. Caroline is off tonight so we're gonna have a long clean-up on this one."

"Yeah but we will be going home eventually. Unlike this guy." Vinny blew out a breath and raked his fingers through his hair in normal Vinny fashion. "I better call Vera and tell her I'm gonna be late."

Shadows of Doubt

"I'll call it in while you do that." Lou followed Vinny through his entry hole and they made their way to the car. The onslaught of black and whites began piling up with the red glow of flashing lights washing over everything within a half-mile. Lou had no idea who the assholes had been but she was certain they had picked the wrong people to piss off. Now she wanted to know why.

As Caroline walked up the path to her parent's bungalow she tried not to be so anxious. Instead, she replayed her day with Lou in her head and chuckled aloud at their shenanigans. They had a lovely breakfast then did a bit of shopping before they headed back to Lou's place and watched some old movie that Caroline couldn't remember the name of. It was a good day, until she had to leave. Stalling as long as she could, Caroline finally knocked on the bungalow door and waited. It was her mother that answered.

Katherine Devereux was a stunning woman with gilded hair that cascaded in waves around an angelic face of peaches and cream. Her lithe frame reminded Caroline that she was grateful for inheriting more than her mother's eyes, after eating all those pancakes.

"Caroline!" Her mother squeaked as she wrapped her arms around her daughter. "Oh my, I am so glad to see you!

"It's good to see you too, Momma." Caroline hugged her mother back just as tight.

Katherine shoved her daughter back and gawked. "Heavens, you look absolutely fantastic! I don't think I remember seeing you so lovely in all my life!" Her mother's southern drawl was so thick that Caroline couldn't help but giggle. "Come in darlin'! Come in!" She all but ripped Caroline's arms off as she yanked her into the bungalow. "Charlie! Our little girl is here!"

The first thing that Caroline noticed when her father came into the room was the silver strewn through his blond hair. There hadn't been so much of it when she had left home. His face still reminded her of Clark Gable even in his Georgia Tech sweatshirt and faded bluejeans. It suddenly occurred to her that both of her parents were unusually casual, something they never were. Her mother was wearing a high end cocoa colored jog-suit which was extremely odd since her mother thought it blasphemy for a proper southern lady to wear trousers. Her parents were different.

"Hi Daddy." She beamed a smile at him. He never said a word, just walked straight up to her and hugged her tight. It took everything she had not to start blubbering.

"Oh, this is so wonderful!" Her mother did the blubbering for her.

The buzzer at the door startled them all, sending the three of them into a burst of giggles. Katherine wiped her eyes as she went for the door.

"I hope you don't mind, but I just ordered room service. Real casual. I figured we could get cozy and munch a bunch while we caught up." She opened the door and directed the young man to wheel the cart into the living area. It took several minutes, but after unloading of its goodies, Caroline's father tipped the boy and showed him out.

"Well I just can't wait to hear all about your life here in Los Angeles." Her father spoke for the first time. "Your uncle will be over later, after we eat and have had time to catch up."

"That will be nice, Daddy. I haven't seen Uncle Richie in so long." Caroline sat down on the couch and scanned the feast that had been delivered. The coffee table and serving cart had everything from buffalo wings to caviar and God help her, cream puffs.

"Go ahead and dig in, Sugar Pie!" Katherine urged her daughter. "I had the bartender at the main hotel make us a pitcher of sangria. That sound good to you?"

It shamed her but Caroline was wondering who the hell these

people were. They were not her prim and proper parents. 'That sounds real good Momma, thank you."

Caroline's father sat down next to her on the couch and shoved up his sleeves. "Well let's dig in baby girl, and start fillin' us in on California life." He nudged her with his shoulder then grabbed a plate.

It seemed like they had been eating, talking and laughing for days but when Caroline looked at her watch, it had only been a couple hours. She got up and helped her parents clear the table of all the dishes. It was shocking to her that the three of them had polished off as much food as they had. Just as her father was returning from wheeling the serving cart full of dishes into the kitchen there was a knock at the door. Caroline knew it would be her uncle but when she noted the odd look her parents exchanged, she wondered. Her father smiled at her, then rushed to get the door. Her uncle Richie hadn't changed one drop from the last time she saw him. His hair was the same silver blond mixture as her father and his jovial face made her smile instantly.

"Uncle Richie!" She leaped up and bounced into his arms. "It is so good to see you!"

Her uncle let out a booming laugh that reverberated through her. "It's even better to see you, baby girl!" He stepped back and gave her a kiss on the forehead. "Goodness you are all grown up now, aren't you?" It was only then that Caroline noticed the man that came in after her uncle. He had a slight smile to his face and seemed very familiar to her. She backed away from her uncle and looked carefully at the stranger. "Oh! Francis, this is my niece, Caroline. Just think of him as extended family, sugar."

Frank stayed back a bit and stood with his hands clasped behind him. He bowed his head to her in greeting. "It's a pleasure, Miss Devereux."

"Hello." Caroline could not figure out why the man seemed so familiar.

"Come and sit, baby girl. As much as I would like to reminisce and all that, we have some important matters that cannot be delayed." Her uncle sat down in one of the chairs by the coffee table and she noticed that both her parents faces were suddenly very somber.

"What the hell is going on?" She demanded.

"Now honey, don't get all riled." Her mother ushered her to the couch. "We have some family things that we need to talk about. Important things that we've put off for far too long. Just relax and drink your wine while we explain." She handed her daughter a glass.

"All we ask is that you listen and keep an open mind, please." her father added as he took her hand.

"Ah right, here it comes." She rolled her eyes and took a big gulp of her wine before she set them straight. "I am telling you all right now, I am not moving back to Savannah! I have a life here!"

Katherine sighed and stroked her daughter's arm. "No baby girl, we aren't going to try to make you come home. We know you have a life here. That's sort of why we need to do this now."

"It's all our fault ya see..." Her father interrupted. "... we should have done this years before you left. When you were eighteen. That's the normal rule but we just kept putting it off."

Caroline wanted to be angry, thinking that her family was going to try and abduct her or something but instead of feeling rage she was getting calmer and more relaxed.

"Alright you two, stop it. We need to get to it and stop going on and on about crap." She always admired her uncle's no-nonsense attitude. He never tiptoed around anything. He just came straight out and told it like it was. "Caroline, I need you to listen to me. I am going to tell you a story and you need to promise me you will sit and listen with an open mind, alright?"

At the moment Caroline felt oddly alright with just about anything. She was warm and fuzzy. Very comfortable, sagging into the couch. "Did y'all drug me?" She would have been furious if she could but she was too relaxed for the fuss.

Katherine patted her daughter's hand "Just a little alprazolam, sugar. To keep you from freaking out, is all."

"Oh, well that's okay I guess." She heard the familiar stranger snort at her words. "What's so funny? And how do I know you?" Caroline noticed her accent had gotten thicker as the anti-anxiety drugs hit her system.

"Francis, it ain't funny so hush." Her uncle ordered halfheartedly. "Alright, so I guess I just need to get to it. You paying attention, Caroline?"

She sat up straight and leaned towards her uncle to listen. "Uh huh."

"First of all, I should tell you that I am not your uncle, I am your grand-daddy."

She cocked her head sideways at him. "That will make more sense to you after I'm done telling you the story. Now please, only interrupt me if you are completely confused, alright?"

Caroline was already confused but she focused on her uncle and nodded. "Alright, uncle Richie."

Richlieu took a deep breath and looked carefully at Caroline as he began his story. "Thousands of years ago there was a small village, not far from the old city of Babylon. It's still not clear what happened because there wasn't technology like we have now, and everything since then is dust. Long gone for any kind of testing. Anyway, what we do know is that the first night of the lunar feast, what we now have come to believe was a meteor that crashed at the edge of the village. It caused a great big fire but they got it all under control before the feast, so everything was fine. Just a little scarey for a while there. Now ya gotta understand that our lunar festival starts on the night of the new moon. The first night you can't see anything of the moon at all. There's a big feast and prayers and all that stuff. So, on this particular night, things were strange because of the meteor and the fire but it's a holy festival so things gotta go on. Everyone in the village, except some who took grain and whatnot to the city to sell, got together for the big feast. They sat and shared food, said their prayers and so on. Well the whole lot of em' got real sick that night. For days and days people were sick. Some dying, some just sick as dogs. The ones that had gone to the city came back and thought it was a plague that hit the village and some of those people ran away but others stayed and tried to care for the sick. You following me, sugar?"

Caroline nodded to her uncle, absolutely engrossed with his story. "Go on!"

"Right, well, the sickness held on to people for what we call a 'lunation' which amounts to about twenty-nine days. All the way to the time the next lunar festival was supposed to be observed. Only about half of the village survived and even then they were real weak and were not recovering the way they should have been. Now I need you to listen to me here and listen carefully. Don't go all wacky on me alright? Promise me now!"

"Alright, I promise." Caroline was far too interested in the story to care about freaking out.

"It was a few days after the sickness seemed to subside but people were still not getting better. One of the villagers who stayed to care for the sick got cut. She was cutting a piece of fruit for her brother and sliced her finger wide open. Something clicked in her brother and he grabbed her finger and licked the blood clean off of her. He instantly perked right up so she was too happy about that to be freaked out

Shadows of Doubt

about him licking her blood. Now she was a smart girl. She realized that it was her blood that made him feel better so she squeezed more out of her finger and let him drink it. It was miraculous how the color came to his cheeks and he felt so much better! So the girl ran to the others who were tending the sick and told them about what she discovered. Of course some of them thought it was flat weird, but they all tried it. Most cut their hands and fed their blood to the sick directly but a few cut deeper and tried to fill cups for the rest. They found that the more the sick drank, the faster they recovered. But there were only five of them so they had to wait, take turns because they themselves would get too weak from giving so much of their blood.

After a time, and after drinkin' a good bit, the people that survived the sickness got well. But not just well, they got better. They were stronger, faster, could see farther, hear things from a good distance away. They learned things quicker too. You still with me here, Caroline?"

"Yes! She waved a hand at him. "Keep going!" Her uncle smiled then continued telling her the tale.

Richlieu told Caroline that not long after the caregivers stopped administering their blood to the others, they fell ill again but became well as soon as they received more blood. It became clear that blood meant life, so the process of learning came. They discovered animal blood didn't have the same healing properties as human, but it would stop the sickness from worsening for a time. They also learned very quickly that outsiders viewed them as cursed, demons, and tried to kill them. But that was when they discovered that they would regenerate. Normally fatal wounds would heal. The more blood they received, the faster they would heal. Even severed fingers and toes, if held in place, would knit back eventually. The only thing that was certain to kill them was cutting off the head and keeping it away from the body. For without the mind, the body withers and dies. It was when outsiders discovered this type of immortality that they began to be hunted and slaughtered. When only seven of the the changed villager remained they realized they could no longer stay there. They needed to hide and keep their condition a secret. So they took the blood of those that came to the village to hunt them, kept the bodies until their numbers equaled their own, then set the village ablaze. The caretakers fled to the cities and spread a tale that the plague had returned to the village and killed them all.

Some fled to the larger cities to try and learn of anything they could to help them survive while the others, along with the caregivers were nomads for a time. They discovered that not only did they heal but they did not age, unlike their caregivers. And through trial and error, and the whim of the Fates, they learned that their condition could be shared under a very specific set of circumstances and even then it was a fifty-fifty chance the person would survive the turning. Only one caregiver remained unchanged so they knew they had to find others who would understand, help and protect their secret. The seven original infected grew wise and thirsted for knowledge. They split apart with carefully selected caregivers, and headed to far away lands in search of understanding. They agreed to meet back at their old village after a time and when they did, they had a much greater knowledge of their changed selves, their capabilities and weaknesses and where their place in such a tumultuous world was.

The original seven knew they were different from normal people, having evolved and changed physiologically from the normal human being they once had been. So they named themselves the Sanguinostri, which is a Latin variant of 'our people of life-blood'. They learned through trial and error that some people they turned grew power hungry and greedy with the change. Those few believed they were superior and elite. That normal humans were only valuable as servants and a food source. The original seven villagers, the elders, saw this and knew the need for removing the threat they themselves had created. It was from this realization and understanding that laws were set to stone. A vow was made to protect each other and all life above all else, for each was sacred and dependent on one another even if by tiny threads. The seven made the vow, took an oath. Setting it by blood, slicing their palms and letting their blood flow into the earth with their solemn word that if one were to betray, he would forfeit his head to the others. And so The Law of the Sanguinostri was born.

Since that time the seven and their progeny parted ways to learn and grow wherever the winds carried them. They found places in the shadows but always in a position of command, within the greatest empires mankind has ever known. As the empires fell and others rose, the need for growth, additional laws and enforcers became necessary. Ultimately the original seven chose six more and formed the Senatus Imperium, the counsel of masters. Each member of the Senatus was sent to each empire to govern, protect and provide. Those individuals are called Dominor and are the supreme rule over the Sanguinostri in their region. They have their own Aegis Council who are the lieutenants. Soldiers who answer only to the Dominor and the Senatus as a whole. They hold the laws of man sacred as their own but their own are above all. To protect the sanctity of humankind and sanguin-kind, even from themselves.

"So, baby girl, for over two millennia the Sanguinostri has survived by those same laws and vows they made back then." Her uncle began his conclusion to the story. "Above all, keeping our presence a secret from human society is critical, or else we would be hunted, exterminated, or worse, held prisoner, dissected like bugs and used as lab rats."

"Whoa, whoa, whoa, wait a minute." Caroline interrupted. "Keeping 'our' presence? Who is 'we'? What do you mean exactly by 'we'?"

"Well that's the thing, 'we' means your parents, me and Francis over there for starters. But there are those who are just indoctrinated and haven't turned. They are called Stewards, formally. Like you're momma chose to be so that she could have you." He looked at her parents then back at her. "But remember when I said in the very beginning, I was really your grand-daddy?"

Caroline tried to absorb it all. "Yeah, I remember."

"Well I don't exactly look old enough to be, do I? Which is why as times change, those of us that have turned, have to lie."

"So how old are you then? And don't expect me to start calling you grand-daddy now." The room took a collective breath at Caroline's joke. It was a good indicator that if she were going to freak, she would have by now.

"Do you remember in the beginning of the story, the first girl who bled for her brother and that's how they figured that out?"

"Yeah I remember."

"She was my mother, baby girl. It took her nearly a thousand years, but she gave birth to me successfully, and that's a big deal for our kind. But to answer your question, I was born just after Byzas established Byzantium, right about 654 B.C."

"Holy crap!" Caroline goggled. "You are freaking old! No offense or anything."

He laughed outright, his deep booming laugh that she loved. "None taken, sugar pie. Yes I am old, but not as old as some. Caroline, we need to get to the point of me telling you all of this, it's getting late and we are going to need some serious decisions out of you."

She blinked slowly. "I don't understand."

"Well you're parents were supposed to tell you all this when you were eighteen and properly indoctrinate you. We're doin' all that now but its a little difficult because you and your friend Lou have gotten mixed up in Sanguinostri business without knowing it. Those three crimes you girls are looking into off the books?"

"Shit!" Caroline jumped up from her seat. "Shit! Shit! He's one of you guys?"

"Now calm down, missy!" Her uncle demanded when he saw Frank take a step forward. "Just like normal humankind, we have our bad guys too. That's all the jurisdiction of our Dominor, the Aegis Council and all their people. You girls stir things up and put too many eyeballs on our bad guy and its dangerous for us. We take care of our bad guys a hell of a lot stricter than human laws do."

"But what's the deal with the saliva and that keratin I couldn't identify?" She sat back down and Frank took a step back again. She had never noticed him move.

"Those of us that have turned have funny blood, tissue and other bodily fluids. One of the reasons why its so rare for us to have babies the normal way. Once things leave our bodies, they sorta die instantly, or degrade as you would say. We have some of the most brilliant scientists in the world trying to figure it out but so far, no go. You could even try to help us figure it out if you choose indoctrination."

She thought for a moment. "So that would explain why its so necessary for you to have your own police. To pick up where regular cops have no clue what they are looking at."

He nodded. "That's a real strong reason. We have people in all kinds of places keeping eyes open for stuff. Your associate Carpesh being one of them. That's how we learned about the three dead girls and our Dominor and his Council came to be in Los Angeles."

"Huh? Carpesh? Seriously?" Caroline was having a hard time putting the whole of what she was hearing into something she could comprehend. "Wait! Wait! What do you mean if I choose indoctrination? Haven't I been indoctrinated by virtue of you telling me all this?"

"No, baby girl. You have to swear the Oath, Blood-swear. You have to keep this a secret from anyone outside the Sanguinostri and vow to keep us above all else, or die as the price for betrayal. We have to do this right quick because if you can't swear, Frankie here has to wipe your memory of us ever telling you all of this."

"What? Wipe?" She goggled again at her uncle.

"Sometimes the turning gives us special talents. There are mentalists who can read thoughts and hypnotize with a blink of an eye. Some that can read objects and tell you where its been, who's touched it and so on. Then there are some like Frankie here who can erase memories. If you honestly can't swear, then he needs to make it so you don't remember any of this happening."

Caroline could feel the anti-anxiety pill was wearing off and pieces of the puzzle started to fall into place. She turned and looked at the familiar stranger that stood off behind her. She looked at him hard for several moments then almost heard an audible click in her head.

"Holy shit. Carpesh, the Dominor, his Aegis Council..." She pointed her finger at Frank. 'Francis... Frankie... Frank Sullivan?"

Frank smiled at her. She was a smart girl. "That would be me."

"I freaking called you today!" Caroline couldn't stop herself from laughing.

"Huh?" He was puzzled for a moment but quickly placed what she was saying. "That was you? That hung up after asking my name?" He walked toward her and almost started laughing with her.

"Holy shit, it is a small world." She regained her composure and realized the reason he looked familiar was she had seen him on the security footage from the morgue. Another click in her head. "That means... The man with you at the morgue, is that the Dominor?"

Frank bowed his head as he did when he greeted her. "That is our Dom, yes."

Caroline plopped down on the couch and covered her mouth to stifle a gasp. "Holy shit, Lou's Yummy Morgue Guy is the Dominor."

"Yummy what? Caroline's parents, her uncle and Frank all asked in unison.

"Yummy Morgue Guy! Oh she has got it bad for him since she passed him in the hall that day!" It was probably totally inappropriate but she started laughing again.

"Holy shit!" This time it was Frank that said it. He shoved her over on the couch and sat down next to her. "She has a thing for him, too?"

"What do you mean, too?" Caroline looked at him suspiciously.

"Wait, we will deal with that later. You three..." Frank pointed at her uncle and parents. "You never heard that or I'll send Niko to deal with you." The three muttered various things to the effect of not hearing a thing, heard what, and so fourth. "Caroline..." Frank turned back to her. "You need to focus and decide. I can't let you leave here until you decide to take the Oath or reject."

She stood and started pacing. "I need to think." Caroline yanked the rubber band out of her hair and scratched her head as thought the action would help organize her thoughts. "Can I step outside and get some air so I can think at least?" She looked at her uncle and her parents who in turn looked at Frank.

"Yeah but I need to go with you." Frank got up and escorted her out to the garden.

It was cold but the air was refreshing to Caroline. She needed to focus and take everything in even though she had more questions than she could count. She paced on the small patio while Frank kept his distance and said nothing for a long time. This was a twist of fate she had never seen coming.

"Caroline..." He finally spoke up. "I know this is very difficult to comprehend, fantastical even. But you need to understand that who we are, what we are, is good and honorable. We always have been."

Caroline stepped up to him and waggled her finger in his face as she spoke to him. "You would think that finding out my family tree is a bunch of vampires and that the world as I've known it has a whole other world to it that I need to either swear fealty to or die would be what is so upsetting about all this." She snorted at her own statement then haphazardly pulled her hair back into a ponytail.

"The term vampire is such a load of crap. Excuse me but it pisses me off." Frank was the one to pace now. "That term didn't even come to be until like the sixteen-hundreds and the dumb ass who started it was too chicken to turn so he tried to wipe us out!"

She had to smile at his temper. "Really? Is that true?"

"Yeah, its true but I probably shouldn't have told you that yet." He tried to fight back the smile.

Caroline stepped right in his face again and nearly touched his nose with her pointed finger. "I cannot lie to Lou. That's what is making this hard for me. I will not lie to her or keep secrets from her. If you are telling me that's what I have to do then you better wipe or whatever me now."

Frank knew what that sort of loyalty and conviction felt like. He felt it every day of his life with Max and the others. Even though it had been for Max's own good, Frank had felt uneasy about his going behind his back with the Code Pink for days now. Understanding somewhat how Caroline felt, he took a chance and placed his hands on her shoulders. "Listen to me carefully, there are things I wish I could tell you, things that I know." When she looked down towards the floor, he tilted her chin gently so she met his gaze. "I know you don't know me and have no reason to trust me but I am asking you to.

Please believe me when I tell you that I don't think you are going to have to lie to Lou for more then a a few days. A week at best."

Her eyes grew wide with his words "But wha..."

"I cannot tell you." He cut her off. "I wish that I could, but I can't. Just please give me time. I know everything is going to work out." They stood there just like that for several moments, just looking into each other's souls.

"Will you do it?" She asked him after a few moments of considering his words.

"Will I do what?"

"If I decide to turn, will you be the one? Or at least be there?" The look in her eyes was more than he could bear.

"If you decide to turn." He sighed, certain he would regret making such a promise. "I will be there."

She hugged him and he wasn't quite sure how to hug her back. Before he figured it out, she stepped back.

"Okay, lets go do this oath thing. But whatever it is you are up to, you better be all over it and make it snappy." She disappeared into the bungalow before he could utter a word.

For a moment, just a brief moment, he wondered if this was how it started for Max.

Chapter Nine

The day looked like something Michelangelo would have painted. Though a bit on the cold side, the robin's egg blue sky with its tufts of snow white clouds drifting by in dollops made it bearable even with Lou's serious lack of sleep. January was done and the first days of February teased with the hope and promise of the coming spring. Lou and her parents had enjoyed a delicious brunch in the solarium of the country club with the picturesque morning as a backdrop. The previous night's excitement had drifted off into memory as Lou and her parents ate and laughed, listening to Joe recount his adventures during his trip to Bangalore. As she laughed some more, it struck Lou funny how their Sunday tradition had come to be and how grateful she was for it. She had lost a bet to her mother some time ago which forced her to take golf lessons with her. Lou had never thought much of the sport but after a few of those lessons, she was hooked and looked forward to Sundays together very much. Today was especially so given her and Vinny's run in with the grease monkeys the night before. Lou had decided not to mention anything about it to her mother so as not to spoil the day.

Monkey number one had lawyered up and wasn't talking. There was really nothing to be done on Lou and Vinny's part past the paperwork until they were cleared by the department shrink. Departmental procedure demanded it whenever an officer involved shooting took place. The psychiatrist was a good guy that both Lou and Vinny knew and liked. He had spent all of ten minutes with each of them knowing full well they were fine, but stated he wouldn't be able to get the reports in until Monday morning. Apparently the poor guy had been called in while he was moving from his bachelor pad to his single family dwelling with his new bride. He was literally pulling his mattress off the truck when his cell rang for the incident and dropped everything to get them squared away. He ordered them to take the day to decompress and promised they would be back at it bright and early Monday morning. Since the rookie that had taken custody of the jackass in the parking lot was frothing at the bit to do anything on the case, they decided to let him do the grunt work while they followed the doc's orders and proceed with Sunday as usual. Lou with her golf and Vinny with nursery painting. Ok, so maybe not quite so usual after all.

Finishing the last of their coffee, Lou and her mother left the solarium to meet Joe out by the pro shop. He had gone ahead to collect their clubs, get the carts ready and check on their tee time. Shevaun paused in the pro shop as was tradition. She perused the latest selection of golf apparel with Lou giving the nod if something suited her. While her mother admired a cute spring green ensemble, Lou observed the coming and going golfers through the windows. A cart passed by with a couple of familiar faces and a foursome walked up the path nearly doubled over with laughter. It made Lou smile. When another cart came around the bend, Lou's knees nearly gave out. The golf director that Lou knew well was pulling up with Yummy Morgue Guy in the passenger seat.

"Holy crap!" It flew out of Lou's mouth without her realizing.

Shadows of Doubt

Lou's mother jolted at the use of language in the pro shop. Lou's random bouts of cursing on the golf course had been a bone of contention between the women for some time. "Tallulah! Mind your mouth!" She scolded as she approached Lou. "What?"

"Momma..." Lou stammered and whispered at the same time. "It's him! That's him!"

"Who's him? What are you talking about?" Shevaun looked to see who had gotten her daughter all flustered when she saw Max getting out of a cart. "Oh there's Max!" She instantly disregarded Lou's outburst and focused her attention on the man. "I am so glad he could join us!"

Lou looked at her mother as though the woman had a horn growing out of her forehead. "What? You know him?"

"Well of course I do sweet pea, that's Max, Joe's long time business buddy from back east. Our soon to be new neighbor?" Shevaun couldn't understand her daughter's surprise. "We had dinner with him Friday night and invited him to join us. I'm sure I told you! He's a lovely man. You're going to like him very much." Shevaun dismissed her daughter and went to the counter with the spring green ensemble to have it wrapped up.

Lou stood for a long moment trying to process what was happening. "I'll be right back Momma. Meet you outside in a sec." Lou told her mother then made a mad dash for the locker room and hit the speed dial on her cell to call Caroline. She figured her friend would be asleep still so she wasn't surprised when the call went directly to voice mail. "Caroline, shit! I'm at the club and you will absolutely freak out when you hear who my parents have as a fourth for our game! My freaking parents know him! Yummy Morgue Guy is a friend of Joe's!" Lou finally sucked in a breath. "Do you understand what I am saying? I am about to play golf with Yummy Morgue Guy! Wake up dammit! Call me as soon as you get this message!"

It took Lou quite a few minutes to compose herself before she dared leave the locker room. After considerable stares from women coming and going, Lou decided she had a grip and needed to face this man and get it over with. It was ridiculous since he had absolutely no clue who she was, let alone that he had been on her mind nearly twenty-four hours a day since she passed him in the hall at the morgue. She thanked God she had opted for the new fucshia and gray argyle sweater she had gotten for Christmas rather then her favorite Tattoo Golf sweater. With little skulls and golf clubs as crossbones embroidered all over it didn't exactly exude femininity. The gray golf pants with the pretty matching sweater was a much better choice in retrospect. After a final once over, she decided she was looking as good as it was going to get and she headed out. She only prayed she didn't make an ass out of herself.

When Max got out of the golf cart and said his farewell to the golf director, he was relieved that it was only Joe there to greet him. Max had spent half the night getting in the proper frame of mind to deal with this first face-to-face with his detective. Unfortunately the closer and closer he got to it actually happening, the more nervous he became. It was utterly ridiculous for a man of his stature and considerable age to be flustered like this. He used that anger with himself to take the edge off his panic.

"My Dom." Joe held out a hand to Max and smiled warmly. "I hope everything went well after I left yesterday?"

Max scanned the area looking for Lou and her mother. He could only spot Shevaun inside the pro shop, waving to him as she apparently finished with a purchase. "Richelieu seemed to handle things well. Frank said that Caroline took the Oath but things are tenuous pending how things go with Lou. She is adamant about not lying to her best friend. He's sticking to her like glue to keep her in check for the time being."

Joe nodded, knowing this would be a deal breaker. "Well, I have a good feeling about all of this. It's going to work out, I just know it." Joe shut up as soon as he saw his wife exiting the shop.

"Max!" Shevaun gushed, something she never did. "I am so glad you could make it!"

He took Shevaun's hands and kissed her cheek. "So am I. Fortunately things are going according to plan so I was able to steal away for a while."

Just then Lou emerged from the pro shop and came towards them. Shevaun was not a stupid woman and she knew her daughter inside and out. Something was definitely up. She noticed Lou had actually primped while she was gone, with fresh lip gloss, her hair fluffed and not a strand amiss. Her daughter never ever primped, for anyone.

"Tallulah, come and meet Max." Shevaun watched her daughter's reaction to him very carefully. "Max Julian, this is our daughter, Lou."

Max held his breath as his detective came closer, he simply couldn't help it. Reaching out his hand, he smiled at her with a smile he had only once before been able to give. "I've heard so much about you, I feel like I already know you." It wasn't a lie at all.

Lou extended her hand to take his while she repeated to herself in her head 'He's just another guy. He's just another guy'. But when that smile spread across those perfect lips of his, she felt like she would melt into a puddle on the spot. "Er...um..." She blushed. "... I wish I could say the same. I only learned of you joining us a few minutes ago. Forgive my surprise." Christ she was a blathering idiot. Now he was going to think she was annoyed he was joining them.

"Oh?" He felt his heart crack a little at her disappointed tone. "I'm sorry if I am intruding, would you pref..."

"No!" She blurted, then realized she was not only still holding his hand, but was squeezing the life out of it. Quickly she released her hold and stuffed her hands in her pockets in an attempt to look casual. "I mean, no. Its perfectly fine. Lovely in fact." Lovely? She thought to herself. What the hell is that? Was she going to ask him for a spot of tea next? "Uh..." She had to recover quickly. "We can play girls against the boys."

Shevaun tried hard not to bounce up and down as she clearly saw her daughter flustering over Max. There was something absolutely there, finally! She had almost given up hope of her daughter showing an interest in anyone again. "Oh! That's an excellent idea!" She stepped in quickly to cover up her daughter's tripping over her own tongue. "You boys can ride together."

Once it was agreed and everything was settled, Shevaun and her daughter pulled away in their cart while Joe and Max followed to the first tee. Joe couldn't be certain but standing on the patio he thought he sensed something from Max towards Lou. He decided he needed to pay very close attention throughout the day. Shevaun, on the other hand, saw it all plain as day. Her daughter's out of character fluster. The twinkle in Max's eye. She knew within the first five minutes that it was going to be a wonderful day.

The day was turning out to be a disaster, or so Max felt. By the time they reached the fourth tee he had two bogies, a par and a double bogie. It was his worst round of golf so far in about twenty years. To make matters worse, he had barely spoken to Lou and when he had, he was about as smooth and charming as a fork stuck in a garbage disposal. He was furious with himself.

"A little off you're game today ?" Joe asked after Max had driven the ball into the left rough.

"A little?" Max wanted desperately to hurl his driver into the lake, but walked to the cart and stuffed it forcefully into his bag instead, avoiding eye contact with Lou at all costs.

Shadows of Doubt

Lou hurried to the tee to make her drive while Max wasn't looking and to her horror it landed five inches behind his ball. Shevaun simply couldn't stand it and started laughing.

"Real nice, Momma." Lou scowled at her mother. "The damn wind is pulling everything to the left." Lou swore under her breath and headed for her cart.

Shevaun was eventually able to stop laughing when her husband approached. "What is so damn funny?" He asked her quietly.

"Oh Joe, can't you see?" She was grinning from ear to ear.

"See what?" Joe had felt something was amiss but honestly he was so rapt with worry about the situation with Caroline, the rogue and the big plan that he wasn't paying as close attention to the golf game as he would have liked.

Shevaun leaned in close to her husband, laying a hand on his chest. "Those two are absolutely smitten with each other! I would bet the farm that Lou has crossed paths with Max before. She is so flustered, and so is he! It's just hilarious to watch!"

Joe looked over at Max and then Lou and watched with his new perspective, courtesy of his wife. "I'll be damned!" He shouted and Shevaun promptly shushed him. He suddenly noticed that both Lou and Max were doing everything possible to avoid looking at each other and had been for the entire morning. His wife was absolutely right.

"Don't make a fuss! Let's just have a little fun with it, shall we?" She patted him on the chest and winked.

Joe looked at his beautiful Shevaun and grinned from ear to ear. "You are such a wicked woman. Have I mentioned how much I love that about you?" He kissed her quickly then scooted her off to the tee. "Go on darlin', show them how it's done." He cheered her on.

Lou turned in time to see her mother drive her ball long and straight, smack into the middle of the fairway. It made her furious, even if she was on her team. When her father followed suit, she could hear Max grumbling behind her and she wondered if he was feeling the same. That was when she decided things were becoming utterly ridiculous. Almost in an act of defiance, Lou turned and finally looked at him. God he was handsome as hell. His hair had loosened from its previously immaculate style and was falling gently into his face. She wanted to run her fingers through it, combing back the rich, glossy, sable strands. He turned suddenly toward her and caught her gaze. She jerked to avoid eye contact and nearly knocked herself out with her own three iron. Rubbing her forehead to dull the sting, she climbed into the cart and yelled for her mother to hurry up.

Max thought for a moment he had caught her looking at him, then thought of course she was. She was looking at the ass that couldn't swing a club for the life of him. This time it was Max swearing under his breath as he got in the cart and Joe drove them up the path. When they got up there, he saw how close Lou and his balls were to one another and resumed swearing. Not so much under his breath this time. It was inevitable. He simply could not avoid talking to her any longer. Since her ball was further away, he let her walk ahead of him to take her shot. He stood behind her and watched as she addressed the ball. Taking her time to line up her shot. She had a good solid stance, he noticed. Elegant and strong arms with a perfect slight bend to the knees. Christ she was adorable, even with the scowl on her face. He took in the curve of her body, the petite little ears and the way she bit her lower lip when she concentrated. He was so engrossed with taking her in that he hadn't noticed her head turn and look at him. She was staring.

"What?!" She barked.

"Uh..." Good God he couldn't think of anything to say.

She stopped and walked towards him. "You were staring at me so let's have it. What?" She was sick of feeling like an idiot. This was going to stop now before she gave up golf forever.

So this was it, he thought. She's throwing down the gauntlet. "You know our paths have crossed before." There, he put it out there. The elephant in the room, so to speak.

At first she was shocked that he had noticed her at all, let alone remembered. "So you do recognize me, then?" Then it occurred to her that the bastard was enjoying watching her squirm this whole time.

"Of course I do." Recognize her? She was practically all he had been able to think about ever since.

She cocked her head and considered. "Why didn't you say something?" It was a risky question. She wasn't really certain she wanted an actual answer.

It never ceased to amaze him, the feisty spirit he kept discovering as he observed her. "Well now, how would that have gone I wonder? Hello, so good to meet you after crossing paths over dead bodies once or twice." For effect he did a little gentlemanly bow and a flourish with his hand.

"Aha!" She stepped up and pointed in his face. "Once or Twice! So it was you at the crime scene!"

Bloody hell, he didn't mean to let that slip. "Take your shot before the marshal comes and kicks us off the course for holding up play." A good solid tactic he thought. When cornered, redirect and deflect.

She glowered at him, whirled around and went to make her shot.

Shevaun and Joe watched the two from the cart path while they shared a bottle of water. Joe got a little nervous when he saw Lou storm up to Max and get right up into his face. However, his nerves were quickly settled and he nearly spit out his water laughing when Max did his bow and hand flourish.

"Oh dear! He's definitely got his hands full with her." Joe shook his head and passed his wife the bottle of water as they waited for the two to take their shots.

"I wonder what he did to get her all riled like that." Shevaun took a sip of the water then stuffed the bottle back in her bag. "Not that it matters, he better learn quick and get used to it."

Joe looked at his wife thoughtfully. "So you like him then?"

Shevaun smiled as she watched her daughter and Max from across the sprawling green grass. "I do. There is something strong and wise about him. He has a great sense of humor and a good deal of patience, obviously. I don't really know him still but my first impressions aren't usually wrong."

Taking his wife's hand, he kissed her knuckles tenderly and then gazed into her eyes. "He's a good man. If they survive this part of it, there is no one I could approve of more for our daughter."

"Well that's high praise coming from you." She cupped his cheek. "We'll hope for the best then, shall we?"

Joe simply smiled and felt his heart pang. If she only knew how hard he was hoping for the best already. This development with Lou and Max could either kill or cure the whole dilemma so he just prayed they made it through the rest of the day without the two of them wrapping clubs around each others necks.

Lou took her shot, in spite of him, and it was a beauty. Her ball caught a bounce and landed four feet from the cup. She twirled her club and spun around to gloat at Max, feeling more herself again.

"Your turn, big guy." She sauntered back to her cart with her nose slightly upturned at him.

Oh yes indeed, she had definitely thrown down the gauntlet. Suddenly all the insecurity that Max had been feeling melted away and the competition had begun. When he finally took his shot, he turned and grinned right back at her as it landed a foot closer to the cup than hers. He twirled his club and sauntered back to his cart exactly the same way she had done only moments before. The game was on now.

By the seventeenth hole the match was a dead heat. Both Lou and Max had found their game again and were bringing it fiercely. Shevaun had managed to casually feed her daughter all the information she knew of Max without her daughter actually having to ask and Joe had somewhat done the same about Lou. It had been at the ninth tee when Lou had actually started making Max laugh out loud with her ribbing and shortly after she started laughing at Max's clever retorts. The two had relaxed considerably, enjoying the battle of wits and golf. Forgetting themselves and just being in the moment. It was only after Max had teed off at the eighteenth hole that things sunk in with them both. His drive was perfect, landing over the large pond and just a yard or two below the green. Shevaun and Joe both applauded and he turned and took a bow with a smile on his face. He didn't miss for a second that Lou was grinning.

"Alright, I'll admit it. That was a beauty." She didn't find saying it as bitter as she thought it would be.

It was at that moment Max let his guard down and spoke his thoughts without really thinking. "Well it's only natural for one beauty to recognize another." It was a blatant, overt flirt and he said it while staring her dead in the eye so that there was no mistaking the feeling behind it. He watched her fluster and saw her pull her guard back up immediately. "I meant the shot of course..." He tried to recover but it was too late. He had gone too far.

"I know what you meant." She looked down, avoiding eye contact. "Move so I can take my shot." Lou didn't say it with the witty sarcasm he was growing accustomed too. She was backing away from him and he knew they were right back at square one. Shevaun and Joe saw it too, and Shevaun sighed with disappointment. Joe put his arm around his wife as if to console her. Lou made her drive and it landed in the pond. She moved quickly back to the cart without so much as a mutter of a curse.

Shevaun could see the defeated look in Max's eyes and went to him, placing her hand on his as he leaned on his club and blew out a breath.

"Be patient with her. She's suffered greatly in matters of the heart. She's just afraid of her own feelings." Lou's mother smiled at him when he looked at her aghast. It was a rare occurrence that someone could see through him so easily. Had he been so obvious all day? His heart on his sleeve? But then he realized that Shevaun's words were encouraging him not to give up and that meant that she wasn't upset over him having eyes for her daughter. He took her hand and squeezed. A smile of thanks in his eyes. Finally someone knew what he was feeling and it was alright with them. More importantly it was Lou's mother. The one person in the world who meant the most to Lou. It was a relief he couldn't have imagined.

Shevaun said nothing as they drove the cart up the path. She let Lou take her drop, and her lumps, waiting it out until they drove up to the green for the last strokes. When Lou parked the cart and walked around, her mother stepped in her way and put a hand on her shoulder.

"I didn't raise my only daughter to be afraid, and up until now she never has been without good reason." She moved her hand from Lou's shoulder to her cheek. "I've let you be afraid for about six years too long now. Don't let the possibility of joy with your soul-mate slip by because you let old wounds poison your heart." She didn't wait for her daughter to respond. Shevaun turned from her daughter and walked to the green to take her last shot with the boys.

Shadows of Doubt

Lou watched her mother walk up to the green where Joe and Max already were evaluating their shots. It had been a good day, all in all, despite her foolishness, her nerves and fear. The truth of it was that Max had lived up to her own hype. Besides being drop dead gorgeous and a fantastic dresser, he was charming and witty, matching her ribbing tit for tat. She truly enjoyed that part of discovering him. He gave as good as he got and was still a gentleman about it. Her parents liked him too, which was so rare. Even as she watched them up there on the velvet green grass, they smiled and laughed. She could so get used to days like this. But she had decided to try for that once before, many years ago, and was betrayed by the man she thought she loved when he slept with one of her best friends. That was long before Caroline, though. Then after a couple years of licking her wounds she took another chance and almost died twice for it. In many ways she was much stronger for it all, braver in many aspects. But when it came to her heart and even cracking the door to it, Lou was flat terrified. Her mother saw that in her and it shamed Lou that she was disappointed with her. It didn't really matter now anyway because Max had probably written Lou off as one of those chihuahua people she loathed. Skittish, irrational and way too high maintenance emotionally. Lou sighed, grabbed her putter and headed up to the green.

There wasn't time for congratulations after the last putt was made because another group was waiting behind them, so Shevaun ran for the cart and suggested they meet up on the patio. Max was very grateful to her for that because for the first time in more decades than he cared to remember, he wasn't sure how to handle himself. He was grateful to Joe also now for driving slow so he could think.

"So when was it exactly that you started falling for my daughter?" Joe gave him a half smile as he navigated the cart path.

It shocked Max to hear those words, and not the daughter part of the statement. It was the falling for part that kicked him in the gut. The truth of it was it really didn't matter who those words came from, they would have overwhelmed him regardless. "Pardon me?"

"With all due respect, my Dom, it may have taken me getting thumped over the head by my wife to see it, but anyone who takes a second can. So may I ask when? From the two of your banter early on this morning, this wasn't the first time you met. I mean, I know you have been keeping tabs but it's rather unlike you to take such a hands on approach in matters that are usually reserved for the Council."

"Christ." Max blew out a breath. He had already admitted it to Lou so there was no sense in keeping the facts to himself any longer. "We never actually met. We crossed paths in the morgue when I went to see Carpesh and the Talbott woman's body. Then she spotted me at the Winslow crime scene before I knew who she was. But we never spoke. Hell, I was expecting some old codger with a name like 'Detective Lou Donovan'!"

Joe pulled off the cart path into a patch of dirt under a tree and set the brake. He turned to Max with a most serious expression. "I am sure you did a thorough check on Lou, but I am not sure how far you went back?"

"Five or six years I believe. Why? Is there something I should know?" Max's brow furrowed as Joe thought for a moment.

"You need to go back a bit more. I don't think it's wise I tell you now, knowing you as I do. But you need to know. Something that I kept from the Sanguinostri but not for any other reason than it was complicated. Involving you would have put too much at risk at the time. Shevaun's side of the family and the department had it handled once it was done. Perhaps text Frank or Abby so they have it for you when you get back to the hotel."

Shadows of Doubt

"Why can't you tell me now? I could order you." Max was seriously concerned now.

"I know you could. But out of respect for my daughter and my family as a whole, I would ask you please to wait and read it on your own. It will explain many things about Lou." Joe prayed that Max would accept that as enough for now.

"Very well, then." As Joe started the cart and continued to the patio, Max pulled his cell phone from his pocket and sent Abby a text message to pull the details for the time Joe directed. It worried Max immensely but he truly tried to keep himself in check. Something he obviously had not been doing well for the past week.

When they arrived at the patio, the girls were donning jackets and the sun was setting behind a heap of bruised clouds. The cold bit hard as if to remind everyone winter still had a strong grasp on things. Caddies came to retrieve the bags and one paused to ask Max if he would be storing his clubs with them. Lou tried not to be so relieved when she heard Max answer in the affirmative.

"Well boys, congratulations on kicking our behinds. You won fair and square." Shevaun offered a good sport handshake.

Grinning, Max took her hand then leaned down and kissed her cheek. "Hardly fair, I intruded on a customary game. That's unsettling and I should have had better manners than that." He turned to Lou and extended his hand. "Please forgive me."

Lou smiled at him despite herself then took his hand. "Nothing to forgive. Especially if you give us a rematch." She held her breath when she felt him squeeze her hand gently.

There was hope. "Best two out of three perhaps?" Now he held his breath as he waited for her answer.

"You buy dinner next time then." Whoa, did she just say that?

Max breathed again and decided to go for broke, leaning down he kissed her cheek ever so softly, trying not to linger as he inhaled her jasmine and vanilla scent. When he stepped away, releasing her hand, he felt his heart race. Dear God, he was so lost for this woman.

Lou was afraid to move. If she did she feared she would fall sideways. It took her several seconds before she realized she still was holding her breath so she tried to exhale without being obvious about it. "Well, I really should go. It was very nice meeting you, Max." Christ she had a frog in her throat now. "I'll see you two at home later?"

Shevaun nodded. "We'll be along soon sweat pea. I just need to pick up my outfit I bought and check my tee time for the Ladies Auxiliary on Tuesday."

"Want us to bring you something home to eat?" Joe offered.

Trying her best to get the hell out of there, Lou waved Joe off. "Oh no, thanks, I'm still stuffed from brunch."

Max held a hand up in farewell then shoved his hands in his pockets. He absolutely hated seeing her leave but knew if he opened his mouth, something asinine would fly out.

Shevaun looped an arm through Joe's and the other through Max's as they watched Lou dash down the hill to the parking lot. "Well boys, I think we all could use a drink right about now." She tugged to get them moving and the three strolled off to find the bar.

Caroline paced back and fourth in Frank and Abby's suite while Frank made a pitcher of something in the kitchen and Abby clicked away furiously on her laptop. When her phone beeped to indicate a missed call, Caroline looked at the number and grumbled.

"That's the second time she's called. I hate this!" She paced a little faster now.

"Just be patient. We know what we are doing and it's all going to work out." Abby tried reassuring her again but needed to get the search Max had requested done before he got back. When the data she requested popped up, Abby's jaw dropped and she turned to Caroline. "Did you know about this?"

"Know about what?" Caroline marched over to see what Abby was talking about. She scanned the information that was displayed on screen and sighed. "Yeah. I knew about it but I wasn't here during all that. I only know bits and pieces of what Lou has felt comfortable sharing."

"What?" Frank shouted from the kitchen.

"You better get over here." Abby shouted back at him.

Frank came in carrying a pitcher of margaritas and balancing a stack of glasses. He set them down on the table then went to see what Abby was talking about. It only took him a moment before he saw it. "Oh shit!"

"Oh shit is right." Abby hit a key then pulled the CD out of the drive and shut the laptop. "He is gonna go postal when he reads this."

"If we are lucky he'll only go postal!" Frank grabbed the pitcher and poured them all a drink.

"What? Why? I mean I know it's bad but I don't understand." Caroline looked at Abby then Frank. It was totally unorthodox having met both of them less then twenty-four hours before, but after everything she now knew, everything she had been through and the way these two people had comforted her, she felt almost as close to them as she did to Lou. Abby had even offered for Caroline to bunk with her and Frank since she didn't want to be alone until she could talk to Lou.

Abby and Frank looked at each other, Frank giving her a hairy eyeball then Abby furrowing a brow at him.

"Oh come on you two! This is like my sister we are talking about here! I need to know what's up!" Frustration was was wearing all over her face. "Are you two like talking without talking or some weird psychic crap only turned people get?"

"No!" Abby laughed.

"Not at all." Frank sat down in the chair adjacent to Abby. "It's just that when you've been like brother and sister for a hundred years, you kinda get to know what the other is thinking. I mean think about you and Lou after what? Five years or so?"

"Okay, that I get. But then you understand how you would feel if someone was keeping something about the other from you, right?"

"Right. Yeah." Abby looked at Frank again and he nodded to her. "Okay he's less likely to bite my head off if he finds out I told you. But you need to..." Abby looked at Caroline's bandaged hand. "Okay so a Blood Swear probably would suck right now so just swear you won't let on we told you this, okay?"

Caroline winced and held her right hand close at the mention of Blood Swear. "I swear!"

"It happened when Constantinople fell, in 1453. Max was engaged to be married for the first time ever and to him that was as good as married. Up until then, he had never allowed himself to have any kind of relationship because he took his role in the Council far too serious. "I won't go into all the specifics but the basic gist of it is that Max got picked out of his Council to go defend Constantinople and while he was gone, one of his enemies beat, tortured and killed his fiance'. He has not so much as blinked at a woman since. Until now."

"Abby!" Frank shot out of his seat.

"She's going to figure it out soon enough!"

"Whoa!" Caroline plopped down next to Abby. "So that's the second time one of you has slipped on that. Max, the Dominor, really has a thing for Lou?"

"Shit, I should have wiped that from you when I slipped last night." Frank scrubbed a hand over his face.

"Hey! You promised no wiping! That means ever!" Caroline pouted.

Shadows of Doubt

Abby nodded in agreement with Caroline. "That's like way more serious than calling no backs."

"Ah Geez Abby, this is way more serious than calling jinks and no backs!" Frank gulped down some of his margarita.

The door swung open and Niko stepped in. "Olie olie oxen free. Time to open the door back up. Hello Caroline, I'm Niko." He bowed his head politely to her. "He's back and wants that data. Now, Frank."

"How did it go?" Abby looked at Niko hopefully. "Is he in a good mood?"

Niko shrugged. "He sent me out before I could get a read. Frank will be able to tell."

"If he doesn't kill him after he reads this." Abby said as she handed Frank the disc. "Good luck little buckaroo. I love ya!"

"Why? What's on it?" Niko walked in and sat in the chair Frank had been sitting on.

"Easier for him to read for himself. That crap doesn't need to be said out loud." Frank said as he headed out the door.

"I don't want to know the details, so please let him just read it." Caroline insisted. It was only right to allow her friend to keep some sense of privacy. Caroline knew just enough that it killed her to think of Lou having suffered.

Abby slid the laptop over so Niko could read. After a few minutes, he just sat back in the chair and blew out a breath.

Niko thought for a few moments then looked at Abby. "This guy is really pissing me off now. Find out where he's being held."

"Pissing you off, now? What's that supposed to mean?" Abby pulled the laptop back and started clicking away.

"Why?" Caroline risked asking the very large and scary man called Niko.

"Because as soon as Max reads that he's going to want to pay the man a personal visit." He smiled at her which softened the scary considerably. "And when I tell him what's transpired with that guy's former cell-mate and pal over the last twelve hours, it's going to make the outcome of that visit a little more final."

"What are you talking about Niko? What the hell happened?" Abby had stopped typing and was glaring at him now.

Niko rolled his eyes and began relaying the events of the previous evening. From when he decided to do a more covert recon of Lou than Abby had done, to his clean getaway after forcing one asshole to blow his own brains out. He also informed them that his investigation into the two had led him to the subject of Abby's search and how the two were intertwined. Niko was not at all enthusiastic about having to tell Max all of that after he read what Abby had found. What he omitted was the fact that by morning, Detective Donovan's attacker number one would be found hanging in his cell. The Fates had seen fit to put one of their own on duty when he was brought in to holding. Said trustee just so happened to be highly skilled at planting suggestions into feeble, corrupt minds. One less thing Max would need to get his hands dirty with as far as Niko was concerned. "Anyway, to answer your original question, Caroline, I would like to know where I am taking my Dominor and have the arrangements made ahead of time." Niko gave Caroline his best sweet smile.

"Oh." It took a minute for the implications of his statement to sink in but Caroline's eyes soon went wide. "Ohhhh!" Niko nodded and smiled again.

"Well crap!" Abby had finished absorbing what Niko had told them about the two thugs. "If Max wasn't going to go postal before, he sure as hell will when he hears that!"

"I should have wished Frankie luck before he went over there." Niko picked up Frank's half empty glass, refilled it then took a generous sip before looking back at Caroline. "Okay, so you want in on the Code Pink club, huh?" Abby giggled at him.

"Code Pink club?" Caroline looked at Abby but it was Niko that answered.

"Alright, we need to catch you up on all the old episodes so you are up to speed. Grab your drink and relax while we fill you in. I need to make this quick and get in there soon, before Max rips Frank's head off."

Abby hit a key then the sound of a printer went off somewhere in the suite. She closed the laptop and set it aside, grabbed her drink and grinned as she got cozy in her seat. "I love this show."

Frank walked in to Max's suite to find him scanning the reports he had left him on possible leads to their rogue. At first glance, Frank would say that Max looked tense.

"Close the door." He ordered and Frank did so, rather grateful since he knew across the hall Niko, Abby and Caroline were no doubt conspiring. Frank preferred Max not overhear any of that just now.

"How was golf? He asked and by the way Max's head whipped up, lips moved but nothing came out, Frank knew his Dominor was having an internal crisis.

"It was golf." Max finally said, trying to keep his emotions in check by flipping through the reports. Not really reading a single word. "Where is the data I asked Abby for?"

Frank simply couldn't stand it anymore. If Max was going to kill him, so be it. But Frank knew if he didn't let Max get it out now, when he read the data on Lou's stalker, he would seriously go ballistic.

"She's working on it now. Max, my Dom, please forgive me but we've known each other too long to beat around the bush, true?" Frank was really trying to get this out thoughtfully.

Max responded without looking up. "Of course."

"Right, well then you must please forgive me here but it is simply too much for me to sit by and watch you suffer like this." He took one last breath before he got it out. "So what the hell happened with Lou at golf today?" Frank braced himself for Max's wrath.

"I don't know what you mean." The innocent blink was not working for Max very well.

Frank threw his hands up in exasperation. "Max, give it a rest. I know you have feelings for the detective so let it go and just tell me."

"How the hell do you know anything?!" Max took a charging step forward before he realized what he was doing.

"Really Max? Is that how were gonna do this?" It was Frank who stepped forward now. "You think I'm stupid? When was the last time you played peek-a-boo with a total stranger? I know Max. I saw you watching her. There is no way you can deny it so you may as well get it all out before you blow."

Max resisted the urge to smash Frank's face in and stormed out onto the terrace instead. It wasn't that he was mad at Frank, he was mad at himself. Furious with himself was more like it. Having let this woman instantly get under his skin on sight was just wrong on so many levels. Then to lose all rational grasp on himself and think he could hide it from the person closest to him was just poor judgment, something he simply was not allowed to have. He growled when Frank followed him out but deep down he was glad for it.

"How the hell do I justify this? Huh? Even her parents saw it. Her mother saw it within the first half hour! How is this acceptable behavior for a Dominor?"

Just then Abby literally skipped out onto the terrace shoving a piece of paper at Frank, then kept moving towards Max. "It's perfectly acceptable behavior for a Dominor when he is falling in love!" She yanked his collar and pulled him down so she could kiss his cheek. "So get over it and let it out, vent away! We are family and that's what we are here for." She whirled around and plopped down in one of the chairs.

"Ah Christ, you know too?" He raked his fingers through his hair and began to pace.

"You should know by now that Frank and I are Siamese twins, without the whole being physically attached part. The point is what he knows, I know, so don't pretend you're shocked." She gave him an eye-roll and twirled her fingers through her ponytail. "Now let us help."

Max looked at the two of them and should have been livid but all he could see was two of the dearest people in the world to him. They both stared at him with genuine concern and in that moment he wondered why the hell he hadn't told them from the get-go. So, he began. Telling them everything, from the first moment he set eyes on Lou to the minute he left her parents at the country club. He recounted every mortifying detail of it all and told them how he was at a complete loss on what to do next and how that made him furious because he should be focusing on the rogue, not matters of the heart.

"Well, this is definitely serious." Abby pondered all of it. "The thing is, if we can get past this part, you two would probably catch this rogue in like a snap! It's freaking scary how well you two are suited. I totally dig her by the way." She gave Max a big cheesy smile.

"What do you mean you totally dig her? You don't know anything about her except what you've read on paper, how could you dig her?" Abby utterly baffled Max sometimes. But when he saw the flicker of guilt flash across her face he knew she had been up to something. "Abby?"

"So I butted in and sorta met her, somewhat." She started chewing on her thumbnail. "When I went to get the plans signed off I kinda on purpose went to the wrong house so I could see who had you're panties all in a twist." Max slapped his hand to his forehead. "But she doesn't know a thing! It was all brilliant! I got to sit with her while I waited for her mom to come back and we got along super great! Its all good, I swear!"

"Max, you would have picked up on her knowing anything weird today if Abby had blown it, so don't get stuck on that. It's what we do now that's critical." Frank sat down next to Abby. "You really need to read this first though." He held up the disc.

"Is that the data Joe told me to look at?" Max asked as he snatched it out of Frank's hand. Not waiting for an answer, he went inside to load it into his computer.

"Yeah, but its not a happy thing Max." Abby was afraid to go inside.

It took a few moments for the disc to load but soon enough Max was scanning through the information. There were several police reports, medical reports, court documents and crime scene photos. When he read through the first restraining order, he could feel his stomach knot. With every paragraph he read his fury rose. The thought of anyone laying a hand on Lou was almost more than he could handle. Then he began reading the details of the injuries she sustained and flipped immediately to the digital crime scene photos. He found himself looking at pictures of the massive pool of blood on her kitchen floor where she had been found barely alive. Photos of her in a hospital bed, nearly beaten to a literal pulp followed. Bile rose in his throat as he studied the pictures but he forced himself to swallow hard. He bypassed the text and went directly to the images of the second assault and saw the single image of Lou laying on the gurney. Limbs twisted in directions they shouldn't have been able to go. Her face was unrecognizable with all the blood, the intubation apparatus shoved in her mouth and all the bandages wrapped around her head. Lou had almost died not once, but twice.

Max snapped. He shot up out of the chair and kicked the monitor off the coffee table, sending it flying across the suite. Outside, Frank wrapped an arm around Abby and pulled her close as if to protect her while they helplessly listened to the rage spilling out of Max for what felt like an eternity. It was a wonder there were any walls left standing when he finally stormed back out onto the terrace. The fury in his eyes scared the hell out of them. Frank simply held out the piece of paper with the information Niko had instructed Abby to get on the man who had made Lou's life a bloody living hell. Max ripped it from his hand.

As if timed precisely, Niko stepped out of the shadows. "There's a bit more to the story you need to know." Max whirled around and stared at Niko as he strategically planted himself between Max and where Frank and Abby sat. "This sick twist of a shit-stain sent a couple of his pals to visit your detective last night. Sort of a pre-homecoming gift in his warped thinking. They tried to kidnap her but they failed miserably." Niko recounted events once again, including the part he omitted from Abby and Frank about the second assailant that was about to hang himself. "Everything is arranged. We will leave here at six tomorrow morning. The son-of-a-bitch will be waiting in an isolation cell when we get there. By the time your detective makes the connection between that grand poobah of fuck-heads and the two lumps of crap from last night, it will all be over."

Max stood staring into Niko's cool gaze as he took in everything that he had just been told. His rage was boiling within him to the point that his eyes felt hot. After several moments of processing the situation, he was finally able to inhale and blink. Oddly, above the pure primal instinct to shred the source of Lou's pain into oblivion, Max felt the weight of concern pressing on him from Abby, Frank and Niko. It was disconcerting to him that the three of them knew him better than he knew himself. But it was also extraordinarily comforting. It calmed him instantly.

"Alright." It was all Max could say as he began pacing back and forth across the terrace, trying not to jump out of his own skin.

The three watched him for a long moment, guaging his mood. What was said and done in the next few moments would be critical to how Max handled anything further. They all knew he was at his breaking point and were very cautious with the situation.

"So what do we do about winning Lou over now?" Abby broke the silence and took a chance by trying to bring him back to happy thoughts.

"Well, we have a really good source for insight." Frank said as he looked at Abby and Niko.

"What?" Max stopped his pacing and looked at Frank, only semi-back from his full blown rage-fit.

"Not a what, a who." Abby smiled.

Caroline should have been petrified but she wasn't. She walked through the disheveled suite and out onto the terrace with the desperate need to hug this hulking man for having the gut instinct, passion, need even, to defend and protect Lou. So that was exactly what she was going to do. She walked straight up to him, did a little curtsey because it seemed like something you were supposed to do when your face-to-face with what amounted to be your king. Then she wrapped her arms around his thick trunk and hugged him tight. "It's nice to meet you, my Dominor." She said in a choked voice as she began to cry. Her simple, silly and pure act of courage and devotion defused the mortal combat vibe instantly.

Max really didn't know what the hell to make of this stranger hugging him and he sort of felt like panicking when he heard her sobs. He looked desperately to Niko, Abby and Frank for any sort of help.

"Max, meet Caroline Devereux. Lou's best friend, besides her mom that is, and our latest addition to the family." Abby beamed proudly at Caroline. Her courage and sincerity made her own tears well up.

As understanding sank in, Max let his arms fall around Caroline and couldn't help but smile. That took serious guts for her to do.

"Caroline..." Max said in a gentle tone. "...I really need your help here." She shoved away from him and wiped her tears as she nodded and did another little curtsey for the hell of it. "Caroline please stop doing that." Max laughed at the absurdity of her curtseying to him. "We are not that formal around here." He took her hand and led her to sit at the table.

"Okay, sorry." She sniffled.

"No need to be sorry, I appreciate the sentiment, truly." His demeanor had taken a one-eighty from where it had been only a few minutes ago. He was calm and gentle with her.

"So yeah, you do need my insight here." Gathering her composure and determination, Caroline looked him dead in the eye. "Because you have to win her heart and bring her over because I can't live without my best friend. And from what I can see so far, you can't live without her either."

So there it was. The truth in a nutshell, tossed at him by a woman he had only just met. The Fates were truly throwing a whole bunch of weirdness at him lately.

After a very hot bubble bath with a very big glass of wine, Lou had finally calmed down. It took over an hour of kicking herself for acting like such a bitch before she settled on the cold fact that what was done, was done. After calling in to learn there were no new developments with grease monkey number one, whom she now knew to be a parolee named Teddy Monroe, she had made herself a couple of corn dogs, one of her favorite self-pity foods. She put her pajamas and striped socks on, climbed into bed and found a mind numbing B-movie to watch just so she wouldn't start thinking about her day of golf with Max any more. She had tried to call Caroline again but got sent straight to voice-mail. Again. That would have normally worried Lou but she knew that Caroline's parents were in town so she was more than likely still visiting. She would start worrying if she didn't get a call back by ten.

Lou's parents had come in while she was in the tub so they said their good-nights through the intercom system. She really didn't want to face her mother after what had transpired that afternoon. Mostly because she didn't want to have to admit her mother was right. Again. Lou was scared. She ran it over and over again in her head and there was really no reason this Max person should have been under her skin the way he was. Even so, it wasn't the end of the world for Lou to find someone attractive or interesting, that was a normal human thing after all. But Lou was petrified of it. He wasn't a complete and utter stranger. Joe had known him for ages, apparently, so she should have been more at ease with things. But she wasn't. She was scared of so many things and so many of them were in direct contradiction with each other. The whole, "he likes me so run, but does he really like me?" It was just so ridiculous. She really needed Caroline.

Then a simple thing that Lou had overlooked popped into her head and had her sitting up in bed and completely ignoring the movie all together. What the hell had he been doing at the morgue and the crime scene anyway? What would some big shot lawyer, business tycoon guy from back east be doing at the morgue and then at the crime scene of some unknown student/stripper? Lou jumped out of bed, grabbed her robe and headed to the other side of the house to her parent's room. She knocked on the partially open door and when her mother's voice said to come in, she pushed it open to see her parents

Shadows of Doubt

sitting on the floor playing Scrabble in their pajamas. It was a sweet image that almost distracted her from the reason she had come down there in the first place.

"Hey Joe, when did Max arrive in L.A.? Do you know?"

"Well, yeah." Joe gave her a perplexed look. "He came in Tuesday afternoon. He texted me from the airport asking when we could meet but I told him I was in India and would get in touch when I got back in town."

"Do you know when was the last time he was in L.A.?" She had her fingers crossed behind her back.

"Ah shoot, maybe four or five years ago? It was just for a day, though. For the closing of some deal." He cocked his head at her. "Can I ask why?"

"Was just curious. Thanks. Night." Lou closed the door behind her and headed back to her room so completely relieved that Max hadn't been in town when Angela Talbott or Marjorie Scott had been murdered. He may not have been guilty of murder but he was guilty of something, or knew something. Yet another reason to kick herself for putting her feelings before the case. If her head had not been so thoroughly shoved up her own backside, the fact that this guy had been in at both places would have been in the forefront of Lou's mind. She looked at the clock to see it was half past ten and was really pissed that Caroline wasn't calling her back. She picked up the phone and dialed her again, getting her voice mail, again, and leaving another rambling message, again. Tomorrow Lou was really going to kick Caroline's ass.

Caroline was nodding emphatically. "It will work."

"It will totally work!" Abby agreed.

"And how is this different from lying?" Frank asked.

"These are white lies, and it's totally for Lou's own good so that's completely okay." Caroline rolled her eyes at Frank when he just looked at her with a glazed expression. "You are a guy, I don't expect you to get it."

Frank looked at Max and Niko for some sort of solidarity but they looked just as confused as he was. After a couple of hours of hashing things out, Caroline and Abby had come up with a plan to help Max win Lou over. They had ordered room service, a lot of it, and Caroline had tried to explain how Lou rationalized things and why Caroline's plan would work. Abby had understood immediately but the men were still absolutely clueless.

"I don't understand!" Frank rolled around on the floor, frustrated. "If you can lie and not tell her about Max, why can't you just lie and not tell her about the Sanguinostri?"

"Oh. My. God." Caroline threw a grape at his head. "Because they are two totally separate things! Totally different importance values!"

"Wait one minute here." Niko was squinting as thought his brain hurt. "Are you telling me that the whole Max and Lou thing is more important than the secrecy of our kind? Is that what you are trying to say here?"

Abby and Caroline looked at each other then Caroline looked back at Niko. "Well, duh! That is exactly what I am saying! Abby, can you help me out here?" Caroline flopped back into her chair as if she were exhausted.

"You're guys, we don't expect you to understand." Abby stroked Caroline's hair as if to soothe her. "It's not their fault, honey, its that whole Y chromosome thing." Abby looked at the three men and contemplated how to make it very simple. "Okay, its very, very simple. Are you paying attention?" Max actually leaned in closer as if to listen harder. "To a woman, a matter of the heart trumps even the threat of a nuclear attack." All three men looked at each other, completely flabbergasted. "With Lou, the only thing to make a matter of the heart more important is to factor it in to one of her cases. In this specific instance, our rogue." She waited and watched as what she just said soaked in. "So, based on the simple principle that love trumps all, Caroline's first priority is Lou's heart, the Sanguinostri is a second but a happy byproduct if this plan works. Do you understand now?" They all stared at her as if they were deer caught in headlights.

"Oh for Christ's sake! Just do what we say!" Caroline bellowed and got up to pace around the room.

"Wait, I think I sort of understand this." Frank sat up and adjusted to face his brothers in confusion. "You know how women get all fussy about getting the perfect dress, then once they find it, the shoes are like the critical thing?" Abby sat up, hopeful as she listened.

"Yeah, what the hell is that anyway?" Niko asked.

"No, no no. It's not something we can figure out, it's just the way it is and we have to accept it. Kind of like the whole 'Does this make me look fat?' thing is really a rhetorical question if you want to keep your manhood intact. If a girl asks another girl though, then it's expected that they be honest." Frank looked at Abby for validation.

"Yes! That is exactly right!" She flopped onto the floor and threw her arms around him. "You make me so proud!"

Max snorted. "And I want to get involved in a relationship for this shit?"

"Lou is far more practical then most women. We are just trying to explain why I can rationalize lying to help you two get together and why the whole Sanguinostri Oath secret thing doesn't enter into the equation, or even matter. I can totally lie to Lou for the sake of love." Caroline smiled sweetly.

"Aren't you a doctor? A highly educated doctor at that?" Max squinted as he asked her.

"Yeah, so?" She looked at him as if his question had no merit, just as her phone beeped again. "Damn it. Okay I am listening to my messages now and you cannot stop me. We have a plan and we are sticking to it. Agreed?" The four of them muttered in agreement as Caroline punched in the numbers to listen to her voice mail. She stood quietly listening while Max studied all the different facial expressions she made. Abby jumped up and stuck her ear to the cell phone to listen in and Caroline cocked the phone to make it easier for her.

"Hey! I should be able to listen! It's all probably about me anyway!" Max shouted.

"Shhhh!" Abby hushed him while Caroline flapped her hand at him to be quiet. "Awe! Abby looked at Caroline and she nodded back in agreement over something they were hearing.

Max was getting highly annoyed after several minutes of hearing Awe's and Oh's out of the women. "I want to hear what she said!" He demanded.

Caroline pushed a button and looked at him as if he were insane. "I can't betray Lou's privacy by letting you hear those! And I really need to call her back but I wish I could get her voice mail when I do."

"I could order you to let me listen you know." Max stood up and tried to appear imposing.

"You could, and I would. But if Lou ever found out I let you, it would ruin everything for me and you so neener, neener, tough guy!" Caroline accentuated her point by sticking her tongue out at him.

"I think I liked you better when you were curtseying." He dragged his fingers through his hair.

"I could hack it and let you listen." Frank chimed in. "That way she's off the hook, and if I am getting this whole weird woman love rationalization thing, Lou might think it was romantic if she ever found out."

Shadows of Doubt

"Oh Frankie, you make me so proud!" Abby hugged him again.

"That's really quite brilliant." Caroline looked at Frank, completely impressed.

"Do it." Max ordered and Frank pulled a laptop over and started clicking away furiously. "So if I am catching on at all, you need to back me up if Lou ever finds out and explain that I only did it because I was trying to find out how she felt. Okay? He looked at both women.

"By George I think he's got it, too!" Caroline did a little dance.

"Geez, I don't know if I ever want to get this kind of logic." Niko got up and went to the bar.

"Okay, here we go." Frank turned the laptop around so the speakers were facing Max then hit a key to play the messages.

The first message Lou left Caroline started to play and it had been before Max and she actually met.

"Yummy Morgue Guy?" He looked at Caroline but everyone shushed him. The next message started to play.

"Caroline, its Lou again. I totally blew it. I am such a total ass I can barely stand it. This guy has got to think I am a total mental defect. You are going to so freak out on me when I tell you how bad I blew it today. I'm on my way home from the club now to drown myself or smother myself or something. Please call me as soon as you get this."

Max couldn't help but smile, but he felt horrible that Lou was feeling bad. He wanted to go right now and tell her that she could never blow anything with him, ever. But he sat and listened as the third and latest message started.

"Hey woman, where the hell are you? I'm starting to worry. Your parents had better not have kidnapped you and taken you back to Georgia. Listen, I need to talk to you because I am doing my usual mind-screw thing over Max. That's his name by the way. Anyhow, I know I blew it and that's just that. The bigger issue is why the hell was he at the morgue in the first place? According to Joe he had just landed so he had to have gone straight there from the plane. Then what the hell was he doing at the Winslow crime scene? He knows something or he's in it some how. I need you. Call me. Please."

"See?!" Caroline looked at him and gloated. "She is such a cop. The way to her heart is to get you two working on the case together. You indoctrinate the cop, not the woman you love. The rest will just pop, I know it. You just cannot be afraid for her to know how you feel and you have got to stop being afraid of how you feel yourself! So what if you let slip the whole she's beautiful thing. Let it flow if it wants to. She is so worth it."

"I gotta tell you bro, after hearing that last message, I think she's totally right." Niko said as he leaned against the bar.

Max considered the situation for the millionth time. "Bring me a drink, would you?"

"My Dom, the way Caroline has it planned, the worst case scenario is I wipe Lou if she freaks and we figure another way around this." Frank got up and sat next to Max. "I can plant that she got drunk with Caroline so the night is not a total blank but I have to say, after seeing how Caroline reacted when she got read in, if they are anything similar to each other, Caroline is right. Lou's sense of justice will override the rest. Plus I know she's nuts for you so that will kick her in the door whether she likes it or not. By the way..." Frank handed Caroline his cell phone. "...if it's okay with Max, just hit send and it will call Lou's voice mail directly without risking her answering."

Caroline looked at Max pleadingly.

"What do you plan to say?" He asked.

"I thought about that." Her mischievous smile reappeared. "I have it all planned. So we are going to set this for Tuesday night, right?" Max nodded in the affirmative. "Then will you trust me here?"

He thought for a minute as he studied Caroline's face. He had gotten where he was by following his gut all his life and he had only dug himself a hole when he started second guessing himself. The people in the room with him now had done nothing but help him dig himself out of that hole. Caroline, a near stranger to him, had proven the biggest surprise of all. Trusting him implicitly, when he had forgotten to trust himself.

"I trust you." He finally answered. Caroline smiled at him then hit send on the phone.

When she spoke she made herself sound weak and groggy. "Hey sweetie, I am so sorry for missing your calls. I got food poisoning at dinner last night with my parents. Bad clams. Anyway, just give me another day to recoup and I am all yours. I love ya girlie and I'm sorry for worrying you." She made a kissing sound then hit the button to disconnect and beamed a smile at them all. "So how was that?"

Abby clapped and bounced. Frank and Niko were apparently impressed with the performance.

Max looked at her with an eyebrow raised. "You remember part of the Oath was never to lie to me?" Caroline shrank a little and nodded. "That includes those little white lie performances too." He grinned at her and she relaxed.

"Hey, I have an idea to add some pressure here that would work in your favor." Niko said as he handed Max a drink. "I need you to okay it first, though. It will involve a phone call."

Niko sat down in the only open chair and gave Max his idea. The girls both thought it was complete genius. Brilliant psychological warfare and, frankly, Max did too. So after a phone call was made it appeared that Caroline's plan was a green light. Now Max needed to be patient and let certain things play out on Monday. He was even more happy that Niko had made the arrangements to go and deal with the bastard that had hurt Lou since that would give him a nice distraction. The man had to suffer according to Max's laws. Because of the way it had affected Max to learn of everything, he understood now why Joe wouldn't tell him at the Country Club. One thing Max knew without a shadow of a doubt was regardless of what happened, whether Lou rejected him and the Sanguinostri and he had to be wiped completely from her mind, no one would ever hurt Lou again so long as Max could draw breath.

Chapter Ten

Lou had given up trying to sleep around four-thirty that morning. She was angry that she dozed off earlier and missed Caroline's call. She hadn't been able to get back to sleep since. Instead she spent most of the morning drinking coffee and staring across the meadow through binoculars at the construction that was going on. Before she knew who the neighbor was, she could have cared less that they had gotten special permitting and dispensation from the Association to work around the clock. Lou would have been livid and have staged protests to stop it. Now that she knew it was Max's home being built there, she wasn't setting foot anywhere near it. Lou did wish she had paid more attention to those plans her mother approved, though.

To his credit, they were being exceedingly careful not to infringe on the meadow and had graded the plot to weave through the oaks rather than move any. They had also stuck to what she did remember of the plan and she would see about one-quarter of the actual structure. Lou remembered her mother mentioning last week that they had dug down for a huge basement which seemed just silly to Lou what with California and its earthquakes. But as she peered through the lenses it looked like they had not only finished digging, but had already poured the foundation with some seriously massive re-bar reinforcement. She wondered how many times Max had been over there to check on things or if he just had people to do that for him.

"The house finished yet?" Her mother's voice startled her.

"Maybe by lunch." She turned to her mother and smirked at her laughter.

"They are working around the clock on that sucker. Fortunately, they are being polite about noise and keeping it restricted." Shevaun stood next to her and tapped on the binoculars. "Let me have a peek."

Lou passed her mother the lenses and noted that she was all dressed, bright and shiny. "Why are you all dressed so early?"

"I've been drafted to the Park Committee." Her mother turned and grinned at her.

"Park? What park?

"Well, our little Max bought off the Association and all the neighbors by purchasing the acreage adjacent to him. He is turning it into a park for the community." Shevaun resumed watching the construction through the binoculars. "Complete with a little lake and everything."

"Are you shitting me?!" Lou was astounded. "How many acres is that?"

"Roughly thirty-eight or so." Shevaun handed her daughter back the binoculars and went to sit and sip her coffee. "Anyway, a committee was established to approve everything and we have our first meeting this morning, here."

"Who's on the committee?" Lou set the lenses on the fireplace mantle and gave up spying since it was almost eight and Vinny would be there to pick her up soon.

"Well me, Sandra Arthur and Max. But!" She stuck her hand up before Lou could freak out. "Max is having his assistant Abigail sit in for him today instead. You met her the other day."

"Yeah, I liked her a lot." Lou wasn't sure if she was relieved or disappointed that Max wouldn't be there.

"Oh I just love her. She reminds me a lot of Caroline actually." Shevaun could see the dark circles under her daughter's eyes and it broke her heart. "So did you get any sleep last night?"

"Some, sure." Lou started to gather her things. "I need to get downstairs before Vinny gets here." She leaned in and kissed her mother goodbye. "Have fun planning the park. Hey, try to plan for plenty of plants that are food sources for the animals would you? Please?"

Shevaun smiled at her daughter. "It was one of Max's stipulations that the park be planned and designed so that it can be certified as a wildlife preserve. He even has a fellow from the Audubon Society coming this morning to help." She was glad she could get that in for Max. Another little thing to tug at Lou's heartstrings. "Have a good day and be safe out there. Love you."

"Love you too, Momma." Lou headed downstairs just as she heard the doorbell ring. "I'll grab it, get your shoes."

When Lou opened the door she had expected it to be Vinny because he had finally worn out his horn. Instead it was Abby La Rue and Sandra Arthur.

"Morning, Lou!" Sandra Arthur was a lovely petite woman with perfectly coiffed copper hair and deep brown eyes that always smiled. Lou often wondered how anyone could ever be in a bad mood around the woman since she was always so infectiously cheery.

"Good morning!" Abby smiled brightly and hugged Lou without warning. "You alright? You don't look well."

"Good morning, please come in. Uh...Yeah, I just didn't sleep well." Lou suddenly felt very self-conscious remembering that Abby worked for Max and was apparently very close to him.

"Oh no! Was it the construction that kept you awake?" She laid her hand on Lou's arm and looked at her with deep concern.

"No, not at all. I even forget that they are there so don't worry, it's fine." Luckily for Lou, Marta came in to escort the women to the room where they were going to conduct their meeting. "You girls have fun planning the park. My mother will be down in a minute. Marta will take care of you until then."

"Thank you dear." Sandra followed Marta into the other room.

"Lou..." Abby stopped her before she could escape outside. "I know you don't know me very well, or at all really! But, if you need anything please know you can always count on me." She smiled a knowing smile at Lou then turned to follow where Marta had taken Sandra. The woman's genuine caring had made Lou's heart ache a little as she closed the door behind her and headed to the driveway.

Lou was grateful for Vinny's rambling as they drove in to work. He was giddy as hell about the new nursery that, thanks to her uncle and cousins helping move all of Vinny's junk out, they were able to complete all the yellow painting and start shopping for baby furniture on Sunday. It was really nice to see Vinny excited about the situation after his extreme panic the week before and their escapade with the grease monkeys on Saturday evening. By the time they had gotten to Homicide, Lou knew exactly what the nursery was going to look like in excruciating detail. Before Lou had the chance to put her jacket on the hook, one of the other detectives informed them that the captain wanted to see them both immediately. Looking dubiously at each other, they made their way up the hall.

Twenty minutes later Captain Davidson was still handing their asses to them. It was all Lou's fault and she simply had to do something.

"Sir." She abruptly interrupted him. "Forgive me for being rude but I cannot in good conscience allow Detective DeLuca to be reprimanded for something that I did. Please sir."

Davidson regarded her carefully then looked at Vinny. "Detective DeLuca, you're dismissed."

"Captain, I was just..."

"DeLuca!" Davidson cut him off flat. "Don't you have a test to study for?"

Vinny looked at Lou and grumbled before he got up. "Yes sir. Thank you, sir." He reluctantly left the Captain's office, still grumbling as he closed the door behind him.

Davidson looked at Lou in such a way that it made her shift in her seat. "Detective, I am not going to drag this out any more than I already have. You are on desk for the rest of the week."

"But Sir.."

"Lou do you comprehend how much I dislike being called up by LAPD brass and scolded? I mean scolded as though I were eight years old, about my detectives nosing around in their cases?"

"Sir, I was just tying up loose ends so I could hand over a complete file to the assigned officers." She was completely aware he knew that was bullshit.

"Lou, cut the crap. You interviewed the victim's roommate, co-workers and employer when there was absolutely no protocol that dictated the need for such. Now, if you had not come to me just a few days ago with the whole pitch to get me to push for you to keep the other two cases, I might have been able to sell that and actually believed it. You and I know better and you crossed the line. Now get out of here and I expect all your files and desk to be neat and tidy by the end of the week because you are so damn bored of sitting on your ass there. You get me Detective?"

"Yes, sir." Lou didn't apologize. She started to make her way out of her Captain's office without another word but he stopped her before she hit the door.

"Detective.." His tone was decidedly different from just a moment ago. "I need to inform you of one more thing before you go."

Lou turned and faced him once again, itching to get the hell out of there before she had to endure another moment of being dressed-down.

"The suspect you apprehended on Saturday, Teddy Monroe..." He shuffled some papers on his desk in what appeared to be an attempt at stalling.

"Yes sir? He lawyered up. Something pop on him?" Lou took a step closer, curious now.

"Trustees found him hanging naked in his cell this morning. Used his own coveralls." He blew out a breath as he acknowledged her confused expression. "There's still no clue why he attacked you and DeLuca but the detectives that have been assigned the case will figure it out."

"But sir.." Lou tried to protest in vain.

"What part of desk duty do you not understand, Detective?" He cocked his head sideways at her. "Dismissed."

Lou turned on her heel and used every ounce of willpower she had not to slam the door behind her.

When she got back to her desk, Vinny grabbed her by the arm before her butt could hit the chair.

"Come out with me while I have a smoke."

She nearly tripped as he dragged her. "I thought you quit years ago?"

"I did but with the stress of finding out I was gonna be a dad, I bought a pack last week. Don't tell Vera."

When they got outside he looked around to see who was within earshot. "First of all, yeah I heard about Monroe. I'm not gonna bother with that crap right now." When he decided it was clear he marched up and glared down at her. "What the hell was that Lou? We are partners! You can't expect me to feel good about you taking the heat for something we did as partners."

Lou grinned at Vinny, then went and sat down on a bench while he lit up his smoke. "Listen Daddy, things are changing. You know it and I know it. I am too old for you to keep doing this babysitter thing so you need to take your damn test and make lieutenant, sit your butt in a nice desk chair and get home to your wife and baby in one piece every night. I'm not gonna let you screw that up if I can help it."

"Ah geez, Lou." He inhaled deeply of the cigarette, then dropped it and smashed it under his foot forcefully as if taking all his anger out on it. "I didn't want to deal with this just yet."

"Well ya gotta pass the test first, you know." Lou got up and pinched his cheeks. "Stop feeling guilty like your abandoning me or something! You'll still be bossing me around, it will just be official. Now lets get out of the cold and you can buy me a cup of coffee."

Vinny held the door open for her. "God help whoever you get as a new partner. Who's gonna pick you up in the morning?"

She stopped and looked at him. "What, are you planning on leaving Homicide?"

Vinny blinked and thought about it for a second. "Well, no!"

"So why the hell can't you pick me up still? Same damn building." She grinned and walked inside. "Maybe I'll get lucky and get a newbie I can boss around."

Vinny laughed. "Now, that would be fun to watch."

"Hurry up, I need to get to organizing my paperclips." She tried to make light of the situation for Vinny's sake, but she was really in a bad way over all of it. Her captain. The Monroe guy kicking the bucket just like like his partner had. Max. Having this nagging feeling that Max was somehow tied to the cases that she just got chewed out for not letting go. If she was being relegated to desk work, perhaps she could do a little digging and thoroughly confirm Max was nowhere near L.A. when the first two victims were killed. One thing was certain, she had to keep Vinny out of it from now on. He had far too much at stake and way too many years in to screw it up for him now.

Max was very glad Niko had arranged for the helicopter rather than driving to the prison which Mr. Robert Sawyer was currently calling home. The forty-five minute flight was much more tolerable then a three hour drive would have been. As it was, Max was antsy as hell. The prison official had apologized four times for the method of transportation when he picked them up from the helipad and explained that it was for the sake of Max's anonymity and security that they use a prison transport van. It made sense really, far more eyebrows would have been raised if a limousine or town car had pulled up in front of the prison and been waved right in without any record. When they arrived at the level 3 area of the facility, they were greeted by the warden accompanied by two guards and were ushered directly through a back corridor while the warden explained why they were heading to an inmate/attorney conference area rather than the isolation cell as Niko had previously been told. As luck would have it, if you could call it that, an inmate had used his attorney as a punching bag on Saturday. They had refrained from sending in a clean-up crew until after Max's visit, though it had been summarily tidied for the meeting. Max really could have cared less. He just wanted to get his hands on the man that had put hands on Lou. Where that took place was inconsequential.

The warden personally opened the door to the room which looked perfectly clean to Niko save for the minor bloodstains on the ground. A stainless steel table was bolted to the concrete floor and two chairs sat on opposite sides. The walls were concrete block, painted a cheery gray drab with one small cut out window that stood about eight feet off the ground. Gloomy winter day-light dribbled in reluctantly through the steel bars of the window, casting long planked shadows across the walls. Niko walked in first and eyeballed the man that stood in the corner. He wore the trendy prison uniform that was comprised of a chambray denim shirt, denim pants and spiffy white slip-on tennis

Shadows of Doubt

shoes. He was a decent enough looking fellow who was obviously making good use of the prison's exercise equipment. The man stood about six feet tall and had close cropped, dirty blond hair and muddy brown eyes that currently looked at them with a glare that Niko found amusing. When Max finally entered the room, the man's expression flickered with surprise as often was the case when Max entered any room. The sharp contrast between Robert Sawyer's average visage and Max's imposing, perfectly polished presence was day and night. Max had specifically chosen one of his favorite suits so that it would be a favorite for another reason after today. It was the same suit he had worn the first time he had set eyes on Lou. Max didn't look at Sawyer when he walked in, he simply peeled off his leather gloves and folded them in a gentlemanly manner. Niko pulled out the chair for him before taking his place near the door just as the sound of it being bolted shut from the outside reverberated through the room. Sawyer was obviously confused because these men were clearly not his attorneys and it was strict prison policy that a guard be present at all times unless it was an attorney-client visit.

"Who the hell are you?" Sawyer barked at them.

Max sat and crossed his legs, smoothing his slacks. "I don't think that will really matter to you Mr. Sawyer, or may I call you Bob?" He looked at the man for the first time now, contempt seething in his stare.

Sawyer took a step towards the table as if he was going to intimidate Max in some way, hulking his shoulders forward. "You can kiss my ass. Who the hell are you and what the hell am I here for?" His shackles rattled as he tried to lift his hands to further intimidate.

"Niko, would you have the guard come in and remove Mr. Sawyer's chains, please?" Max asked over his shoulder and Niko had the guard in and complying within ten seconds without ever saying a word. Sawyer's expression baffled at the immediate response. "Sit down Bobby." Max continued.

Sawyer rubbed his wrists and glared at Niko, then Max, as the guard left and the door was bolted once again. "I'm fine standing."

Max's fist came down on the stainless steel table with such force that it left a dent. "I said sit!" he bellowed and Sawyer sat without even realizing it. Niko nearly grinned, wondering what the table would have looked like if Max hadn't been restraining himself the way he knew he was.

"Now, that's better." Max's voice resumed its eerily calm and gentlemanly tone. "You are curious as to who I am and why I am here. That's only natural. The who means nothing to you but the why is quite critical actually."

"Yeah, okay so why then?" Sawyer calmed a bit and sat back in the rigid chair.

Max took a moment to study the man who had inflicted such agony upon Lou, both physical and mental. Sawyer looked like a thousand men who might have crossed Lou's path. Nothing at all about his look to indicate he was a psychopath. Couple that with the fact that this man had been working as a court officer, Max could see how Lou would have assumed he was safe to have a meal with. The thought of that sort of betrayal only infuriated Max more and he took a deep breath to keep his rage in check for the moment.

"My associate and I are here about the offense that found you incarcerated in this fine establishment. I might note here that anything said between us is strictly for my own personal information, so by all means speak freely. Nothing you say to me will be held against you once you leave this room, you have my word." Max had to smile at the play on words. Though they were true, the man had no idea that he wouldn't be leaving the room alive.

"Okay, so what? I'll be out on parole by Labor Day so what the hell do I care anyway?" Sawyer snickered.

"Yes, that is a wonderful thing to look forward to, isn't it? You'll still have plenty of beach time with the lovely California weather. Good for you." Max was starting to enjoy this. "But the actual crimes are what I am interested in. The how and why of it to be specific. Would you mind explaining all that to me please?"

"What the hell difference does it make? I'm doing my time, you can't arrest me again." Sawyer leaned on the table now, feeling more comfortable and obviously quite curious.

"I know, which is why you should feel more at ease with speaking freely. It's a personal matter for myself only. Let's just say I have issues with the Detective and would like to know in graphic detail your exploits with the woman." Max had thought about how he would word things carefully. The subtle implication that he was envious of Sawyer in some way would loosen the bastard's tongue.

"Ah, I get it. You must be a defense attorney or something right?" Sawyer grinned and leaned back in the chair again, obviously taking the bait in thinking that Max had a thing for Lou on some equally warped level as he.

"Or something, right." Max grinned at the man. "Now, would you mind recounting events from your side of things? Reports are reports." Max made a dramatic gesture with his hand. "They so lack the color and passion of it all. I truly wish to hear your side."

Robert Sawyer obviously felt he had the upper hand with Max wanting to hear his details so badly. He relaxed his posture considerably and smirked. "Get me a smoke and I'll be happy to tell my story." Niko didn't wait for Max to give him a signal. He pulled the antique silver case from his coat pocket and handed the scumbag one of his expensive cigarettes and gave him a light. "Nice. Pricey I bet." Sawyer noted the obvious and didn't bother to thank him. Niko didn't acknowledge the man and took his place back next to the door. "Alright, so you want to know about the love of my life, Detective Lou Donovan. Damn that girl is hot." Sawyer said almost with reverence as he drew in a long drag of the smoke. "I knew she was mine the minute I laid eyes on her, when she came in personally to get a signature on a warrant. She'll know too once I get out and she sees me. I've been working out, getting in shape." He flexed his arm and grinned. "But I gotta do things smart this time. Watch my P's and Q's with the whole parole thing first. Plus the fact that I'm sure she'll know I'm out. Gotta make her wait ya know? That whole longing and anticipation thing will be working in my favor." He winked at Max.

Though the man was oblivious, Niko could see Max's posture tighten like a bow string with each word Sawyer uttered. With every delusional sentence he spewed, he was adding another nail to his own coffin. Niko just wondered how long Max would be able to stand listening to the delusional bastard before he pounded him to a pulp.

"I am sure you have a very carefully thought out plan, Bobby." Max's voice was straining to keep an even keel. "But I really would love to hear about before. What happened that fated you here, please?"

Sawyer studied the black and gold cigarette then looked at Max as if he had forgotten he was there. "Oh yeah, sure." He drew in another breath of smoke and held it, then exhaled and leaned in on the table as he started to recount his tale.

It would have been disturbing to the average person to hear the story from Robert Sawyer's point of view. He recounted everything so rationally, as if it were perfectly sensible to expect utter devotion from Lou after a single dinner and then to come to the logical conclusion that he needed to make her see, by whatever means necessary, that she was his. The man's twisted sense of romance which was to inflict oppression and terror on Lou was so matter of fact that Max could scarcely hide his revulsion. Sawyer even relayed details of his breaking in to Lou's apartment on several occasions to paw through her things, her intimate things, and that he had even contemplated hiding cameras to watch her but he wasn't that tech savvy. When he had finally gotten to the part of his tale where he gleefully described the sensation of his fists pounding into Lou's flesh, Max could feel the thirst in the back of his throat and the instinctive twitch of his fangs that laid dormant, retracted and hidden just under the surface behind his eye teeth.

It was the primal aspect of his kind, the sanguinarius, the savage blood thirst that he and his Aegis Council dedicated their lives to keeping in check among their people. Max knew this side of himself well and had mastered it so very long ago but also utilized it when it served his purposes, as was his privilege. However, right at that moment his instincts wanted nothing more than to let his fangs fly like a viper and drain the life from the pathetic excuse of a human being that sat across from him. It was the Dominor, the highly evolved brain within the man that prevented him. Allowing the tainted blood of something like Sawyer to sustain him evoked nothing less than disgust from Max. But he surely would indulge in watching it puddle and flow on the concrete floor when he was good and ready.

Robert Sawyer had taken the better part of an hour to tell his tale of sadistic brutality he had wrought upon Lou Donovan. After he had explained the mathematical genius in his timing to precisely hit Lou's vehicle dead center to the driver's side door the way he had, Max had heard enough. Calmly he rose from his chair while Sawyer continued patting himself on the back about his choosing the Hummer for maximum force behind the impact. Max removed his overcoat, then his suit jacket and vest, handing them to Niko who in turn carefully folded and draped them over his arm. It was amazing that Sawyer was so wrapped up in his own reverie that he hadn't noticed Max removing the crisp white shirt he wore. Niko handed Max a hank of cloth that turned out to be some sort of apron which he carefully tied about his waist, to protect his trousers, of course. That was when Robert Sawyer noticed the oddity of things and got up from his chair.

"What the hell? What kind of a freak are you?" Sawyer stammered as he backed into the corner away from the approaching Max.

"I may be a genetic anomaly, Bobby..." Max stepped up and glared down into Sawyer's face, letting his fangs fly as he grinned at him for maximum effect. "... but you, most assuredly are the freak."

Max reached back and cocked his fist as Robert Sawyer began screaming like a little girl. Savoring the first of what would be many, many blows, Max watched his knuckles make contact with the bastard's cheekbone, just as the piece of shit had recounted only minutes ago he had done to Lou. When the screams turned to gurgles, Max paused to afford Sawyer the knowledge of why he was about to die such a painful death.

"Bobby, my name is Maximilian Augustus Julian, since you were curious before. The reason I am so enthusiastically beating you to death is because, well, I'll let you in on a little secret that I have only just moments ago admitted to myself." Max leaned down and yanked Sawyer's head up by what little hair he had left and looked him in his eyes that were severely swollen shut. "I am in love with the woman you so gleefully described torturing and terrorizing. The same woman your former bunk buddies tried to pay a visit to this weekend. Oh, they are both dead by the way." Max felt Sawyer losing consciousness and gave him a solid smack on the cheek to wake him back up. "You still with me? Stay with me here just a little longer." Max saw the pulp of a man acknowledging him and continued. "Now, by your own admission it is your personal life's goal to see Lou dead if she will not accept your delusion of adoration, and you see..." Max saw the glimmer of understanding pass through Sawyer's eyes. "... that is in direct conflict with my personal life's goal which is to make sure Detective Donovan lives a long and blissfully safe life with neither a want or need for anything." Max let go of the man's hair, letting his skull bounce on the concrete floor. "I should thank you for that personal revelation Bobby, but I won't. Enjoy your swift trip to the underworld and give Hades my regards, would you?" With one last jolt of rage, Max let his fist fly one more time and heard Robert Sawyer's skull crumble under the weight of his fury. Max straightened and wiped his hands on the apron then looked at the mess of blood spatter he was wearing and grunted.

"The warden has his personal shower at the ready for you my, Dominor." Niko spoke for the first time since they had entered the room.

"Well that is very thoughtful, and necessary I'm afraid. Do we have a good cleaner set up in town yet? I really made a mess of these trousers didn't I?" Max's casual demeanor about the situation was something Niko got a kick out of. It was his Max, the Dominor he admired, swore fealty to and loved like a brother.

"We have a real good one. They can take care of the loafers too, no problem." Niko informed him as he opened the door so they could get on their way.

"Excellent!" Max said cheerfully as he turned his back on the parasite once known as Robert Sawyer and headed to clean up all traces of the unpleasantness before they headed home.

The morning had dragged on at a snails pace for Lou. She had done the digging she needed and verified for certain that Max had not been in town to have been involved in the Scott or Talbott murders. That was something, at least. By one-thirty she had caught up on all her paperwork. Both her in and out boxes were empty and to her chagrin, her paperclips were even organized. She had absolutely no clue how she was supposed to keep busy sitting on her ass for the rest of the week. By two-thirty she had started on Vinny's desk, while he was sitting at it, and he was about to beat her senseless with his stapler.

Frustrated, Vinny yanked his pen cup out of her hand. "Lou, go get a broom or something, I am trying to study here!"

"The janitor is using it. I gotta wait." She said in all seriousness and proceeded to sift through his out box.

"Donovan." Their Captain called from the doorway. "Come get a cup of coffee with me. DeLuca, you too."

Vinny looked at Lou suspiciously. "What the hell did you do now that you didn't tell me about?"

"I haven't done anything!" There was no way that her captain could know that she had been snooping on anything related to the cases. She could have been cleaning up loose ends on old files. Even running something for one of the other detectives.

Vinny grabbed the files from his out box out of her hand, then headed to the break room with Lou following close behind him. When they stepped inside, the Captain gave the two deputies that were sitting at the table eating their lunch a look so they scooped up their sandwiches and hustled out of the room. Before Lou could say anything he held up a hand and sat down.

"Sit please. You're not in trouble already, so sit." He took a sip of his coffee while they both took a seat, then he looked directly at Lou. "I just got a call from the warden up north. He thought you should hear it from me rather than him."

"Hear what sir?" Lou tried to search her brain for who she had put away recently that could warrant a sit down with the Captain.

Shadows of Doubt

Davidson wasn't sure how this would affect Lou, so he just decided to be out with it. "Robert Sawyer was murdered this morning. Apparently some of his fellow inmates decided to smash his head in during shower time but no one is copping to having seen a thing. Not even the guards."

Lou really didn't know how to respond to him. The thought of the man who had made her life a living hell for over a year being dead really wasn't registering.

"How bad of a beating?" Vinny asked, apparently pleased by the news.

"They had to positively identify him by his prints. His head was bloody mush and they had to be careful while scooping it up. Those were the warden's exact words by the way." The Captain actually grinned at the idea. "Less work for the parole board if you ask me." But he could tell Lou was going to a bad place. The memories of what the man represented to her couldn't help but mess with her head, he knew that. "DeLuca, take your partner home. This is a lot to deal with. A lot of bad guys dropping dead all at once. We can celebrate later."

Vinny noted the blank stare on Lou's face and nodded to the Captain. "Yes sir. Come on kiddo, I'll buy ya a drink."

They drove almost the entire way to Lou's house in silence until she looked at him and started cracking up. It kind of disturbed Vinny to watch her do such a belly roll to the point he was glad she was buckled in or else she would have hit her head on the dashboard.

"You okay, Lou?" He tried to focus on the road and not her hysterics.

She caught her breath a second. "Did Davidson actually say they had to scoop his head up?"

Vinny wasn't sure he saw the humor in it as clearly as she did. "Yeah, that's what he said."

"Yeah..." She resumed laughing. "... I know its wrong, and warped but..." She snorted, then tried to compose herself enough to finish her sentence. "... I just had this visual of a guard using a pooper scooper like I use for Angus' cat box! Ya get it? Scoop up a piece of shit?" She snorted again and could barely catch her breath.

After he took a moment to understand what she had said, Vinny saw the humor and started laughing with her. He wasn't laughing simply because it had been funny, no. Vinny began to laugh because he felt a sudden lightness of heart, knowing that she was going to be alright. A certain weight had been lifted off him realizing that he didn't have to deal with the bastard getting out on parole and becoming a threat to her again. He laughed nearly as hard as she did, tears streaming down his face and his side beginning to hurt. When he nearly hit the barrier arm at the guard gate to her community, they both could only laugh harder and had to wait a few minutes before proceeding after the guard raised it for them.

When they got inside Lou's house they heard her mother beckoning them into the kitchen. Joe was flipping tortillas on a skillet and Shevaun was stirring a huge pitcher of mojitos with a big fat smile on her face.

"You're uncle called and told us about Sawyer. Joe and I decided it was cause for celebration, as morbid as that may sound, but I don't care!" Shevaun made a dinging sound with the spoon on the pitcher. "It's mojitos and tacos tonight! Vinny, why don't you call Vera and invite her up?"

"Ah that's nice but she's at her sister's doing some baby shower planning or something like that. I'm in though!" Vinny hopped up onto a stool at the counter and grabbed a glass.

Lou walked around the counter to give her mother a kiss on the cheek then walked around to see what Joe was doing. "Hey Joe,

Shadows of Doubt

whatchya know?" She hopped up to kiss his cheek after reciting one of the little traditional lines they had between the two of them.

"Nuthin' do Lou, how 'bout you?" He gave her the traditional response and grinned as he flipped another tortilla.

"Hey Momma, you mind if I call Caroline and invite her up?" She asked as she skipped over to her mother and grabbed a glass.

"Oh! Please do! We have plenty." She did a little dance while she filled Lou's glass.

Lou joined her mother's little dance as she dialed her friend and waited for her to pick up which she did after the fourth ring.

"Hey girlie! How are you?" Caroline sounded much better than she had on her message and that relieved Lou a lot.

"I had a shitty day and a great day all at once. Sawyer got smooshed today in prison!" Lou could hear voices in the background. "Hey where are you? You have company? You sound much better than on the message you left."

"Oh, no no!" Caroline coughed and Lou could have sworn she heard someone shushing in the background "I mean, no its just the television and yes, I am feeling better. Now what about Sawyer?"

Lou had a weird vibe that Caroline wasn't all that surprised to hear about Sawyer, but she shrugged it off to her being under the weather. "Yeah he got whacked in the shower and is dead as a doornail. So you're off the hook having to go to his parole hearing with me. Hey, my parents are doing a little impromptu celebration over it. You wanna come up and have tacos and mojitos with us?"

"Oh sweetie, I would so love to but I don't think I'm up to food and drink just yet." Caroline adjusted her voice to sound a little ill still. "Hey can you give me a rain check? It's only been a few hours since I last hurled. How about you come over after work tomorrow and we do another celebration? I should be good to go by then."

"Sure thing, girlie. You get some rest and feel better, okay?" Caroline did still sound a little off so she understood completely her wanting to lay low.

"You bet! You okay, Lou? Really, I mean?" Caroline listened for any hint of anything in her friend's voice.

"I don't know honestly. Got a lot of stuff to tell you that you need to kick my ass for but right now, family has things upbeat so I don't have to think about it. Today was straight crap and so was yesterday to be honest. Lou grinned as she watched Vinny, her mother and Joe all dancing in the kitchen with no music. "I'm going to take advantage of the silly people here so I can try to sleep tonight."

Caroline heard the sadness in Lou's voice and it broke her heart. "Okay sweetie pie. I got all you're messages so we will sort it all out, I promise. Things will be better tomorrow, I swear. See ya then, okay?"

"Okay, girlie." Lou smiled. "Love ya oodles." She clicked off before she could hear Caroline tell her she loved her back. She knew she did, she was like her sister. Lou went to hang her jacket and holster on the hook next to Vinny's then headed in to the kitchen to join the silly dance, grabbing her glass along the way.

Caroline could tell by their brief phone conversation that Lou was hurting. She wasn't sure how bad the whole Sawyer thing was affecting her but she had a feeling Lou's distress had nothing to do with with him, but with Max and work. Having the LAPD brass rat Lou out to her captain was cruel but it was a smart move in reminding her of the bureaucracy and limitations she had within the scope of being a normal cop. When Caroline and Max hit her tomorrow with the whole Sanguinostri being bigger than that, and how justice needn't have jurisdictional borders, it would ring a lot truer and louder with her. After the two days of learning everything Caroline had learned about her lineage and the Sanguinostri, she had no doubt in her mind that her life had a far more noble meaning than it previously had. Lou would feel the same way, they just had to get her to listen. She tossed her cell phone on the coffee table and stared at Frank and Abby.

Frank was sprawled out on the couch with his laptop on his chest, clicking away and antagonizing Abby about something or other, but he paused long enough to see Caroline staring at them. "What?" He demanded.

"You two are worse than a pair of Pomeranians sometimes!" She started pacing. "Lou could totally hear you yapping in the background. I had to lie and say it was the TV!"

"Sorry." The two said in unison.

Caroline rolled her eyes and looked out the open door. "I need to talk to Max." She whispered and gestured toward his suite.

"Come on in, Caroline." Max yelled from across the hall.

She blinked in shock. "How the hell did he hear me?"

"It's part of being one of us. Turned, I mean. Super hearing, sight, sniffer, the whole senses thing." Abby smiled at her.

"But if he could hear me, why couldn't he just listen to Lou's messages on my cell while we did?"

"It's a frequency thing, now get in here." Max yelled again.

Frank and Abby giggled as Caroline headed in to Max's suite where he, Niko, the men named Finn and Connor were busy on either phone calls, typing away on laptops or sifting through papers like Max was. They all looked very dangerous and way too handsome for Caroline's own good.

"How is she?" Max looked up from his papers.

Caroline sighed. "Not good. She's way low. I hate that we kinda kicked her while she was down with the whole captain thing but I know it is going to help." She sat down on the ottoman next to Max. "I know it's none of my business but she told me about Sawyer."

Max looked around the room and the other men stopped what they were doing and cleared out immediately. "What did she tell you?" He asked only after the men had gone.

"She said he got smooshed is all, and that I was off the hook going with her to the parole hearing. But, I mean I know that you went there and all…"

Max leaned forward and looked her in the eyes. "Just ask me, Caroline."

"Was it you personally? Or did you have it done like Niko did with that Monroe jerk?"

"Do you want me to answer that honestly or give you something you can stomach?"

Caroline rolled her eyes. "I'm a coroner remember? I can stomach anything. I want to know exactly what you did, for my own sake."

"I won't tell you if you are going to tell Lou."

She shook her head. "No, I get that. This isn't something she needs to know. This is strictly for me."

Max sat back in his chair and gave her a very short version of the morning's events, summarizing his having beaten Robert Sawyer to a pulp with his bare hands. He watched her expression very carefully as he spoke but her face stayed blank all the way through to the end. When he finished telling Caroline what she wanted to know, she got up off the ottoman and stood over him, apparently surveying him. Then, without warning she leaned down and kissed him on the forehead.

"Thank you for telling me." She smiled at him and he thought he saw a tear welling in her eye. "Sweet dreams, my Dominor!" She said then skipped out of the room, just like Abby often did. Once again he found himself utterly speechless.

Shadows of Doubt

The raven haired beauty carefully strapped to the chair was a very special find indeed. Not like that Jade Winslow who had been a weak moment in his endeavors. He should have thought that out more carefully, like this one. Ah, she was exceptionally special and lovely in her haggish, over-used whore sort of way. Yes, he had to admit that she was more ashy than porcelain fair. Her skin was also neither smooth nor lustrous but was sagging and slack from her habitual drug use. But he, being the eternal optimist, preferred to think of her as well loved, as they often say about a child's toy. It sounded much sweeter to him than the reality of her. He had to admit she had truly been charming and very much a pleasure to lure into his web. She had melted so easily into his hands at the promise of just a bit of encouragement, care and of course money. He giggled at the ridiculousness of the name she gave him, Katarina Purrs she said and was very serious about it. Such a silly girl with her short, spiky, over-dyed black hair and her equally overdone black smokey eye makeup that had long since smeared down her cheeks from her incessant weeping. He really wished she didn't weep so much. Perhaps it was because he had kept her longer then the others, spoiling the newness of everything. Well, it couldn't be helped. Things were developing in his little adventure that he scarcely expected and as with all things, one must adapt quickly or perish.

The woman was so tired that her head would have surely bobbed had it not been strapped to the back of the chair. She was exhausted from struggling to breathe with the ball-gag in her mouth. She was exhausted from the stench which she had realized a few days ago was from her sitting in her own urine and faeces. Most of all though, she was exhausted from waiting to die. She had no illusions that she would make it out alive from this nightmare and if truth be told, she was glad for it. She was exhausted before she ever bought in to the man's lies about wanting her to star in his new series of adult films. He had just seemed far too polished to be one of those creepy freaks that would ask for a preview performance or an up-close and personal audition before they cut her a break. With those guys she at least got a few bucks, a drink and a fix out of it. This guy though, he had his own personal agenda and she knew with the first of the thousand cuts he sliced into her flesh that it included her death. So when she opened her eyes to see him standing in front of her again, only this time he was naked with just a black silk robe hanging open, she prayed it would be the last time and he would finally end it.

"Good evening my precious kitten. I trust you had a nice rest?" He said as he sauntered closer, letting his robe brush her shredded bare leg. The odd sound of plastic peeling off the soles of his feet as he stepped seemed louder than it usually did to him. It was too quiet. She wasn't whimpering. She wasn't struggling in the least, which was a pity. He missed the flare of those nostrils when she struggled. Yes, he had dragged it out too long, he conceded that now. The luster lacked and the bauble was no longer shiny. When he had finished circling he stopped in front of her and watched her eyes. They were weary, no longer afraid. "Such a pity, our courting is over my dear. Though I will remember you fondly, your purpose will better serve me with you dead than alive. Nothing personal, though."

She only saw him cock his arm back. A glare of something shiny and then a blur before she was finally free.

Chapter Eleven

The sound pierced her brain like a molten hot ice pick and she strug-gled to find the source to stop it. Dear God stop it! "What?!" She screamed into the phone once she figured out how.

"Lou, ya need to sit up and wake up." Vinny's voice registered somewhat through her post sleeping-like-the-dead fog. "Sit up Lou, don't lay back down. You gotta get up!"

Lou sat up in bed, eyes still closed. "Why for dammit? It's still dark out!"

"Open your eyes Lou and look out the window."

Lou realized her eyes were still shut so she opened them to see it was dawn and there was light out. "Oh."

"Get up and get dressed. We got a body in Westlake Village and I am halfway to your place. Dress warm, it's freezing out."

"Hey but I'm on desk duty." She rubbed her eyes. "Or did I dream that?"

"Lou. Get. Up. Now. Christ how are you ever going to get a new partner that puts up with your crap?"

"I'm up!" She yelled back at him as she tried to get out of bed but wound up tripping and falling on her face. "Ow, crap!"

"Lou?!" Vinny heard the crack and started to panic.

"Shit I think I just gave myself a black eye. Or broke my nose or something really unattractive." She looked at her hand and saw blood. "Ah Christ, there's blood."

"A geez Lou. Hang up." Vinny clicked off and speed dialed Shevaun and filled her in then clicked off and drove a little faster.

Less then two minutes later Shevaun was running into Lou's room to find her exactly where Vinny figured she would be. Laying face down on the side of her bed holding a stuffed frog to her face, apparently to staunch the bleeding.

"Hi, Momma" She said through the doll.

"Oh for pity's sake Lou you have got to stop being so difficult to wake up! Let me see you!" Shevaun pulled the stuffed animal off of Lou's face to see a rapidly blooming black eye and her nose gushing blood. "Dear God in Heaven!" She tried not to shout and stuffed the frog back in Lou's face. "Keep pressure on it."

"How bad is it?" Joe came in with a mug of coffee in one hand and an ice pack in the other. "Can you get her up in to one of the chairs?"

Shevaun hauled her daughter up and got her into a chair while Joe set the coffee down and ran to get a cloth for her nose.

"Wow, and I thought yesterday sucked." Lou said, muffled through the frog. "I gotta get dressed. Vinny is on his way to get me."

"Yeah, yeah, well lets stop the blood flow first, shall we?" Joe took the frog off her face and winced at the sight of her, then gently pressed the damp cloth to her nose. "Keep pressure on this and put the ice on your eye."

"I'll get a brush and get your clothes ready so when the bleeding stops you can just jump in them." Shevaun dashed into the closet.

"Sorry guys. Thank you. I love you both lots!" Lou felt like a total idiot with her poor parents running around because she had fallen out of bed, again. "Hey maybe I should get rid of those bedside tables. Or pad them."

Shadows of Doubt

After a few minutes, Joe came back into the room with a clean cloth. "Vinny is downstairs getting coffee, so don't worry. He said take your time."

"Thanks Joe. Sorry for waking you guys up so early." Lou had looked at the time and it was barely six.

"You can pay me back by going to the gala with us on Friday." He flashed her a wicked smile, knowing damn well she couldn't refuse after all this. "Okay, let me see this now." He very gently peeled back the cloth and it appeared that the bleeding had stopped. "Better, good. Now be gentle Lou! If you just mash it to wipe the blood off it's going to start bleeding again, you understand?"

"I do. Can I have a slug of coffee to get the taste of blood out of my mouth?"

"Out of your mouth?" Joe looked at her nervously.

"I may have... Well you look and tell me." She smiled wide for him and he gasped as Shevaun squeaked. "Ah crap, I knock out a tooth?"

"Drink some coffee and swish. Might just be blood you swallowed from your nosebleed.

Lou did as he said but felt the loose tooth when it hit the rim of the mug. "Crap. Mom can you call and see if I can get in to the dentist this afternoon? Please? I don't want to keep Vinny waiting any longer." She got up and headed to the closet, wobbling because she was still holding the ice pack over her eye. She stepped out a few minutes later in jeans and a gray turtleneck but only partially in her boots. "Joe, I hate to ask, but if I bend over my nose will start to bleed again. Can you yank these suckers on for me?"

Shevaun came up behind Lou and gingerly brushed her hair to try and erase her bed head. "Swish with some mouthwash gently and you should be good to go. No brushing though!" She paused while Joe yanked Lou's boots on for her and fixed the cuffs of her jeans.

"There, you almost look like nothing happened!" Joe said with a grin.

"I gotta keep you guys on you're toes somehow!" Lou said jokingly as she went into the bathroom to swish as her mother suggested. She made the mistake of looking in the mirror. "Ah Christ, I am so cute." The black eye was only just beginning and it already looked like she had a head on collision with a mack truck. "Vinny is gonna have so much fun with this one." She gently wiped the blood from her nose then her face and realized she had no time to try and conceal the damage. Defeated, she walked out of the bathroom and stared at her two adorable parents. "I really do love you guys. No clue why you put up with me." She gathered up her things and Joe helped her put her coat on then kissed her gently on her uninjured cheek.

"Stay safe out there. I love you too." He smiled at the wounded misfit.

Her mother kissed her softy as well and smiled. "Love you sweat pea. Be safe."

"Will do. Seems I only injure myself at home!" She put the ice pack back on her eye and headed downstairs. Carefully.

The entire ride to the crime scene was a lecture from Vinny about her being more careful during the waking up process. He had gone on and on about making sure whoever her new partner was, Vinny needed time with them to train them properly. She simply took all of it because she was actually afraid if she said anything her loose tooth would fall out in mid sentence and she would never live it down. Even with the delay of the morning's mishap they managed to beat the coroner team to the scene.

"Aw, it's here? You didn't tell me that. I love this course." She took a quick look at her eye in the visor mirror and really wished she hadn't. The bruising was deepening and encompassed not only her eye but her cheekbone as well, confirming Vinny's theory that she had landed half her face on the table and the cell phone was responsible for the nose. "I'm telling everyone you hit me." She informed him as she got out of the car.

Vinny chuckled. "Fine, that will mean the Captain wins the pool. He had five years before I finally beat ya down."

"Don't make me laugh, I'll snort blood all over you and my tooth will come flying out."

They walked up the pathway to the Lakewest Golf Course and were met by a uniformed deputy who escorted them around to the first hole and to a sand bunker near the cart path. The first thing Lou noticed was that the area around the body had been raked perfectly. Not even a squirrel print marred the sand. The naked body of the woman had been laid out carefully with her hands covering the pelvic region in the same manner Angela Talbott had been left. The woman appeared to be a rough forty-five years with dull black hair that was cut very short and choppy. She had no make-up on and her eyes were wide open and clouded over. Her face was heart shaped and despite her being dead, looked like she hadn't been much of a sun person. Her lips were over inflated with collagen or silicone or some other puffing agent. Lou really couldn't understand why anyone would want to have their lips look like an innertube. The grisly part of the crime had two parts. First was the fact that the woman's clearly silicone enhanced breasts had been surreptitiously cut. The full circumference of each had been carved with four straight, overlapping lines that formed what could best be described as giant asterisks. The second unavoidable aspect was that the woman's legs had basically been carved so it looked like she wearing thigh-high fishnet stockings. The slices were meticulous, almost as if the assailant had measured or even sketched the pattern and traced the lines with a very sharp blade. The cuts were just shallow enough to leave a decent impression of netting. The thick band marking, where the stockings would stop on the thigh, were apparently achieved by peeling that portion of skin straight off. It was truly monstrous in its precision.

"No one's touched the body or gone in the bunker?" Vinny asked the uniforms.

"No sir." The deputy that had led them in answered. "The groundskeeper found her when he came to prep the bunkers for the first round of golfers and he found her just like this. Said that the sprinklers go off at three in the morning and that would have erased any rake marks so whoever put her here raked afterward and it was after three."

"Cohen and I have been guarding the bunker since we arrived." The second deputy continued and Lou noted his name tag read Grace. "We were the first on scene."

"Sirs..." Cohen spoke up now. "I recognize her, actually."

Lou turned to Grace's partner and saw the coroner team making their way up the path over his shoulder. "How do you recognize her?"

"Ma'am, she's an old timer porn star actually." He blushed at the implication of his information. "Her name, well screen name at least, is Katarina Purrs." The two other deputies stifled their snickers.

"Seriously?" Lou asked him.

"Seriously." Vinny answered and Lou's head spun around to look at his blushing face.

A crowd had started to gather behind the police barricade as she watched Caroline and Carpesh make their way to the edge of the bunker.

"Morning kids." Lou said with a smile then noticed the look of horror spread across Caroline's face. She remembered her own battered face and quickly stopped smiling.

"What the hell, Lou?" Caroline stepped up to examine her injuries closer.

"If I had a dollar for every time you've said that to me." Lou grinned and winced when Caroline touched her black eye.

"A wake up call." Was all Vinny had to say to get Caroline's eyes rolling in understanding.

"Holy Mother of God." Caroline muttered as she caught sight of the victim over Lou's shoulder.

Lou looked back at the bunker. "Yeah, this one is really a sick twist."

"I gotta make a call real quick before I get in there." Caroline stepped away and made her call then cornered Carpesh as he came up with all their kits.

"Hey Lou." Vinny got her attention. "We need to move the perimeter back a lot. This guy had to come the same way we did to drop her. These lookie-loos are just gonna muck-up any possible evidence over there."

Lou nodded in agreement. "Yeah, we need to get the whole damn parking lot secured. The fairway and the path too. No way he came through these course-side houses to do the drop."

They called in for more uniforms to help with the canvass, secure the first hole and the parking lot completely. They also requested additional forensics to help sift through the sand even though Lou felt that was going to be a dead end. When the manager came out flaming mad about the expansion of the scene, Vinny threatened him with the penalty for impeding a police investigation and told him to go have breakfast somewhere. Caroline and Carpesh had carefully gone into the bunker to tend to the dead but were finding no trace that wasn't simply part of the golf course. The fingerprint scan had yielded that the deceased was in fact legally named Katarina Purrs and had quite a few recent pops for solicitation and possession of controlled substances. Seemed Ms. Purrs liked prescription drugs. Just not her own.

The kicker was that there was no blood, again. Lou wouldn't know for sure until they were done with the body but she would bet the farm there wasn't much blood to be had in the victim either. A grid search was started from the top of the first hole, working down to the parking lot and other than the stray golf ball stuffed in a bush, broken tee or cigarette butt, they were coming up with nothing. Lou and the rest of the searchers walked in their line, step by step as a unit, scanning the earth for any trace of anything. When they passed the pro tee box Lou noticed media vans pulling up outside the perimeter and a considerable crowd growing. She scanned the nosy faces that had come to see death at their back door. Despite all her time on the job, Lou would never understand that. She stumbled forward when her eyes caught sight of Max behind the tape. Fortunately the deputies on each side of her caught her fall otherwise her nose would have been bleeding again. This was ridiculous and when he looked her dead in the eye, she knew that he knew he was caught.

She stepped out of the search line and looked for a way to circle back around the crowd so that no one would notice, then tucked her badge away so the bloodhound reporters wouldn't sniff her out for a statement. She cautiously wheedled her way through the crowd and came up behind Max, grabbed his arm and yanked. It was sort of like grabbing the barrel of a tank with one hand and trying to tow it. When he turned around and looked down at her, his scowl made her think that yanking a man who was over a foot taller then her, and could probably snap her like a twig with his thumb and forefinger, probably wasn't such a good idea.

"Come on!" she stiffened her spine and growled at him.

He didn't resist but instead let her drag him around to the other side of the pro shop keeping the scowl on his face intact.

"What the hell are you doing here? And don't even try to be evasive or witty, I want answers!" She stood with her hands on her hips glaring up at him.

Instinctively he raised his hand and gently brushed his fingertips over the black and blue on her cheek. "What the hell happened?" He demanded, ignoring her question.

"I fell." She said, swatting his hand away and blushing with embarrassment. "Now don't change the subject! I want answers! You were at the morgue for Talbott and the other crime scene because of Winslow. Now you're here for this one. I want to know why and what you know, dammit!"

He simply couldn't help himself and grinned as he stood there and watched his feisty detective, her demanding posture and that adorable glare complete with her lower lip jutting out. That lip that he wanted nothing more than to kiss at that very moment.

"Hello? Anyone in there? Stop looking at me like that and talk!" The way he was looking at her was disconcerting and made her remember that she hadn't been able to brush her teeth. She stepped back and put her hand over her mouth then winced when she bumped her loose tooth.

He bent down and cupped her face gently with both hands and looked at her like no one had ever looked at her before. "What? What is it? Are you alright?" His voice was fraught with panic.

Again she swatted his hands away and took another step back. "Would you stop that! I'm fine! I just knocked my tooth loose is all. Stop changing the subject!"

"You need a dentist right away." He pulled his cell phone out of his pocket and started to dial.

She yanked it out of his hand and looked at him like he had two heads. "I have an appointment later. Now would you stop fussing with me and talk to me, dammit!" She slapped the phone back into his hand and glared at him.

"You're right. We indeed need to talk. I'll have a car pick you up in front of the station at four. Lost Hills?" He looked at her intently.

For a moment she had a mind to slap cuffs on him and force him to talk down at the station, but there were complications going that route. The least of which being that she might not make it to the station with him since he looked yummy beyond belief today in his heathered taupe suite that fit him like no suit should fit a man, and be legal.

"I have plans tonight." She said defiantly but he only smirked at her response.

"I know but this takes precedence. We'll talk then." He took another moment to gently cup her battered cheek in his hand, scowling at the injury. "Take care until then, please." He turned and headed back toward the street, then disappeared into the crowd.

She had marched back up to the crime scene both annoyed and bewildered. Didn't he understand the implications of what she was saying to him? Why in the hell had he been far more concerned about her injuries? It was baffling but she tried to put it out of her head so she could do her job. When the coroner team was finished and Ms. Purrs was being taken away in her body-bag, Caroline approached Lou while snapping off her gloves carefully as her right hand appeared to be bandaged.

"You two make a cute couple." Caroline grinned at her and pulled on a pair of knitted mittens.

Lou snorted. "Oh yeah, real cute. Mr. Tall-Dark-and-Suspect and me with my hamburger face, nice toothed dragon breath disaster walking!"

Her friend snorted then focused. "Lets get the formalities out of the way. Let me tell you what I told Vinny. Time of death was between seven and ten last night with preliminary cause being exsanguination from the severing of the femoral artery of the left thigh. The surface lacerations appear to be inflicted over a good bit of time but I can't be certain until we get her back to the shop."

"Can you make a guestimate?" Lou was pretty sure she knew but wanted Caroline's take.

"I don't like to do that but I would say that whoever did the fishnet work started at least three days ago." Caroline knew exactly where Lou's head was going with all this but kept her mouth shut.

"So he probably grabbed her right after he dumped Winslow. Dammit." Lou clenched her teeth but winced at the pain from her tooth.

"Lou, we can't be sure this is our guy. It could have been some sort of porn star rage or retaliation or some psycho spurned fan. Let's wait and see what we get after the autopsy." Caroline needed to try and stall Lou on the rogue track. This new murder really was putting a wrench in her plan and she needed to try and keep things going the way they had mapped it out.

"Caroline, you and I both know this is our guy. No blood! None in her. None at the scene. She's a woman of dubious reputation just like the others. But I understand where you are coming from and you're right. I need to keep my emotions out of it and work this one by the book and on it's own merits."

Lou took a few minutes to tell Caroline about the captain benching her because of her continuing to investigate the cases that were turned over to LAPD. Caroline seized the opportunity to toss in a few utterances about stupid bureaucracy and ridiculous jurisdictional issues. They were perfect seeds to plant for the plan to work.

"Hey listen..." Lou paused and moved closer to Caroline. "...about tonight, I need to make the dentist then something popped up that I have to deal with so I'll call you later okay?"

Caroline was a little nervous that her plan was going to shit with Lou backing out on meeting up with her later, but she had to go with the flow or it would raise a flag to Lou. "No problem. Just call me if you can get free." She gave her friend a reassuring smile. "Take care of that tooth soon."

Lou chuckled then let Caroline take off to deal with Ms. Purrs. It would be at least noon before they were finished at the scene so that worked out okay with the time her mother had been able to get her in to see the dentist. It was just a matter of conning Vinny into swinging her by there before they went to the station. She figured a caramel macchiato and a double cheeseburger while he waited would be a fair bribe.

The dentist put a thin bar on the back of her teeth to brace the loose tooth to the good ones. He said it would take a few months for the root to strengthen but after that she would be good to go and they could remove the bar. You couldn't see anything, but she spent the entire ride to the station completely ignoring the black and blue that dominated the right side of her face and obsessing over whether or not the tiny wire that was behind her teeth, covered with enamel colored bonding agent, made her look funny. Even as they walked to the communal desks at Lost Hills, she stopped him for the hundredth time.

"You sure it doesn't look funny?" She asked, as he nearly walked right into her.

Vinny threw up his hands. "Lou, for Christ's sake you look like a blueberry with perfect teeth. How's that?"

She closed her mouth and pouted. "Well, there's no need to get nasty about it!"

As they rounded the bend they were met by Gabriel Lincoln, the Watch Commander in charge for the shift. He gave them an eyeball and directed them to an unoccupied office.

"What's up, Gabe?" Lou asked, knowing the man very well, as did Vinny.

"Look guys, this really sucks but I got a call from your captain over at Homicide Bureau about ten minutes ago." He sighed and looked really uncomfortable with the situation. "Lou, he wants you back at the Bureau since you're on desk duty unless I can give you busy work here."

"Are you shitting me?!" Lou could feel the hot molten lava of blood flood into her brain.

"No, I wish I were. Vinny, you're supposed to grab one of the guys here to assist you but Lou is prohibited from working the case with you due to her recent reprimand. But I'm going to lunch and will be gone at least an hour and a half so this conversation will not have taken place until at least three. Follow me?"

Lou couldn't speak. The anger was swirling around her so fast that she couldn't find a solid word to grab on to.

"Thanks Gabe, we appreciate it." Vinny shook the Watch Commander's hand then turned Lou toward the door so they could utilize the time wisely. "Get your ass moving, kiddo."

By quarter after three they had been able to compile a list of known acquaintances to question, addresses, last known place of business and current residence as well as a rough preliminary time line before her captain called her directly at the desk. She had tried to get a word in edgewise but only managed to say 'sir' about four times through the entire conversation. He flat didn't care and wasn't budging. By the time he hung up on her she was so livid that her head was pounding due to her blood pressure being through the roof, which only made her face throb more.

"He's not letting up is he?" Vinny asked as she slammed the phone back into it's cradle.

"Freaking protocol and departmental procedure." She huffed as she leaned back in the rickety chair. "This whole crap about my damaging interdepartmental relationships and lack of regard for politics is going to make me vomit!"

"Look kiddo, you know I am going to keep you in the loop on this regardless. So don't sweat it!" He tried tossing a bone to console her.

"That's not the point!" She was literally pouting.

"Listen…" He sighed, not liking what he was going to say. "I don't mean to salt the wound but I'm going to have to arrange for a uniform to get you home."

Lou's anger was tamped instantly remembering that Max said he was going to have a car waiting for her. She looked at her watch and realized it was almost four already. "Don't worry about it. I have a ride." In a moment that made Vinny wonder if Lou was bi-polar she sat up and smiled at him wide. "Are you sure it doesn't look funny?" She said through her teeth.

The black town car had been waiting as promised and the apparently mute driver had taken her to the hotel without uttering a single word the entire ride. Lou had instantly recognized the man that was waiting for her in the lobby as the same man who had been with Max on the morgue security tape. He wasn't nearly as tall as Max and a bit overbuilt for Lou's tastes which made him feel even more mean despite his extremely jovial and warm greeting. He had introduced himself as Frank Sullivan and was more than happy to meet her as he carefully herded her into the elevator and pushed the button to take them to the penthouse floor. When the lift doors opened she noted the doors to all the suites on the floor were propped open. The elevator was flanked by two enormous men who were dressed in black suits and were obviously armed to the teeth. Lou was apprehensive about getting out of the car until she saw Abby peek her head out one of the doors down the hall and wave at her with a huge smile. This was really odd but curiosity won out over caution.

Frank directed her down the hall to the opened door across from the room Abby was in. When she stepped in, four more hulking men were seated all around the living area reading papers, working on their laptops or other such busy things. All four of them paused and looked up at her, then each flashed a brilliant smile with hi's and hello's followed by 'Detective Donovan'. It was more than odd, it was flat weird and Lou had no idea what to make of it. There was equipment spread out that made the living area of the suite look like an FBI of Secret Service operation. When that thought occurred to her, Lou's eyes went wide with the possibilities. Frank escorted her out onto the terrace where she barely felt the cold due to all the patio heaters that were set up sporadically. When she spotted Max and Caroline, of all people, seated at the round garden table, she nearly fell over.

"What the hell is going on?!" She charged up and glared accusingly at both of them.

"Can I get you a drink, Detective?" Frank asked from behind her and she simply scowled at him. "Right. Maybe later then."

"No, get her a drink Frankie..." Caroline told him. "...something like a mojito. She's going to need it. Maybe a pitcher even? Please?" She batted her eyelashes at the man and he grinned at her before he went inside to accommodate the request.

"Frankie?!" She gawked at Caroline. "What the hell? What the hell?!"

Max rose and pulled out a chair for Lou, trying to contain his grin. "Please sit Detective." He gestured with his hand in a gentlemanly manner but she only gawked at him too. "Sit? Or would you prefer to stand there gaping for an hour or so?"

This was the Max she had had so much fun bantering back and forth with on the golf course two days ago and despite the fact that she was livid and in shock over everything, she couldn't help but notice her heart flutter as he continued grinning at her in that smugly adorable way that he did. She sat with a 'humph'.

Caroline knew Lou so well that she could practically hear what was going on in her head and had to stifle a giggle. The chemistry between Max and Lou was intensely palpable and Caroline knew there was no way Lou would be able to walk away from this.

"Alright Caroline, this is your show, so let's get it on the road." Max sat back down next to Lou.

"Can't we wait for the cocktails? Loosen things up a bit first?" She tried batting her eyelashes like she had with Frank and to Lou's surprise, it annoyed her when she tried it with Max.

"No, we cannot." He scolded her. "Time is of the essence here and you know it. Besides, Joe is probably talking to Shevaun as we speak so lets get on with it."

"Wait a minute here!" Lou wanted to get out of her chair and stomp. "Joe is talking to my mother about what?" She nearly got whiplash looking from Caroline to Max and back again. Max placed his hand over hers in a calming gesture which she normally would have ripped away and quite possibly popped him in the nose, but she didn't.

"It's all fine, please don't panic, Please listen to what Caroline has to say then we will get to everything, I promise." He looked her tenderly in the eyes as he spoke and gently squeezed her hand to reassure her. She didn't know why it helped her to not freak out, but it did. He did. He nodded to Caroline to start.

"Okay sweetie, well, you remember how I had dinner with my uncle and my parents the other night and how I told you I had food poisoning?" When Lou nodded at her she continued. "Well, I didn't really have food poisoning and I am so sorry I lied! But I had some seriously heavy shit laid on me by and about my family that I had to deal with and couldn't talk to you about it until now." Caroline looked at Max and he nodded to her with a smile. "What I need to tell you is pretty heavy duty but it involves you similarly to how it involved me. But it also has stuff to do with these cases and all kinds of things that I just know you will be glad for afterward. But I need you to have an open mind and remember it's me that's talking to you and telling you all this. Can you do that for me?" Caroline took the same tactic that her uncle had in explaining the Sanguinostri to her and when Lou said okay, she told her the whole story. The same story her uncle had told her with a few minor modifications here and there that suited Lou's logic better.

When Frank came with the pitcher of mojitos, Lou barely noticed he was there and sat staring at Caroline, absolutely rapt with interest. She hadn't noticed when he poured them, when Max slid a glass into her hand or when she had drunk half of it. In fact, she hadn't noticed much of anything as every word Caroline uttered sank in and made connections in her head. It was only after Caroline had explained that Joe's family had been Sanguinostri since well, forever, that Lou finally spoke up.

"So Joe opted not to turn or tell my mother any of this to protect her and me? For all these years?" She looked at Max when she asked and he simply nodded. "So this is what he is talking to her about right now? Is that what you meant earlier?" Max nodded again and remained quiet. "Go on." She said as she looked back to Caroline. The implications of everything slowly sinking in. It was then that Caroline started a cursory explanation of the vast infrastructure of the Sanguinostri and how mucked up the West Coast had gotten, thus Max and the Aegis Council shifting bases. She explained how they all worked as a single unit regardless of what actual agency they worked for in the normal world, as it were. That they all held justice in the highest regard without political bureaucracy or red tape of any sort. When Lou raised her right hand to drink from her freshly refilled glass, she realized that Max had been holding her other hand, and she his, but for how long she really couldn't say. She started to think when it was they had started holding hands but something Caroline had just said snapped her back to the real situation at hand.

"Wait a minute!" Lou pulled her hand away from Max and looked at them. "Did you just say that the LAPD detectives that are handling all three of those cases are your people? Sanguinostri people?"

Max leaned back in his chair now and looked at Caroline. "This is where it might be best if I take over, Caroline." She nodded at him, then gulped her drink nervously. "Yes Detective, we arranged for Sanguinostri officers to take charge of the cases. Due to ineffective management, which I am in the process of rectifying, we do not have such a solid presence within your agency. Only a few select people who have risen in rank to more administrative positions."

"Then why the hell can't I work on the cases? If you're the grand poohbah with all your higher standard, black and white justice without loopholes and red tape and all that other crap that I am sick to death of! You're obviously telling me all this for a reason, so fix it!" She actually poked him in the shoulder in a demanding gesture and heard someone snort and laugh inside the suite.

"Well, it isn't all that simple now, is it?" He cocked his head sideways and smiled at her.

"Well it should be! Just make it be!" She mocked him and cocked her head in the same manner he had at her.

"Lou, we are talking about my people here..." He placed his hand gently on her knee as he leaned in to speak carefully to her. "...an entire genus of people that I must protect and keep secret from the masses at all costs. I need you to understand that and be clear about exactly why it is we are telling you all of this."

"Lou, sweetie." Caroline interrupted for a minute. "These are my people too. My family. That was why my parents came into town. I had to learn and accept that and vow to hold them above all others. I couldn't do that, even though it's my parents we are talking here, unless it included you, too."

"We hold humankind in the highest regard. We are all intrinsically linked, but our people..." Max gestured to Caroline and himself. "... must come first for the sake of our most basic survival. The secret must be kept and protected. We must be kept and protected and in turn a great part of that is the protection of the average person as well."

"So you want me to swear my life for the protection of the Sanguinostri? Above all other oaths including as a police officer?" She looked at him intently.

"It's not necessarily one or the other. It's in addition to. Of course with ours being the first priority." He made it sound so simple.

"So I would have to lie to Vinny." Her partner sprang to mind instantly and she got up to pace.

Max sighed. "We need good people but that is something you need to consider carefully before you ask me to involve him. It's a domino effect so to speak."

Lou thought about her partner, his wife and their baby on the way. When she thought about him she understood Joe's reasoning for keeping it all from her mother and her for so long. She understood it all, oddly enough, and it made perfect sense to her.

"I need to talk to my mother. Now." She spun towards Max and demanded.

Max nodded, understanding. "She and Joe are on their way as we speak. She demanded the exact same thing of him before she would make a decision."

"What about my uncle? My cousins?" She hated the thought of ever lying to her uncle.

Max had thought of all this before Caroline had come up with her plan, which he had to admit was working out brilliantly. But he had come to terms with himself, and admitted to Frank, Abby and the others that he would pretty much agree to whatever terms Lou set for him in order to have her agree to be indoctrinated. "That will be for your mother and you to discuss and decide. But I am open to whatever you need to be true to you're heart in all of this." He stood up and walked to her, taking her hands in his. "I want you to be happy, Lou. I don't want to make your life miserable or more complicated than it already has been. I am not going to force you to live a life you cannot be content with. That is the exact opposite of what I want for you."

She looked up into his eyes and knew without a shadow of a doubt that he meant every word he was saying. God help her, she trusted him completely.

"Tallulah." The sound of Lou's mother's voice had her spinning around so fast she got dizzy, but she saw Abby leading her out onto the terrace.

"Momma!" She ran to her mother and threw her arms around her.

"Are you okay, sweet pea? I know this is all a bit hard to take in." Shevaun smoothed Lou's hair back and tucked a few stray strands behind her ear, looking at her with great concern. "Joe is so worried that you hate him now!"

"What? That is ridiculous!" If anything, Lou had a greater love and respect for Joe given everything he sacrificed to protect her mother and her.

"Let me give you ladies some time to yourselves and I'll see to Joe and perhaps some dinner." Max brushed his hand across Lou's back ever so lightly as he walked past her and smiled softly to Shevaun as he turned for the door.

Lou grabbed his hand before he could go and he whipped around, wide eyed at her gesture. "Please make sure Joe knows I love him? And don't go too far away, please?"

His heart skipped several beats at her requests and he flashed her such a smile that he felt like the sky wouldn't be able to contain it. He nodded and squeezed her hand before she let go. He caught a glimpse of Caroline before he crossed the threshold and she was bouncing in her chair, grinning from ear to ear.

Shevaun dragged Lou to the table, holding her hand tight as they sat, then she took Caroline's hand in her other. Are you girls alright? Caroline, Joe told me you took the Oath, are you okay? Your parents must be so relieved!"

"I am wonderful, truly Mrs. McAllister. Especially now that you and Lou are here. You two were my only deal breakers on this." She pulled her chair in to sit closer to them.

Lou pushed her glass in front of her mother then took Max's and drank deeply.

"So I guess we need to make a decision here, don't we?" Shevaun spoke up after taking a healthy sip from her drink. "Quite an intense whammy we got tossed in our laps. The funny thing is, it's not as overwhelming as it probably should be, ya know what I mean? The truth is, and I don't mean this to put any pressure on you baby but, you're the only hitch in the giddy-up here."

"What do you mean me?" Lou goggled at her mother.

"Well its your willingness to put this above your job and all. Even thought it's the whole 'protect and serve' thing but on such a more ginormous scale now, isn't it?" Shevaun looked over at Caroline. "Who knew? But anyway, for me its simple if you're taken out of the equation." She shrugged her shoulders then took another sip of her drink.

"Again I ask, what do you mean, Momma?"

"Sweetheart, Joe has been carrying this around with him as a secret to protect us for over twenty-five years. He loves us that much and has sacrificed for my sake and the sake of my daughter. You and I know what a good man he is and if he holds the Sanguinostri in such high regard, well it's just a no-brainer for me. Bring it on I say! Plus all the good they do, protecting us from them and ourselves. I think we could learn a lot from them if you ask me."

That was something Lou had been thinking about since Caroline started telling her the story. Over the years, Lou had seen the true depravity that humans were capable of. The greed and lack of conscience that surrounded her on a daily basis even on mundane levels. Animal testing, litter bugs, kids stealing other kid's shoes, crappy tippers. Hell, in Hollywood alone she was sure there were women who would murder to get their hands on one drop of Max or Abby's blood if there was a chance at chasing one wrinkle away for good. How sick was it for that to have occurred to her? All of this may have been tossed at her mere minutes ago, but some things were always crystal clear to Lou.

"Yeah but too many normal humans are so greedy and power hungry they would exterminate them while trying to get what they have." Lou said with a tone of disgust. "We have to protect them Momma, don't you think?"

"I do! I absolutely do!" Shevaun patted her daughter's hand. "Not sure about the whole turning thing although Joe says they have a test they can do to see if you're blood is favorable to it and all."

Caroline nodded "Yeah they are actually running mine now even though my family line has a ninety-eight percent survival rating."

"I'll tell you it sure wouldn't suck having to not see another wrinkle crop up on this face again!" Shevaun and Caroline laughed.

"You would turn, Momma?" Lou asked. Her mother's statement confirmed her own argument she was having in her head.

"Oh if I knew I wasn't going to croak in the process? Live a thousand lifetimes with Joe? You bet your ass I would!" She answered without hesitation.

Lou considered the possibility of her mother and Joe never getting ill. Always being as they were in her life. Never having to face the possibility of losing them. It really was a no-brainer. All of it was when she really considered. Okay, having to keep the appearance of proper protocol might be tough but being able to handle her cases with all those resources at her disposal? No red tape or bureaucracy?

"Excuse me a minute, I'll be right back." Lou got up from the table as both women looked at her oddly but Caroline squeezed Shevaun's hand and gave her a nod.

Before Lou got to the door, Max walked out and looked directly at her, as if he had known she needed him. It was amazing how Lou felt her chest loosen, as if she could breathe again as soon as she saw his face.

"I need to ask you..." She started.

"Anything." He smiled down at her.

"What about Vinny? I don't want him put in the same position that Joe was put in when he met my mom." He could tell this was weighing on her. "I can handle lying to him but I need him protected somehow. Can you help me with that? Lou looked at him in earnest.

"I've thought about that while considering all of this. His wife is expecting their first child, correct?" Lou nodded and he continued. "And he is going to be taking the Lieutenant's exam? So he'll be relegated to desk work as your superior, is that correct?"

"Yes, that's the plan at least."

"Well, I can make certain that plan succeeds. Even fast track it if you wish. Perhaps down the road you'll see him as a viable asset, but until you say so, and no one else but you, we can make sure he is safe and happy behind a desk." He brushed the back of his hand gently across her bruised cheek.

"You would do that? You would do that for me?" She placed her hand over his and held it to her cheek a moment.

Max sighed. "Let's face it Lou, there isn't a whole hell of a lot I wouldn't do for you and I think you know that, deep down in your gut."

She smiled up and him then bolted over to her mother.

"Okay, so we do this together then? I'm not sure about the whole turning thing but I can decide that whenever right?" She looked at Caroline first, then back to Max.

He smiled. "If and when you are ready. It's your choice." His smile faded and his expression became very serious. "You need to be certain of this, Tallulah. This is not something you can take lightly. I need you to swear to me and the Sanguinostri, the Oath by Blood, and mean it with your life. Make no mistake of that, Lou."

Lou understood the weight of the decision she was faced with and nodded. She knew deep in her bones it was right, almost as though she had just been handed a missing part of herself that she hadn't known was missing until now. "Momma?"

Shevaun looked at her daughter thoughtfully and smiled, then turned to Max. "So do we have to dress up for this? And do we do it before dinner or after? I'm starved!"

Lou threw her arms around her mother and Caroline did the same, wrapping arms around her two most favorite women. It wasn't but a second later that Joe came rushing out of the suite and tossed his arms around them all, crying tears of joy.

Once things had settled, Max and Caroline admitted they had been optimistic about what Lou and Shevaun's decision would be. With

Joe's permission they had made preparations for the ceremony to be held at the McAllister home with an intimate celebratory dinner to follow. With the help of Marta the housekeeper, whom Shevaun and Lou both had been shocked to learn was a full turned Sanguinostri, everything was ready when they arrived. Max had assumed Caroline, Frank and himself would be the only others in attendance but Shevaun had insisted that Abby, Niko, Finn, Connor and Yuri all join them. A simple call from Max had insured there would be enough food to accommodate the extra guests.

When they arrived at the house, Marta greeted them exuberantly, barely being able to contain her joy over the occasion. There was a waiter and a chef in the kitchen and the formal dining room had been set for what appeared to be royalty. After taking their coats, Marta ushered them all into the family room that had been partially rearranged and dressed with glowing candles and a roaring fire in the fireplace. Both Shevaun and Lou excused themselves briefly so that Lou could get out of her dirty jeans she had been wearing since the crime scene and Shevaun had said she wanted to wear something a little less ordinary. It was their moment so no one minded the wait. Joe led the guests to the bar and fixed everyone a drink. He was barely able to contain his delight over the fact that everything was working out as he had never dared to dream possible.

"I must say it was Caroline's brilliant plan." Max conceded that appealing to the cop had been the perfect strategy.

"It wouldn't have been so simple had it not been for coordinating mother and daughter at the same time. And those unexpected heartstrings didn't hurt to tug on either." Caroline winked at Max.

"Let's leave all that alone now, shall we?" He wasn't really asking so much as telling, and Caroline got the message loud and clear.

Shevaun returned first which made Max a little nervous, knowing full well that Lou wasn't one to fuss with her appearance. Her mother had changed into a simple but lovely amber velvet tunic with three-quarter sleeves, simple black knit trousers and velvet ballet slippers in the same shade as her tunic. She had bounced down the stairs and literally bopped up to the bar, ordering the bartender to fix her a drink. Joe was all too happy to oblige. Shevaun glanced around the room and smiled, then noticed a small table set by the hearth and the object that sat on top of it.

"Joe, isn't that the carving knife you said belonged to your great, great, grandfather or something?" She pointed.

"Actually yes, that wasn't a total lie." He smiled sheepishly. "That is the knife that has been used to perform this ceremony in my family for over one thousand years. It was carved by my great great grandfather from the horn of a now extinct species of goat that once lived in the Carpathian mountains." He smiled as he slid her drink across the bar to her.

"Over a thousand years?" She looked at him aghast.

"Yes my love, approximately." He reached for her hand and kissed her knuckles gently.

When she remembered to blink, she squinted at him. "How many other priceless things do you have around here that I have been oblivious to?"

"Some." Joe grinned. "It's going to be so much fun telling you all the stories."

Max was truly happy for Joe finally being able to speak freely about his life, his history, his family with the woman he adored. Life was far more worth living when you had someone to share it with.

No sooner then than thought floated across his mind, the Fates tossed out their impeccable timing again with Lou walking into the room toward him. He noticed she had done something to her hair and she looked softer for it, despite the fact that the black eye and bruises on her face were even deeper then they had been before. She had donned a simple cashmere sweater and matching cashmere pants in a rich milk-chocolate color that suited her completely. Nearly all traces of the tough detective had vanished and the impish woman that had his heart neatly tucked in her pocket stood only a few feet away, smiling at him softly. She was simply the most beautiful thing he had ever seen.

"Shall we get this show on the road before we starve to death?" Lou grinned and sauntered up to Caroline, giving her a bump with her hip in a cheeky gesture.

Max drained the last of the whiskey from his glass and turned to Joe. "I think it's only proper that you conduct the rite," he said to him.

Joe looked at Max in shock. "My Dom, I couldn't possibly..."

"I'll stand with you Joe, but you have waited for this privilege for far too long. It's only right." Max moved to stand by the small table where the ceremonial knife rested and motioned for everyone to gather around.

Abby, Frank, Caroline and the boys all sat about on the ample couches and watched as Joe guided Caroline and Shevaun to stand in front of the fireplace with them. There was no rehearsing or practice run to the ritual. It was one of those odd little anomalies that when someone took the Oath, the rite was burned into their memories forever. Every word and action was embedded crisply and permanently. So when Joe had them in proper position, he turned so he could face them both. He knew exactly what was required and began without pause, holding his hand up so his right palm faced them.

"Upon our hands we have what is often referred to as a lifeline. This is as it's known to the Sanguinostri as well. For we hold each other's lives within our hands and are bound by blood to one another in all things, above all else. It is for life, our people, our life-blood, that we exist, and we shall give of our own life, our own blood, to keep it so."

Joe paused and waited while Max turned and picked up the blade with great care and respect. He held it up as if in offering to the sky, closed his eyes and spoke in what Lou recognized to be Latin. Once Max finished the invocation, he placed the blade against his right palm so that the curve edge lined up perfectly with his own lifeline. Lou felt a warmth filling her as she watched his movements. The reverence in each gesture, in each syllable he uttered. Then she watched him press the blade into his flesh until his blood began to flow. Max never flinched as he passed the blade to Joe who then began speaking in Latin as well and pressed the blade to his own hand and made the same cut to himself. He turned to Shevaun and spoke soberly, asking her if she came of free will and in absolute surety of her choice that once committed to in blood, she could never take back. Lou's mother never hesitated as she held out her hand and said yes. Once the cut was made, Shevaun looked to her husband as he clasped her hand in his. A tear streamed down Joe's face as he beamed at her like Lou had never seen before. Max stood close behind Joe, reaching around to encase husband and wife's hands in his own. Both men closed their eyes and Max spoke again in the language Lou recognized, but could not understand, all the while Joe held on tightly. Once Max was done, Joe kissed Shevaun softly as another tear rolled down his cheek.

When Lou had gone up to change she had been second guessing the situation. She had even told herself that she needed to be prepared for chickening out at the last minute. Ultimately she promised herself that she would walk away if that was what she felt she needed to do. But when it came her turn, she forgot all of that. Everything fell out of focus except for Max's face. The pounding of her heart drifted into silence and all she could hear were the words he spoke. She heard everything he said with such depth and clarity that it filled her entire being with an ethereal calm. Regardless of whether or not she understood the language, she understood what was being said. When it came time for her to make her Oath, it was the simplest, most natural thing she had ever done. There was absolutely no hesitation, no fear and no doubt. In fact, she was eager to get it out. To commit and stand with those who had stood for so long before her. In that split second when her own blood flowed, the depth and breadth of what the Sanguinostri was became crystal clear in her mind and soul. Lou knew she finally belonged to something beyond her preconceived notion of family. She knew she truly belonged to something that was unconditionally worth spilling her life-blood for.

Everything had gone better than Max could ever have dreamed. Shevaun and Joe had insisted that he sit at the head of the table, as the Dominor should. The food had been exceptional and the company more so as he scanned the faces that surrounded him. He decided these were the faces he cared about most on this earth. Even Marta who sat with Yuri and Finn at the end of the table, telling off-color jokes that had the two men blushing. Lou, Niko, Abby and Frank were discussing the finer points of Glock versus Sig for their personal choice in combat pistols. Caroline, Joe and Shevaun were chatting about the upcoming gala at the museum and how fun dressing up was going to be. There were smiles everywhere and laughter bounced off the rafters. Max sat back and took it all in as something he could completely get used to. Its not that he didn't enjoy his friends back in D.C. or Toronto, he did. But these people had showed him so much, some of them in a such a very short time, of how hope, compassion, love and faith can overcome anything.

"Wait a minute…" Lou's urgent voice interrupted his musings. "…that gala thing you want me to go to is at the Museum of Art? The Byzantine thing?" She asked Joe.

"That's the one. It's being thrown by one of our elder Sanguinostri, Albert von Massenbach. Max served with him on the Aegis in Britain."

Lou looked at Max. "Oh?"

"Yes, I did. After I moved from Rome to Britain but before I was elevated to Dominor. I was certain at the time that Albert would have been elevated because he was far better at politics than I was." Abby snorted and Max only smiled. "Albert was a good sport, we worked well together. He decided to retire himself from governance when the Dom position for Britain consolidated with France so that I could handle North America. I've seen him a few times here and there at various galas and functions over the decades. He's done well for himself in antiquities, and shipping, I think. I'm looking forward to seeing him Friday. A very pleasant fellow."

Lou just goggled at him for a minute. "How the hell old are you?"

"Lou!" Shevaun scolded her daughter as laughter erupted from the far end of the table.

"He's older than my uncle, I know that much." Caroline said with a raised eyebrow as she stuffed another shrimp in her mouth.

"Really?" Shevaun was curious now after having an idea how old Caroline's uncle really was.

"I know my birthday on the modern calendar is April 21st. How about we settle there?" Max smiled uncomfortably.

Abby quickly stepped in and tried to clip the inquisition. "Maybe we can leave it as Max knowing that Rome was not built in a day." She grinned towards him and he nodded to her in thanks.

Lou flapped her hands about and leaned back in her chair. "We got off topic here. Let's get back to the gala. I'm going over all this rogue stuff in my head now that I really know what's going on." She turned to face Max and looked at him intently. "You know Winslow was doing volunteer work for her professor, cataloging for that event?"

Ah, there was his detective, he thought with a grin but quickly focused on what she was saying. "No, I actually didn't know that." He gave disapproving glances to Frank, Abby and Niko.

"Hey! Don't be looking at me!" Abby was clearly defensive. "I've been dealing with the new Council, new agents, freaking regional planning, building and safety inspectors!." She pointed at the two men who had been in charge of compiling data on the victims. "Rogue data is on them!"

"Well, anyway..." Lou ignored the finger-pointing and continued. "...the professor that Winslow was volunteering for was hand picked to work on this exhibit. She and two other professors from different universities. This professor was super reluctant to give me any data other than Winslow was pretty much saddled with cataloging things as they arrived and had been doing so for weeks. If she wasn't in class or at the strip joint, she was working on this gala exhibit."

"Why the hell does it have to be Byzantine?" Niko grumbled, having a personal connection to the topic of the exhibit.

Abby tossed a roll at him "Don't start that again!"

Max ignored them both and looked at Frank. "When did Massenbach come to Los Angeles? And who was with him?"

"I think it was four or five months ago, but I'll verify." Frank consulted his Blackberry. "I'll have to check my records back at the hotel to give you a list of his entourage, but I know that he had seven with him when he landed, and has thirty-two on record right now. I looked into all of that when you got the invitation, though. Before Winslow turned up dead."

Max thought for a moment. "Talk to all of them again. Perhaps one of them crossed Winslow's path or has some sort of detail that will be helpful, that was overlooked the first time."

"None of those people that loan their collections to museums ever has anything to do with the actual exhibit, you know that Max." Niko raised a valid point. "They just dump their valuables on one facility or another and take the bows. Highly unlikely they ever had direct contact with Winslow."

"I realize that, but get the detective dossiers on all of them and have them delivered to her as soon as possible anyway." Max looked back at Lou. "Abby will make sure you have copies of everything we have on the rogue as well. You'll need to keep me up to speed on your findings. I would prefer daily briefings." Abby and Caroline snorted at Max's handy way of keeping in touch with Lou, but hushed themselves quickly.

"My findings? I won't find shit unless this rogue is hiding in the supply closet at the bureau. My captain has me sitting on a desk for the week." Lou grumbled and slumped in her chair.

She looked to Max like a little girl who had just been scolded. She hated being on the sidelines, it was very obvious, and she made no attempt to hide her disdain of it.

"I wouldn't worry too much about that." He grinned and sipped from his glass.

Chapter Twelve

Anticipating taking the train in to the office, since Vinny was working the case she should have been working on, Lou had gotten up very early. She peered out through the binoculars at Max's construction while she drank her coffee and wondered what it would be like living so close to him and her new extended family. The previous night had been really wonderful, even if it was shocking and hard to take in at first. But dinner had been truly enjoyable with the mundane chatter and silliness. Even the discussions on her unknown suspect and learning things about him that filled in gaps and created even more.

The serial freak had been murdering women off and on for the better part of two and a half centuries. He had been a thorn in Max's side for all that time and one in hers for only the past couple of weeks. She really wasn't sure how the hell she was going to make a difference in catching this guy if they hadn't been able to yet. Max had insisted that she would be invaluable and that her fresh perspective alone would be the turning point. Whatever. Aside from the rogue, she had been informed that she would be playing an integral part in the actual law enforcement aspect of Max's operations in Los Angeles. A secret agent within the department, as Caroline had put it. That made Lou laugh even now.

It was just after seven when her cell rang and she heard Vinny's muffled voice calmly telling her to wake up on the other end.

"I've been up for half an hour already." She grinned.

"Well good! We can grab some pancakes before we head over to, get this, Spank Me Productions." Her partner said it with a snort but still sounded like he was talking through a pillow.

"What are you talking about?"

"Ms. Purr's last known place of employment. She had a contract at that porn studio."

Lou could hear him lay on his horn. "Vinny you sound funny, are you talking on a cell while driving? That's illegal you know?"

"Vera got me this headset thing. It's hands free." He shouted obscenities at someone who had apparently cut him off, again.

"Vinny, I'm on desk duty remember? Captain's orders?" Lou hated reminding him of that.

"What? No, he called me around nine last night. Said to make sure you and I checked the studio out before we came in. I asked him about you being benched but he said that was over, said you would know why. You don't know why?" Vinny suddenly sounded like he was falling down a hole as he muttered more obscenities. "I dropped my headset, I can't hear you Lou. I'll be there in about a half hour. I gotta fill up the clunker first. Hanging up now!"

Lou hung up and stood there a moment, puzzled. She wasn't clear on what her captain had meant but she had an idea that needed following up on.

"You awake, sunshine?" Joe popped his head in to see if Lou was up.

"I am." She smiled at him. "What are you up to?"

Joe walked in with a mug of his famous coffee and swapped it for the one she was holding. "Thought you might like this before you took off."

"Thanks! This is just what the doctor ordered. Mine sucks." Lou drank deeply from the mug then looked back at Joe. "Hey, so you're real deep in the Sanguinostri stuff right?"

"That would be one way of putting it." He grinned.

"Would you know who everyone is? I mean like Captain Davidson or some other high up in the department?"

"Yes, Davidson is one of us. He's a Steward though, not turned." Joe confirmed what Lou had only just suspected and she could only roll her eyes. "I think Abby will be providing you with all the contacts you'll need. Although Max may want to do that personally."

"I don't understand why, if Davidson is one of us, he would bench me." She knitted her brows trying to make sense of it.

"Well honey, at the time, you weren't one of us, were you? Remember, he's brass, not out in the trenches, which means he mitigates and manages. We can't have civilians running around possibly revealing things that could wind up throwing a light on us. I'm sure the second you were indoctrinated Max gave Davidson the go-ahead to let you work."

"But Vinny gets to work the case and he's not indoctrinated?" The logic was not clear to Lou.

"Yes, that's true but Vinny didn't put the cases all together did he? You did. If not for you and Caroline he would never have put the cases together so he's not entirely a worry is he?" Joe tried to make it sound not too terribly insulting to Vinny's detective skills. "Plus there's the whole matter of his looking to take a desk and get off the beat. He's far more focused on that right now."

"So basically you're saying I was benched because I'm so damn good?" She batted her eyelashes as she finished her coffee.

Joe grinned at her and felt so happy at the fact that they were actually having a conversation of this nature at all, after all these years.

"Basically. Now I'll let you get on your way, but remember, when you get any pangs of guilt about fibbing to Vinny, it's for his own protection."

Lou nodded, understanding it all very clearly. "I know that. I don't have a problem with that at all. It's like you did for Mom and me, for love. I understand that completely." She took that opportunity to hug him tight. To reassure him that she loved him and didn't harbor any bad feelings over his keeping such a secret from them for so long.

Joe hugged Lou tightly and tried not to cry for the hundredth time since yesterday. He was just so relieved and happy to have both of his worlds merged into one. Finally. Joe had feared for so long that if he told Shevaun and Lou, they would hate him and leave him. He wouldn't have survived that.

When Vinny pulled up into the driveway, Lou bounced over to the car and hopped in. It took her about four seconds of looking at him for things to really register, then she burst out laughing.

"What?!" He demanded.

"Vinny..." Lou tried to control herself but it was almost impossible. "That is not how you wear that hands-free setup."

Looking at her technologically challenged partner, she could not contain her laughter one bit. Vinny had the earbud portion exactly as it was supposed to be but the microphone section that was several inches down on the cord, should have been clipped to his shirt. Instead, Vinny had the cord wrapped over the top of his head and the microphone was stuffed in his other ear with the clip attached to his earlobe. It was no wonder the man had sounded muffled when he called. Lou took a moment to arrange the device properly while her partner just watched with total irritation.

"There was no diagram or instructions! The little picture on the side of the phone shows a regular headphone set up. So how was I supposed to know!" He jammed the car into drive once Lou had finished. "What happened to you're hand?" He asked, noticing the bandage.

Lou had already thought of a brilliant explanation for her wound. "Ah someone freaking put a knife blade up in the dishwasher and I stuck my hand in, not looking."

"Ouch! I've done that before. My hand smelled like liverwurst for a week."

Lou looked at him with her eyebrow raised. "Liverwurst?"

"Yeah. Might have been psychosomatic but I think it's because Vera doesn't rinse the dishes very well before she stuffs them in the washer. That's a pet peeve of mine, ya know."

Lou could only shake her head. These were the moments she would miss when Vinny took his desk. The odd little quirky conversations they had throughout the day that made her laugh. But Vinny was going to be a father and his family needed to come first. It was also better since she had to keep secrets. This way she wouldn't feel so guilty about it.

They arrived at Spank Me Productions just before nine and if it were not for the name and the numerous framed posters for the various productions hanging on the walls, it could have been any administrative office anywhere. Decorated in cool grays and blues with shiny chrome accents, it was a nicely polished facility, on the surface. They had been asked to wait in the main lobby until someone could escort them back. It seemed the person they needed to speak with about Katarina Purrs was very hands on with the production end of things and was currently on set in the back of the facility. After several minutes of waiting, an amazonian woman who reminded Lou a lot of the weather anchor she detested came to lead them back. When they finally arrived on set, if you could call it that, they were greeted by a woman of about five feet ten inches in height who was dressed in a very sharp gray tweed pantsuit. Her gold hair was pulled back tightly into a knot and her keen eyes peered through thick black framed glasses. She introduced herself as Tawny Peters and apologized for having to meet them on set but that the death of Purrs had made a mess of scheduling.

"She had one last shoot on her contract and we were supposed to start today." Peters explained. "Since she screwed us out of that too, we had to shuffle things to minimize losses. Once we book talent, we book production staff and they get paid whether or not we shoot."

"What do you mean by screwing you out of that, too? There were difficulties with Purrs?" Vinny inquired of the woman, trying desperately not to gawk at the scene behind her that appeared to be a bastardization of a children's story.

"Difficulties is an understatement! That woman was a hag!" Peters composed herself by pulling off her glasses and pinching the bridge of her nose before she continued. "Her heyday as an adult film star died with legwarmers but thanks to a not so indiscreet indiscretion on the part of our CEO, she had an iron clad contract for 250 leading roles. "Taming the Cougar" was her last one and was supposed to start shooting today. Now we need to recast it in a hurry before we lose serious cash. I know that sounds cold to you but the woman was a skank of the highest proportion, and in my business, that is saying a lot!"

Lou refrained from laughing at the woman's statement as well as at the woman that suddenly appeared behind her dressed as an x-rated version of a red-headed rag doll. "Can you think of anyone who'd want to harm Purrs or would be willing to take her out to land her role?"

"Oh God who wouldn't want to?" Peters snickered then took a sip from her bottle of water. "But for that roll? Hell no. It was written

Shadows of Doubt

specifically for her, to accommodate the multitude of sins that her pill popping, coke-snorting, martini swilling to the extreme of excess had wrought on her body. I mean you saw her, right? Someone got a telephoto of her body posted online last night and I am telling you she looked better dead!"

Vinny winced. "That's a little harsh, don't you think?"

Several production assistants that were eavesdropping all said "No" at the same time.

"See!" Peters exclaimed as she flapped her arms. "Anyone, and I mean anyone in this business is going to tell you that woman was a hag and a misery to deal with. She slept with anyone and anything that got her high, drunk, a buck or something shiny to drape on her over-siliconed carcass. I know you are going to ask me for names but there simply is not enough ink and paper in the universe."

There were chuckles and snorts from numerous people on set over Peters' last sentence. Lou and Vinny looked at each other in amazement over the resounding disdain apparently everyone in the company felt for Katarina Purrs. The rag doll woman wearing a wig made of red yarn walked over to them to add her two cents.

"Hey, Tawny is absolutely right about Kat. She was a biatch and a hag. I'm Candy by the way." The woman said it with a cheesy smile that she probably had meant to be charming. "You're going to have a long list of suspects if you look inside the industry here. But I do know she had a couple creepy fans that she always would go on and on about. They sent her letters and emails and stuff all the time that she would just go on and on about. Her adoring fans and shit, ya know?" The woman actually snapped her gum. A cliché' in the flesh. "I hadn't seen her in a couple weeks but she came in while I was shooting Bambi's Big Adventure and was all pissy about June at the front desk giving out her new email address to some weirdo fan that was going on about if he couldn't have her, no one would." She snorted loudly. "Like that guy's all stable and has any taste or anything. But I know June was real upset about it. Maybe ask her?"

Vinny and Lou thanked them all for their cooperation and stopped to check with June about Candy's story. June was far too mild mannered and sweet to have been tied up with Purr's death. When asked about the fan, she was clearly rattled. She had felt horrible about falling for such a rouse. A gentleman had called representing himself as a reporter from a reputable entertainment rag who was doing a piece on retro pornography and it's lost art. Lou and Vinny both thought that June should have known it was a bullshit story right then and there but to June, it had seemed like something Ms. Purrs would have lapped up like warm milk. June agreed to forward Purrs' contact information to him via email, which she had, and Purrs went through the roof over the whole thing being a fraud. In what appeared to be true Katarina Purrs form, she was less than interested in her information being given out than she was livid there was no real story and that he was just an obsessed fan. June was able to provide Lou and Vinny with the man's email address and Lou discreetly texted it to Frank to see if he could come up with a name attached to the account faster then their techs at the station could.

Since they had opted to skip breakfast until after their visit to Spank Me, they headed to their favorite pancake joint on the west side. Halfway through her short-stack, Lou got a text back from Frank with the name Toby Bender. As luck would have it, Mr. Bender just so happened to reside within ten miles of the diner.

"Guy's name sounds like he should be in porn. How'd you come up with that info before me?" Vinny asked as he tossed the tip on the table.

"A hacker friend. Techs will come up with it eventually but this gives us a head start." Lou yanked the check out of Vinny's hand and raced for the cashier.

"Hey!" He shouted after her, but he was too late.

When they pulled onto Bender's street they saw several LAPD black and white's as well as the coroner truck.

"Uh oh." Vinny said under his breath.

Lou nodded in agreement as they parked then got out of the car. When they flashed their badges and informed the uniformed officer at the perimeter why they were there, he directed them to apartment 4C, which just so happened to be the apartment of one Mr. Bender. They rounded the corner just as Carpesh was coming out of the apartment, barking orders at the techs and nearly running into Vinny's chest.

"What, watch where you..." When Carpesh registered Lou's presence his demeanor changed instantly. "... Detective Donovan!" He smiled at her brightly. "Er... and Detective DeLuca. What a surprise to see you here. Forgive me, I wasn't watching where I was going."

"No problem, sport." Vinny hulked his shoulders to appear more intimidating to the rather small Carpesh. "You okay there?"

"Oh yes, no damage!" Carpesh chuckled nervously.

"What's going on here Carpesh?" Lou interrupted Vinny's alpha-male act.

"Ah, oh! Toby Clifford Bender, deceased. Isn't that odd that his first name is actually Toby? Not Tobias? With such a formal middle name?" Carpesh wandered off topic.

"Yes, that is odd but how is he deceased?" Lou brought the apparently A.D.D. Carpesh back to the question.

"Oh yes, yes! So far I would have to say a clean cut case of suicide. Hung himself from the curtain rod in the only bathroom of the apartment. Quite a sturdy curtain rod for such a shabby place, don't you agree?" Peter Carpesh was a pleasant man but Lou could see now why Vinny had his slang name for him.

Vinny rolled his eyes. "Yeah, you'd be right about that. Who's the lead officer on this? Do you know?"

Carpesh turned and stuck his head back into Bender's apartment and called out to someone inside. Turning back to Lou and Vinny he smiled again, very brightly at Lou. "Peretta is the lead, he's coming. I best get back to work now. Its a pleasure seeing you both again. Let me know if I can be of any assistance." Carpesh scooted past them and disappeared around the bend.

Moments later a mountain of a man came out of the apartment, peeling off his gloves. He was classic Latin coloring with eyelashes that looked like they were fake, they were so damn thick. Lou couldn't help but stare.

"Detective Donovan?" The LAPD homicide detective extended his hand to her immediately and she broke from her eyelash envy to shake the man's hand.

"Yeah, this is my partner, Vinny DeLuca." She pointed and the man offered his hand to Vinny.

"A pleasure. I bet I can guess what brings you to my crime scene." He said with a blinding smile. "Let me get you some gloves and booties then we can get you inside." Detective Peretta walked around the corner then came back within moments holding out the required accessories.

When they entered the apartment, Lou instantly felt the strong urge to shower. It was not dirty as in dust or grime, it was dirty as in creepy twisted pervert lived there, which was obviously the case.

"Whoa." Vinny gawked at the images of Katarina Purrs that were hung, taped or tacked to nearly every inch of wall space.

"Yeah." Peretta nodded. "That's exactly what I said when I walked in."

The images of Purrs appeared to be blown up stills from her older films that depicted her in assorted lewd positions. Bender had obviously taken great care to pick all his favorites, even having some matted and framed. The studio apartment was small and dark with what little you could see of the walls being painted a ruby red. The brown shag carpet was strewn with black area rugs that appeared to be homemade cut outs of over-endowed women, like those mudflaps you see on eighteen-wheeler trucks. Nearly every counter top, table top or other flat surface had some sort of naked lady kitsch on it. Even the lamps that sat on each of the black plastic tables flanking the heavily abraded sofa were in the image of naked women holding umbrellas.

"I wonder if he liked naked women?" Vinny jested, making everyone in the room chuckle.

The coroner techs were just lifting Mr. Bender into the body bag when Vinny and Lou got to the bathroom which was also decorated in the naked lady theme. Toby Bender was five and a half feet on a good day and was just as creepy looking as his apartment led you to anticipate. He wore a 1970's baby blue tuxedo, complete with ruffles. His hair was slicked to a high sheen and parted severely to the left. The early aroma of decomposition mingled with the overabundance of bad cologne to complete the pathetic scene.

"Guy dressed for the occasion, I see." Lou had seen enough as the techs zipped him up.

"So over here is what I think you two will be interested in." Peretta led them to the tiny computer desk in the corner of the main room of the apartment. The evidence marker drawing their attention to a carefully handwritten note on stationery with the same naked lady silhouette as the area rugs. In it, Bender had professed his adoration for Katarina Purrs as well as his devastation over her rejection of him.

He further went on to say that he had killed her and marked her so he would be able to recognize her in her angelic form when he met her in heaven. He concluded with a brief notation of how he hoped he looked nice for her as he was wearing his favorite suit.

"Seriously?" Lou boggled over the note. "This twit whacked Purrs then offed himself?" It was very neat and tidy for public consumption and Lou wanted to call it for the crap that she knew it was, but Peretta placed a hand on her shoulder before she could.

"It would appear so." He said to her, giving her a hairy eyeball to shut her up. It bit at her hard.

"Well hell, that sure brings an abrupt end to this. I was enjoying the freak show, too." Vinny appeared to be very disappointed.

"I'll have copies of all this sent to you right away so that you can close your files on it." Peretta headed for the door and nodded to the forensics tech that was standing by to bag and tag the note.

"Thanks." Vinny said as he followed Peretta out. "This all works out pretty damn nicely if ya ask me. I got a thing Friday so I won't feel so guilty taking the time with this wrapped up."

"You got a thing?" Lou asked as she followed the men. "What thing?"

"Well..." Vinny turned to her with a guilty look. "... I need a favor actually, kiddo."

"I'll leave you two to talk while I finish with my guys. Yell if you need anything." Peretta winked at Lou as he took off around the corner.

"What, Vinny?" Lou grumbled at him even though the source of her ire wasn't him.

"Well when the Captain called last night, he told me he got me a spot in Friday's testing for the Lieutenant's exam." He stuffed his hands in his pockets and shuffled his feet.

"That's great!" The reality of things hit Lou and she calmed down quite a bit. The necessity of the cover up coming into focus. "So what's the problem?"

"Well Vera has had morning sickness ya know only it's morning, noon and night sickness. Not to mention the friggin cravings! I'm on a first name basis with the guy that works the night shift at the mini-mart. So studying has been hit and miss for me. I was hoping I could take a personal day tomorrow and hide out at you're uncle's to study, and you would cover for me so Vera thinks I'm working. I don't want to hurt her feelings but I'm nervous as hell about this test."

Lou grinned at her partner and grabbed his arm, linking hers with his. "You bet!"

He blew out a breath, obviously relieved. "Thanks kiddo, I appreciate it a lot."

They headed down the stairs and toward the car. "No worries. Besides, this way I'll feel less guilty about taking Friday for this stupid thing I have to go to." She didn't think it was stupid at all, but had said that for Vinny's benefit.

He looked at her with a raised brow. "What thing?" He mimicked her tone from moments ago and she snorted at his uncanny impression of her.

"An art charity fundraiser something or other, with my parents. Caroline is going with her family who came into town for it. She and my Mom want to go to some salon and get all girlied up for it. Bad enough I gotta go after work with Caroline tonight and get some fancy-shmancy dress I'll only wear once."

"Hey!" Vinny stopped in his tracks. "Get one you can wear to my kid's wedding! Get a second use out of it eventually!"

Lou couldn't help but smile at him. "That is a genius idea. I'll keep the wedding in mind when I am picking it out."

"Detective Donovan, a word if you could real quick?" Peretta yelled from the steps of the apartment and Vinny looked at him funny.

"Be right back, get the heater running." Lou jogged back to the steps.

"My sincere apologies that you were not briefed on this. As soon as I arrived on scene and read the note, I called our Dom and informed him." Peretta scanned the area to make sure that no one would overhear them. "It's a serious stroke of luck that this freak wants to claim responsibility for Purrs. I was planning on contacting you as soon as I headed back to the station on this but, well, you just showed up!"

Lou looked at Peretta suspiciously. "You mean the note wasn't a plant?"

"No! Not at all! This is legit all the way." She could tell he wasn't bullshitting her.

"Serious stroke of luck is an understatement. Thanks for letting me know." She turned to head back to the car.

"I look forward to working with you in the future, Detective." Peretta smiled as she walked away.

As she and her partner drove off, Lou could only think that her selfishness in wanting to scream cover-up almost cost Vinny study time for his test. She knew she would catch the rogue and that Max would make him pay dearly. So what difference did it make if some creepy, greasy freak took the public wrap for Katarina Purrs if it protected everyone all around? She would just have to make sure she caught the true murdering bastard before he could claim another victim.

Lou ducked out of the building under the pretext of a stomach ache from the pancakes she had for breakfast which baffled Vinny because it was only a short-stack. When Lou felt she was safely tucked away in the back of the parking lot across the street, she called Max's suite in the hope that someone other than him would answer, that she could throw her fit at and they could give him the message. Unfortunately, Frank didn't wait long enough for her to get started before he handed the phone to Max.

"I'm certain you think this was staged Detective but I assure you the note and Mr. Bender's suicide as well as everything you saw at the crime scene was one-hundred-percent genuine." Max got it all out before she could say one word. It was highly deflating. "Detective? Are you still there?"

"Yes, dammit, I'm still here!" Her tone even sounded deflated and she knew he could tell.

"Good..." Lou could have sworn he sounded a little panicked. "...then to support my case I would suggest you look at Mr. Bender's rantings on certain blugs so you can see that I am telling you the truth. Frank will text you with the web addresses."

"Blugs?" She thought for a moment. "You mean blogs?"

"What?" She could hear him muttering under his breath then heard Frank whispering in the background. "Yes yes! Blogs, whatever they are!"

Lou grinned at Max's obvious embarrassment. "It's okay, I know old guys like you have a tough time adapting to these newfangled sources of communication and information. You should have seen Vinny this morning with his new headset for his cellphone."

"Very funny, Detective." Max grumbled. "And Vinny looks easily fifteen years older than I do. Now take advantage of the bone the Fates have thrown us with Bender and lets focus on the real murderer, shall we?"

She considered for a moment. "Blood-Swear?" She recalled Abby and Caroline telling her it was the most sacred of all swears to the Sanguinostri.

"What?" He sounded surprised by her request.

"Will you Blood-Swear that Bender's suicide is for real and has no Sanguinostri prints on it?" She posed it clearly for him.

"If that's what you wish, I'll come by this evening and do so." He hadn't hesitated.

"Nah, that's okay. The fact that you're willing is good enough. See you Friday." She hung up before he could say a word, and headed back across the street.

By the time she got back to her desk Frank had sent her several web addresses to various blogs dedicated to the worship of Katarina Purrs and other vintage porn stars. All of them had Purrs' murder as the hot topic and there were plenty of comments from readers who both loved and hated the woman. Another consistency was the poster who went by the screen name of 'Toby_Purrs4Kat' basically spamming each site right about the time the media broke the story of her death. The numerous posts were filled with his professed love for Purrs and his grief over having had to kill her because he loved her too much to let her go. Apparently, in his mind, as evidenced by much earlier posts that spanned over several months at least, he and Purrs were involved in a torrid romance. His last post on each site was within several minutes of one another and they apologized to everyone for taking such a gift from God away from her fans and that he was leaving to meet her. Lou was willing to bet that Bender's time of death was right around the time of the last post.

"This kid was a freaking drama queen!" Vinny startled her, having been reading the screen from over her shoulder. She would have to remember in the future that he was real stealthy like that.

Lou smirked. "No kidding. I keep expecting to read 'Goodbye cruel world' in one of his posts."

"Well, he wanted the attention, he sure got it." Vinny reached around her and typed in one of the local news channel web addresses into her browser. "Media is already all over it and we haven't even filed the paperwork."

Once the page had finished loading, the headline read 'Uber-Fan sticks it to Porn Diva' and had a picture of Toby Bender that made him look even creepier than he did when they were loading him into the body bag.

Lou grumbled. "I'll bet you lunch someone got paid real well for the tip."

"That's a sucker bet." He scooted back and looked at her. "Hey, that must mean your tummy feels better!"

She almost forgot she had used that as a lame excuse earlier but caught herself and nodded. "Probably better skip lunch though just in case. Let's get all the paper work ready on this so when Peretta's stuff comes in all we have to do is file it."

"So young, yet so wise." Her partner grinned as he went back to his desk to do just as she suggested.

Peretta had called at around three-thirty to apologize for the delay in relaying the reports to them. The coroner was waiting for the toxicology to come back before they would formalize cause of death. Lou had to admit that the level of courtesy and cooperation was a refreshing change and would probably be hard to get used to. When Caroline arrived to pick Lou up for their shopping excursion just before five, she confirmed Peretta's story with her and stated things should be wrapped up on their end by the morning. Given that, and the late hour, Lou assured Vinny she would make sure everything got filed properly and he needn't worry about taking the day to study. Especially since she was taking her own personal day on Friday while he took his test. When he was content with the plan they checked in with their captain to give him their report as it stood. Satisfied with the situation, Captain Davidson sent them on their way for the evening, telling Vinny to study hard and good luck on Friday.

"Donovan, I'd like a word before you go." The Captain informed her and Vinny gave her a nervous look before he left. Once Vinny had gone and the door was closed he motioned for Lou to sit. "I wanted to talk to you and mostly apologize for having to sit you out of things temporarily. Now you understand that I had a duty above and beyond this desk to uphold."

Lou nodded. "I understand sir. It was a little disconcerting to learn of you're association, I'll admit."

"You have no idea how frustrating it has been for me, not having anyone on the front lines to be able to work with and handle things that I am clearly not in any position to handle as a captain." It was odd for Lou to listen to him speak so casually and freely. He usually was so formal, which as her captain he should be, but this was yet another breath of fresh air for her today.

"Sir, may I ask why you didn't request people be recruited to assist you?" It may have been asking the obvious but she wanted to hear it from him. "I mean, I am new to all this but from what I gather, the Aegis Council has protocols for just that."

"I did!" He tossed his hands up in frustration. "I mean, I went through the proper channels with the local agent in charge and was waiting. That bastard Gilroy. I never would have guessed he was that corrupt and was just tossing requisitions into the trash. I just assumed the Council was bogged down and would get to me when they could. Anyway, the point is I am sorry and I appreciate your understanding. When you have time I think we should grab a cup of coffee and collaborate on our own protocols here since we will be getting at least a couple new recruits now that our Dom is taking personal control of things."

Lou stared at her captain, confounded. "Sir, I don't see where my input would be proper given you're the veteran Sanguinostri here. I appreciate your consideration, though."

Davidson cocked his head and looked at her for several seconds, then grinned as he spoke. "Lou, our Dominor hasn't told you yet, has he?" Davidson laughed a deep and hearty laughter. "That explains all the sir's and shit! Well isn't this funny."

"Sir?" Lou was baffled.

"There it is again! Okay, he really hasn't told you so I guess I better. This is going to be priceless." Her captain leaned in over the desk and looked at her with a gleam in his eye. "Yes, I am your captain in this law enforcement agency. But our Dom has made it very clear to all the stewards and agents that you will be in charge of any Sanguinostri criminal investigations from here on out. So technically, and make no mistake I am thrilled about it on so many levels, you are my boss with only the Aegis and our Dom above you."

"What?!" Lou couldn't help but shout which made Davidson roar with laughter.

He wiped a tear from his eye. "You need to have a talk with our Dominor so you are better informed of your station, my dear."

"What the hell? I'm nobody! Why the hell would he do that? I don't know what the hell I am doing!" Lou shot up from her seat and started pacing the office.

"And I am here to help you with anything at any time!" Davidson got up and went to her, placing a comforting hand on her shoulder. "Don't worry! You will adjust quickly and frankly I think he made an excellent choice." To Lou's complete and utter shock, her captain's smile was sincere.

"I don't know why the hell you would be okay with this. I am not okay with this. It's just a ridiculous mistake! I'm going to get this straightened out immediately." She started to head for the door.

"Lou!" He called to her before she stormed out. "Maximilian Julian doesn't mistakes."

She rolled her eyes. "Right, like in his picking the agents to run L.A.?"

"Gilroy was a brilliant Agent in the beginning and for a good while after. He just became lazy and corrupt as so many do in Hollywood. I will stand by our Dom's choice on Gilroy regardless of how it turned out." He spoke sternly now, clearly very protective of Max. She smiled at him because that was as it should have been.

"I stand corrected. It still doesn't mean I am qualified for what he expects of me. Let alone not telling me! Thank you for the info, Captain. See you tomorrow." With that, Lou left the office, then the building, barely waiting until she was in Caroline's car before she dialed the hotel. Once again it was Frank that answered the phone. "Is he out of his freaking mind?!" Lou shouted into the phone and got no satisfaction from Frank as she could hear him call Max to pass her off to him.

"Hello Detective." His voice was rich and warm on the other end but she didn't let that deter her.

"Are you out of your freaking mind?!" She shouted the slightly modified question again.

"About what, this time?" He asked smugly and it only made her more angry.

"What the hell are you thinking, putting me in charge of anything? I don't know shit! You know, that explains everyone being so damn nice and accommodating today! I should have known something was up!"

Lou continued to rant at Max for several minutes as Caroline drove them to the boutique where they were going to get her dress for the gala. Caroline was grinning from ear to ear because she had just won a weekend at her favorite spa over Lou freaking out over being put as lead for Sanguinostri criminal investigations. She had known exactly the first words that would fly out of Lou's mouth.

"I'll be collecting on that bet in a month or so!" Caroline spoke loudly so Max could hear her through the phone.

"What bet?" Lou eyed her suspiciously.

"Tell Caroline I said shut up and get me the information. I don't welch on a bet." Lou could hear the irritation in Max's voice.

"What bet?!" She demanded of them both.

"Detective, as much as I enjoy you berating me over one thing or another, I'm afraid we are going to have to continue this conversation Friday evening as I have several people waiting for me on a video conference. Until then." He clicked off before Lou could tell him she didn't give a shit who he had waiting. Which in retrospect she realized was a good thing.

Caroline explained the bet while they got a parking spot and Lou could barely contain her annoyance as they flipped through dresses at the boutique. Even when she went into the dressing room she was so wrapped up in her frustration over the situation that she had barely paid attention to what Caroline had shoved in her hands to try on. When Lou finally stepped out and demanded Caroline look at the dress she could have cared less about, Caroline simply smiled wide.

"That's the one." Caroline gestured to the woman who was assisting them. "She needs it taken up at the hem a touch. Turn around for me Lou."

"Are you serious?" Lou huffed and did a quick turn. Stopping only when she caught her own reflection in the mirror on the wall.

Begrudgingly, Lou had to admit it was indeed perfect. It was simple, not fussy, with its clean lines of bronze silk charmeuse that reminded Lou of one of those dresses that Jean Harlow or Ava Gardner would have worn. With a slightly off the shoulder portrait collar, perfectly fitted bodice and bias cut skirt that flowed like a soft breeze.

"Well, hell." Lou hated to admit it, but Caroline had been right. "What shoe..." She started to ask as the woman handed her a pair of classic pumps in the same exact bronze silk as the dress.

"Best to let the person be the statement with the dress as the exclamation point rather than muck everything up with overly-fussy shoes, don't you agree? I believe you're a size seven?" The pleasant woman said as she leaned down to help Lou into each shoe.

"Yeah, I guess you're right." Lou conceded as she stepped into the shoes that completed the look. The woman immediately began pinning the hem to the proper length.

"If you girls want to go and grab some dinner, I can have this hemmed for you within an hour or so?" She finished with the last pin then admired Lou's reflection.

"That would be fantastic. Thank you Camilla! Once again you come through for me!" Caroline kissed both cheeks of the boutique owner, then smiled at Lou. "Go get changed, Princess Charming, then you can bitch at me over pasta."

Lou grumbled but did as her friend ordered.

Chapter Thirteen

*Thursday morning had come far too early for Lou's liking and she real-*ized while waiting for her train to arrive that she had gotten spoiled with her partner picking her up so frequently. When her train finally pulled in at the Chatsworth station she was only one of a handful of people to hop on to the nearly empty commuter. She found an isolated seat away from everyone else so that she could thumb through the file Abby had sent her on their rogue the day before. Like it or not, for the time being she was who Max had on the chopping block as head of crime for the Sanguinostri. Whatever the hell that meant. She sure as hell wasn't going to blow it if she could help it. By the time her train hit the Burbank station, things started to get crowded so she packed up the sensitive material and pondered what she had just skimmed over. Lou chuckled to herself over her paranoia, noticing she was clutching her messenger bag like someone was going to actually snatch it from an armed cop. But there was a teeny tiny tingle at the back of her neck that made her feel like she had reason to be paranoid and she started to casually scan the train methodically looking for the source of her tingle. There was the usual aversion of eyes as there often was on public transportation. A few obviously gang affiliated fellows and one dodgy looking guy who Lou chalked up to starting his first day of sobriety. The rest of the crowd appeared to be normal commuters just like her and really didn't set off any alarms. Still she had a feeling that she didn't like so she stood up and took a defensive posture just in case as she waited for the train to hit Union Station so she could make her transfer.

The train finally came to a halt, the doors opened and Lou got off with the horde without incident. She moved to the platform to wait for the Orange County line which would take her on the last leg of her morning journey.

"Morning Lou." She nearly jumped out of her skin when Niko stepped beside her and said hello.

"Christ, would you not do that!" She swallowed hard to get her heart back in it's proper place. "What the hell are you doing here?"

"I had a funny feeling. You had a funny feeling. So here I am." He smirked down at her. She hadn't realized how damn big the guy really was before, or how dangerous looking either.

"What do you mean, funny feeling?" She decided to play dumb, sort of.

"You know, you had it. I can tell you did, so lets not screw around with it." Lou looked at him intently and noticed he was not looking at her any longer but peripherally scanning the area. He was really slick at it too.

"Thought I was just being a paranoid weirdo." She admitted as she tried to mimic his scan but only succeeded in giving herself a headache.

Her train pulled up and he ushered her on, directing her to an empty set of seats. When the last of the passengers piled on and the train headed out, he leaned in and spoke to her quietly.

"One of my things, gifts you could say, is that I get dreams." He paused a minute to look down the aisle at something that caught his eye.

Shadows of Doubt

"Dreams?" Lou remembered Caroline and Max telling her that people will develop skills after they turn but she wasn't sure what Niko meant about dreams.

Once he determined the object of his attention was nothing, he leaned back in and continued. "Yeah, they are like premonitions but very narrow. I dream of how someone is going to feel at a specific moment in time. Last night I dreamed of you're feeling something was off during your train ride."

"Okay but like I said, I may have been being paranoid." She whispered.

"Nope. When I dream it I feel it, but objectively because I don't know the state of mind or emotional crap of the person I am dreaming through. It's a clean read. You're not being paranoid."

Lou wasn't sure if that made her feel better or worse but she had to shove it out of the way regardless. Brooding on it would only cloud her observations. "How do you do that?" She had to ask him.

"What? Dream?" He looked down at her now.

"No no, the looking everywhere without looking like you're looking?" She realized how ridiculous that came out. "You know what I mean?"

"Years of practice, little one." He smirked and resumed scanning, if only to rub his talent in.

"Don't be a snot, tell me!" She poked him in the shoulder as a little sister would a brother who was teasing her.

"Ow!" He rubbed his shoulder and frowned down at her. "Violent little sprite! There's one reason you won't be able to do it! You're too tense and angry!"

Lou huffed. "Sorry." She slumped slightly and looked forward feeling guilty.

"You're a detective, you're very observant. So what's the big deal?"

"Observant is one thing. Doing it without anyone knowing you're observing is different. People think I'm glowering at them when I observe." She sat up as the train came into her stop. "I want to be all covert observing like you are."

He looked at her and grinned. It was like having a little kid asking him how to be like him when they grew up. "Come on, I'll explain while we walk you to the bureau."

As they walked, Niko explained to Lou the finer art of relaxing and taking things in. While it sounded mostly like crap to her, she tried to follow his tips and in the process noticed the reflection of a black sedan in one of the mirrored buildings they were coming up on. It was trailing them by about a block but at a dribbling pace which could only mean it was following them.

"Black sedan at seven o'clock" She interrupted him.

Niko beamed proudly at her. "That's just Frank. Nice catch though."

Lou looked back at the sedan and the headlights flashed twice. She waved back. "Why is he following us?"

"Because we know you like the walk from the station and I need to get back somehow, now don't I? Give me your phone." He held out his hand.

"Why for?" She questioned even though she was already digging for it.

"For why so you can text me when you're ready to head out tonight." He programmed his contact information into her phone, then gave her a wide smile when he handed it back. "Don't even think of soloing it or I'll sneak up on you and scare you so badly you will embarrass yourself horribly in public. Perhaps even in front of Max!" He made a Gene Kelley-esque little twirl as he turned and started for the sedan. It was then Lou realized they were in front of her building. Lou decided at that moment that she and Niko were going to be excellent friends.

The vein on the side of Max's temple was pulsing so profusely that Abby literally backed up for fear of it touching her. To say he was angry was the understatement of the century.

"Why in the hell did you even take a single breath of air before informing me of this?!" He bellowed as he hulked over Niko who looked as if he couldn't be less concerned about Max's tirade if he tried. He even was picking lint off his trousers, almost ignoring Max.

"My Dom..." Frank tried to intercede.

When Max's head whipped around to glare at Frank, both Abby and Frank jumped back. "Do I look like I'm talking to you?! Trust me, you will know when I get to you!" Max spun back around to resume glaring at Niko. "I want an answer dammit!"

Niko casually looked up at him. "And when you settle down, I'll be happy to answer, but you are answering the question for me with the way you are freaking out at this very moment."

Max took a step back, never taking his eyes off Niko and was quiet for several seconds before he let out a horrendous roar, then plopped on the couch.

"Feel better now?" Niko wasn't being sarcastic although he could have been with good reason. "I didn't tell you because I know how you feel about her and you would have only freaked and popped a vein which in turn would have pissed her off royally." Niko got up and plopped next to Max on the couch, draping an arm around his shoulders as he did. "This is the twenty-first century Max. She's a tough cop, not an oppressed girl at the mercy of her tyrant father, like Nila was." Max winced at the mention of his long dead fiancee's name. "This is like brand new to you so forgive me if I remember that my place is looking out for your best interests. In a nutshell, it wasn't necessary to tell you about my dream and if I had, you would have made an ass out of yourself in front of her and we simply cannot have that, can we?" Niko patted Max's shoulder.

Max grumbled. "Really pisses me off when you're right."

"I know, it's a burden someone has to carry, though." Niko got up from the couch with one last pat on Max's shoulder. "Now I'm going out for a smoke to give you time to feel like more of an idiot, then we'll go over security for the gala."

Max watched Niko walk out on to the terrace then turned his attention to Abby and Frank. "When did you all take to treating me like I'm five years old?"

Abby snickered and sat down next to him, patting his knee with the slightest hint of condescension. "When you started falling in love and acting like a five year old. But it will be our little secret, m'kay?"

Max could only laugh.

After Niko came back in he told Max all about the dream, how he explained it to Lou and that all in all it had been a nice bonding experience for the two of them. It had made Niko laugh to see the knee-jerk flash of jealousy cross Max's face and it made Max even more embarrassed with his behavior

"Honestly Max, it may have been nothing more than a curious steward wanting to get a look at her but I just wasn't going to take that chance and still don't plan to. She's going to text us when she's ready to go and I'm going to personally see she gets home safely. I vow to you she will get there safely." Niko reassured him.

"I know. It is probably nothing but I hate to think of that son of a bitch using her to get to me." Max got up and began to pace.

"No one but us and the immediate circle knows of you're feelings for her!" Abby chimed in. "There is no reason for anyone to use her in that way."

"You need to understand something..." Max turned to make sure he made eye contact with each of them. "... Purrs' was left on the golf course not two days after I was with Lou and her family playing golf.

Shadows of Doubt

All the other murders in L.A. have been in LAPD territory and up to Sunday, Lou had been working out of the Lost Hills station. Purrs not only lands in Sheriff's jurisdiction but a few miles away from Lost Hills. It is a message, however subtle. It is still a very strong message and we cannot be so foolish as to ignore it."

When Max put it that way he made a very, very good point and they all got it. When Frank immediately took out his cell and started typing, Max demanded to know what he was doing.

"I'm making sure we have eyes on Lou, her building and the McAllister compound twenty-four-seven." Frank didn't bother to look up, only kept texting.

"Alright, then let's get our ducks in a row for tomorrow and tomorrow night." Max was pacing again.

"Both Caroline and I will be with her and her mother tomorrow doing the girl thing, getting ready for the gala." Abby said as she spun around on the bar-stool. "I'm sure Frank and Niko will have eyes on us as well so she will be covered there."

"Absolutely." Frank backed her up. "Cohen and Dern are thirty yards to the west of her building and all is quiet. Davidson has eyes on her inside via camera." It suddenly occurred to Frank. "You know I can probably get that feed here if it's web based."

"Do it." Max turned to Finn as he walked into the suite. "Make sure our cars pick up the McAllisters and Lou as well as all the Devereux family tomorrow night. Give Joe and Richelieu the actual photos as well as names of the drivers and the armed escorts for them all so that they know who to expect. I don't want a single hole for this scumbag to squeeze through on this." Finn nodded and headed back out of the suite to make the arrangements. "Do we have a copy of the guest list as per protocol?" Max turned to Abby.

"One of von Massenbach's people faxed over a semi-final guest list about an hour ago." Abby checked her PDA. "Deadline is six tonight so they will send the final before seven. They have followed all the protocols that they are required for your attendance."

"Good, alright..." Max raked his fingers through his hair and glanced around the room. "Then lets get some work done on the fifty-million other balls we have up in the air so we can keep my mind occupied so I don't throw another spazz-fit like I did earlier."

They all laughed and chortled at him, gathering around the coffee table to do just as he wished. They had a few hours to accomplish things before Max would see Niko and Frank take off to get Lou home safely. Just before they started going over new data that might help point them in the direction of their rogue, Frank spun a laptop around so Max could see the four frames being transmitted to the display. In the bottom left-hand corner he saw Lou. She was sitting at her desk, chair dancing to some unknown music being piped into her ears via her MP3 player. She drummed her pencil and index finger on the stack of papers she was reading and Max felt all the tension melt away at the sight of her. He looked up at Frank and smiled with approval. "Thanks."

"Welcome. I can probably get this streaming on your cell too if you want!" He grinned when he realized what a stupid question that had been. Of course Max would want.

Lou had given them forty-five minutes notice before she was ready to head out and sure enough, a stereotypical black SUV was waiting for her when she walked out of the bureau. It surprised her how glad she was to see it and realized what an idiot she must have looked like when she noted she was almost skipping toward the car. Lou was sure she turned several shades of red when Niko got out of the passenger seat to open the back door for her. He was grinning at her even though he didn't say a word. She thanked him and got in. It was awkward for all of two minutes until Frank glanced at her through the rear-view mirror and smiled.

"So how was you're day, Tallulah? Did you play nice with the other detectives?" He snickered as he said it.

"Do you know what happened to the last person that called me that other than my mother?" She looked out the window as she asked.

"Actually I do!" She could hear Frank's smug grin in his voice.

"Ah!" She nodded. "So you actually want to be a soprano then."

Niko snorted and slapped Frank on the shoulder. "A soprano, that's funny."

Frank grimaced as he rubbed his shoulder, catching Lou's snicker in the rear-view mirror as he did.

"Actually my day was good." Lou eventually took Frank's question semi-seriously. "I finished going over the files you and Abby gave me on the rogue and did some cross referencing. It looks like his first victim in L.A. was Marjorie Scott for sure." She decided to talk it out with them when she noticed the freeway they had just gotten onto was a parking lot. It would make the time go by faster. "He definitely has a pattern of picking women of questionable character although the London files call them 'unfortunates'. What is that all about anyway?" It was a rhetorical question really, she didn't pause long enough for either Frank or Niko to answer. "The fact that he's stuck to that type all these years means he has some beef with skanky women. Either his mother, sister, wife or lover turned out to be damaged goods and he hasn't gotten over it. And the cutting is significant as well, even if he covers… oh hey! That reminds me!" She scooted up to peer at them from between their seats. "So what's the deal with feeding? You guys have fangs and bite people like vampires or what?"

Frank grumbled loudly and scowled at her which amused Niko immensely.

"Come on man, it's only natural for her to go there. The whole vampire thing is within her time so don't take it so damn personally." Niko rolled his eyes at Frank then shifted in his seat so he could face her better. "We mostly drink out of glasses like normal people these days..." Now it was Lou rolling her eyes at him. "... but yeah. Promise not to freak?" Niko eyed her suspiciously.

"If I were going to freak I think I would have done that by now, don't you?" Lou huffed.

"Alright then." Niko made a soft hissing sound while he appeared to be yawning but no sooner than he started, Lou saw fangs spring forward from what appeared to be the roof of his mouth. Similar to vipers she had seen on the wildlife channels. He smiled wide and she couldn't help but lean in closer to look. "Aren't you glad I brushed my teeth before we came?" he jested as she inspected his fangs.

"That is so freaking cool! Does it hurt to flip em out? They are kinda like landing gear!"

Frank jerked the car to the right slightly as he burst out laughing. "Landing gear?!" Lou only glanced at him for a second before turning her attention back to Niko.

"Nah it doesn't hurt." He yawned and hissed again as he retracted his fangs. "I imagine like wisdom teeth coming in all at once, or sort of. For those that are Blood-Born, they are always there at birth but don't pop out until adolescence so they need to be bottle fed, literally along with milk, like normal babies."

Lou blinked several times. "Blood-born? You mean you can reproduce full blown turned babies?"

Niko nodded. "It is very very rare and difficult. Because our blood is like antibodies on steroids. So when a fetus survives, its a big deal and the kid is usually massively stronger for it."

"But that makes no sense, I thought you don't age?" Lou was having a hard time computing things.

"With Blood-born, they develop and age like a normal child until their bodies reach about twenty-four to twenty-seven in age. Then it slows to the sloth pace like for the rest of us. We actually do age but its like dog time but in reverse. Approximately a couple hundred years or something to a normal human year of aging. I've never known of a turned Sanguinostri to ever die of natural causes, lets put it that way. That's why there are restrictions on turning, a screening process, permission, so on and so forth."

"So Joe would have to get permission to turn, and my mom too? If they decided to? They could not be allowed?" The thought of Joe and her mother being denied the option suddenly upset Lou very much.

"Oh no." Frank spoke up. "Joe's family has been what we call Grand Stewards to the Sanguinostri for over a millennium. The Senatus charged special dispensation for all Grand families ages ago so that they are automatically sanctioned but it has to be overseen by a their Dominor."

"Oh." It was all so fascinating to her. "But I'm technically not his family. I'm not even adopted!" Lou hadn't made a decision whether she was going to turn or not but as with the panic for her parents being able to have the option, she suddenly felt that same fear for herself.

Niko sensed her upset and put a hand on her arm to calm her. "He will never admit it but that's one of the reasons why Max is placing you as Principate for criminal investigations. That insures your right, should you choose to make that decision."

She thought about that for a moment. "One of the reasons?"

Frank and Niko looked at each other briefly. "You're a damn good cop for starters, but lets not get into all that now. Fishing for compliments doesn't suit you." Frank knew he skillfully diverted Lou from that line of questioning when she swatted at him. "Hey! I'm driving here!"

"Alright then, I need you guys to explain this whole Principate thing and what I'll need to do, etcetera and so forth. Since it appears I will die of old age before we get home, you may as well start now." Niko and Frank were founts of information that Lou decided to exploit to the fullest extent possible. She needed to be prepared for this so called position should she decide not to fight Max on it.

By the time they arrived at the McAllister compound, Lou had a list of to-do's three pages long and her to-get's were extensive as well. Frank had told her he would train her on all the technical things and help her acquire a proper computer system with biometric security and higher encryption levels than the Pentagon. He would make sure she was networked and had a cell phone separate from the one she was using that would be untraceable to anyone outside of the Aegis Council. Niko had informed her that they were looking in to property on the ridge above Lou's neighborhood to build a tactical headquarters but until then she was welcomed to join him for combat training any time. He even jested that he would help her learn all of his superpowers like his observation skills. Lou had nearly jumped out of her seat with excitement at the offer and demanded to know how soon they could get started.

"Whoa there, cowgirl!" Niko chuckled. "You have the girlie thing to do with the gala tomorrow night. Why don't we get together this weekend and set up a schedule that suits us both?"

Lou grumbled when she remembered the whole gala affair but she knew it was important to Joe and now that she was Sanguinostri, and supposed to be stepping up to some level of position in it, she knew it was important for her too. "Okay, sounds like a plan." She started to get out of the SUV. "You guys hungry? Want to come in for dinner? My Mom and Joe had a meeting to go to over Max's damn park so it would be nice to have the company."

Shadows of Doubt

Frank and Niko looked at each other, knowing full well that Max would worry if they left her alone.

"Got any leftovers from the other night still?" Niko asked.

"A ton and they're going to go bad if we don't polish them off." She hopped out of the truck, surprisingly glad they were staying.

Frank threw the truck in park and killed the engine. "I got dibs on those artichokes!" He shouted and bolted for the door.

Lou laughed as she ran with them and headed into the kitchen. Marta came in to investigate the ruckus they were making. When they told her it was a leftover raid she started fussing over them and insisted on making them proper plates. Lou took the opportunity to sneak away for a second and check in with Vinny before it got too late.

"Hola, kiddo!" He sounded very chipper.

"Hey! Can you talk freely?" Lou wondered if Vera was lurking.

"I'm still at you're uncle's place. Vera's at some pregnant yoga thing with her sister so your aunt invited me to stay for pot roast! You know I'm a sucker for her pot roast."

"You're a sucker for food, face it." She grinned when he chortled at her statement of the obvious. "How was you're study day? Ready for tomorrow?"

He sighed on the other end. "I better be. These guys even made flash cards for me. Just keep your fingers crossed and a candle lit, okay?"

"You know it. Make sure you call me as soon as you get out and remember to breathe and stay calm." Lou could hear her aunt yelling in the background.

"Hey kiddo, that's the dinner bell. Have fun with all your foo-foo stuff tomorrow."

"Will do! Give everyone there a kiss for me there."

"How about you're aunt only? Not kissin' Seamus' ugly mug." He snorted at the thought. "See ya kiddo, sweet dreams!"

"Night Vinny, good luck tomorrow!" She shouted then clicked off and headed back into the kitchen.

When she walked into the chaos, she stopped and leaned against the wall just to watch a while. Niko and Frank were teasing Marta incessantly over her dirty jokes from the other night and Lou couldn't help but grin. These huge, mean looking guys were becoming something like big brothers to her. Something she never thought she would have wanted. For the umpteenth time so far this week, she was very surprised at how happy it all made her.

He stood surveying the room. Triple checking to make sure that all was in it's proper place. The floor was meticulously covered in plastic and the smell gave him a shiver of anticipation. Plastic sheeting had been draped to cover every wall carefully so that not a single drop of blood or flake of tissue could accidentally slip underneath. A new chair had been prepared with all the customary straps that were so integral to his work. Even the little table off to the side was covered in plastic and all his accoutrements were neatly arranged just as he liked them. Everything was as it should be. Ready and waiting for his new, very special fly to be caught in his web.

It had all come together so brilliantly. He hadn't anticipated finding anything worth troubling over when he had come out west. Media reports always glorified the Golden State as being all perfect, bright and shiny people with their blond hair, golden tans and casual living. The truth is that it had become a cesspool of corruption under blue skies and abundant sunshine. There wasn't a palm that couldn't be greased or soul that couldn't be bought for the right price. Both Los Angeles and San Francisco were fraught with opportunities for the discriminating tastes of the sick and twisted. The business of catering to the dark underbelly of debauchery was thriving and he reveled in it. It was a shame he was going to have to cut his stay so soon but it was best for now. Just a few more days then off to new happy hunting grounds and new adventures. He still had one adventure here and he was so excited for it.

Ambling about his workspace, he toyed with the various options he had in obtaining his next fly. The one minor sticking point was that she wasn't an unfortunate as all his others had been. That was a difficult thing to reconcile within himself. Regardless, all the signs pointed to her being the perfect choice. No denying she had nearly been handed to him on a silver platter. He actually caught himself giggling out loud over it. Just one more day and she would be sitting in that chair, straining for breath. Her teeth would dig into the rubber of the ball-gag. Her fingernails would chip and split from scraping and clawing at the wooden arms of the chair. Certainly she would weep a little and pray to whatever god she worshiped for a way out of the nightmare. It made him giddy every time he thought about it. There would be no way out for this fly as there had been none for any of the others. She may not be an unfortunate but she was nothing special when it came down to it either. She was a whore waiting to happen like the rest of them. Like all of them. The only thing that made this one special is that the illustrious Dominor thought she was. And for that simple fact alone, she would die a long, slow and exquisitely painful death.

Chapter Fourteen

Abby inspected Max's tuxedo first, checking that not even a speck of lint could be found on it. She had his cashmere overcoat already prepared and just needed to get them into his room before she left. She was so excited when Caroline invited her to join her, Lou and Shevaun for a long leisurely day of getting all dolled up. Abby couldn't remember the last time she had had that luxury. Being Max's girl Friday and the only girl at the top tier with the Aegis Council, she usually was the last to get ready for anything. However, Max had been within earshot when Caroline invited her and he was insistent that she let the boys fend for themselves for a change and she take the day to indulge herself. It was really nice when he acknowledged her sacrifices and let her know that he realized how much she did for them. Not that she needed such petty validation, but it was nice just the same. Once she found his ensemble for the evening satisfactory, she scooped everything up and headed across the hall to his suite so she could set it out for him.

She was excited for the day to come with the girls as she skipped down the hall. Abby had prearranged with the spa, after Caroline invited her, to have top-drawer accommodations for all of them. Her treat. She would spare no expense for her new girlfriends and was even having a champagne brunch delivered to their private suite. She could afford it after all. Besides the boys, she rarely spent her money on anything since most everything, including any residence, was handled by Max and his extensive empire. She had been collecting a hefty salary for her position for gods knew how long and had even had to break it up into numerous different bank accounts over the last few decades to avoid complications. It was going to be so much fun spoiling girls for a change rather then the boring boys who only really cared about tech toys.

Max had been up and out for a while when she entered his room just after seven. She arranged his clothes, shoes, freshly polished cufflinks etcetera on the mahogany valet stand in the corner of his room. She even put a handkerchief over his shoes so they wouldn't get dusty while they sat out all day.

"Aren't you supposed to be taking care of you for a change today?" Max had seen her skip into his room with her arms full and came to see what she was doing.

"Just appeasing my conscience before I go." She grinned and gave a last smoothing over to his coat. "I'm just hanging the boys things on their hooks and then I am outta here!"

"Any instructions for me before you go?" He grinned now, knowing full well she would have a laundry list of things for him not to forget.

"Well, now that you mention it!" She pulled a piece of paper out of her pocket and handed it to him. "Its all laid out so you can't screw up." As he scanned the paper she noticed he seemed to be a little uneasy so she placed her hand on his arm and tried to get a feel for him. "What's wrong?" She asked.

"Nothing!" He knew he answered too quickly.

"We can do this the easy way, or the hard way, your choice." She sat down on the bench at the end of his bed and gave him the look that meant there was no way she was leaving until he answered. Grumbling, he sat down next to her.

"Tonight is important. I have all my bullshit duties as Dominor that I have to do but all I can think about is Lou. How is she going to react to something like this as her first real exposure to me and the Sanguinostri as a collective? How am I going to be able to temper what I have to do with what I want to do? What if this all turns Lou totally off? I mean, I don't have any illusions that she has feelings for me but it would be nice to have a shot, and tonight could ruin that."

"Hmm." It was a reasonable concern, she knew. "First of all I know she has feelings for you, we all can see that, even her mother. As for the rest of it, I think she understands your role and how important it is. Caroline and I have had discussions with her about the structure of things, so I know she has a clue. She's a very down to earth person, Max. She is not petty or easily put off by things so just be yourself tonight. Don't be nervous and standoffish towards her. You're not a stuffy dictator, you're fair, generous and a good man who takes his role very seriously. That is something she needs to see and needs to factor into her equation of you. Just make sure you come back to her between obligations so she knows you balance things well."

Max looked at Abby and thought for a while before he smiled. "When did you become so wise beyond your years?"

Abby snorted and hugged him. "I know, such a young two-hundred and something years, but an old old soul."

He laughed and hugged her back. "Thank you. Now have the guys grab their own stuff so you can get the hell out of here. I have a car waiting for you downstairs and we have transpo already set up for tonight."

"Oh! The limo we have here? That way we can all ride together and drink more champagne since no one has to drive!"

"Of course. I already called and had it brought around for you." He kissed her on the forehead then got up to head into the other room.

"Try and relax, its all going to be perfect. I know it." She smiled at him as he looked back at her before he left the room.

Despite the protests made by Frank and Connor, Abby gathered her things and began stuffing her hands into her mittens. Max scolded the men for not knowing how to tie their own ties by now and told them to leave Abby alone.

"I'll be back by five to get changed so you can save your panicking for then. All your stuff is ready to throw on, so just remember to shower and shave!" She took a moment to look them all in the eye as she said it. "Now I am off, so no calls unless it's something of global proportions." She blew kisses to them all and headed for the elevator.

The men stood staring at each other for a long time after she left, as if completely clueless what they were supposed to do next.

"Oh for pity's sake!" Max shook his head in disgust. "Its barely eight in the morning. We have hours before we have to worry, so someone order breakfast and let's see if we can accomplish something before we need to get ready."

The other men grumbled briefly then began the ritual morning debate of what to order from room service. It took about seven minutes before they decided on a smattering of everything and then focused on work until it arrived.

Lou had woken up early, forgetting she was taking the day to go with her mother and Caroline to the spa to get ready for the gala. Caroline was bringing Lou's dress and shoes over with her own so they could play dress up and all go to the event together. Lou just had to kill a few hours before she got there. She had tried to go back to sleep but the more she thought about the gala, the more nervous she got.

Shadows of Doubt

Other than the Sunday golf thing, Max had only seen Lou in her work grunge and while that was really more her style, she suddenly felt like there was a lot of pressure to clean up well and mind her manners. He was putting a lot of faith in her abilities if he was planning on making her Principate or whatever it was. She was going to have to prove herself to a lot of people who were all going to be at this thing. Of course that all sounded excellent as an excuse but that really wasn't the truth of it.

Max had floated her boat since the moment she laid eyes on his shoes and everything attached to them. She knew it, Caroline and Vinny knew it, her mother knew it. But now she knew who he was, what he was and that he was a seriously important man, especially in this new world she was knee deep in. How in the hell did she think he would ever notice her? He had been around for God knows how long and only been engaged once so that woman had to have been very special. He had serious standards, clearly. Max had rubbed elbows with kings and queens, presidents and supermodels. She was just a jean wearing, boot hoofing cop. Sure he had seemed to flirt with her before but maybe that was all pretense to get her indoctrinated and recruited as an operative. He had been snippy with her on the phone the day before, but she hadn't exactly been charming and flirty like Caroline was in her sleep. Did she really care if he noticed her in that way? Oh, who the hell was she kidding, of course she did.

She studied herself in the mirror as she brushed her teeth, picking herself apart inch by inch. She had bags under her eyes and she barely noticed the green of her irises because the whites were so damn bloodshot. She should have kicked the guys out earlier last night but she had been having too much fun. The non-black and blue portion of her skin tone was even, though a bit on the pasty side. She could definitely stand getting a little sun. She wondered if the spa did that spray-tan thing or if that would rub off on her dress. She would have to remember to ask. Her hair was a stylish cut, she thought, though there wasn't much to be done with the boring auburn mop anyway. Her bangs definitely could use a trim since she could barely see through them unless she brushed them to the side, which when she did just then she saw the condition of her hands and winced. She couldn't remember the last time she had a manicure and she had remnants of black nail polish on her toes from Halloween. Alright so she had to admit to herself that maybe a spa day wasn't such a bad thing after all.

"You realize your bathroom is as big as my apartment?" Caroline startled Lou so badly that she started to choke from nearly swallowing her electric toothbrush. "Oh God! Sorry sweetie, are you okay?" Caroline thumped on Lou's back and handed her a towel.

When Lou finally caught her breath and wiped the toothpaste off her face, she glared at her friend. "For someone who hates it when people sneak up on them, you sure are good at doing the same damn thing!"

"I am so sorry!" Her friend grabbed another towel to mop some of the toothpaste out of Lou's hair. "I was sure you heard me and your mom talking out there. She let me in, then I helped her cart coffee and morning noshes up."

"Oh! Any of Marta's croissants out there?" Lou suddenly forgot all about almost choking to death.

Caroline grinned at her. "Most definitely. Hey Lou, would you mind if Abby joined us for girls day getting ready? I kinda feel bad for her being stuck with all those guys all the time."

"Not at all! That's a great idea. It's kind of like having two of you around." Lou grinned then headed for the croissants.

"Great, because I already invited her." Caroline followed her out.

Shevaun was walking out of the closet as they headed for the goodie tray and was already perfectly polished and ready for the day.

Lou looked at her mother and wondered why in the hell the woman needed a day at the spa.

"I definitely must have gotten more of my father's genes." She muttered.

Her mother went for her coffee mug. "Oh stop that! You know I hate it when you say things like that!" She took a sip of her coffee and grinned at her daughter. "I absolutely adore your dress. You have to wear that topaz suite your grandma left you."

Lou was drawing a blank on two fronts. First, why in the hell would her grandmother leave her a hotel room and second, how could she possibly wear it. "Uh..."

Shevaun scoffed. "The copper brown chandelier earrings with the matching bracelet and ring?"

"Oh! That would be perfect!" Lou had forgotten all about the set her grandmother had left her several years ago. "So a suite is like an ensemble?"

Shevaun and Caroline just rolled their eyes at her before they turned to head for their chairs.

Caroline's phone chirped to indicate an incoming text which she began to read as soon as she plopped down. "Too fun! Abby has commandeered a company limo for us and is on her way now. I would have invited my momma but she's had like the entire staff from her salon at home flown in for this. Daddy actually bunked with my uncle last night. The women have the place overrun with girl junk. You know she brought five different gowns with her because she couldn't decide which to buy? She bought them all!"

"Wow!" Lou was baffled by all the fuss. "So this thing is that big of a deal?" She could feel her nerves flaring up again.

"Apparently so, from what Joe has told me." Shevaun broke off a piece of scone and studied it. "It was a big deal to begin with because the man who's giving it has like the largest collection of Byzantine artifacts, jewelry and other priceless things." She finally popped the piece of scone in her mouth and chewed quickly, then swallowed. "But now that Max, being like the king of all of North America is going to be there, its an ultra big deal so everyone on the continent is flying in for it."

"Well, that is so cool!" Caroline gaped. "It's like the red carpet of all red carpets for the Sanguinostri!"

Now Lou's stomach was doing flip flops and if she thought she was nervous before, what her mother had just said and with Caroline's gawking, it had literally made her hands start to shake. She put down her mug and went in to her closet to change, hoping that would buy her some time to compose herself. She had already showered and all that but noticing how posh and polished the women in the other room were, Lou figured plain old gray sweats and mukluks wasn't going to cut it. She rifled through her things to find an appropriately fashionable jog suit like Caroline had on, then heard Abby's voice in the other room. When Abby came into the closet to say hello, she could clearly see that Lou was freaking out.

"First of all, breathe." Abby ushered Lou to sit on the bench in the closet. It wasn't exactly a closet but more of a dressing room that Lou felt was better suited to someone who coveted closet space as so many women do. Abby knelt down in front of Lou and looked at her intently. "You're nervous about tonight."

Lou cocked her head sideways at Abby. "Are you reading me?"

"I have ultra puny reading skills so don't freak out. I really just get the vibe. If I try any harder than that I give myself a headache. Now what are you nervous about? You can tell me! Let me..." Abby looked past Lou, making Lou think perhaps she had a touch of Attention Deficit Disorder. "Oh crap, your dress is gorgeous! You are going to absolutely knock him out tonight!" She bounced up to get a closer look at it. "Oh Lou! This is brilliant! Did you have this made for you?"

"Uh, no. Caroline picked it out for me yesterday."

Abby turned to goggle at her. "Are you kidding me? How is it possible you found something so utterly perfect for you in one day?! I hate that! Why can't I do that!"

Lou had to admit, Abby was absolutely darling and had made her feel better already by approving of her dress. She also noticed that Abby was wearing similar sweatpants to the ones she had on, and they were tucked into sheepskin lined boots exactly like the ones Lou had planned on wearing. This was a woman who was the closest to Max next to Frank and Niko from what she had been able to deduce so far. Lou was suddenly feeling much better.

By ten o'clock the girls were being ushered to their private accommodations at the spa and handed soft and squishy robes and slippers to change into. The facilities were sumptuous in golden pink and mocha hues that glowed and gleamed off of every surface. There were overstuffed chairs, overstuffed couches and an equally overstuffed table that was covered in fresh fruits, pastries, pitchers of juices and full tea and coffee service with Lou's coveted Kopi Luwak brewed to steamy perfection. Margaret Beechum, the manager of the spa, had greeted them personally when they came in the door and with a snap of her fingers had staff fawning all over them.

"I hope that everything meets with your approval, Ms. LaRue." Beechum flashed her over-bleached smile at Abby. "If there is anything else you need, just inform one of your technicians and they will take care of it for you. I'll be just a moment away, should you need me." With a wave to everyone, the glossy Margaret Beechum closed the door behind her.

"Abby! What on earth did you do?! This is beyond decadent!" Caroline did a little twirl in the middle of the room.

"This is far too extravagant, we can't let you do this, Abby." Shevaun shook her head as she took in the luxurious surroundings.

"Oh stop! It is so my pleasure! I never get to do anything over the top, and who better to do it with but my girlfriends!" Abby grabbed Caroline's hands and they twirled together.

"This coffee is Kopi Luwak! Abby, you are a goddess." Lou was already sipping from a cup and Abby giggled.

"Ladies..." The technician named Lana quietly clapped her hands together to get their attention. "If you all would step into the dressing room and get changed, I'll escort you to the mud room for your Dead Sea Soak."

"Mud room? Dead Sea Soak?" Lou looked at Abby curiously.

"Oh yes, its the works for us today ladies!" Abby literally bounced with excitement.

"Now lets get you all ready for your treatments!" Lana clapped again, not as quietly as before. "We had best get started or you ladies will be late for your gala!"

One by one the women filed into the dressing room and came out looking like cotton balls. After a few minutes to relax and enjoy the treats on the table, they were ushered to their next stop on the pamper train. Once Lou had settled into one of the four tubs of black goo, she had to admit it was really nice. There were gauzy curtains to separate each tub for modesty but once everyone was in, the technicians pulled them back so they could all chat and make fun of each other. They soaked for half an hour or so then they were given plastic wraps of a sort so they didn't have to traipse to the shower naked. Even if they were covered in black goo, it was still a little awkward. The steam room had felt glorious and made Lou very sleepy. If relaxation was the goal, this place had it down without a doubt. She paid little attention to the others' chatter as she leaned back against the warm tile and let herself drift like the steam that surrounded her. She was going to have to remember to come back and do this again.

After soaking, steaming, being wrapped like mummies, then scrubbed with a finely granulated salt, it was nearly one o'clock and time for the airbrushing. They were all back in the suite but a partition had been set up at the far end of the room along with a low platform. Inga, the tanning specialist, handed them all g-string bikini bottoms only. They were made out of dental floss and a half sheet of paper towel at best. Inga informed them it was optional whether they wore it or not, whatever they were comfortable with. Lou was seriously reconsidering. It didn't take a detective to figure out that she was going to be next to naked in front of a total stranger while they got up close and personal with the air brush.

"It will be fine, Lou!" Caroline coaxed her. "Abby and I are doing it, I've done it a bazillion times before. It's no biggie, I swear."

"I assure you, Miss Lou..." Inga stood and looked at Lou very seriously, her thick accent and broken English adding levity to the situation whether she meant to or not. "I am professional. Before I found my calling, bringing peace and glow to all peoples, I was a nurse in Germany. So I tell you truth that I have seen all shapes and sizes. It is only the glow that matters."

After such a sincere statement from Inga, considerable convincing from the girls and that glass of champagne that didn't hurt the cause too much, Lou went for it. She had to admit the experience wasn't nearly as humiliating as she had expected.

By three o'clock Lou was set in pin curls and was able to see the full bloom of the airbrushing. She was really glad she had done it. Her skin was not only soft and luminous but it did indeed look like she had spent a few days basking in the sun. When she looked at her mother and the twins, as she had taken to calling Caroline and Abby half way through the day, they too looked like they had been with her on her imaginary tropical excursion. They were all in the middle of hairstyle development when their make-up artists started on them. Caroline's platinum locks were rolled up in curlers that were as big as coffee cans. Abby's hair looked like it had been attacked by a box of straws and her mother looked like she had stuck her finger in a light socket. She explained to Lou that she was in mid-tease, whatever that was. Lou had been talked into highlights and a trim, especially the bangs, which she was all too happy to have cut. The girls had spent a long time discussing the appropriate style for her and had gone so far as to describe her dress to both the stylist and the makeup artist. Caroline had even showed them a picture she had taken with her cell phone. Lou simply could not understand why color coordination on her hair was so damn important, but she figured they knew far better than her.

"The boys should be finishing up with their manicures right about now." Abby informed her as she sat in the chair next to her while the straws in her hair were carefully removed. "I left strict orders for the manicurist to beat them if necessary to make them submit." She smiled sweetly at the genius of her plan.

Lou snorted and the stylist that was taking out the pins in her hair growled at her to hold still. "Somehow I cannot see Niko submitting to a manicure." Lou ignored the woman at her head but tried to stay still anyway.

"Oh I'm not worried about Niko, he gets a manicure at least once a month. It's Frank and Max that are going to moan and groan over it." Abby rolled her eyes with annoyance.

Caroline chimed in from her seat on the other side of Abby. "I would have thought Max was a manicure guy."

"No no, Max is a man's man, I am sure. Dressing impeccably of course but being fussy about his hands? I can't see that." Lou's mom tossed in her thoughts.

"And you would be right!" Abby grinned at Shevaun. "I force mani-pedies on those guys once a month. I cannot stand snaggle toes or grungy hands on a man. I simply will not have it if I have to be around them all the time."

"And we thank you for it!" Caroline tipped her champagne glass toward Abby. "Nothing worse than holding hands with a guy who has cheese grater hands."

They all laughed at Caroline's analogy for a rough handed man but were promptly scolded by their respective stylists for bobbing around in their chairs. Forty-five minutes later they were allowed to turn around to look at one another and more importantly to look at the finished product of themselves.

"Lou..." Caroline gasped as her friend turned to face them. "You look amazing!"

"Wow! You are just a knockout!" Abby concurred.

"Oh stop you guys!" Lou got up out of her seat to go take a look at herself in the mirror.

"They are not kidding sugar pie, you look so beautiful, I may cry!" Shevaun's eyes welled up but the make-up artist snapped at her not to ruin her work.

Lou walked over to the mirror and took a look at herself. Her dark auburn hair had been lit up subtly with soft copper highlights in all the right places. They had done pin curls on her which had made her nervous but the finished product was soft tousled waves like the leading ladies from the 1920's. Like her all time favorite, Greta Garbo. Her make-up was soft, not overdone at all, but definitely glamorous. She couldn't help but smile at herself. She turned from the mirror and looked at her stylist and make-up artist who were holding their breath waiting for her to say something.

"You two are geniuses!" I love it!" She told them.

The stylist and artist bounced up and down and hugged each other while Lou realized how selfish she had been not looking at her salonmates. Caroline looked stunning as ever with a her shimmery platinum locks swept into a sophisticated up-do. Her make-up was fresh and perfect for her. Abby's flaming tresses were a mass of cascading ringlets that were pulled up on each side and fastened by combs that were encrusted with jewels. Her eyes were smokey and alluring with a hint of forest green on the lids. Lou could only imagine all the socks that would be knocked off when Abby walked into the room tonight. It was her mother though that took her breath away when she looked at her. The strawberry blond was swept away from her face in graceful glossy loops. Her lips were polished with the perfect shade of red lipstick and her eyes were done in an understated sultry kohl. She was simply gorgeous.

"Okay so we must swear not to cry and screw up all their hard work!" Shevaun ordered.

"Shit!" Abby squeaked when she looked at the clock. "It's four-fifteen! We need to hurry!"

The stylists all shrieked as if the world were coming to an end and started gathering little bottles and stuffing them into plastic bags. The make-up artists did something similar, gathering the lipsticks and glosses, mascaras and little compacts and put them into silky little black pouches. The four women tore off their protective smocks and clamored for shoes, jackets and purses. As they filed out the door, each two-man team that had worked on each of the women presented their bags of gifts to them and wished them a wonderful time at the ball. If the day was any indicator of the evening to follow, Lou knew it was going to be a blast.

Shadows of Doubt

It had finally quieted down in Max's suite after all the bitching and moaning the men had done over Abby arranging a proper barber and manicurist to come to them. Once sufficiently buffed and shorn, the men left to their respective quarters to finish getting ready. It was half past six and the quiet wasn't really a good thing for Max. The chaos that accompanied having his top people around tended to keep him grounded. Focused on one matter or another that needed to be handled. He was excellent at juggling the chaos that accompanied governing, it was much like playing godfather to everyone. When it came to tending to himself and acknowledging anything of his own on a personal level, he lacked considerably. In his mind it was about his duty to others first and foremost, until very recently that is, and whether he liked it or not.

After a long hot shower he pulled on his robe and meandered about his room. He couldn't remember the last time he cared about his appearance for an event, and even now he felt silly for being concerned. He did love his clothing, his suits and shoes especially. They were his secret weakness from long long ago when he was lucky for any scrap to cover himself with. When he was able to afford his first pair of sandals, he swore he would never ever go unshod again. So he had to admit he had another weakness, his secret pedicures with Niko once a month. That too was something he did because of his early years, before his turning. The first fifteen years of his life had been barefoot and barely a day had gone by that his feet were not bloody. Surely his indulgence was justified. He wandered into his bathroom and stared in the mirror at himself, long and hard. No matter how many centuries passed, he would always see the slave boy he once was. He wasn't certain why women had found him attractive over the years. Truth be told, he hadn't cared lately, and certainly not about just any women, only Lou. His naturally tanned skin was courtesy of his Greco-Roman heritage and he had to admit that the proper shave had been a wise idea on Abby's part. He honestly felt his features were average. Not a weak jaw, he would concede that and perhaps a relatively straight nose despite it having been broken more times than he could remember. All in all he saw nothing special when he looked at himself. he was a big man, but that didn't count for much, nothing to make a woman like Lou weak-kneed by a long shot. Max didn't see his chiseled features the way Lou did, or the eyes of warm honey. He didn't see the symmetry the way she did, he just saw plain brown hair, light brown eyes and two arms and legs of the slave boy grown into a man.

He grabbed a bottle of goop and poured some into his hand, then worked it through his towel-dried hair until it was glossed back and off his face. He brushed his teeth and used the skincare products that Abby had lined up on the vanity and numbered with huge white stickers. So far he had completed everything on her list, right down to the spritzes of the cologne she left him, so it was time to get dressed and be done with it already. By the time he was nearly dressed and fastening his cufflinks, he had worked himself into a nervous pitch and it was infuriating him.

"You're thinking too much." Abby startled him as she walked into his room. "If it makes you feel any better, so is she." She grinned at him as she approached to help him with his cuffs.

"You look stunning as ever." He smiled as he admired her finery. Her hair was a mass of curls and the combs she wore were rich in jewel tones that matched the twinkle in her eyes. The deep forest green velvet gown she wore was lovely on her and reminded him that she wasn't the little girl he always saw her as.

"I do, don't I?" She grinned at him. "You know I love these kind of things. I think I have dresses stored up for the next ten events in anticipation."

"I am sure you have more than that, but it's the shopping for them that you love, don't think I don't know it."

"And this would be another classic example of why you are my wise and beloved Dom." She started on his tie once she finished with the last cufflink. "The boys are ready when you are."

Max sighed and fidgeted while she fixed his tie. "Do I look ridiculous?"

How the man was not riddled with conceit over how gorgeous he was would always baffle Abby. "Ridiculous is definitely not what comes to mind. You look dashing, I promise." She grabbed his jacket and helped him into it as he snorted.

"I'd settle for presentable." He turned to inspect himself in the mirror. The bespoke tuxedo fit him perfectly and the three button with vest was Abby's personal favorite, which is why she set it out for him.

"More than presentable, so lets get a move on and present you already!" She grabbed his gloves and overcoat and headed for the door.

When they entered the living area of the suite, Finn, Connor, Yuri, Niko and Frank were all there waiting. Properly pressed and polished. It was times like this that Abby remembered she was constantly surrounded by magnificent looking men. Too bad they were all virtually her big brothers.

"Abby give that to me!" Max ordered as he snatched his coat and gloves from her. "You are the lady, I should be fetching your things."

"Allow me." Finn stepped up, holding Abby's wrap up for her to step into.

Abby grinned. "Why thank you!"

"I have your bag." Frank waved the small clutch that was encrusted with the same jewels as her combs.

With a deep sigh, Max waved his hand toward the door. "Then I guess we are off."

Niko chuckled and slapped a hand on Max's back then pushed him out the door.

Lou had been standing in front of the mirror for at least ten minutes and still was unable to calm herself. She felt ridiculous. Like she was looking at a stranger in the mirror and that Max would laugh the minute he set eyes on her. There was no way in hell she was going to this gala. Unfortunately for Lou, there was also no way in hell her mother or Caroline would allow her not to.

"Whoa!" Caroline gasped as she walked in to the closet and saw Lou all dressed and ready to go. "You look utterly amazing!"

Lou looked as if she had stepped off a movie screen in her bronzed dress and matching shoes. The earrings and bracelet that her mother had suggested could not have been more perfect. While Lou did in fact feel pretty, it was too far off the beaten path from her normal jeans, lip-gloss and go. Insecure was far too light of an adjective for how she currently felt.

"I can't do this." She said as she turned to her friend who in her mind was the most beautiful woman she had ever seen, besides her mother, of course.

Caroline wore siren red satin that was cut just low enough to be tasteful with a slit up the side that was just high enough not to be tacky. Giant pearls surrounded in diamonds adorned her earlobes and on her wrist was a matching three strand bracelet. The up-do she had chosen along with her bare shoulders just added to her already long and graceful stature. Lou felt small and drab next to her.

"You can and you will! So come on, we are going to be late." Caroline grabbed Lou's coat and bag then shoved Lou out of the closet with a body check.

"Ow! Seriously?" Lou nearly fell over.

"Seriously. Now move, we don't have time to cover up another black eye, so move before I send for your mother. They are waiting for us at the door."

The look on Joe and her mother's face when she came down the stairs made her feel a little better. They were smiling proudly like they had when she walked up on stage at her graduation from the academy. Her stomach stopped flopping but continued the flipping.

"You look so beautiful!" Joe gushed when she finally made it to the door.

"I feel ridiculous." She huffed as Joe helped her into her coat.

"Of course you do sweetie pie, you'll get over it." Her mother gave her no solace as she ushered her out the door.

Chapter Fifteen

Limousines and town cars inched their way up the boulevard with the direction of traffic cops to take their turn letting off passengers that ranged from rock stars to foreign dignitaries to homicide detectives. Lou watched the searchlights pan the sky from out the car window and cringed at the logistical nightmare this event must have been for local law enforcement. When the top hat and tails clad valet opened the door to the limo, Lou stepped out onto the sidewalk to the barrage of flashbulbs from the paparazzi that lined the barricades on each side of the pathway. It was a bloody zoo.

They were immediately met by a formally dressed gentleman wearing a headset who was typing and stabbing his finger at his tablet while trying not to look immensely frazzled. To his credit, he knew precisely who they were and escorted them up the pathway to the reception area where a horde of guests were already mingling and sipping from cut crystal champagne glasses. After being relieved of their coats by another attendant, they stood at the top of the steps before descending down into the sea of other guests and took in the spectacle of it all. The reception area was actually the front gardens of the museum that were tented for the occasion like a circus big top, but in creamy white rather than primary stripes. Soft string music played just below the din of chattering guests and tinkling of water from the myriad of fountains that jutted up out of the streams and ponds that were dotted and woven throughout the gardens. Huge gilded freestanding candelabras that stood at least eight feet tall and held candles the size of Lou's leg, were placed strategically about and gave an ethereal glow to the setting. Clearly no expense had been spared for the event.

Lou looked out at all the people, the beautiful and finely dressed people and wondered once again, what the hell was she doing here? It was precisely then that something instinctual led her eyes to his. Across the throng of people, at least thirty yards away, Max beamed a smile at her that made her feel warm and instantly lightheaded. Dear God, he looked like something off the pages of a magazine and she had to grip the railing to steady herself. Max was surrounded by people nearly clawing to get to him, but he seemed not to notice or care as he started to make his way toward her. She had forgotten her mother, Joe and Caroline and descended the stairs to meet him without thinking. Lou hadn't noticed the thousands of eyeballs that had landed on her, clearly wondering who had captured the attention of their Dominor. Max could care less about protocol or manners and could only think about getting to Lou. She took his breath away when he saw her.

When they met at the bottom of the steps, he extended his hand, which she took without thought. He drew her closer and breathed in her jasmine and vanilla perfume as though it were the only thing that could sustain him.

"You are the most beautiful thing I have ever seen." It slipped out of his mouth without hesitation.

Lou blushed instantly and grinned despite herself. "You clean up pretty good yourself." Her eyes met his and they both were lost for several moments. The whole of the affair melted away into the distance as they took each other in. Not a word was spoken between them but volumes were said in that stare.

Shadows of Doubt

"Uh, hello?" They both started as Caroline butted her way in. "Remember us?"

Lou's face grew hotter as she turned to Caroline and her parents. "Sorry."

"Caroline, you look ravishing." Max took Caroline's hand and politely kissed her knuckles, turning to Shevaun to do the same. "And you my dear Shevaun, look magnificent as always." He smiled brightly to Joe. "To borrow a recent quote, you clean up pretty good too Joe."

Lou chuckled as Max greeted everyone and couldn't help but notice how he postured himself close to her as if tucking her under his arm. It made her feel warm and lightheaded again.

"Where is the gang?" Caroline asked him as her eyes scanned the crowd looking for signs of the others.

A waiter approached them to offer glasses of champagne, which they all were happy to accept. Max took two glasses and handed one to Lou with a beaming smile. She didn't think there was enough champagne in the world to calm the flutter in her stomach.

"As you all are fashionably late, I am sure they are moving about the garden politicking as per proper form." Max sipped from his glass.

After a carefully measured sip of her own, she looked up at him again. "I'm certain you have a good deal of that to do yourself. Please don't feel obligated to hang out with us."

Max looked down at her with a whimsical grin. "I don't think I could ever classify hanging out with you as an obligation. More an indulgence." Shevaun and Caroline grinned at each other as they watched the invisible sparks flying between Lou and Max.

"It's quite remarkable all those in attendance tonight." Joe observed. "A veritable who's-who of Sanguinostri. Have you seen Albert yet?"

"No, not yet." Max absentmindedly turned to face Joe, placing his hand on the small of Lou's back without thinking. Lou nearly melted into a puddle at the sensation and bit her tongue to refrain from humming aloud. "His assistant told us when we arrived that he will be making some grand entrance once all the guests have checked in. I shouldn't imagine it will be much longer." Max nodded and smiled as people passed and greeted him with a degree of reverence that only added to Lou's fluster.

Lou had begun to notice the eyes surveying her and it was becoming a bit disconcerting. When a couple finally approached them that looked like old world royalty, the woman looked down her nose at Lou as she extended her hand for Max to take. She was a good bit taller than Lou, probably due to the impossibly high stilettos she was wearing. Her skin was pale as porcelain and her long mane of hair was equally pale. It was styled to sweep around the nape of her neck and cascade down in front in rolling waves. Her dress was a nude satin that was so tight it left nothing to the imagination, which was probably the plan all along. Her ears and neck dripped in diamonds that were obviously real since the woman was definitely the type who would never have stood for anything imitation. The only color she wore was the red lipstick that was far too bright for her skin tone but her continued pursing and pouting made it clear to Lou that the woman felt it was the perfect shade.

"Maximilian..." The snobby woman spoke. "...we had expected to see you much sooner after you arrived. Naughty boy staying away from me like that." Lou found the woman's voice grating with overly seductive tones.

"Corinne." Max greeted the woman, taking her hand and barely touching his lips to her knuckles. "A pleasure to see you. I've been very busy since my arrival and haven't been able to make the rounds as of yet. Allow me to introduce you..." Max released the woman's hand and stepped in closer to Lou, drawing his hand up her back while the

Shadows of Doubt

other skimmed her arm as he nudged her more in front of him. "Lou Donovan, my companion and newest Principate." The woman's eyes nearly popped out of her head at the declaration and Lou wondered what the implications of being referred to as his companion were, but simply smiled brightly at the woman who appeared to be trying not to choke.

"Lou, this is Corinne Corgan, an old friend and devoted patroness of the arts." He looked at Lou and gave her a reassuring wink that went unnoticed by the goggling Corinne.

"Good to meet you." Lou extended her hand.

Corinne reluctantly took Lou's hand in hers very briefly and obviously only for appearance's sake. "Yes, likewise I am sure." She studied Max's face carefully as he looked at Lou, and raised an eyebrow.

"And these are her parents, Shevaun and Joe McAllister, as well as Caroline Devereux, of the Richelieu Devereuxs" Max turned slightly and gestured to the three.

Corinne's eyes goggled again at the mention of Richelieu. "Really?!" Her voice squeaked slightly.

Joe and Shevaun shook the woman's hand politely but Caroline had Corinne's number and relished dealing with her type.

"Really." Caroline said smugly. Obviously knowing something about the woman that Lou didn't. "Corgan? Aren't you the Corinne Corgan from the Falsbey films?"

Corinne instantly puffed up. "Why yes, one and the same. You're a fan of my work?"

"Well, actually I just took a historical cinema class as a filler in college. I remember you from a paper I did on the failure of burlesque on film. Too bad things didn't catch on for you back then." Caroline smiled at the woman cheerfully.

Shevaun hid her laughter under a cough as the steam almost visibly rose off of Corinne's face.

"Corinne, darling..." The man who had gone unnoticed by the group stepped in as if trying to diffuse a bomb. "The Duke has been asking for you since he arrived. I think it's cruel for you to keep him waiting any longer. If you all will excuse us." He ushered the fuming Corinne away from them and as soon as she was gone, they all started to laugh.

"Pompous bitch." Caroline declared as she took a solid gulp of her champagne. "I always hated her type growing up. My momma taught me early on how to deal with the likes of her."

"You'll need to learn to ignore those bitches, Lou." Abby said as she suddenly appeared next to them. "They are so old and crusted with self importance that they forgot how to be discreet about their jealousy." She reached for Lou's hand and squeezed reassuringly. "And this guy is oblivious to it most of the time so you gotta thump him on the head when someone is being so overtly rude."

"That was very overt." Max admitted. "I despise having to deal with that woman." He scowled and swapped his empty champagne glass for a fresh one as a waiter walked by.

"Well it would be nice to know if I am allowed to be rude back to them or if I'm required to play nice with the shrews?" Lou glared across the crowd at the woman as she tossed her head back with phony laughter over something a short, fat, bald and shiny man had said.

Max couldn't help grinning at Lou. "You have my blessing to be rude right back to anyone that annoys you" He skimmed his hand up and down her arm again which gave her goosebumps. "Remember though! You still have to deal with your normal strain of politics within the departments as always. I can't step in there on a daily basis. The normal world still turns as usual."

"I understand all that and am used to it. Don't worry." She tore her eyes away from him briefly to catch Corinne scowling at her from across the crowd. She simply couldn't help herself and stuck her tongue out at the woman who gasped in reaction. "It's nice to be able to do that though."

Max erupted with laughter, nearly doubling over and drawing even more stares from the other guests. The sight of Lou in all her sophisticated splendor resorting to such a juvenile, albeit effective, tactic, was priceless.

"Okay, enough fun and games, we need to make some rounds and introduce all of you to key people and get it out of the way so we can enjoy the rest of our evening." Max regained his composure and looked to Abby to lead the way.

"Probably wise to start with the east coast admin." She led them away from the base of the steps and into the throng.

Forty-five minutes later Lou had forgotten more names than she could remember. Everyone she had met after Corinne had been genuinely glad to meet her and very kind. She had stuffed at least a dozen business cards in her purse with all the givers insisting she contact them for any reason if they could ever be of assistance. Of course there was a new level of brown nosing which she found highly amusing. At least it was sincere with kindness rather then poorly veiled attempt to gain favor from Max. Lou had just finished listening to a bad joke told by the agent from the Department of Justice when she heard a tap on a microphone from the sound system that had been piping in the stringed music.

"Ladies and gentlemen, esteemed guests and friends, our Dominor..." Lou found the source of the voice perched at the top of the entry steps. He was a pleasant looking fellow though he appeared a bit worse for wear with his tie askew and his hair slipping out of place. He placed his fist over his heart and nodded to Max as he addressed him. "It is my great pleasure to introduce our host and benefactor for this exhibit, Sir Albert von Massenbach." The man stepped aside from the microphone and began applauding, which cued everyone else to applaud.

It suddenly occurred to Lou that all in attendance were Sanguinostri only. Even the media that had been allowed to cover the event must have been. She would have to remember to ask Max about that later. For now she spied the man that was evidently throwing the shindig step up to speak. He raised his hands up in a gesture to stall the applause. He was hardly an aristocratic looking man despite his finely tailored clothes. His wiry ginger hair was pulled back tightly into a pony tail and secured with a black ribbon. Complete with bow that reminded Lou of how men may have worn than in the seventeen hundreds, right along with stockinged feet. His facial features were obscured, thankfully she thought, by a well groomed beard and his eyes reminded her of a dead fish. This man was not at all what she had expected as the host of such an elaborate event.

"Dear friends..." He finally spoke once the applause had died. "...and my Dominor." He made an overly fancy bow, complete with rolling hand gesture towards Max. Lou could hear Niko chortle at the move from behind her. "It is my greatest honor that you all have joined me this evening! I am humbled to see all the faces of so many dear friends and even dearer loved ones..." To Lou's delight, he waggled his eyebrows toward Corinne, making her fluster uncomfortably. "...at the unveiling of my most prized collection that I have allowed the museum to exhibit for the next year. Many of you who know me are well aware that the antiquities contained in this collection represent a very fond period of time in my long lived life." Lou sensed Max tense at the words. "I was very fortunate to have held on to so much when the Empire fell. Even more fortunate to be able to retrieve so many other pieces back from the clutches of oblivion to which precious and beloved things were lost to quite a few of us."

Shadows of Doubt

There was no mistaking the glance directed at Max when he said this. It stirred Lou to look at Max's expression when he did, and she saw the well disguised anguish in his face. Lou turned to Abby with a questioning look and saw that she was frowning. When Abby met Lou's gaze she held a finger up to her lips in a gesture of silence. Something was definitely up with this guy and Max.

"Now that I have rattled on long enough, I invite you to step inside and enjoy the exhibit! Take your time and explore everything, then I shall meet you all on the other side for a lovely midnight supper I have had prepared in honor of all of you! My dear friends! Please enjoy!" He finished his monologue and the crowd began another round of applause. Once von Massenbach stepped away from the microphone, Max was swarmed by his Aegis Council and Lou headed for Abby.

"What the hell was that about?" Lou demanded.

"That was crap is what it was, and I would have never expected it from Albert." Abby grabbed Lou's arm and pulled her further away from Max and the other men before she continued. "You remember Max was engaged once, a long time ago, right?" Lou nodded, remembering. "Well..."

Abby went on to tell Lou the tale of Max being sent to defend Constantinople when the Empire began its fall and how his fiance had been murdered while he was gone. She explained how it had devastated Max and that it was common knowledge among the Sanguinostri not to bring up the matter if it could be avoided. Clearly von Massenbach tossed an unwarranted and painful jab at Max but it was unclear exactly as to why.

"The fall of Constantinople? That was what, nearly six-hundred years ago? You mean this guy has an ancient bug up his butt that would warrant salting such an old wound?" Lou couldn't imagine harboring all that animosity for such a long time.

"It would be news to me but I can assure you that we will find out shortly." Abby guided Lou to where her parents were standing with Caroline and her family then took off like a shot. Max joined them a few minutes later and Lou watched the other men disperse into different directions. Max seemed to be fine to her but her heart ached for him a bit, knowing that underneath that calm, cool and completely unflappable visage, he had hurt.

As the they and the crowd made their way into the exhibit, Frank, Niko and the others came by one at a time to whisper into Max's ear. Lou tried to use the tricks that Niko had taught her about peripheral observation but other than getting pissed at all the women tossing moon-eyes in Max's direction, nothing seemed off to her. Lou tried to seem interested at the information that Richelieu would relay with each piece they came upon in the exhibit, but she honestly could have cared less. She was glad when they came to the end of it and were guided by more fancily dressed ushers into a tent that was fashioned into the finest ballroom Lou could ever have imagined possible. The floor was made up of three-by-three foot squares of cream and gold tiles polished to such a mirror finish that the three gigantic chandeliers that hung in a row down the center of the tent were reflected perfectly. Each of the several dozen tables that lined the perimeter of the tent were gilt with giant candelabras at the center, golden china and more cut crystal stemware. At the far end of the tent, Lou could see an entire orchestra that was currently playing some sort of waltz. The usher directed them to a table and Lou saw her new friend, Corinne, standing on the other side engaged in a clearly heated argument with another usher. When she saw Corinne point at a seat, Lou caught that she clearly was not happy about sitting at the same table as her.

"Let's take the high road sweetie pie and mingle a bit more while Corinne regains her composure." Lou's mother was clearly as amused as she was.

Shadows of Doubt

It was a little upsetting when Lou realized that Max had been seated at another table than she was, but she couldn't complain too much. She had anticipated barely seeing him at all during the event given his position, but he had nearly stuck to her like glue all night. When she caught sight of the back of him across the dance floor, huddled with Niko, Frank and the others, she smiled inwardly and headed over.

"I thought that was handled while I was dealing with Sawyer?" Was all Lou heard come out of Max's mouth but it made her stop cold behind him. Max read the expression in Niko's eyes and whipped around to see Lou standing there.

"Lou..." He started.

"Dealing with Sawyer? Robert Sawyer?" She looked at him with a blank expression.

"Lou I would have told you if I felt it necessary..." He was at a loss for what to say that would help his case.

"Necessary?" It was a rhetorical question. "So dealing with Sawyer, meaning killing him?" She asked him flat out. No pretense.

He wanted to reach out to her but didn't dare. "I listened to his side Lou." By her reaction, she hadn't expected him to tell her that. "I listened to his version of reality. He was all too happy to tell me."

Lou shifted her stance, clearly uncomfortable with Max knowing the details of her humiliation. "And?" Was all she could come up with.

Max looked carefully into her eyes before he said another word. "He had sent those two cretins to that restaurant to do gods know what to you. He had no problem telling me what he had planned for you himself once he was paroled. Lou, I simply could not let that happen. Please forgive me." He could see her eyes welling and risked reaching for her hand but she stepped back.

"Excuse me, I seem to need to powder my nose, as they say." She turned and moved away as fast as she could without attracting any more attention than she already had. It occurred to Lou she had no idea where she was in relation to any facilities. When she spied a group of women heading down a hall she knew the pack was headed for a restroom so she followed after them. She simply needed a minute to gather herself and make sense of what she had just heard.

Max wanted to charge after Lou but he knew better. She hadn't slapped him or punched him, which was a good sign, but he knew that she was a woman of laws and justice, not of revenge or retribution, which was often his duty to hand down in his world. He hadn't wanted her to learn all of that yet. To see the darker side of his role as Dominor so soon. Not that his dealing with Sawyer had anything to do with being Dominor but was a pure, primal need to protect and avenge Lou. Max had hoped she could see the good things he was responsible for, the safety and security that he made certain his people had. This was very bad indeed.

"Just give her a little time, she will understand once she has a minute for it to sink in." Abby placed a hand on his arm in a reassuring gesture.

"You should go and see to her." He looked at her with urgency.

Abby shook her head. "No. We need to give her a minute and some space. If I go she will know you sent me and that would only make things worse. She'll be back."

Everyone started to take their seats for dinner so Abby steered Max to his place before she headed to Lou's seat where her parents, the Devereuxs and horrible Corinne sat with her footman. Abby had decided she better fill them in before someone went looking for Lou and raised eyebrows at the empty seat. When she sat, Shevaun and Caroline looked at her questioningly so she relayed what had transpired as quietly as she could.

Niko took Abby's seat next to Max for the time being, smiling politely when he got stares for disrupting the boy-girl-boy-girl seating arrangement.

Shadows of Doubt

"My Dom, she just needs a little time to think it out." Niko could tell he was sick of hearing that already but continued anyway. "I've had the opportunity to spend time with her. See first hand how she thinks, her logic. She is a sharp girl, no doubt but more than that..." He looked Max square in the eye as he spoke. "She has the mind of an Aegis, my Dom. She has a truer sense of justice than most, and a keenness to get a stronger hold on it. Don't underestimate her capacity, my brother, she will surprise you. She certainly has surprised me."

Max was taken aback by Niko's words. He was not the type to give praise lightly, if at all, and for him to compare Lou's sense of justice to that of the Aegis, well, it was truly extraordinary. They were snapped back to reality as the waiters came around to serve the first course and Max clearly noted Lou had not taken her seat yet. Abby remained in her spot and saw Max looking, giving him a soft smile as she picked up a fork and started eating. Good, he thought, Lou could come sit by him when she came back and eat Abby's food.

Food was the last thing on Lou's mind as she sat in the bathroom stall of the ladies restroom. She had gone in there to compose herself after the stunning revelation that the two grease monkeys that had attacked her were sent by Robert Sawyer and that Max had killed him. Had the monkeys really killed themselves or had Niko or one of the others used their special gifts on them? Did it really matter either way? She should have been upset, shocked or something to that effect but when she finally sat down and thought about it, she wasn't. A great deal of things that should have bothered her as of late simply did not. She wondered what the hell that meant exactly. To add to her guilt over not being upset, she found the gossip and chatter of the women coming and going in the ladies room far more interesting than Sawyer and his minions' demise. Lou was the hot topic among the single Sanguinostri females, and how Max seemed to have eyes for her that none of them had ever seen before. Some of the women were excited and wanted to learn more of the presumed couple while others were even worse than catty and would have liked to see Lou drowned in one of the garden ponds. It had been difficult for Lou not to laugh when she heard two women cheering for Lou when they were told by a third woman that Lou had stuck her tongue out at Corinne to her face.

Lou felt her position in the stall was akin to being a fly on the wall and she was actually enjoying herself. She heard the door to the restroom swing open and a woman announced dinner was being served, then the mutters and grumbles of several women as they meandered out. When the last woman exited, the silence reminded Lou why she had come in there in the first place and she remained seated, thinking long and hard about it. Max had found out about Robert Sawyer and had gone to talk to him directly about what he had done to her. Over the years Lou had thought about coming face to face with the man again herself and knew, unequivocally, that she would kill him without batting an eyelash. The only thing that bothered her was that she hadn't the first time he attacked her. So, knowing that and now knowing that Max had actually afforded the man the chance to tell his side which she sure as hell wouldn't have done, how could she be angry? Add to that Sawyer sending two goons after her, then actually telling Max he had intended to find Lou again once he got out? Wouldn't she have wanted Max to prevent this if he could? Wouldn't Lou herself have done the same thing if someone were threatening her own family? Caroline or Abby even? No, Lou wasn't upset with Max over killing Robert Sawyer in the least when she considered all of it. She was more shocked and embarrassed that he knew about what had happened to her if truth be told. When it came right down to it, she was moved by his actions. That he cared about her at all was a feat in itself but enough to eliminate the man that had caused her so much pain? That was something else entirely. Right then all Lou wanted to do was run to him and wrap her arms around him and tell him how grateful she was. She knew she had to tone it down a lot for the gossips but she had to get out of there and let him know at least that she wasn't upset or angry. Thankfully, when she walked out of the stall she was alone in the restroom, as she had thought. Lou took a hard look at herself in the mirror and was grateful that her makeup was still in place and her black eye hadn't started peeking through. With a quick wash of the hands and a quicker swipe of lip gloss, she headed for the door quietly so as not to raise eyebrows when she snuck back to the ballroom. The hallway was clear when she looked out so she proceeded with caution down the tented corridor. She paused a moment to spritz herself lightly with some perfume so she didn't smell like toilet bowl cleaner, when she suddenly felt a sharp sting in her neck. She tried to reach to feel what had bitten her but her body instantly felt heavy and she couldn't find her voice to even say 'owe' as the tiny bottle of perfume slipped out of her hand. She thought she felt someone grabbing her but the world swirled out from under her and everything went black.

By the time the second course was served, Max couldn't stand it any longer. Lou was not the type of woman to brood, let alone for this long. He looked over to Abby and when she caught his glance, he jerked his head for her to go. Abby got up immediately and headed for the ladies room to check on Lou. It only took about three minutes before Niko started whispering into his wrist and Max noticed security moving from one side of the room to the other at a fast clip. Yuri, Finn and Connor got up from their seats and nearly ran in Abby's direction while they touched their ears, clearly channeling in their micro receivers. When Niko pushed his finger to his ear also, then whipped out of his seat, Max knew something bad was happening.

"Christ, no." He pleaded as he followed behind Niko and fished his own receiver out of his pocket, twisted to turn it on then stuffed it in his ear.

What he heard was each security sector chief sounding off, acknowledging whatever order Niko had just given. Max tried to grab Niko's jacket as they ran but Niko brushed his hand away and ordered him to move it. They raced down the tented corridor that Max had seen Lou disappear down less then half an hour ago and found Abby ordering the dozen security agents that were half-circled around her to start a perimeter search. When she turned and looked at Max, there was utter panic in her eyes and he noted she was holding Lou's purse in one hand and a tiny bottle in the other.

"I found these on the floor right here." Abby held them up slightly. "We checked the ladies room and there is no sign of her."

"Who the hell had eyes on her?!" Max bellowed.

"My Dominor..." One of the security team stepped forward. "She went into the restroom twenty-eight minutes ago. I stood right there until eight minutes ago when one of the waitstaff suggested I grab a plate before they were gone." The man shrank to the reaction on Max's face but he continued to relay his movements. "I walked through those double doors down there and waited in line to grab food with some other staffers and when I came back, Ms. LaRue was here and well, I became a dead man walking, sir."

"Well at least you got one thing right!" Max charged towards him but Niko stepped in the way.

"This is wasting time, we deal with him later." Max stopped, realizing Niko was right. "You..." He pointed at the moron. "... go assist the surveillance team review the footage for the last ten minutes and stay out of the way if you feel the urge to be incompetent again."

Niko looked at Max hard now. "We are locking everything down. I have security doing a table by table head count to see who, if anyone is missing. Yuri and Finn are putting eyes on every staff member and security personnel to make sure no one has gone unaccounted for. If she is on the premises we will find her my Dom, I swear to you."

"And if she's not?!" Max knew it was the rogue, without question. He had taken Lou. "If that bastard has already gotten her off site?! What the hell then?!"

"Then it will take a little more time, but we will find her and get her back." Niko put a hand on Max's shoulder and squeezed. "Settle my Dom. I need you here with us. Focused."

Max looked at Niko then at the others who were staring at him as if his head were about to pop off. Abby had tears streaming down her cheeks and Frank was squeezing her hand. Niko was right, he needed to get it together and deal with what needed dealing.

"Abby, once the table check is done, calmly and quietly get the McAllisters and the Devereuxs back to the hotel and lock them down tight. Shevaun is going to freak out so only tell her once you are out of earshot from the gathering." He fished a handkerchief from his inside pocket and handed it to her. "I need you to handle them so put on your game face." She nodded as she took the cloth and blotted her eyes. "Finn, get Richelieu. I don't care if he's insulted, I want you to read him and make sure he's not involved. Once you know for certain, have him set up a war room in his bungalow and I want communications to all operatives synched within twenty minutes." Frank headed to fetch Richelieu immediately just as Connor came up the hall.

"You are not going to believe this." Connor started.

"Just tell me!" Max barked at him.

"The only people missing are von Massenbach and Lou." There was a collective gasp after Connor said it.

"Albert?!" Max could hardly believe it. He hadn't understood the dig that Albert had made toward him earlier and this had made even less sense. It was incomprehensible that Albert harbored ill feelings over Max being chosen as Dominor after all this time, and to be committing these murders as a result of it. "That makes no sense. Why the hell would he act out like this because of our past? To kill innocents? It goes against everything an Aegis stands for, retired or not. It simply doesn't make sense." Max scrubbed his hands over his face while he tried to grasp the situation.

"Ah shit, why didn't I see it before?!" Niko yanked his hair in frustration and Max turned to look at him. "Its about Nila!"

Max stalked toward Niko. "What the hell does Nila have to do with any of this?"

"Christ, I thought you were being paranoid!" Connor said as he squatted in the hall then blew out a breath.

"What the hell are you both talking about? I don't have time for this! Lou doesn't have time for this!" Max was starting to lose his grip again.

"Max, I don't believe it was a coincidence that just you and I were sent to Constantinople." Niko began to put the pieces together and talked it out to Max. "I had seen the way Albert looked at Nila but thought little of it because he and I knew you would crush him like a bug if he ever acted on it."

Conner stood up and interjected. "It was right after you two were betrothed. I heard him talking, not very flatteringly, about Nila and had words with him over it. I hadn't realized it was out of jealousy until just now."

"The weeks leading up to the final assault..." Niko continued. "...when word was getting back to Constantine, before Mehmed made him the final offer. I had seen Albert holding private counsel with our Dom. It seemed odd then but so much was going on that I let it pass for the time being. Then when we got home and learned of Nila, everything else seemed petty so I pushed it out of my mind."

"You're saying Albert convinced Zarath to send us to Constantinople? Because of some sort of jealousy?" Max couldn't believe it even as he said it.

"There is one way to find out." Connor said as he pulled out his cell phone.

"What are you doing?" Max asked him.

"Calling Zarath." Connor shrugged. "What could it hurt?"

"This is preposterous! He probably doesn't even have a phone!" Max began pacing the hall.

"Actually, he even has a Facebook page." Niko informed him just as Frank returned with Richelieu.

"What the hell is going on?" Richelieu demanded as Finn stepped up and took his hand. "What do you think you are doing?" He started to struggle as Max stepped in front of him.

"It's necessary. I apologize but this is necessary and I am asking for you to submit, as your Dominor."

Richelieu saw the fear and sadness in Max's eyes and submitted to Finn immediately. It took only a few moments before Finn let his hand go and Niko proceeded to inform him of what was going on and what was needed of him. Richelieu paused for only a moment to grab Max's arm.

"We will find her." Was all he said before he bolted down the hall.

"Well..." Connor said as he stuffed his cell phone into his pocket. "...that confirms that. Zarath confirmed Niko's suspicions after all this time. He even went so far as to say that it has been one of his greatest regrets and one of the reasons he retired and fought for your ascension. He feels that if he never had sent you, never had let Albert convince him that you and Niko should be sent, Nila and you would be living a quiet happy life this very moment on some island somewhere."

Max would have roared with rage if he could have. If Albert had manipulated Zarath into sending him and Niko away, then he surely was the ax that had severed Nila's head. It made sense now that he knew. The way Nila's body had been found in the alley where known whores peddled their wares. Albert had even tried to console him over it. All this time the bastard had been responsible for all of it.

"He must have been in love with her. Spurned by her before the two of you came together." Frank placed a hand on Max's shoulder. "I didn't know your history really, but I know that the few times I have seen him and you together, his jealousy leaks out a little. It must have secretly driven him mad once you were elevated to Dom. The fact that you hadn't been destroyed by losing Nila, and were even stronger for it. Somehow killing women that in his warped mind reminded him of her. A perversion. An exact opposite of what she really was."

Max shook his head in disbelief. "But now he has Lou. She is so different from Nila. Of course I loved Nila but Lou is so different, so much more than I could have ever hoped for." Max could feel his chest caving in with panic.

"And we will get her back!" Niko reminded him. "Frank, call Abby and get her on a list of every piece of toilet paper that Albert has bought or rented within a thousand miles of here." Frank simply nodded and pulled out his phone. "Connor, pin down the vehicle Albert came in, then check where it is now and if it's not here, where it went, where it's been and for how long."

Max looked at Niko. "This whole damn exhibit was him giving me the finger and when he got wind of Lou meaning something to me, that was the double finger."

Niko nodded. "Maybe so, but now we are going to shove those fingers right up his own ass."

On a normal day Max would have chuckled at that. He turned to Finn instead. "I want everyone in this building to know that Albert von Massenbach is wanted for capital crimes against the Sanguinostri. I'll call the Senatus myself. I want the people that dealt with Albert setting up this event and the person in charge of this damn museum in front of me ten minutes ago. Someone find me a room I can work in."

While everyone scrambled to comply with Max's orders, he called the Senatus and informed them of what was happening and that they could verify with Zarath the information from the past. Max was not one to be frivolous with his judgments so they found no reason to doubt him now. He was given full rights to pursue the matter as he saw fit by unanimous vote right there on the conference call. Each of the other Doms also offered their own personal assistance and stated they would inform all of their people that Albert was a criminal and was to be apprehended on site, dead if needs be. While Max appreciated the sentiments and compliance without hesitation, it was of little consolation when he thought about Lou. He paced up and down the hall that had guards on either side, preventing anyone from coming or going without Max's permission. All Max could think of was Lou and the dead women by Albert's hands. The brutality of the murders made sense now that he knew of Albert's rage and hate. He looked at his watch and based upon the time frame given by the moron who was supposed to keep eyes on Lou, she had been gone for almost an hour now. He prayed to every god he could think of that she was still unconscious and that Albert hadn't begun his sick and twisted acts on her. The only thing certain that Max had to hold on to was that he would feel Albert's blood flow through his fingers for this.

Fifteen minutes later, and after a five minute argument with Abby about how his coming back to the hotel which was full of their equipment and only three miles away was the most prudent course of action, Max was in the Devereux bungalow with Abby, Caroline, Joe and Lou's mother. Shevaun was a wreck and had obviously been sobbing just prior to Max coming in. Now, however, she was trying to calm down and focus.

"What do you have, Abby?" He asked as he hovered over her to look at the three computer monitors she had running at once.

"He has nothing in his name personally so it's been a matter of hunting down his various companies and fronts. Frank is next door with Rich coordinating searches with the guys, as we get addresses." Before he could ask, she swung around in her chair and scooted to the other table that had four additional monitors hooked up and running scans. "The limousine was a little tricky but we are on that now. Seems Albert was a busy little bee while we were all sipping champagne. Five different drivers were found sound asleep at the wheel in the back lot and the license plates had magically vanished off their rides. Clearly he's using one of those plates for cover. I got those plate numbers by cross referencing the Vehicle Identification Numbers so now I am scanning all the Caltrans traffic cams within a ten mile radius of the museum for any hit on any of them. It's just taking forever because their system is bogged down with Friday night traffic."

"He had to get her out of there somehow without being noticed. Someone had to have helped him." Max said as he dragged his fingers through his hair then ripped off his tie and jacket in frustration.

"Wait..." Shevaun got up from her seat. "Lou said that one of the victims had been doing cataloging of items as they came in for the exhibit, correct?"

Max walked over and took Shevaun's hands. "Yes, what strikes you about that?"

"Lou felt that victim was always different from the others..." Caroline turned in her seat and looked up at them as she chimed in. "She and I went around about that since she didn't feel being a pole dancer was enough of a lowlife for our guy as the other women were."

"Well that woman would have been in the back of things. The guts, unpacking crates as they came in." Shevaun picked up again. "What if she had stumbled upon his plot for the gala and that's why Albert killed her?"

"It wouldn't jibe." Caroline shook her head. "Winslow was killed on Tuesday. You and Lou didn't get found out until after Sunday. No way Winslow stumbled upon some plan to smuggle Lou out of the event then. Max didn't even know who Lou was until after Winslow was dead."

"She's right." Max sighed.

Suddenly Abby spun around again in her chair to face them. "But he would have known about Corinne!"

Max looked at her as if she were insane. "What about Corinne? I can barely tolerate the woman."

"Yes but only we know that or have known that! You have always been far too polite to put that wench in her place. So she always goes on and on about this secret thing you two have! Oh! Oh!" Abby spun around in the chair again. "And I know for a fact that she knew the day you got into town because she called me personally to set up a lunch date with you! But I blew her off as usual!"

Caroline's mother spoke as she entered the room. "So if she was spreading some bullshit story about you fawning over her to all the Nostri-lites..."

"Nostri-lites?" Max asked her.

"It's a name we have for all upper-crust socialites and divas of the Sanguinostri." She smiled sheepishly.

"Then Albert may have been planning her demise all this time and when he found out about you and Lou, he changed targets." Caroline finished her mother and Abby's line of thinking.

"Alright so assuming this is all fact..." Max began his ritual pacing. "...we know the why, who and when of the plot but that still doesn't give us the where, as in where he has Lou now! That is all that matters right now to me! Caroline, based upon what you know about the previous victims, I know you and Lou went over it pretty hard..."

"Yeah we did but we had too many holes because we didn't know about the Sanguinostri then."

He nodded, understanding the dilemma. "But you had an idea of time the girls went missing and time of death. When the wounds were inflicted and so forth?"

Caroline squinted as if she were trying to figure out what he was thinking. "Within a reasonable estimation, yes. Why?"

"I want you to search for any drug or toxin that could have been used to incapacitate the women, but that would allow them to be conscious before the first wounds were inflicted and..."

"Wouldn't show up on any toxicology postmortem!" Caroline finished his sentence as she made a dash for one of the computer set ups.

"Figure it out. Then figure out where he could have gotten it or if he had it shipped and I want to know how much time she has before she comes to. I don't want her to wake up alone with that son of a bitch!" Max stormed out of the bungalow and headed for the other to fill them in and get filled in.

When Max walked into the war room he heard buzzing, beeps and hums coming from all the equipment Rich had brought in. He saw Frank sitting in front of six monitors that had been fastened together with modular piping. He and Rich had headsets on and were talking into cell phones as well. Rich handed Max a headset as soon as he spotted him.

"Dom is on the Comm." Was all Richelieu said once Max put the headset on.

Max heard the crescendo of voices all at once saying "My Dominor." Then they were quiet.

Shadows of Doubt

Max was not new to this. It was how things worked in a time of action. "Status?" He said, his voice being transmitted to every operative at once.

One by one each team reported in. Relaying their current position or findings as of that moment. Abby was always the one to check in last. After she informed him of the new locations that teams one, two and three were being dispatched to, he heard an unfamiliar voice calling "Team Fourteen reporting..." And smiled despite himself when he realized it was Caroline.

"Five possibles on the toxins. I am running any and all purchases over the past four months with the assistance of Team Thirteen."

"Basis for four month limitation Fourteen?" Max asked her.

"My Dom..." Caroline answered without pause. "Subject von Massenbach arrived in Los Angeles exactly three months, twenty-six days ago. It is unlikely that he would have entrusted the procurement of such a critical component to his plan to anyone."

Max nodded in agreement even though she couldn't see him. "Agreed. Critical thinking Fourteen, keep me posted of your findings." Under different circumstances he would have laughed at her falling right into line on the operation just like a veteran. Now, he was just grateful to have another good mind at work finding Lou. The sensation of a cold hand on his shoulder blade startled him and he spun around to find Shevaun standing there. He quickly muted his line and gave her all his attention.

"What is it?" He asked her as he took her hand gently. He was certain she hated him. It being all his fault that her daughter was in the clutches of a homicidal madman. "Come sit and talk to me." He led her to a pair of chairs out of the way.

"Abby explained all of this to us, about Albert and his actions against you." A tear fell down her cheek and it broke his heart. "She told us about your fiancee and everything."

Max wiped the tear from her cheek and sighed. "I am so sorry, Shevaun. I should have never allowed my feelings to get away from me. If I had kept things under control, Lou would never..." Shevaun placed her hand over his mouth before he could say another word.

"This is not your fault, Maximilian! You are not responsible for the actions of a lunatic! I don't ever want to hear you apologize for falling in love with my daughter ever again, do you understand me?" Her eyes were fierce with her demand.

He placed his hand over hers and kissed her palm softly and for the first time in nearly six-hundred years, his own tears fell silently.

"Max, I didn't come in here to make you sad. Listen to me now, I have been thinking about everything Abby said. Everything that I know trying to make sense of this and it occurred to me that we might be thinking too typically here."

Max looked at her thoughtfully. "Explain please?"

"Well think of it, think about all the other victims now that you know the who and why. There has to be some commonality that you didn't see before. Some sort of pattern or story even that this son of a bitch is trying to tell you." Her eyes were still fierce, but he saw a light of hope that he often saw in Lou's.

"How would this help?" He wondered aloud.

"Because it would help you think like him. Just as any good detective gets inside the head of their suspect to find the hole they hide in. They are sloppy when they are cocky. They think they are too clever and you haven't gotten it yet, so why would you now?"

Max stood up and resumed pacing. "So where he takes them may be something obvious that I would have known. Should have known if I understood what he was trying to accomplish by all these killings."

"Exactly." Shevaun stood up and placed her hands on his chest. "I think it's going to be simple now that you know it's him and why it's him. I just need you to calmly think it all through. Lou needs you to."

Max looked at her for a long time and considered. He looked at his watch and took a deep breath. It was just after two in the morning and Lou had been gone for just under two hours. Was it significant that Albert had planned a midnight supper for his guests? Had he planned to take Corinne at midnight just as he had Lou? He bolted into the other bungalow.

"Abby, was there anything off about Lou's food?" He demanded as he screeched to a halt in front of her.

"How the hell would I know? She never got to eat remember?" She looked at him bewildered.

"Abby!" He shouted at her, making her cower slightly. "You ate Lou's food! You were sitting in her seat!"

Abby's eyes grew big as saucers. "Oh shit, that's right! But our metabolism is entirely different from human. I wouldn't have reacted to almost anything he put in her food."

"Abby have you peed since you ate?" Caroline asked as she made a dash for the kitchen.

"Well no, there hasn't been time!" Abby blinked with confusion.

"Go pee Abby!" Max ordered as Caroline returned from the kitchen with a small glass and handed it to her. "Pee in the glass! What do you need Caroline?"

"I got it, it will be on its way." She was dialing frantically on her cell phone. "Carpesh?" She nearly screamed into the phone then headed back into the kitchen as she barked orders at the skittish man.

"You tell him I said move!" Max shouted loud enough so that he knew Carpesh would hear him.

Shevaun had been right. Calming and thinking about events had led him to the probability that Albert had done something to Lou's food that would have lured her away from the crowd. It was just a stroke of luck that she had gone to the restroom on her own and not because of something she ingested.

"You're not going to like what I am about to say." Caroline said to him when she returned, holding a piece of cellophane in one hand.

Max grimaced at her. "Just say it, I think I am already going there in my own head anyway."

"If he drugged her food, then he's just smart enough to have calculated that into whatever dose he gave her when she came out of the bathroom." Abby returned from the restroom and handed the filled glass to Caroline, which she promptly covered with the cellophane. "Since she didn't ingest anything, she will be coming to sooner than that calculation."

"How much sooner?" both Max and Abby asked her at the same time.

After setting the glass in the small refrigerator, she came back and looked at both of them. "If it was one of the five possibles, at most, half the time. Maybe three hours down?"

Max looked at his watch and noted the time. She had been gone for approximately two hours and seventeen minutes. He had under forty-five minutes to put the pieces together as Shevaun suggested and get to Lou.

Chapter Sixteen

Albert knew she wouldn't be conscious yet but he was so giddy, he just had to peek in to make sure. As he headed down the hall to his workroom, he reflected on how everything had gone like clockwork. Well, almost. Considering he had an entirely different fly in mind just days ago, he couldn't complain too much about one or two minor hiccups. His little minion had taken care of the tedious work for him while he waited patiently hidden in the hall. He had to admit that she took a lot longer to come out of the restroom than he expected. He even thought perhaps he had put too much of the sedative in her salad and she fell asleep in there, or worse. Too much of the root and she would have gotten violently ill rather than just nauseated. The point was to get her to go into the restroom, but she had taken forever to come out. When she finally did, all the fretting was for naught. He had snuck up on her with the pressure syringe so fast she never knew what hit her. It was almost disheartening that she went down so fast and without a struggle. However, considering the fact that all of his other guests were just several yards away, faster was better in this instance.

He opened the door quietly, looked in and was disappointed but not surprised that she wasn't stirring. Checking his watch then going over his calculations in his head on the half-life of the drugs in her system, he was certain she would be out cold for at least a few more hours. It was just as well. He had a few things he needed to tend to so that he could be completely focused on his fly. Besides, they were simply no fun when they were loopy from the drugs so there was absolutely no rush at all. He closed the door, not bothering to be quiet about it, and headed back to take care of his loose ends.

Lou couldn't move, couldn't see and something was in her mouth that made it difficult for her to breathe. At first she thought it was the typical disorientation she'd have when she first woke up. Hell, she had given herself a black eye just the other day. But this was different and somehow she knew it, even in her groggy state. It was silent as a tomb, which is why for a moment she thought perhaps she was still asleep, having a bad dream. She forced herself to stop and think. Focus rather than fuss. She began remembering. First she remembered leaving the bathroom, then digging in her purse for her perfume, then the stinging sensation on the back of her neck and everything fading to black after that. Lou remained perfectly still as she thought it all out and did a check of all her extremities. Each arm felt slightly numb but she could feel her forearms and wrists being held to the arms of a chair with wide straps. Her legs felt the same numbness and they too were strapped at her ankles. She could feel the belt-like strap across her waist and another across her upper chest. It was starting to sink in and she reminded herself to stay calm, still and quiet. Lou realized she was blindfolded because she could feel her eyelashes rubbing against the cloth when she blinked and more than likely it was a ball-gag stuffed in her mouth. Her head wouldn't move at all because it too was strapped to the chair but it was when Lou realized she was naked that she knew she was in trouble.

He had her, the son of a bitch. Stay calm and think, she told herself as she tried to remember everything she could about the previous murders and the victims. Knowledge was power and that was the only form of power she was going to get at the moment. When she thought about what she and Caroline went over on the victims, she remembered they had come to the agreement that their suspect waited and took his time inflicting pain. He wanted them to suffer, so they wouldn't have been unconscious when he started. Buy time and play coma girl, she thought. They will notice she's gone from the gala. Someone will look for her and they will figure it out. Her mother, Max, the two of them would notice. But Max thought she was angry and might not go looking for her. He may even think that she had left because she was too upset. No, he had arranged for security. No way in hell he would let her take off without keeping tabs on her. He would send security to the house, see that she hadn't gone home. Right, that takes time so back to coma girl to buy that time for them to get a clue. Whoever this was that had her, he wasn't in the room now or he was far enough away she couldn't hear any breathing but her own. She thought about trying to rock the chair to get a feel for how sturdy it was. Perhaps try and crack it sideways by tipping over. No, he could be watching on a video camera or other surveillance, waiting for her to stir so he could come in and get started. Stay calm, play possum and pay attention to every little thing to try and gain an advantage somehow. And start praying.

The instant Carpesh arrived with cases of equipment, Caroline started transforming the bungalow kitchen into a mini-lab. They hoped they wouldn't have to waste time sending samples to the big lab and could narrow things down from where they were.

Abby spun around in her chair after clicking off from a call. "Okay I have two new bits of info. First, since we locked the party down tight, the caterers didn't have a chance to clear all the salad plates so they were able to get mine, or rather Lou's. You want it brought here?" She looked to Max and Caroline.

"Do we have anyone at the lab right now?" Caroline looked at Carpesh.

"Yes, we have Duke there. I'll have him wait at the entrance to meet the delivery." Carpesh started dialing the tech in question to have him standing by.

Abby's fingers flew as she sent the instructions out via text to her guys. "Okay now for the bad news..." Max looked at her with a good bit of panic in his eyes. "We found the limo in a back alley off Flower, downtown. Slimy dead guy in the driver's seat who was not dressed as a proper driver, according to Polis, and all the stolen plates were in the back save for the one he mounted on the car as a diversion."

"What the hell does that mean?" Max sat on the edge of the table scowling at her. "He didn't take her out in the limo?!"

"I am already running all surveillance to identify any vehicle that took off within our time frame." Abby tried to look hopeful.

Max grumbled and started pacing again. "Alright, we need to think about this carefully using all the bits we know and I need to go back and think about everything like Shevaun said." He looked over at Lou's mother who was staring at nothing while nursing a cup of tea. "I know she's right, I just can't clear my head enough to get a hold on it."

"You need to go back in your head, now that you know it's him and why." Shevaun said as she came out of her fog. "Think about him back then and factor in what you know now about him. Like he's a sadistic, cruel and devious bastard that's hell bent on making you hurt and look bad for his own personal satisfaction."

"Christ, it's so hard to see him that way." Max rubbed the back of his neck as he thought about it all. "He was a noble warrior and a good Aegis, or so I always thought!"

"Yes and he counted on that all this time." Lou's mother got up and stood in his face now. "Now you have to rethink him. Pull in anything that stands out in your memory knowing what you know of him now. It could be something innocuous or seemingly frivolous that you overlooked before. He knows you so he has been boring under your skin for decades. He knows how. Only you know those buttons he's pushed, so only you can figure it out."

Max nodded at Shevaun and sat down in a chair to go over his memories. Thinking all of it over in his head, with all of the data he had just found out. It did put a completely different complexion on the past.

"Abby..." Caroline called out to her from the mini-lab. "Did you feel nauseous at all?"

Abby considered a moment. "Well yeah, but that's to be expected given what's going on, right? Why?"

"Because I'm finding some metabolized trace in your urine but I'll need to confirm as soon as the samples are identified from the salad. It might not be entirely nerves or stress induced." Caroline peered into the microscope that Carpesh had brought. "Look at this and tell me if you're seeing what I'm seeing?" She asked Carpesh.

"What is it?" Max asked as Carpesh looked at the sample.

"I think I have identified traces of Midazolam as well as Psychotria Ipecacuanha but toxicology is not my thing so we will confirm it with the guy at the lab." Caroline looked over at Carpesh and waited for his input.

"Yes, it appears to be the same to me, which would have been very clever indeed." Carpesh looked up from the microscope and nodded at Caroline. "I concur with your findings."

"What the hell does that mean?" Max demanded.

"Well from what I gather of you guys, I mean turned Sanguinostri, you really metabolize things differently since your mainstay is from blood. I mean, am I correct in assuming that's where your systems get their main sustenance?" She looked from Max to Abby then back again.

"Sort of, but for the most part, yes." Abby answered. "A lot of the normal food we eat kinda just goes through us which is why we can eat like pigs and drink like fish. But given we can't actually study our own bodily fluids other than pee, like you have there, we can't say for certain even now, how we process things."

"Drugs, alcohol, poisons and such basically have no effect on our systems." Max spoke now, filling in some blanks. "Its impossible for us to get drunk or high as something in our system blocks absorption. Same goes for fats and what not. Only what our bodies absolutely need for proper function, based on the individual metabolism, is allowed to actually get into the system. The rest is passed through, so to speak. But we haven't found a way to successfully analyze anything beyond that since our blood, saliva and the like degrades before we can get a handle on things. It's some form of self preservation reaction that we haven't been able to crack yet."

Caroline was fascinated to learn all of this. "You say basically have no effect? That's not saying that some things can have an effect?"

"There are some herbs, fruits, plants and the like that can affect us temporarily." Max thought for a minute about what she was asking. "But nothing that could inflict real harm or damage."

"What about Ipecac syrup?" She asked.

Max furrowed his brow. "The emetic?"

"The road-sick plant!" Abby shouted as she jumped out of her seat. "The syrup is pretty innocuous to us but the actual root can make us queasy. I know because I used it on Frank once after he pulled a nasty practical joke on me." Abby looked at Caroline. "Yeah my nausea could be classified as a result of eating the root."

"Then I am certain the lab will confirm that there was Ipecacuanha in the salad, and traces of Midazolam." Caroline didn't have a doubt. "He must have added the Midazolam when he switched from

Corinne to Lou. Just enough of both to make her have to get up to use the restroom and a little loopy so she wouldn't see him coming."

"But she never ate the salad." Abby reminded them all. "I did."

"Right but he doesn't know that!" Max spun around to look at Shevaun. "It was just luck that she got angry with me right around the same time she was supposed to eat the tainted salad, and went into the bathroom anyway!"

"He's going to want to wait until everything burns out of her system before he starts playing with her." Caroline knew there was really no soft way of putting it. "And he would have dosed her in the hall with something strong and long lasting so he would feel safe getting her out of there without a fight. Probably Rohypnol if I were to guess."

"Assuming you're right, how long until she would come to?" Max prayed for a big number from Caroline.

"Well he's smart. I'm assuming he's done his homework on these drugs but he will probably err on the side of caution with a little more rather than a little less since he didn't want to get caught getting her out of the party." Caroline dashed over to one of he computers and began typing furiously. "Hell, it's a long half-life on Flunitrazepam, I would say at least six hours, but it could be upwards of ten even depending upon the dosage he gave her. He thinks she ate the salad, though, so he would factor that in."

"Caroline!" Max shouted at her but caught himself immediately after. "I'm sorry but I need the best guess you can give me."

Caroline nodded in understanding. "He probably knows there can be respiratory complications mixing the Flunitrazepam and Midazolam regardless of quantities so I would say five, splitting the last hour to be safe."

Max looked at his watch and did the math. "She's been gone just over three hours now so we have two hours to find her before he starts. Abby, do you have anything on the other vehicles leaving the museum yet?"

"Three possibles that I am just starting to run down now." She answered him without hesitation.

"Check the traffic cams around where the limo was found. Cross-reference those three possibles. It will more than likely be some innocuous mini-van or something like that and he will hang on to it until he's done so he can transport her out of where ever he has her now." Max saw the panic in Shevaun's eyes when he said it. "But we are going to get to her long, long before he does that, I promise." Max laid a hand on her arm in a reassuring gesture. "I am going next door to do a status, then I need to think for a minute. I'll be in the garden if I am not in the war room."

After a status rundown from all the teams, there was little new information to be gleaned. Abby was running down the vehicle and trying to sniff out the front company Albert was using to lease, rent or to have purchased his hidey-hole under. That was the critical piece that Max felt Shevaun was right about. Something in his memory, some little thing would tip him off as to where to find Lou. Max walked out into the pitch black of the garden and looked at the stars that shone brightly in the cloudless night sky. It was cold as hell and he found that odd since he was used to Washington winters. The dead of night wrapped around him as he walked through a row of rose bushes that had been pruned down to nubs. He imagined it would have been silent all around him if not for the comings and goings between the two bungalows. Lou was in the dark, he thought, and she was all alone with a madman. He pushed the image out of his head and scolded himself for letting his emotions play into things. Lou was not the focus of Albert's rage, she was a means to his end was all. It could have been Corinne or even Abby had Max never laid eyes on Lou. It was about him, or really Nila choosing him over Albert, when you got to the root of it all. Max had had no clue that Albert had any interest in Nila whatsoever and she had never mentioned any advance he may have made on her. Nila had been the daughter of one of the regents, middle class by today's standards at best. Women were very different and were treated very differently back then. It had been her gentle and quiet nature that drew Max's heart and he sought permission from the Senatus to indoctrinate her since her father deemed her worthless to do so himself. Max thought of how different Nila was from Lou and how different he was now from who he was then. It saddened him to think that he may not have truly loved Nila as much as he thought. That perhaps she was a charming caretaker who would tend to him as a good wife was expected to in those days. Nila was lovely, kind and gentle but fragile and easily subdued which Lou certainly was not. Max thought about Lou's fire and defiance and it made him smile.

A thought occurred to him that made him bolt inside at once. It seemed so obvious he hardly thought it viable but anything was worth a shot at this point.

"Abby!" The three women in the room jumped in surprise.

"Christ, you scared the shit out of me." Abby sank back into her seat. "What?

"Sorry ladies but Abby, I need you to run all permutations of the name Nila and perhaps my name in your searches." Max leaned over her shoulder as she typed. "It will probably be some kind of refuse company or trash, anything that might be dirty, even a cleaning company."

"Yes! Yes! Now you're thinking!" Shevaun got out of her seat and moved to watch the screen with Max.

"I get it, you both are nothing more than trash so use your names to front a company to hide behind?" Caroline was reasoning it out.

"Shit!" Abby exclaimed.

"That is it!" Max said as he grabbed his headset and began getting locations for all dispatched teams.

"AnilaMax Exterminating Services, for all your pest problems. The catch phrase for the company on their website is 'We take extermination to the Max!' How freaking loud and clear is that?!" Abby turned and looked to the other women in disgust.

"Address, Abby!" Max demanded.

"I already sent GPS coordinates to your phone." She said with a soft smile.

Max tore off his vest then grabbed the house phone. "I need my motorcycle brought to the front immediately." He ordered, then slammed the phone back down on the hook. "Abby, send GPS to Niko and the others..." He opened a case that Frank had brought in hours ago and took out a Katana sword that was housed in it's sheath and was securely attached to some sort of back-strap, holster type apparatus. Max slung his arms into each loop so that the weapon sat snugly between his shoulder blades. He reached over his head and grasped the handle of the blade and pulled straight up to unsheathe it and test that it was properly secured, but easily accessed. When he felt comfortable with it's placement he grabbed his leather jacket off the couch and pulled it on so that the weapon was completely concealed underneath.

"My Dom..." Abby got up and approached him with a serious expression radiating on her face. "...you're not planning on going in without Niko or back-up are you?" It wasn't a question so much as a plea.

"Abby, he is too arrogant to think that I've found him and he's been out of the game for too long to remember how demanding I am about keeping in shape and on my toes." Max smiled at her. "You think I can't take him myself?"

Abby didn't dare try and answer that. Either way she would sound like an idiot. "Watch your back. Don't accidentally slice Niko's head off when he gets there, please."

As he turned for the door, Shevaun stepped in his path and placed a hand on his chest. "Be careful, please. But bring my baby back to me."

Max put his hand over hers. "I vow it."

She stepped out of his way and he was out the door, running up the path to the main building of the hotel. A quick glance at his watch had him praying that Caroline had been right with her calculations of the sedatives. The bottom estimate of four hours had just passed and Lou could very well be coming to already. Max picked up his stride as he ran around the side of the hotel to the entrance and saw the MV-Augusta ready and waiting for him. He fished some bills out of his pocket, not looking whether they were singles or hundreds and stuffed them into the valet's hand before strapping on his helmet. He pulled his cellphone out of his pocket and pulled up the GPS coordinates that Abby had sent him and got his bearings as to where he was headed. He just prayed that he would get there in time.

Lou had dealt with enough victims, sifted through enough depravity and waded through enough bloody crime scenes to know the capacity for evil certain people had. Dealing with it and living through it, however, were two totally different things. She had been the victim of a crime before but this was on a whole other level. Although, if Sawyer had been a creative psychopath with sadistic tendencies, he might have come up with a similar scenario. Her mind was going a mile a minute which was a good thing given the fact that every time she thought about where she was and how she was utterly helpless, it was a little hard to keep calm. She had to keep reminding herself that how she was staged was designed for maximum panic and fear and she could not afford him one ounce of either, no matter how bad it got. He wanted her scared to death, whimpering, begging and more than likely screaming. She had a gut feeling that the screams were what really got him off.

In the eternity she had been sitting, strapped naked to that chair in blind silence, she had run through the files of the rogue's four victims in her head. She had only seen the Scott crime scene photos but the others she had seen up close and personal and knew the guy that had her was a sick twist. Snatching her up was not a crime of opportunity and it had been a really risky move. It was a reasonable expectation that Lou would visit the restroom at some point in the evening so that took patience. But why? What purpose did she serve in the line of victims? That was something she couldn't get past as she sat there and tried to make sense of it. In the off chance he took the ball-gag out of her mouth, she could try to get under his skin enough to get the upper hand somehow. So what was it that she knew for certain about this guy and all his victims? Lou knew that he had started in London ages ago just after Max had been elevated to Dominor status, but that the killings stopped there right before he was sent to North America. There had been sporadic murders all over Europe over the following years but never two consecutively in any one place until now. Lou thought about that for a while, the long gap between sequential murders. In London there had been ten women murdered, but she questioned that number given that the lack of forensics, technology, record keeping and communications were less then reliable. It could have easily been twice that number and they wouldn't have had a clue. The ten though, those were the ones he wanted known for certain. At least known to the Sanguinostri and to Max. That is when it clicked. With the echoing of Max's name in her thoughts it became clear that he was the one the rogue was taunting. With everything Lou had been brought up to speed on, not just with the rogue but with the Sanguinostri corruption on the West Coast, Max having to come out and deal with everything personally, the rogue knew. That was the entire point in his coming to Los Angeles to start up his spree again so that he could rub it in Max's face as he had been doing all along. Some sort of superiority complex in having eluded Max all these years? Lou had no clue of Max's history really to come up with any candidates for who would have a grudge against him. She was certain having lived as long as he had, there would be an extensive list. The problem was that she had only heard of one dig against Max since she had met him and that had been just that evening. Shit. It was just that simple wasn't it? The only person who Lou knew of having anything against Max was also the person who had an all access pass to his own party and could easily come and go with little to no notice from staff. Dammit all to hell, she thought, wanting to scream it but not daring to flinch an inch. If Abby and the guys had no clue why good old Albert would have given Max a verbal dig, they sure as shit wouldn't be suspecting him as the rogue. His staff maybe, which she knew Max had already been checking out, but wasn't sure how far he had gotten. All she could do was hope and pray that he pieced it together, and fast. In the meantime she had to try and remember everything she could about this Albert freak.

She had read a little about him when she was looking hard into Winslow but she was a civilian then, not Sanguinostri. She was at a serious disadvantage. Fortunately her little revelation had calmed her a good deal. It wasn't so difficult to breathe and she felt like she had a tiny grasp on something useful. Putting the fragments of knowledge she had together to form a strategy in case she got the chance to talk to him, was key. He liked to hear them scream so he would have to take the gag out eventually. Suddenly a new smell drifted into the room and it made her heart pick up a little faster. She listened carefully and tried to tune out the pounding of her own heart. She heard a door up ahead of her and to the left opening, what sounded like like a couple of soft crunches, then the door closed. He was there.

"Are you awake yet, my dear?" The smug tone in his voice made her legs go hot with anger but she didn't flinch. "You should be awake by now."

She heard his footsteps but they sounded off, as if walking on paper. She considered carefully her observations of the room that she had tried to make in her blind state. She was able to smell plastic, wood and bleach but the plastic had been the most prominent smell. When she thought it through, she decided that was the sound she was hearing in his footsteps, walking on cellophane. Christ he must have had the floor covered in plastic wrap of some sort which would make for handy dandy cleanup. The wood was probably from the chair, especially if the straps had been fastened to it recently. The bleach, well that had to have been a remnant from secondary cleanup. She could smell him getting closer. His cologne was far too overdone for a man. She knew he was going to see if she was conscious and she really would rather he not know she was. Niko's relaxation thing popped into her mind and she focused on remembering what he had taught her. She let her breath rise and fall naturally. Let the weight of her body fall into the chair, letting her body sink and let go. She focused on that grounding and when Albert pulled off her blindfold, she was too heavy in her own space to let her eyes react or flinch. She needed to remember that if she got out of this alive, she owed Niko some serious thanks.

"Hmm. You are out still. Pity. Perhaps I didn't calculate properly with the champagne. That would make sense since I have no idea how much you drank." His footfalls moved away from her and to the right some and she could hear him sigh and mutter something in what she thought might have been German. "Stupid fool. I probably should have asked him what he did with my bag before I killed him." His inane laughter following his comment to himself grated Lou like fingernails on a chalkboard but she stayed heavy and limp in spite of it. She heard him sigh again then move from right to left. The door opened and closed again and the wafting of his cologne began to dissipate. He must have gone looking for whatever bag it was he was talking about.

Lou waited a few minutes and listened before she risked opening her eyes so she could take stock of her surroundings. Fortunately the light was dim so the shock wasn't so bad and her eyes adjusted relatively quickly. The room was medium in size and was in fact completely covered wall to wall in plastic. It looked like he had hung white shower curtains around the perimeter and covered the floors in cellophane. If he did have a camera trained on her, it was shooting through plastic so he wouldn't see anything clearly. She noted the table to her right that was covered in plastic also but on top she saw several knives of all different shapes and sizes as well as an old fashioned straight razor. The straps that held her were far too thick to rip and there was no way to get her hands on that razor to cut through them. What she could see of the chair she was strapped to led her to the conclusion that it was not going to split apart very easily. She was stuck and stuck good. Her only weapon was going to be her wit and a cool head. She resumed the exercise Niko had taught her and let her peripheral vision see the edges of the room as best as possible since turning her head was not an option. There was nothing there but plastic walls and plastic coated floors. Resigned she had gained all she could from looking, she closed her eyes and went limp and heavy again, just in the nick of time too as she heard the door open.

"Here we are, my dear. Sadly, I do not have the luxury of time for you as I did with the others. I've been recently informed that my ship will be sailing sooner rather than later. So, we need to get you up and at it the artificial way. One little zip of this and you should be right as rain in fifteen minutes or so. Just enough time for me to slip into something more comfortable."

She felt the pressure syringe at her neck and tried to stay calm. If he saw her heartbeat quicken by the movement of her carotid artery in her neck, she was blown. The sting was nominal, she managed not to flinch and a few moments later she heard him walk away again. Now what the hell did she need to expect from that shot? Not like she was in short supply of adrenaline or anything. Maybe she would scare him to death with her heart leaping out of her chest at him. Christ, she thought, if anyone is coming for me, you better make it real quick.

Several minutes later, she began expecting his return. Maybe it was the drug he had given her, maybe it was her own stubborn stupidity, but in the split second that it took Albert to turn the doorknob, Lou had come to a decision. The fact that it may have been the last decision she would ever make might have had something to do with it but she decided in no uncertain terms that she was not going to go quietly or be another one of his victims if she had one ounce of fight left in her. She opened her eyes and glared at the door as it opened. Every ounce of rage and hate that she had within her radiated in her eyes and it was clearly not what he was expecting to find when he came into that room. At that moment, Lou would have tried to bite through that damn ball-gag if it weren't for remembering her loose tooth. By the expression on his face she had no doubt that he knew if looks could kill, he would have been a dead man. The funny thing was the calm that came with her rage. It was rather liberating and peaceful all at once. He approached her with obvious caution and the irony of the situation hammered Lou in that instant. She started to laugh, even with the gag in her mouth. Albert had completely proven Max's point. The whole thing that had gotten Lou to go into that restroom in the first place. The instant that Albert opened the door she felt the very same rage envelope her to the core of her being. The same rage that Robert Sawyer had met up close and personal. The thought of what Max would do to Albert once he got his hands on him, well Lou only knew what she would do so guesstimating was what had her laughing. No matter what Albert did to her, how slow or fast he killed her, she had the last laugh knowing Max would find him and pay him back a thousand times.

"Are you laughing?" Albert was truly perplexed and this only made Lou laugh more, which caused her to snort because she couldn't draw in a proper breath and the vicious cycle of the laugh fit ensued. "You are laughing!" Good God she could barely stand it and tears started streaming down her face from her hysteria. Albert was seriously annoyed as he stomped in wearing some ridiculous shiny black robe. Lou suddenly pictured him with Corinne in that robe and nearly wet her pants laughing, except she wasn't wearing any pants.

When he reached her he studied her for a moment to truly see that she was laughing and by all accounts she was laughing at him. This was utterly unacceptable! He would demand to know what she found so damn amusing! He reached behind her head and unfastened the ball-gag and Lou sucked in air with a gasp. But to his extreme horror she immediately resumed bellowing with laughter. It was by no means fake laughter, she wasn't forcing anything. Something had truly struck her as hilarious and given he was the only thing that was in the room it must have something to do with him.

"What in the hell is so damn amusing?!" He demanded, his eyes filled with annoyance and at the same time, uncertainty.

Lou gasped for more air as she continued to wail with laughter but caught her breath long enough to manage a few words. "Hold my side, it hurts!" She resumed laughing but he did not find anything funny so he backhanded her across the face, drawing blood from her lip. Her laughter dimmed to a chuckle when she tasted the blood, then all that anger and rage flooded back and shone once again in her eyes as she licked her lip and grinned. "Oh Albert, we were just starting to have fun and then you have to go and spoil it." She specifically took the same tone he had used when he thought she was still unconscious.

The clarity her rage gave her was calming and another piece of the puzzle clicked as she observed his posture. Little man envies big man. Classic old story. The dig that Albert had made to Max earlier in the evening, the entire Byzantine exhibit. He hated Max and it had started long before the whole passing over as Dom thing. So what else was it, she had to remember, put things in sequence, use it to hurt this man the only way she could before it was over. She needed to see him suffer before he killed her. That would make it okay. If she could just die knowing she had gotten a few good shots in for herself and the other women he had broken.

"You think you're such a clever girl, but by virtue of you being here we can clearly see that is not the case."

He started feeling smug again, Lou could see it. "Eh, everyone's entitled to an off day." She snickered and kept her eyes on his. Letting every ounce of fury radiate in her gaze.

No matter how he tried to hide it from her, she was unsettling him by not being afraid. "You are not exactly in a position to be so saucy, my dear."

"Another thing we will have to disagree on, Al." She purposely shortened his name and said it with a tacky exaggeration that she knew he would hate. "I find there is no position that couldn't use a little sauce."

Shadows of Doubt

"My name is Albert. You would be wise to remember that." He turned his back on her for the first time, letting her know for sure that she was getting to him.

"Oh what's the sense in being so uptight, Al? I mean this is supposed to be your fun time! Lighten up a little." She grinned at him in a viscious way when he turned around to glare at her for calling him Al again.

"Do you have any concept of what I am about to do to you? The pain I plan to inflict? If you thought about it for one second instead of playing your little game, you might reconsider what flies out of your mouth!" He reached and grabbed whatever knife was at the ready and stormed toward her, shoving it into her face.

She didn't flinch. She kept the same grin and let it spread to her eyes. "Oh I am completely aware of what you plan to do. I've seen your handiwork, remember?"

He straightened quickly and regained his composure somewhat. Remembering she did in fact know what he was capable of doing. "Then you are either incredibly brave or ridiculously stupid." He turned again, fidgeting with the blade.

"Doesn't really matter because it's not what I do or say that I find so funny." She watched him carefully and tried hard not to blink.

"Then what, pray tell, is it that you find so amusing?" He walked to the edge of the room and leaned against the wall.

"Well for someone who fancies themselves as so superior, that should be easy for you to figure out." She tried to move her head to see him but the strap prevented it. "You may as well loosen the strap on my head. You're not going to get a scream out of me and I am well aware I am not getting out of here alive. Unless you are over there to avoid eye contact because you're the coward I know you are."

He had moved across the room and had her face in his hand faster than she could blink. "I am anything but a coward!"

She had obviously struck a nerve when she noticed he had let his fangs fly. "Geez you guys are fast. Hey, mind the makeup." She matched his glare. "Spent a whole day getting all dolled up, you could show some respect here."

He scowled at her and let her face go. Reaching behind her head he unfastened the strap and threw it across the room.

"Oh hey! Thanks!" She turned her head, loosening her neck muscles, and smiled. "Much better. Now, where were we?" He only snarled at her and began pacing the room. "Oh yeah! You being a coward! Well of course you are Al! Going around slicing and dicing women because you can't get over a girl wanting someone other than you?"

This time the backhand came so fast she didn't have time to really brace herself. Of course she expected it, but it may have hurt less if he had done it to the unbruised side of her face like he had before. She held her head in place for a minute as she swallowed the pain, then turned to face him again. It had been a calculated guess but a correct one. Albert had definitely had a thing for Max's fiancee and she clearly ignored every advance Albert had made. Now if she could just remember what the hell her name had been. The drugs he had given her must have been messing with her memory.

"Long time to carry a torch, Al. Especially for a woman you snuffed out yourself." Another calculated guess that had paid off. She could see he was shocked she had figured it out. "Kinda pathetic that you haven't moved on after what? Five hundred years or something?" She snorted and laughed.

He raised the hand that had the knife this time but caught himself and lowered it slowly as he glared at her. "I should just cut your tongue out and be done with your drivel."

"You could." She nodded in a sing-songy manner. "But you would be pissed you never found out what was so funny before you did."

Shadows of Doubt

"Fine!" He whirled around and resumed pacing the room. "Illuminate me on what you found so comical."

She chuckled as she thought about it all again. "You totally screwed yourself Al." The hilarity of it started to well up in her again.

"I have done no such thing. You haven't the slightest clue what you are talking about!" He waved the knife at her as he spoke as if to intimidate her somehow and she only found it made him look more ridiculous.

"See, that's the problem right there, Al! You are so self involved and wrapped up in your own ass that you can't see where you have made your greatest blunder! You know..." She started to lose control of her laughter again. "...my only regret is that I'm not going to be around to see how it plays out."

He stalked toward her, clearly annoyed to almost a breaking point. "What the hell are you blathering about?! Spit it out already! I'm growing weary of your fooling around!"

She caught her breath and looked at him again. "Okay, let me ask you something first?"

"Whatever, just be done with it already." He was fidgeting with the knife again.

She made a decision to try a bluff. It wasn't as if she had anything to lose. "Was it when Max went to deal with Sawyer that you were tipped off about us?" Albert's eyes went wide at her use of the word 'us' and she felt less silly about her little lie.

"You know you were far better at keeping your relationship a secret than he was." His smug grin returned and he seemed almost delighted at her false confirmation of their having a relationship. "His having you watched, building so close to you, then not being able to stand that Sawyer character living any longer. So pathetic. But you! You kept things so professional right down the line." He sliced the air with his knife to accentuate his point. "I almost doubted you had feelings for him at all until I saw you two together at the gala. Then when he introduced you to Corinne as his companion! Ah! Pure vindication!" He skipped a few steps then whirred back towards her. "It was almost impossible to contain my excitement and wait along with the plan. But, here we are!"

"Yep! Here we are indeed, and you just happen to be there, a dead man walking." She grinned at him with that death look she felt she was getting really good at.

"What the hell are you talking about?" His annoyance at her interrupting his happy moment was clear.

"You cannot possibly be that stupid, can you?" She started laughing again. He charged at her, fangs flying once more as he leaned in low and pressed the blade to her skin. She never flinched and simply stared into his eyes matching glare for glare. She kept her voice calm and low, with just the right edge of smugness to it. "By now, Max has told the Senatus all about you and word has been passed to every Sanguinostri on the face of the earth that you are the rogue murdering scumbag they have been hunting. You think they are going to take kindly to you spitting in their faces while you've been fulfilling your own sick twist version of love unrequited?" She laughed in his face, loud and hard. "You pathetic moron. You have lost everything you have worked so hard to shove under his nose! You can never go back to anything you own, or think you own! If you make it out of the city alive, and that's a huge if, you will have everyone clamoring for your head!" She could see that it was starting to sink in that he hadn't calculated so brilliantly after all. "You think Max was pissed at Sawyer? Oh, Al! What the hell do you think his state of mind is now that he knows that you took his Nila and me!" She tossed her head back as far as she could to laugh, pretty sure that it would be the last thing she ever did, when she saw him stalking towards her with the knife raised.

"You bitch!" He bellowed as he stormed toward her, but she still didn't flinch. She stared him right in the eye as he steadied himself to slice her throat wide open and be done with her.

Lou refused to close her eyes. Refused to meet death trembling in fear. She smiled wide and focused in on him as he raised the knife and even tried to puff her chest out to meet his blow. As his arm came down she saw a glint that didn't seem to be his blade but she didn't want to take her eyes off his as he ripped through her. She refused to go screaming as the others had. He would get no satisfaction from her as she felt the knife slice across her shoulder and her chest rather than her neck. She was a little confused because she was certain he had been aiming for her neck, but then more confusion flooded her as she saw Albert's arm, complete with knife in hand, fall at her feet. She looked back up at him and saw the look of shock on his face as he looked at her, and the black blood spurting out of his shoulder that no longer had an arm attached to it. She blinked once then saw Max knock Albert sideways, out of his way so he could get to her. It was then that Lou felt the searing pain in her chest and could feel blood coming up in her throat. She looked down at herself and saw the blood pouring out of her chest. It was all slow motion now as she saw the horror on Max's face as he clasped his hands over her wound. She could feel his strong hands pressing into her skin as she looked up into his beautiful face and smiled at him before it all was gone.

Chapter Seventeen

Everything was extraordinarily bright and she couldn't focus on anything because of the glare. The first time she tried to sit up, the pain had knocked the wind out of her and that was the clincher that she wasn't in Heaven. There wasn't supposed to be any pain in Heaven, right? She blinked to try and get the brightness to settle so she could see where she was as she felt around to get an idea. She could feel the IV in her arm, the soft sheets and blanket over her and she felt the fluffy pillows under her head and shoulders. Her eyes finally started adjusting and she recognized the foot-board as her own bed's, and the large glass doors off to the right that looked out over the hillside were her own balcony doors. She was home? That couldn't be possible. She knew she took one hell of a hacking and could never have survived that.

She tried to sit up again to see beyond her feet and it looked like her entire room had been rearranged. It was then she noticed the sofa at the end of her bed that was facing her, and the sleeping bodies parked in it. To her utter amusement there was Max. Although completely gorgeous as usual, he looked like he had seen better days. And there, curled up under his arm all cozy was her mother, complete with his head resting atop hers. There was something profoundly moving to Lou at the sight of the two sleeping there. The giant and the fairy queen watching over her. More then that, it was the most important person in the world to Lou who had been so all her life, and the new one in her life, whether she liked it or not. She could have watched them sleeping like that forever, so peaceful, but the pain that radiated in her chest caught her hard and she winced aloud, stirring the two instantly.

"You're awake!" Lou's mother jumped up immediately and rushed to her side, pressing some sort of garage door opener looking device that was on her bedside table as soon as she got there. "Oh sweetheart, are you okay? How are you feeling?" Shevaun smoothed her daughter's hair back, then kissed her forehead.

Max was a bit standoffish as he stood up and looked at Lou from the foot of the bed. His eyes were filled with worry and fatigue as he gripped the foot-board and just stared at her. Lou tried to speak but only a croak came out and she suddenly realized she would kill for a cup of coffee.

"Don't talk yet! I'm sorry, I shouldn't be making you talk." Her mother fussed with the sheets, straightening them as Lou saw a man in a white coat walking in followed by Caroline.

"Good, she's conscious." The man said as he pulled a stethoscope out of his pocket.

"Hey girlie!" Caroline's eyes were full of tears as she hovered behind the man who was now listening to Lou's heart. "This is Doctor Craig, he's been taking care of you since we brought you home from the hospital."

Brought her home? How long had she been out? She needed to ask so many questions but her mouth was so damn dry. She tried to make spit to get a word out and thankfully Max realized what was going on.

"She needs ice chips." He said as he turned and raced out of the room so fast she could feel the breeze he created.

"Oh honey, he has been so worried, just beside himself as we all have but Max..." Her mother took her daughter's hand and squeezed gently. "...he hasn't left your side since he found you."

Lou closed her eyes and tried to remember what had happened but most of it was a haze. She remembered seeing Max's face and the horror in it when Albert had swung at her, but after that she could only remember the feel of Max's hands on her chest then everything going black. How badly had she been cut? She wondered.

"Everything sounds good." The doctor announced as he took her wrist to take her pulse.

Max came back in the room like a bolt of lightening with a cup and spoon in his hand of which he promptly handed to Shevaun.

"Thank you." Her mother smiled at him softly as she took the cup of ice chips. "Here sweetheart, try this." She fed Lou some of the chips that tasted like manna from Heaven. The cold crunches of ice melted on her tongue and soothed the dryness instantly. As she saw Joe, Abby and Frank enter her room, she opened her mouth for another spoonful because those chips were just so damn good.

"Well?" Max looked at the doctor with unveiled irritation.

"Everything seems good so far." He placed Lou's hand back on the bed and turned to the growing crowd. "We keep her on the intravenous fluids, antibiotics and pain medication for at least another two days. Keep her in bed, resting, no stress whatsoever, and she should be just fine by next week."

"I'll come back in the morning..." The doctor started to say.

"You will stay here until she is off the IV." Max told him.

"Well, it's not really..." When Max looked at the man, he shut up instantly. "Absolutely my Dominor, as you wish." The doctor looked down at Lou and she rolled her eyes at him with a grin that made him laugh. "Alright, I'll let you all visit with the patient but remember, not too long! She needs rest and calm." His voice was stern as he looked at her visitors before he left the room.

All the faces were looking at her as if she was about to die and it was starting to freak her out.

"Stop looking at me like that!" She finally said. "He said I'm going to be fine so quit looking at me like I am going to knock off at any second."

The faces instantly lightened, all but Max's. He stood there watching her like she was a ticking bomb about to blow up in his face. She looked at him and cocked her head sideways, at least as best she could.

"What's with you Mister Grump?" She raised an eyebrow when he didn't respond. "Hey gang, can you give us a minute?" She looked at her mother first and she nodded and smiled knowingly, then got up.

"Come on boys and girls, lets go check with the doctor what we can feed our patient and whip something up for lunch." Shevaun lead them all out of the room while Max simply stood there, continuing to stare at her with that pained expression on his face.

"Max, you are seriously freaking me out. What is wrong with you?" Lou demanded.

"Wrong with me?" His eyes went wide at her question. "Nothing is wrong with me! You, on the other hand!"

"What? What's so wrong with me that you are looking at me like I'm going to implode?" She could see by the look in his eyes that he didn't want to answer the question. "Get me a mirror." She told him but he just continued to stand there. "Get me a mirror or I'm gonna get up and go look for myself!"

He grumbled but turned to do as she asked. After hearing him fumble around in her bathroom for a minute, he came back with a hand mirror and sat down on the side of the bed next to her.

"I am so sorry." he said as he handed it to her.

Lou expected a horror the way he was being so dramatic so she took a deep breath as she looked. Oh yeah, her face was toast for sure. Her old black eye was entirely refreshed to a lovely raspberry black and the other side matched nicely, though the swelling explained why her vision was off. She had really expected that though, given how hard the bastard had whacked her. She also had expected a slash across her throat but there was no bandage there as she examined herself. Lou suddenly realized she had no idea what the hell she was wearing and thought that should have occurred to her before everyone and their cousin came sauntering into her room. But she figured her mother would have made sure she was properly covered given Max was there and all. So upon further inspection, it appeared she was wearing some sort of one-shouldered toga style nightdress that was fastened over her right shoulder. That made sense when she looked to see the heavy bandages that covered her left shoulder and continued down and across her chest in a diagonal direction. She looked at Max and scrunched her nose as she thought a moment.

"Turn around." She said to him.

"What?" It wasn't what he was expecting her to say, obviously.

"Yeah, I know you saw me buck naked but that was different, so turn around!" She made a turning gesture with her right hand and he did as she asked.

Lou resumed examining herself and pulled the nightdress away from her so she could see just how far the bandages went. Apparently Albert had cut her crossways from left shoulder, across her chest, breast and all, then down to the bottom of her right ribs. The bandaging was so heavy that she had no clue how deep or thick the slash was.

"How deep did he go?" She asked as she put the fabric back in place to cover everything. "You can turn around now." Max didn't turn around and didn't answer. "Look at me!" She managed a semi-intimidating growl and he finally turned. She saw the tears in his eyes that he was fighting.

"I almost lost you." Was all he could manage.

"Max..." Lou reached and took his hand. "... You didn't. I am here and I am going to be fine. I just want to know and I need you to tell me."

He laced his fingers with hers and stroked her hand gently with his other hand. "He nicked your heart and lung. I was able to put pressure long enough for the med-team to get you patched so we could air-lift you out." He took in a deep breath before he continued. "You were in surgery for eleven hours."

"Wow. What the hell day is it? How long have I been out? How did you get me home?" She started hurling the questions at him in her normal fashion and it eased his gut to hear her as her normal self.

"They had you in a drug induced coma because of the pain and you needed to stay still. That was for three days but then you wouldn't wake up. After three more days, I talked with you're mother and Joe and we felt that bringing you home might make you feel safer so you would want to wake up. That was two days ago"

"Holy crap! So I've been out for like nine days? What's today?" She was utterly shocked.

"It's Tuesday." Max hated telling her how much time she had lost. "Vinny should be here any minute actually, it's after five and he's come every day after work."

When Lou thought of the implications, she realized she must be catheterized and that just utterly embarrassed the hell out of her, with him sitting right next to her.

"Get the doctor and my mother, now!" She shouted at him and pulled her hand away.

"What?! Are you alright? What hurts?!" His face went white.

"Just go! Please!" She could see he was about to freak out and she swallowed her mortification so that he would calm down. "I have to pee if you must know! Now go!"

He was so relieved that she was alright and it was just her normal stubborn pride that he gladly went and fetched the doctor and Shevaun as she asked.

Fifteen minutes later, and much to the doctor's dismay, the catheter was out and Lou was hobbling to the restroom with her mother under one arm taking the brunt of the weight and the rolling IV stand on the other for stability. When Lou was done, she had her mother stop in front of the wall mirror so she could get a good look at herself. Ironically, her bandage reminded her of those sashes that the beauty pageant contestants wear because that was the length and breadth of it. But her face was so black and blue, she was not anywhere near the realm of a beauty. Christ, she thought, it was over a week and she still looked this bad. It was probably a blessing in disguise that she didn't see herself then, or remember anything of that last week. Her mother could sense Lou was getting upset and promptly ushered her back to bed.

"Can you get Max for me please, Momma? I need to know what happened." Lou asked as she relaxed and let her body sink into the soft bed and tried to tune out the pain.

"You bet. Be right back." Shevaun kissed her daughter's forehead before heading out to get Max.

When he came back into the room Lou could tell he had washed his face and slicked his hair back with water. The rich brown was glossy with the dampness and she just wanted to run her fingers through it, but she kept a lid on that little impulse. He sat back down on the bed next to her and took her hand again. She really liked the way her hand felt in his and thought she could get used to it.

"Feel better?" He asked her with a half smile.

"Much, thanks. Now what happened? Is he dead?" She looked at him intently at tried to read the look on his face.

"We will get him. He won't get far and everyone, every last Sanguinostri knows I want his head on a platter."

"He got away?! You let him get away?!" She tried to sit up, but the pain speared at her and made her wince. She let herself sink back into the bed as he tried to soothe her.

"I couldn't let you die! I wouldn't! Given the same choice now, I won't! So be mad at me all you want!" He tried to look smug but he was too worried about what she thought of him for all of it.

"So you whacked his arm instead of his head so he couldn't slice my throat?" She was remembering as best as she could and he only nodded in reply. "Alright, I guess that's okay. He said something about his boat sailing sooner rather than later. Hey! Have Finn read me! He can see things I may be missing!"

"Lou, we will get him, I promise you that." He wanted to touch her cheek but he didn't risk hurting her with her face as badly bruised as it was.

"I know why, I figured it out. He hates you because Nila loved you and not him." She didn't dare look him in the eye as she said it. She didn't want to see that he still loved Nila and still mourned her after all these years.

"Yes, we figured that out too. It was hard to comprehend but I never knew he harbored such hate for me and..." He tried to find the right words. "... I am so sorry I got you involved in all of this. That I caused you such pain and suffering."

She looked at him now, surprised that the pain she saw in his eyes wasn't for Nila but for her.

"What are you talking about? You think you did this?" He looked down, avoiding eye contact. "Don't do that, you look at me!" She yanked on his hand and he looked back into her eyes. "Albert is a nutjob who used his former prestige to hide behind while he did his own little crazy dance across the world. He picked me because he thinks you have some sort of thing for me but he could have easily picked Abby or even Caroline! This was not your fault. I don't want to ever hear you say anything so stupid again!" It was hard to miss the grin that spread across his perfect lips but she tried not to let it get to her. "What are you grinning at?"

"Your mother said almost the same exact thing to me while you were missing. It's because of her that I figured out where he had you." He rubbed his thumb absentmindedly across her fingers as he held her hand snugly. "And you must know by now, Lou, I very much do have some sort of thing for you."

She could feel her face get hot and her breath hitched when he said it. "Yeah well I should imagine any guy would after seeing me strapped naked in a chair." She tried to make light of it and chuckled nervously.

"I covered you immediately, I promise. As soon as I could, I got my jacket over you so you were covered before the others came in." The childlike quality in his face as he reassured her of her modesty was almost more than she could stand. But it was an effective dodge tactic obviously by his reaction.

"Thanks, I'm sure it wasn't a pretty sight." It was cruel, she knew it but she couldn't help herself. She had to rib him a little and she could tell it worked.

"I... uh..." When he saw the grin hit her eyes he furrowed his brow. "That's just mean! Of all things you should know I am a gentleman and would never exploit such a grave situation for a cheap thrill!"

"Oh! So now I'm a cheap thrill!" She had to laugh but it hurt incredibly to do so.

"Stop being such a brat, you're going to hurt yourself just for the kick of watching me squirm!" He let go of her hand and tried to adjust her pillow to make her more comfortable.

"I can't help it..." She hissed through the pain. "You just set yourself up so badly for it." She drew in a deep breath as the worst of the pain passed.

He brushed her hair from her face, smoothing it very carefully. "I'll argue with you when you're better. Hardly a fair battle with you in this state." She turned her head to look at him again, pinning his hand with her cheek. Her face fit so perfectly in the palm of his hand. He hoped it wasn't hurting her. When she smiled he knew it was alright, and he happily left his hand right where it was.

"So what does everyone think? I mean its not like the department could know the truth so what's the story?" She blinked lazily and listened for his reply.

"Well that is a little convoluted and I am sure we will need to go over certain things later, but bottom line is you took the suspect down. He got a good swipe in on you before he dropped. Since your captain was at the gala, you had gotten word to him for back up. Evidently he was a tad late but got to you in time. Viola', here you are." Max grinned down at her and his heart broke to see her looking so battered and bruised.

"Suspect? What suspect? Bender doesn't get to go down in infamy?" Her eyelids began to feel ever so heavy.

"I found Albert's little henchman propped up sitting in the hall. Dead as a doornail with one of Albert's knives sticking out of his chest. We just did a little rearranging and he'll be pinned with the other murders. Bender still gets to live in infamy for Katarina Purrs' demise." He reached over with his other hand and stroked her hair. He could see that she was about to fall asleep. "I know its difficult for you, having to cover all this up with a lie, publicly. I'm very sorry about that. I promise you, though, Albert and any soul that helped him over the years will see justice.

Lou yawned and grimaced at the pain of it. "Oh I know. I'm good with it." She let her eyes close and snuggled into the palm of his hand. "Hey is your house done yet?" She tried to keep her eyes open but just couldn't.

"Not yet." He watched her fight the sleepiness that washed over her and it made him grin.

"Bummer. Maybe my Mom will let you stay over so we can talk more later. I might fall asleep on you. Sorry, just so sleepy." She barely got the last word out before she was out cold, sound asleep with her head still tucked in his hand.

"I am not going anywhere, ever." He risked leaning down to kiss her cheek softly then propped himself as best he could without disturbing her so that she could sleep as she was. If he had his way, he planned to keep her in the palm of his hand forever.

About the Author

A native Southern Californian, Mell Corcoran resides just outside Los Angeles with her family, two cats, a hoard of wild frogs, bunnies, squirrels and any other wild animal that happens to wander in the yard. Yes, she is a huge animal lover and has been known to stop traffic to help critters cross the street.

For many years, Mell's day job has been in the legal profession but she has always had a strong passion for writing and a deep love of literature, regardless of genre. It was this passion that finally led her to focus her energies primarily on writing.

Mell and her mother, who also happens to be her best friend, are well known for their shared love of a good mystery and crime fiction. This shared interest is what inspired the special relationship between her characters, Lou and her mother Shevaun. When she is not dreaming up new plot lines for a juicy murder mystery, Mell can often be found attempting to play golf or laughing with her family.